C000247309

Published by Pusstifer Books, 2023

ISBN 978-1-9161372-0-2

Tigger and the tantric princess

By Clive Akass

Illustrations and front cover by John Storey

Contents

Part 1: The kidnapped princess

Part 2: Travels with Henry

Part 3: Showdown in Solung

Note on the songs and text

I have taken liberties with the geography of India to depict the location and character of Solung, where much of this story is set. Readers familiar with the Himalayas may recognise elements of Kashmir, Kulu, Nepal and Darjeeling, but Solung does not represent any one of these places either politically or geographically. Like the characters I describe, it exists only in my imagination and (I hope) that of the reader. However the dialogue with revolutionaries and quotes from their propaganda in chapters 22 and 34 are taken with little change from conversations with militants in Bengal, and pamphlets and posters that they were distributing. The character of the dacoit hunter NRJ is based on a magazine interview, now sadly lost. All the songs in this book are available for streaming or download from major music sites. For more information, and news of future books by me, go to http://www.cliveakass.co.uk

Part One

Rescue in the mountains

Prologue

My name is Tom the fatalist,
no earthy trade I tend.
They say that I'm a vagabond,
call every man my friend.
Vain hope that rides
on taking sides,
it's only policy.
The partial views,
the senseless news,
will die with history.
Travel on you roaming kind.
Don't let those sun-cast shadows turn you blind.
The clouds will pass,
the sun will rise.
Don't let the darkness close your eyes.
(Henry's song, to be continued)

A time would come when Tigger would smile at the thought of his first impression of Henry the Hippy. No-one who knew Henry would call him regal. Yet that evening in the late summer of 1972, shortly after sunset, when Tigger and the princess dragged their tired bodies into a clearing where he presided over a roaring fire, it seemed as if they had stepped into the magical abode of a mountain king. Henry sat alone, hair cascading down his back, naked save for a loincloth and a necklace of curiously pitted beads, legs crossed, back straight, deftly manoeuvring a pot to rest on three stones placed strategically in the fire. The firelight striking the night-shrouded pine trees gave the impression of a vaulted hall, with shimmering sides composed of the elfin barrier between light and darkness. Sparks shot up like stars in homage. Henry lit a bedi, a tiny cigar favoured by peasants.

"Enter the mercenary and the damsel in distress. So you've managed to get away from the guerrillas," he said.

"Terrorists," corrected the princess. "They're terrorists. At least, they terrify me."

"And I'm not a mercenary," Tigger said. "I'm a hero. I've just rescued a princess. I'm the stuff fairy tales are made of."

"You get paid for it, don't you?"

"Even heroes have to eat." Tigger sat next to the fire and eyed the pot significantly.

"We could start with some tea," Henry said.

Marvellous what you could read from an accent. English. Street London vowels but educated, probably more so than his parents. And friendly, despite his barbed greeting. That was a relief. "You must be the foreign sadhu people told us about," Tigger said.

"I wouldn't call myself a sadhu. I'm just hanging out."

"That's all sadhus ever do," said the princess, who had a poor opinion of the average Hindu ascetic.

"I guess you could say the same of hippies. People call me Henry the Hippy."

It was surreal, bantering with this stranger as if they were in a London coffee bar. They were half lost, half way up a mountain god-knows-where in the Himalayas and in fear of their lives. Tigger did not want to fence with words. He had been carried along by the momentum of events; now, suddenly, his body felt like it was giving up.

He had gone pale, the princess could see that. "You should lie down, Tigger," she said. And then to Henry: "He's had a hard time."

"So I see."

Henry rolled out a straw mat invitingly and Tigger fell across it, muttering thanks. Almost immediately he fell asleep. Henry woke him a couple of hours later with a meal of rice, dahl and curried vegetables.

"The princess tells me that you really have been a hero," he said as Tigger tucked in.

"I was shooting my mouth off. She has been doing most of the rescuing. I just blundered about."

"I wouldn't be here if it were not for you and your friends Tigger," the princess said. "You are all heroes to me."

"I always wanted to be a hero," Henry said. "I wanted to be Biggles. Do you remember Biggles books, Tigger? Did you read them?"

"Every one I could lay my hands on."

"Who is Biggles?"

Tigger tried to explain the impact of the stories that had fed the fantasies of British schoolboys growing up in the shadow of two world wars. Biggles fighting deadly dogfights in glorified boxkites over the trenches of World War One. Or adventuring in the quaint aircraft of the thirties when (if you were Biggles) you could fly almost anywhere and see what no man had seen before, and tread where no man had trod. Biggles, forever young, knight of the Spitfire, battling Nazi aircraft in World War Two. Bane of bullies, invulnerable might-with-right incarnate.

"Biggles made war seem like school games," Henry said. "He helped psych a whole generation of boys into becoming cannon fodder. He could have done for me and Tigger too, if there had been a war on when we came of age."

"It's a bit much to blame Biggles for the dead of the war," Tigger said drily. "But you could say Biggles got me into this. My boss is a real-life Biggles, and when I walked into the office only last week back in London, it was like I'd walked straight into a Biggles book."

1 The kidnapped princess

In fact, Tigger had not walked into the office. He had run up the stairs and burst in, to the irritation of the celebrated aviator Edward FitzDougal, who was sitting at his desk quietly cataloguing some newspaper cuttings.

Dougal said: "Do you always have to come through that door like a rhinoceros on heat, Tigger? You'll break it down one day, and my eardrums with it."

Everyone called him Dougal, even the newspapers. An entire wall of the office was taken up by a publicity shot of him at the controls of a Spitfire on a wartime airfield, ready for takeoff. He was famous even then. Next to him in the picture was a second Spitfire, piloted by a man who now followed Tigger into the room, rather more slowly. Charlie Naughton, still Dougal's sidekick thirty years on. The name of their company was on the door: Dougal Air Charter.

"Everything go OK, Charlie?"

"No problems." Charlie sank into an armchair.

"About as exciting as a milk round," Tigger said. "Eighteen drunken fitters delivered to Aberdeen, all set for the oil rigs. Deserts, uncharted wastes, jaunts into the unknown... that's what I expected when I took on this job. I'm wasting the best years of my life as a glorified bus driver."

"Another one crazy for excitement," Dougal said. He nodded towards a figure lounging on a settee on the other side of the room. "Gosh here has been chafing at the bit all afternoon."

4

All that could be seen of Gosh were his sharply creased cavalry-twill trousers and polished brogues. He spoke from behind a copy of *The Sporting Times,* in the languid drawl affected by officers of his old regiment. "I'm bored stiff, old boy. If I'd wanted to do milk runs I'd have signed up as milkman."

"This is good, healthy work," Dougal said with some asperity. "If you don't like it, take your boredom somewhere else."

Tigger was beginning to regret opening his mouth.

"Calm down. I was only fooling," Gosh said, putting down his paper. "Can't you find any chance for excitement in those cuttings, a war maybe, or a dragon to be slain?"

Dougal's habit of collecting curious newspaper items had indeed been known to have interesting results, but not for a very long time. "You need a new interest in life," he told Gosh. "You should take up a new hobby, like counting the blessings of peace. People die in wars you know."

The fact was that both Gosh and Tigger had joined the company because of Dougal's reputation for adventuring. Every schoolboy in the country knew his story, not least because a highly successful film had been made of his early life, in which he was shooting down Messerschmitts at the age of 17 in the Battle of Britain of 1940. After the war he embarked on a series of adventures that kept him in the papers. He cracked an international air-piracy racket. He found an heiress lost in the Amazon. He fought bandits in Central America. But his most dangerous exploits were done covertly for the government. Charlie accompanied him on most of these missions. Their transport company was originally set up as a cover but they took on some conventional work to give it credibility, always owning one aircraft and chartering any others they needed. This work had gradually become the mainstay of the company and the only work they had had for months involved ferrying people and equipment for oil companies. Charlie preferred it that way, and Tigger was beginning to suspect that Dougal did too.

Gosh had worked with Dougal on and off for years. Few people knew his real name – the one his family, an obscure branch of the aristocracy, had inflicted on him. It was so long and eccentrically spelt that people gave up trying to pronounce it. His initials were far easier, so he was stuck for life with being known as an exclamation. Tigger's pet theory was that the unmanly nickname had affected his character — that he had strived all his life to be the reverse of what might be expected of a Gosh. Before taking up flying, he had served in one of the army's toughest, not to say brutish, units. He left after a back injury condemned him to a desk job but he was still more active than most men. His muscles were evidence of serious work in the gym, and he had what on the streets they called attitude. Gosh looked and spoke like a gentleman but, whether or not his name was to blame, he was a bruiser.

Dougal looked delicate by comparison. Average height, hands as soft as a woman's, he looked a good ten years younger than Charlie and considerably slimmer. His hair showed flecks of grey but it was as thick as the day he first took to the air. Time showed most in deep lines round his eyes, which had seen so much death and destruction.

A buzzer sounded on his desktop intercom, followed by the disembodied voice of the receptionist they shared with other offices in the building. "A Mr Raju Sinouk is asking to see you. He doesn't have an appointment."

Dougal looked puzzled. "Sinouk? Never heard of him. You may as well send him up." Putting the phone down he said to Gosh: "This could be the answer to your prayers."

A young man dressed in a smart grey suit entered the room. He looked Indian, with a touch of the far East in the shape of his eyes.

"Mr Sinouk? Will you take a seat?"

The visitor looked uncomfortably at Dougal's companions. "I have come to see you about a very delicate matter,"

6

he told Dougal. "I would prefer to speak to you alone." His voice suggested an expensive English education.

"These are colleagues of mine. You can trust their discretion."

"The fewer people who know about what I have to say, the better. If you accept the proposition that I'm about to put to you, you will be free to choose what help you need. I think that I was followed here and I may put you in a danger just by speaking to you."

"We are not unused to danger. But if you prefer..."

Tigger was already picking up his things to go. "Come on, you two. Let's get some lunch."

ooo

"I am sorry about that. I am not used to this cloak-and-dagger business and I don't like to take unnecessary chances," the visitor said after the others had left.

"Neither do I. That's why I'm still alive."

"Perhaps I should introduce myself properly. My name is Prince Raju Sinouk, son of King Sung of Solung. You know Solung?"

"I know *of* it. North East India. Next to Bengal."

"You are better informed than most people outside South Asia."

"Not that well informed. I didn't know it still had a king. I thought it became absorbed into India."

"Many people in India would like it to be. So would some in Solung, but nowhere near a majority of the people. When India got independence from Britain it was given the right to trigger a plebiscite in Solung to let the people decide whether to become part of the new nation. India never agreed a date because it knew it would lose the vote. There is still a good chance that India would take over Solung if the country became unstable – particularly if the instability threatened to spill over the border."

"Is this relevant to why you have come to see me?"

"It's a factor."

"So you are not offering simple charter work?"

"Not exactly. I am afraid this will sound rather dramatic. I want you to rescue a princess." The prince smiled uneasily.

Dougal's face did not move.

"Go on," he said, lighting a cigarette.

"Princess Sita is a distant cousin of mine. Ten days ago she disappeared while out horse-riding. Two days later, my father received a ransom note for one crore rupees."

"I get confused with these India numbers. That's how much?"

"Ten million rupees... rather over half a million pounds. The kidnappers also demanded the release of three convicted terrorists."

"So it was a political job?"

"Politicians, bandits... there is not much difference when referring to the fellows who pulled this off. I'm sure some of them believe they are fighting for a better world but they don't hesitate to line their own pockets while they are doing it."

"You know these men, then?"

"Only by repute."

Dougal caught a slight hesitation in the reply but he did not remark on it. "In my experience, a man's reputation depends very much on who is doing the reputing. Who are these people?"

"They call themselves the People's Army and we know they're the military arm of a group called the Revolutionary Marxist Party – the RMP. We can't prove the link, and the RMP would invite arrest if they admitted it. There is political freedom in Solung but private armies are obviously beyond the law. The RMP has only a small membership, but terrorist acts committed by the People's Army – mostly attacks on small landowners – give it an influence disproportionate to its size."

"Has the kidnap of the princess affected the political climate?"

8

"It could do. At the moment, it has been kept a secret."

"Why?"

Yet again that slight hesitation. "The PA — the People's Army — have been unusually quiet about it, perhaps with an eye on public opinion, and my father has been trying to keep the political temperature down while we play for time. He believes the PA does not really want a settlement. It is trying to provoke the government into oppressive measures that will polarise the country and help precipitate a revolution."

"What is the king's status – does he run the country?"

"We are a constitutional monarchy rather like that in Jordan. There are two houses of parliament but the king has a veto on any law passed. He also appoints judges and army commanders and is himself commander-in-chief with the power to declare war."

"That's hardly power to the people."

"As my father says: 'Better an imperfect democracy than perfect chaos.' I don't expect the arrangement to last forever."

"You'll do away with the monarchy?"

The prince shrugged. "I don't know what we will do. We'll find our own way. Much of Solung is feudal, with poorer people depending on the rich and powerful. This means that the richest or the strongest tend to get elected. Both major Solung parties indulge in vote buying and intimidation during elections. The result is that there are many stupid, short-sighted people in parliament..."

"Tell us something new," said Dougal.

The prince smiled wanly. "Some MPs are little more than robber barons, or their puppets. Without my father as arbiter, the country would soon tip into chaos. Happily most people in the country realise this. The arrangement suits all the mainstream politicians because they don't trust their rivals enough to risk giving them full executive power."

"Where does the People's Army stand over India? Aren't they just going to invite an Indian invasion if they push

Solung into chaos?"

"They don't care. They have strong ties with revolutionary movements across the border in Bengal. They would like to spread the revolution throughout India."

"You think that is feasible?"

"Who knows? India is under a lot of stress. Bengal is far from the only Indian state with powerful revolutionary organisations, and there are strong separatist movements in several areas."

"People have been predicting the collapse of India since independence but it keeps tottering on. I'm sure it will survive the kidnap of one young woman."

"I wouldn't want to overstate the risk but it is not negligible, especially with the possibility of foreign involvement. China already has links with the People's Army. Russia has long tried to extend its influence into India."

"Both countries are heavily involved in the Vietnam War. You don't think they have enough on their hands there?"

"Who knows? I'm just saying that the situation is volatile, to say the least."

Dougal sat back in his chair and lit another cigarette. "So what exactly do you want me to do?"

"We know where the princess is being held... in a mountain village accessible only by a couple of paths."

"And you don't want to send the army in?"

"There is no knowing what would happen to the princess if we launched a full-scale assault. And the signs are that the People's Army *wants* us to attack. Our soldiers would constantly have to distinguish between loyal villagers and fighters. Innocent people would suffer. Some at least would blame the government. We could have a civil war on our hands."

"Doesn't your army have special forces to deal with this sort of thing? A group capable of mounting a small, surgical operation?"

"The generals are keen to try but they have no-one with experience of this sort of thing. I don't want to risk it."

"Have you asked the British government for help?"

"We've had talks, but as a former colonial power it can't be seen to be involved. It's too tricky politically. You are famous even in Solung, and we know you have done this sort of thing before. My father suggested that you might take on the job. Your Foreign Office seemed happy with the idea."

Dougal shook his head. "The obvious way to launch an operation would be by helicopter. We don't do helicopters."

"I'm assured that it would be possible to use other types of aircraft. I don't want to go into details now."

"Do you have an air force?"

"We've never needed one until now, though the army has a few transport planes. We do have the makings of an air force, of sorts."

"What do you mean?"

"We have four fighter aircraft but they are antiques and we have no trained pilots."

"Antiques?"

The prince smiled. "Of a type you are familiar with. Spitfires."

For the first time since the prince arrived, Dougal showed surprise. "Spitfires!"

"My father got them cheap when the British left India because it would have cost your country more than they were worth at the time to ship them home. Daddy thought they would be a good investment and kept them in mothballs for years. When the People's Army agitation started, he got them armed and ready for use. We hoped to interest you in training up pilots when this business is over."

Despite the seriousness of the conversation, Dougal smiled at the prince's lapse into Indian English, the dated use of 'daddy'.

The prince went on: "As if the situation were not quaint enough, there are four Messerschmitts in the country, attached to a flying club owned by my father's brother-in-law, Sanjeev."

"You are not expecting us to take them on to get to the princess?"

Again there was that hint of a hesitation. "Hardly. Sanjeev is her uncle."

"Spitfires and Messerschmitts... I am beginning to wonder if you are pulling my leg."

"The facts of my story can be verified by a call to the official Solung representative in London."

Dougal was silent for a while, then shook his head. "It seems to me that if I help you, I could end up having to take sides in a civil war. I've seen too many wars to want to become involved in one again. Why doesn't your father simply pay the ransom?"

"It's government policy not to do deals. They don't want to encourage more kidnaps. Daddy can't be seen to make an exception for a princess."

"And the princess will be killed if she is not rescued?"

"We think she is too valuable an asset to be wasted on an empty gesture. If they do kill her, they will choose their time carefully with a particular political purpose."

"You realise that if a rescue attempt went awry she might die anyway?"

"It's a balance of risks, isn't it?" the prince said. "We know where she is right now. She might be moved at any time to somewhere we could never find her. If we are going to try a rescue, it is now or never."

His voice faltered and for the first time, Dougal realised the strain he was under. "Leave your number with me and I'll discuss the matter with my friends," he said. "I am afraid that the answer is likely to be no. I hope that is not too much of a blow. Do you know the princess personally?"

"Our wedding was to have been announced today," the prince said quietly.

2   A threat from a stranger

"A kidnapped princess! Spitfires! Messerschmitts! How could you turn the job down? What's wrong with rescuing a princess?"

Charlie's quiet voice broke into Tigger's protests. "Steady on, laddie. This isn't a game you know. Dougal knows what he is doing."

"I'd bet that if this were twenty years ago you would both have jumped at the job."

"You can't run about the world playing Sir Galahad these days. It was a simpler world twenty years ago," Dougal said.

"You were twenty years younger, too."

They were silent for a few seconds, aware that a mark had been overstepped. From somewhere outside came the sound of a news broadcast... another bomb in Northern Ireland, more fighting in Vietnam. Three pairs of eyes fixed on Dougal, who drew slowly on his cigarette. But Dougal rarely lost his temper when actually provoked. He said coolly: "I had twenty years less experience, too."

"Tigger and me could have a go," Gosh said. "I could call in a couple of people from my old army unit if necessary. There's no need for you and Charlie to be involved."

Before he could say more, a buzzer sounded and the receptionist's voice came over the intercom: "The gentleman rushed past, sir!" Then the door burst open to reveal a man who looked as if he had stepped out of a thirties gangster film. He was of medium height, almost swamped by a trench coat with a wide collar, both hands held in pockets suggestive of weaponry, trilby hat at a rakish angle over a handsome Asian face. He stood in the open doorway, feet apart.

"Where is the boss of this outfit?" he said.

Dougal viewed him with distaste. "It is usual to knock before entering a room. You might also have announced yourself to my secretary, so that we could know who we are talking to. We might have thrown a party for you."

"I am not here to be polite," said the man. "And I have no interest in you knowing who I am. You have been speaking to the so-called Prince of Solung."

"I cannot see that it is your business who I have been speaking to," said Dougal.

"You cannot see that it is my business because you are meddling in affairs that are not of your concern. I have no quarrel with you. I have come to give you a friendly warning. Forget the Prince of Solung. Forget Solung. Forget me."

"And what if I choose not to heed your warning?"

"You British have a saying: accidents will happen."

"You are threatening me?"

"I am advising you, as a friend. I like you. I can see that you are a man of principle and good sense."

He spoke with a jocular insolence for which Tigger felt a sneaking respect.

"My heart is warmed by your concern," Dougal said. "But as a man of principle, I dislike people who burst into my room without knocking. And as a man of taste, I do not like your style."

"And I don't like your face," Gosh added, punching one hand into the other, menacingly. "A couple of taps on the nose would do it wonders."

The stranger ignored him, clearly taking this as a joke. Tigger knew better. One more peek out of the man, and Gosh would flatten him. Best to tease them both.

"Down Gosh, down!" he said. "Be a good dog and don't bite the man. You'll put him off his act."

The stranger kept his eyes fixed on Dougal. "I take it that you will ignore my warning."

"You can take nothing but your leave."

The man paused for a few seconds, as if wondering how to leave with the last word. Finally, he said: "You are like a lot of overgrown schoolboys. You think you are playing a game. If you are not careful you are going to find that the game is all too real."

"I've met enough skunks like you to have lost that kind of illusion," Dougal said.

The visitor's next move was so unexpected that it was over and he was out of the office before anyone could take in what had happened. He took off his hat, threw himself to the floor, touched Dougal's feet, and said quietly: "I salute the god in you, my enemy." Then he stood up, brushed himself off, bowed slightly to Dougal, and left the room as calmly as if he had just delivered the milk.

"An odd man, but clever and dangerous," said Dougal. "He won't frighten easily. Tigger, slip down the fire escape and see if he meets anyone outside. Don't bother to follow him."

"What was that last bit about?" Gosh said as Tigger left.

"He sounds like a religious fanatic. Unusual for a Marxist revolutionary, if that is what he is."

Tigger came back into the room a couple of minutes later. "Cool as you like... he strode straight into a waiting Bentley, complete with chauffeur and CD plates. I've got the number."

"Good work. Get on to Meekin at the Yard and ask him to trace the number for me. He owes me a favour." Dougal caught sight of Tigger's face. "What are you grinning at?"

"I thought we weren't going to get involved..."

"I'll not allow myself to be bullied by a jumped-up sewer rat who thinks he's civilised because he runs around in a big car," said Dougal. "Trace that number. I'm going to call on the prince."

Tigger looked over at Charlie, who raised his eyes to the heavens and gave a deep sigh.

By the time Dougal returned to the office, Tigger had

discovered that the Bentley used by the stranger belonged to the embassy of an oil-rich country well known for supporting revolutionary movements.

"That is worrying," said Dougal. "It could mean that Da Silva is on to a supply of arms, though he may just have borrowed the car to give us that impression."

"Da Silva... is that his name?" asked Tigger.

"The prince recognised the description. He's well known in Solung. Da Silva is thought to be the driving force behind the People's Army. He's quite a character. Born in Solung, but with a name like that he probably has Portuguese blood somewhere way back. Intelligent, free with his money, brave, and utterly ruthless. Seems he turned to revolution when he went on a scholarship to university in Delhi. The city kids there ribbed him for being a country boy. He got his own back by passing out top, came to study in London, and worked here for nearly 15 years in marketing, of all things. He was very good at it by all accounts and it seems he dresses flamboyantly as a way of self-promotion. I guess that's why he came in looking like Bogart on a bad day."

ooo

The airmen were used to taking off at a moment's notice and had few preparations to make. That evening, Tigger went to the local pub with Charlie, who was going to stay in England and contract out the company's commitments. Tigger drank little but liked to talk to the older airman while he had his regular evening pint. They sat in a corner, silent for a few moments, Tigger oblivious to the glances he was getting from office girls popping in for a drink on their way home, no doubt wondering what to make of this interesting-looking young man with the blue eyes and swept-back fair hair. His tee shirt and clean well-worn jeans gave little hint of what he did for a living.

Tigger was looking intently at his companion. "Do you mind being left behind, Charlie?"

"I'm getting past gallivanting about. You'll find that these

16

jobs are not all excitement."

There was more to it than that, Tigger knew. He could imagine the conversation Charlie had had on the phone with his doting wife, who lived in fear of Dougal dragging him off yet again into mortal danger. Dougal's old comrade was upset, Tigger could tell. He was chain-smoking, and his hand shook slightly as he sipped his drink. Charlie would tell him about it. They lapsed into silence again, gazing at the bustle around the bar.

Finally, Charlie said: "What do you think, Tigger? It sounds good, rescuing a princess, but how do you know what is going on out there? Maybe the guerrillas are right. I've seen India and I know what goes on there. I'm no communist, but sometimes I think that any system would be better than the one India's got already. People starving. Every man's uncle taking bribes. There's no way that place can work, the way things are now."

"Solung is not India."

"I'd be surprised if it is much different."

Tigger thought for a few seconds. "As far as I am concerned, a woman needs help and I can help her. I'm not involving myself in politics."

"You'll be playing politics whether you like it or not. But I can't tell you. If I were your age, I would go too. You'll learn. I bet that you'll come back thinking differently. If you see fighting out there, you'll never want to see any again, I'm telling you. Some men get to like war, but you're not the type."

"You're certainly right on one point, Charlie. You couldn't talk me out of going. I hate to admit it, but at the moment I don't care whether I am right or wrong. I've got to do it. A jaunt like this doesn't come more than once in a lifetime."

"Unless you are Dougal."

The enormity of the venture was beginning to strike Tigger. He asked: "Does Dougal get afraid?"

17

"Everyone does. Fear paralyses some people but Dougal seems to be able feed on it. He's galvanised by it. I was never like that. I always wanted to pull back, to step aside."

"Like this afternoon? You thought he was right when he turned the job down."

"I did and I do. There's something about that prince's story that doesn't quite add up. Dougal knows it too. He admitted to me that he thought the man was holding something back. But these jobs are never what you expect and where would any of us be if we were always sensible? Dougal wanted to go all the time, you know that. He turned the job down because he knew what I would say, and he knew I would be right."

"I'm glad he changed his mind but I was surprised that he did it just because Da Silva threatened him. It was like something out of a kid's story."

"Da Silva just gave him the excuse. Mind you, he didn't like the idea of Gosh taking the job on. Gosh was quite capable of rushing off and offering his services, and you might have been daft enough to go with him. Dougal wouldn't trust Gosh to lead a job like this. He's too hot headed."

Charlie lapsed into silence, staring into his beer, weighing his words. "I want to tell you something, Tigger. You remember that film we were involved in?"

Of course Tigger remembered. It was about the Battle of Britain, and it was the first time he met Dougal and Charlie. They had all flown Spitfires for the battle sequences. Dougal connected with Tigger immediately – perhaps because both had been orphaned in their teens, and maybe Tigger reminded him of the young men he flew with in the war.

"You didn't know Dougal before, so you wouldn't notice, but he's never been the same since," Charlie said. "He never used to be so moody. The film triggered something in him, I'm sure. Too many bad memories."

"But what about that first film, the one about his early life? Didn't that affect him? That had war scenes in it too."

18

"He never watched it. Never wanted anything to do with it. It made him angry, the focus on him. You'd understand if you'd been through what we went through. So many good men gone. We take the credit and they did the dying. It doesn't seem right. But the war scenes were not the half of it. The film dragged up all the stuff that happened to him before the war. You know about that?"

"I saw the film. He's never talked about it to me. It never felt right to ask."

"I've known him 30 years and he's only ever spoken to me about it once, after a good friend of ours got killed in the war. It was the only time I ever saw Dougal drunk, and the only time I saw him cry. It was also the first time I realised that he had signed on under age."

"Didn't he look too young?"

"We all looked young. No-one suspected until later in the war, when he was recognised by some high-up who knew his family in India. The top brass could hardly sack one of their most successful pilots, and by that time he was old enough to fly legally. So they told the press and made him a celebrity instead."

Tigger knew the story but he wanted to hear it from Charlie. "Was Dougal actually born in India?"

"Born in England. Brought up in India. An idyllic childhood. Servants. Out in the wilds. His dad was some sort of colonial administrator. Bought an aircraft to help him get about, and taught Dougal and his brother Danny to fly when they were barely big enough to see out of the cockpit. Totally against the rules, of course, but it was in deepest India and they could get away with it."

"Danny was older?"

"Two years. Their parents died of a fever days before war broke out. Two weeks later, the brothers were on their way to Bombay to take a ship to England when their train crashed and Danny was killed. Dougal told me it was the worst moment of his life."

19

"I couldn't believe that scene in the film. Dougal standing there by the crash, pretending to be Danny, almost within sight of his body. Just to get into the air force."

"The way Dougal told it to me, it was like attempted suicide. At that moment he didn't want to live. He was likely to get killed if he enlisted, and taking his brother's identity would get it over with more quickly. He'd planned to join the RAF as soon as he could anyway."

"It's one thing to think up something like that and another thing to carry it off. Especially when your whole world has just collapsed."

"That's Dougal all over. He's crystal clear, cool as cucumber, in a tight spot, but there's a lot churning away inside. He shuts it off, like he shut off Danny's death. It's as if the adrenalin focuses his mind, so there is no room for his troubles to get in."

"Is he hooked on the adrenalin? Is that why he keeps doing all this stuff?"

Charlie shrugged. "You tell me. He doesn't need to. He has money. The company is ticking over nicely. I thought he was beginning to settle down, and then this happens. He can't resist it. What worries me is that his luck is bound to run out some day. People see him as an expert on these jobs but he just barges in and wings it. It's always worked. He's taken risks and got away with it. You could do that in the old days. But now... I'm afraid everyone has upped their game."

"Are you telling me he is not up to it?"

"I'm telling you what you are letting yourself in for. If I had the choice of anyone in the world to take me on a mission like this, I'd pick Dougal. He's got experience and bottle, and that can take you a long way. He'll see you all right, I promise you. But he's not as tough as he seems. He needs looking after. That's what I'm trying to tell you. I won't be there to help. Keep an eye on him for me, will you?"

3   A deadly beginning

Two days later, the airmen arrived on a scheduled flight at the small civil airport that served Satpur, capital of Solung. The old military airstrip where they were to be based was within the airport perimeter and they arrived to find technicians testing a radio link with the control tower. Outside a hangar stood an old Dakota transport plane which had been put at their disposal by the Solung army.

Four Spitfires, apparently in perfect working condition, were lined up on the tarmac. "They are my joy and pride," said Babu, the former RAF mechanic who had looked after them since they came out of storage. He beamed on being congratulated for his work. "My son doing much, too. He grow up learning Spitfires. Every bit knowing. He first-class mechanic."

Babu pushed forward a young man, who smiled awkwardly. "This Ganesh, my son. You Dougal, Tigger, Gosh... you all my sons. You save Princess Sita, you all my sons."

"You know about the princess?" asked Dougal, sharply. The kidnap was still supposed to be secret.

The prince butted in. "Babu is practically one of the princess's family and he still does work for them. His family has served with them as retainers for centuries and they paid for Ganesh's education at an English-language school. Incidentally Ganesh has taken some flying lessons but we've yet to let him loose on a Spitfire."

"I know the princess when she baby," Babu said. "She sitting on my knee. I see her grow and play. I see her beautiful young lady. Now I see her mummy and daddy weeping. I am very sad man."

"Well, we'll have to see what we can do to cheer you up," said Dougal. "You've done a good job, Babu. These planes look good on the ground. Now we'll have to see what they feel like in the air."

To Tigger, raised in the mythology of World War Two, no aircraft could touch the romance of Spitfires. As a boy he was in awe of the men who flew them in battles with Nazi bombers and Messerschmitt fighters above besieged Britain, in full view of the people they were trying to protect, like the legendary warriors who fought to the death outside the walls of besieged Troy. He knew that the reality of war was horrific, yet it still held for him a kind of pornographic attraction, simultaneously fascinating and repugnant. The ritual battles of the sports field bored him; stories of the battlefield had him gripped, and battle in the air had an awful purity, uncluttered by the complications of the world. The death, the blood, the pain, the distress, the horror, the despair, were below the airman; and when death did reach out to the sky, it fell flaming to the earth and did not pollute the emptiness in which only the fit and able could chance themselves.

Tigger felt a surge of exhilaration as he climbed into one of the Spitfires and prepared to take off. The tiny cockpit seemed to fit him like a second skin. "You have to fly the aircraft as if it were part of you," an instructor had once told him. The words echoed in his mind as the Spitfire roared along the runway and lifted off into a cloudless sky. The engine was his muscle, the control cables were his nerves, his will was the will of the aircraft. Tigger was the machine and the machine was Tigger.

ooo

Satpur was the size of a small English town, a jumble of sun-baked buildings surrounding an area of ancient temples, set on the banks of a river fed by streams from the nearby mountains. There were few cars. Carts drawn by men, oxen and buffalo plied the narrow streets, but most carrying was done by men and women, bent double with loads slung across their backs from coloured bands stretched across their foreheads; children played half naked in muddy pathways as their mothers washed pots, collected water at public springs, chatted in doorways, or pounded the dirt and life out of clothes on riverside rocks. There was a pervasive, earthy stench foreign to modern cities: piss and shit, rank tobacco, woodsmoke, decaying food, spices, incense, and animal sweat.

The prince was inclined to be apologetic as they drove through the city after the test flight. "I am afraid that this must look dirty and primitive to you. We have a lot of work to do."

"Our cities were much the same little more than a century ago," Tigger said.

They drew up outside Satpur palace, a high-walled building in the city centre. A guard, scruffy in a threadbare uniform and bearing an ancient musket, saluted with more enthusiasm than grace, then pushed open a large, brass-studded wooden gate.

"We are not strong on military display," the prince said dryly as they passed through into a cobbled yard, surrounded on four sides by a large building made of masoned stone and huge carved beams. Each floor of the building was ringed on the inside by a balcony, so that the whole had something of the look of an Elizabethan theatre.

They were ushered straight through to the king, who was dressed in a grey suit that appeared rather too hot for the climate. He looked like an older version of his son. Hanging from the ceiling above him was a large elaborately embroidered drape attached to a cord which was tugged back and forth by an unseen minion to provide some surprisingly effective royal cooling. Around the king sat various relatives and advisers, all dressed in gleaming white cotton suits.

The king's voice seemed to have been lifted straight from a 1935 BBC recording, complete with crackle. "Squadron Leader FitzDougal! You are most welcome. I have heard much about your exploits. Saw a film of them, you know. I was at Oxford with some of your comrades. Driscoll... you know Driscoll?"

"We have met. Your son has explained some of the background to what is happening here but there are some details I would..."

"Driscoll... a courageous man, they tell me. Killed in '45. Never would have made a scholar, of course... more guts than brains. Were you at Oxford, FitzDougal?"

"Sadly, my education was interrupted by the war."

"I have great memories of the place. You've heard of Lord Eardley? He was at my college. Went on to be a great man. I remember meeting him at dinner...."

The prince looked discomfited. "Excuse me, daddy, but we don't have time to talk. These gentlemen have to be shown to their quarters."

"Of course. Of course. Perhaps they would like a drink. Whisky... warm up the vitals, eh? Or perhaps tea?"

"Tea would be welcome," Dougal said.

The king flicked his fingers in the vicinity of his right ear, and a turbaned servant scuttled off to disappear behind heavy curtains at the rear of the room.

"Your man has done a great job with the Spitfires, though I am not sure that we are going to need them," Dougal said.

"Spitfires... magnificent machines. Mind you, there are some who say the Me 109 had the edge in the Battle of Britain. The designs never had a true trial of strength in their most advanced form... "

The servant scuttled back and laid tiny cups of tea next to the airmen. "Sugar?" asked the king.

"None," said Dougal.

"One," said Tigger.

"Two," said Gosh.

"That's what's so fascinating about what we have here, don't you think?" the king said, resuming his flow.

"Fascinating?" Dougal's voice had an edge.

"My brother-in-law Sanjeev has some Messerschmitts at his flying club, you know. There can't be many places left where MEs are within scrapping distance of Spitfires."

"From what I understand, there is no possibility of a confrontation with them," Dougal said.

"Of course. Of course. Sanjeev is not going to get in your way. But he's very proud of his pilots. They are a pretty wild bunch by all accounts and they stage mock dogfights using what-do-you-call-ems... photo guns. I'm sure he would love you to join in with the Spitfires, see how his boys fare against a man with experience of the real thing."

"Forgive me your majesty but I have been in too many dogfights to be able to treat them as a game. I've come here to rescue a princess, not compete in a fighter pilots' cup final."

Dougal's asperity was lost on the king. "Yes. We've got to do something about young Sita. Headstrong girl. Probably brought it all on herself. She's alive and kicking, my spies tell me. The kidnappers probably got more than they bargained for, eh what?"

The prince did not like the way the conversation was going. "Daddy... perhaps we should allow these gentlemen to make themselves at home before we talk more."

"Quite right, my boy. I forget myself. Not often I meet any English gentlemen these days. Reminds me of old times. Now when I was..."

The airmen had stood up, their tea untouched. "Daddy... I'll see you at supper," the prince said, evidently accustomed to cutting short the parental recollections.

If the visitor's hurried departure was ill-mannered, the king did not seem to notice. As the prince ushered them out, they could hear his father telling the courtiers: "I bet he could teach Sanjeev's boys a thing or two."

When they were clear of the room, the prince said: "I should have warned you about daddy."

"Bit much, old boy, treating us like new players in a football team," Gosh said.

"Don't underestimate him. He is very shrewd and he uses that silly-ass act to stay aloof from all the factions here – but it *is* an act. Just look at his purchase of those Spitfires. They are worth a fortune, just as relics, but they are saving a fortune on the cost of a modern air force."

Dougal stayed on for supper at the palace to discuss business with the prince, leaving Tigger alone with Gosh, who regaled him with gruesome stories of his army days. Tigger had heard most of them before and they did not make for comfortable listening now. "Can't you talk of something else?" he asked, after Gosh had given graphic details of an incident in which he had killed a man with his bare hands.

"Not got the stomach for it, old boy? You'll have to pull yourself together if you meet those guerrillas, or they'll have your guts for garters."

Realising that he was being wound up, Tigger saw a chance to change the subject. "I'm wondering whether we have more than guerrillas to worry about. Didn't you think it was odd the way the king kept going on about those Messerschmitts?"

"The man's a fool. His precious princess is in the hands of killers and he is prattling on about us playing dogfights at the family flying club. He needs to get his priorities right."

"I wonder. Charlie told me he thought something about all this didn't quite add up. The same thing struck me when the king talked about his brother-in-law's fighter pilots. Remember Prince Raju told Dougal that Solung doesn't have any. If the king is as shrewd as his son says he is, I'd say he was doing a pretty good job of putting us on our guard while avoiding awkward questions."

ooo

They awoke the next morning to the feeling of having stepped back half a century. It had been too dark the previous evening to take in their surroundings. Now they found themselves in a large bungalow in a former British army camp near the airstrip. Built for visiting officers, it had changed little from British times: large, airy bedrooms with shuttered windows that opened on to a shady veranda with cane chairs and tables; the bedroom doors all led to a dining room containing a single, long wooden table; armchairs, worn from use, dated from the thirties; bookshelves still contained the reading material of a generation back, with pages yellowing into history: green and orange Penguin paperbacks, old Agatha Christies, a strident exposé of the German menace, a Hindustani primer. The stuffed head of a once-celebrated racing horse took pride of place on a wall, alongside pictures of past officers and forgotten polo teams, the faces caught in the flush of a youth long since lost in private memory or the grave.

From the veranda, they could look across a dusty plain, patched with tiny fields, to where the Himalayas exploded into the sky. Moving across the landscape was the ubiquitous traffic of the subcontinent: carts and buffalo, women in sarees with burdens on their heads, clerks on bicycles, rickety buses. To Dougal it was all as familiar as childhood. He took for granted the obsequity of the bungalow's several servants, each with a caste-dictated job: sweeper, cook, gardener, and waiters who served with a style marred only slightly by their scuffed shoes and grubby white costumes.

The prince arrived shortly after breakfast bearing satellite pictures of the area where the princess was believed to be held. "It's humbling to have to ask a foreign country for pictures of one's own. These are from the US government."

The guerrilla-held village lay at a height of about four thousand feet, poised above a river that plunged in a series of rapids and waterfalls down a steep valley. The pictures showed buildings grouped around an open square. An area in a high tributary valley about four miles away was ringed in red. The prince explained that here the valley shelved into a flat area that had been cleared for use as a contingency airstrip during the war when Japan threatened the borders of

India.

Dougal, who already knew much of what the prince had been telling them, said: "Are you absolutely certain that the strip is still usable?"

"You will receive confirmation from a man you are about to meet. Actually, he insisted on seeing you. I would have liked to have kept him away."

"Why?" asked Dougal suspiciously.

"Krishna Baba is a little eccentric. You must understand that people who in your country would be regarded as cranks hold enormous sway here. He is seen as a holy man."

Dougal exploded. "Cranks? You're not asking me to listen to a crank?"

"I said you may *see* him as a crank," said the prince, a little irritated. "Someone from Solung might think the same of the Pope, dressing up in fancy dress, calling himself God's anointed, and blessing people."

"Quite right, too. I wouldn't ask the Pope about the safety of an airstrip. But then I'm not a Roman Catholic."

"All I ask is that you suspend judgement and listen to what he says."

The conversation was interrupted by a servant, who ushered in the oddest-looking man Tigger had ever seen. Krishna Baba was very thin and very short, though his greying hair was piled up to add six inches to his height. He wore only an orange loincloth and a red waistcoat; an embroidered bag was slung from one shoulder. "*Namaste*," he said, placing his hands together in greeting.

This was to be Tigger's only meeting with Krishna Baba, and he was to recall it many times in conversation with Henry the Hippy. His reaction now was one of faint amusement.

After introductions were exchanged, the prince said: "Krishna Baba speaks little English, so I will have to translate what he says."

The prince deferred unselfconsciously to the little man as

28

He knew immediately that he had overshot the target area.
(see page 35)

they conversed in Solungese. Finally, the prince said: "Babaji says that normally the airstrip is unusable by aircraft because it is occupied by buffalo herders and their animals. Da Silva and the People's Army feel safe because they know we have no helicopters and they are watching all other possible routes into the valley."

"So how are we going to get in there?" asked Tigger.

"A friend of Babaji's, a hermit who lives nearby, is arranging for it to be cleared ready for use as a landing strip. He will ensure that the herders move their buffalo to a higher valley for a couple of days to get them out of the way. It's apparently been done before."

The prince hesitated. "Krishna Baba insists on me telling you that the arrangement was made before the kidnap. He predicted the kidnap."

"You're asking us to stake our lives on this mumbo-jumbo? Has your holy man seen the airstrip and how does he know it will be clear?"

Krishna Baba, who evidently understood much of what was being said, smiled as if at a private joke. He and the prince conferred again. "Babaji says he understands that you are bound to doubt him. He suggests that you drop someone by parachute to check his story."

"I can't ask anyone to do that. Apart from the danger of a drop in the mountains, whoever went would be stranded if the strip is not clear."

"I'll do it," Tigger said. "I've done the training."

"I won't let you risk your neck. I'm sure that Krishna Baba is sincere but I'm afraid I can only act on hard information."

"You should not assume that Krishna Baba is sincere on all points," the prince said. "He has a peculiar sense of humour. You can trust him on essential points."

"Are you seriously asking me to trust a man on the assumption that he is lying? I'm not surprised this place has problems. It's run by madmen."

"He has his little jokes," the prince said.

Tigger said: "He would look pretty foolish if we went to the strip and found nothing had been done."

Krishna Baba resorted to English. "I go with parachute. Tigger go with parachute. He lost. I lost. This good."

Dougal exploded. "Good to be lost?"

Krishna Baba waggled his head. "No problem. Strip is clear. You coming. Plane coming. All good."

Tigger smiled at the idea of this crazy little man at the end of a parachute.

"This is no joke," Dougal said.

Gosh spoke for the first time. "We have no choice, old boy. Unless we pack up and go home. Personally, I don't feel like going back with my tail between my legs and Da Silva smirking all the way to the revolution."

"If anyone jumps, it should be me."

"You have the most flying experience," Tigger said. "It's best if you do the flying. Landing on the strip could be tricky. Gosh can't jump because of his back. It's got to be me."

"You certainly won't do it with Krishna Baba. He'd break his neck," Dougal said. "I don't like it but I can't see any other way out."

Krishna Baba began to speak rapidly in Solungese. The prince translated: "Babaji says Tigger is a brave young man but he will have moments of fear, and fear is a great teacher. For you, Dougal and Gosh, learning is difficult because your heads are too full. But Tigger can learn because he is innocent, and the innocent are blessed."

"I always said I was innocent, yer honour," Tigger said.

"We don't need a sage to tell us you are young and impressionable," Dougal said. "He's spotted you for a sucker. When I was a boy out here you couldn't move without meeting one of these people. I deal with things and facts. I understand them. At the moment, the fact is that we have little time to stand around philosophising."

"So I'll make the jump as soon as possible," said Tigger.

If Krishna Baba understood any of Dougal's remarks, he showed no sign of it. "All finished? I going," he said, closing his palms in blessing. The prince left the room with him.

Tigger said: "What do you make of him saying the airstrip was cleared before the kidnap?"

"That's how these fellows work," Dougal said. "They build up an atmosphere of superstition around them, and people are willing to believe the most ordinary events are miracles. There'll be some explanation, I'll bet."

"The obvious explanation would be that he is in league with the kidnappers and knew their plans," said Gosh.

"Then why should he make a point of telling us? He probably knows the area is relatively clear anyway, and made up that story to impress us. What I don't like is Tigger having to risk his life to prove him right or wrong."

ooo

It was agreed that Dougal and Tigger would take off in the Dakota just before dawn the next day so as to be over the mountains at first light. Babu, who had been brought up in the area, would go with them to point out the airstrip.

The airmen were not worried about using the 30-year-old Dakota, although they made sure to give it a thorough checkover. Its delicate art-deco lines disguised a robust design that was the workhorse of Allied forces during the Second World War. Solung was far from the only country where they were still in service. To Tigger, it was a classic machine and he looked forward to flying in it, though his sleep that night was disturbed by thoughts of where the flight might take him.

Babu picked them up in the early hours, and drove carefully under a moonless sky along a deserted road, knowing that at any moment an unlit bullock cart or a stray animal might loom out of the darkness. His son Ganesh, who looked much younger than his 21 years, had come along for the ride and they decided that he might as well come on the flight too, because he knew the mountains as well as his father and his younger eyes might prove useful. Another reason, which they were too polite to mention, was to reduce the chance of misunderstanding; Ganesh spoke fluent, charmingly accented English.

As they entered the airport, they drew curtains round the car's side windows to avoid prying eyes. Babu drove them straight to the Dakota which stood ready on the runway.

"You plane starting," he said cheerfully. "I take car. Parking. Two minutes, I coming."

Tigger was to remember incidentals of the next few seconds with the capricious clarity that can come when confronted with the terrible. A blast came just as Ganesh clambered after Dougal into the Dakota. By its flash, and even as it bowled him over, Tigger registered Ganesh's foot stopping mid-step, and the aircraft rocking, and the startled look of the mechanics lounging around. He was aware of Dougal rushing out of the aircraft and past him; then he followed, his mind and body still reeling.

The car was in flames, and Babu's body could be seen sizzling obscenely, like a Sunday roast, in the front seat. Nearby stood a smouldering wooden cart which had been carrying an urn of tea for airport workers. Next to it, writhing in agony from cuts and burns, lay the man who had been pushing it. Tigger, struggling to mitigate the horror in some way, noted that at least the man's face and eyes seemed untouched. Ganesh was sobbing and screaming a few yards from the car, a mechanic fighting to restrain him from making a futile attempt to extricate his father. Dougal, ashen and tight-lipped, appeared with a first-aid box and gave the injured man a shot of morphine. Clear-headed under stress, like Charlie had said.

"Can I do anything?" Tigger asked.

"Calm Ganesh down if you can and get him on the plane. I'm going to talk to the airport supervisor and see if he can seal the place off for a couple of hours, so the wrong people won't know exactly what happened."

"We are still going to fly?"

"It's the only way to keep them on the hop. News of this will be all over Satpur by this evening. If we go now, we may be able to maintain surprise."

To Tigger's relief, Ganesh had calmed down considerably and went willingly to the aircraft. "I'll come. It's what daddy would have wanted," he said, tears rolling down his face. By the time he had sat down, the shock seemed to have sent him into a trance. He nodded dully when Tigger asked if he felt capable of picking out the right valley. With a mechanic's help, Tigger managed to start the engine of the unfamiliar aircraft and a few seconds later Dougal was at the controls.

"Any idea what happened?" Tigger said, as the aircraft roared into the pre-dawn sky.

"Car bomb. The swine booby-trapped the car. Looks like it went off when Babu braked to avoid the cart. An inertial trigger. We were lucky Babu was such a careful driver or it might have got us on the way here."

"You think it was Da Silva's work?"

"Probably one of his men."

For the next few minutes, Tigger tried to forget about the bombing and concentrate on present dangers. They were completely at the mercy of the aircraft's instruments as they headed up through low mist towards the mountains. One small fault in the reading of a dial, and they would smash into the foothills. Soon they were above the mist and could see the mountain peaks sticking up like islands in a cotton-wool ocean. Dougal had taken a detour to approach the valley without flying over the kidnappers. When he banked round to make his approach, the peaks were silhouetted against the pink glow of dawn. Ganesh, red-eyed and speaking with difficulty, was brought forward into the co-pilot's seat. To the airmen's relief, he confidently pointed out landmarks, and soon spotted a high lake which fed a stream leading to the small treeless plateau where the airstrip was.

When Dougal was sure Tigger knew where to jump, he banked the Dakota round to repeat his approach. "Ganesh... you'll have to close the hatch after Tigger jumps," he said. "Make sure you don't fall. You'd better put on a parachute, just in case."

Tigger helped Ganesh with his chute and stood by the open hatch; his heart beat faster when the jump zone came into view. Closing his eyes involuntarily, he pushed himself through the hatch and to his horror his backpack snagged on an unseen protrusion. For a couple of seconds he hung half in and half out of the aircraft, then the blast of air tore him away and he felt thin cold air clutch at him, and his parachute jerked, and he was dangling in the serenity of space. He knew immediately that he had overshot the target area, and looking down he feared that he would land among the pine trees; but his forward drift carried him over a ridge, and brown scrub-covered earth rushed towards him, and he was frightened. It was not flat earth, waiting to receive him. It was a slope so precipitous that it threatened to tip him on to the rocky bed of a river far, far below. His feet touched earth, and he was pitched uncontrollably onward.

4   Ganesh drops in

After several seconds of sliding and bumping down the slope
he felt a tug on his parachute; then he hit something with
such force that the air was knocked out of his body. It took
him some time to recover his breath and realise what had
happened. His parachute had caught between two rocks and
he had swung round in its harness to slam into an outcrop
300 feet above the valley floor. Now he had lost his momentum, he seemed to be in no immediate danger: the scrub-
covered slope was not so steep that he could not scramble
up. But his relief did not last long. He heard a shout from
below and saw a man climbing up towards him. Was it a vil-
lager or a guerrilla? Frantically, Tigger struggled to extricate
himself from the parachute but by the time he was free the
man was almost on him. To his astonishment he heard the
words: "Tigger, are you OK?"

It was Ganesh.

Tigger closed his eyes, shook his head, and looked again.

"Phew," said Ganesh, looking at the jammed parachute,
and then the rocks below them. "You were lucky!"

"Ganesh! How on earth did you get here?"

"I saw you had missed the airstrip, so I jumped after you.
You'd never find your way there without me." He paused
and tears came into his eyes. "And I want to get those people
who killed daddy."

"Did you tell Dougal you were going to jump?"

"I shouted but I couldn't wait or I'd have lost you. My
parachute was on so I jumped. Are you OK? We'd better
get out of sight."

Tigger could move, although he felt bruised and shaken, and he was relieved to find that the contents of his backpack had survived the fall – including, crucially, the radio he would need to contact Dougal. They hid the parachute behind the rocks in which it had jammed and followed goat trails up the slope to the shelter of a forest, where they sat down to take stock. Ganesh did not appear to think he had done anything remarkable in jumping. He had seen Tigger tumbling down the slope but he had himself landed safely by the river and feared the worst when Tigger did not move.

They were on the far side of the river from the village held by the kidnappers, and Ganesh reckoned they were a four-hour walk from the airstrip.

"We had better get on our way. Is there a path?"

"I'm not familiar with this side of the river. The only people who come here are loggers and goatherds. But there must be a path. There always is."

"We'll just have to climb up until we find it," said Tigger.

The path turned out to be only a short distance above them. They agreed that Ganesh, who could pass as a local, should walk a couple of hundred yards ahead of Tigger and warn him to hide if he saw anyone coming. In the event, no-one passed them. After about three miles, Ganesh stopped and motioned Tigger to catch up. They had reached a point where the path plunged a couple of hundred feet downwards to where a stream from a side valley joined the river, which was spanned by a narrow wooden walkway slung below two cables. Next to it was what at first sight looked like a pile of rubbish: scraps of plastic and old tins bashed flat and spread over some rocks. Closer inspection showed that this was the roof of a makeshift shelter.

"I know this place," said Ganesh. "We have to follow that side stream to get to the airstrip. There is a shorter route up the main valley but it's a steeper climb and would mean crossing that bridge."

"Is there someone living in the place down there?"

"It's a family of Tibetans. They sell *chung*, a kind of beer. They live out here because no-one is allowed to sell alcohol in the villages."

"Can they be trusted?"

"No idea. And there may be other people inside the shop. It's bigger than it looks from here."

"Then I guess we'd better stay this side and try to avoid the shop." Tigger pointed to a faint track branching off from the path in the general direction of the side valley. "Do you think that will take us in the right direction?"

"You can't always trust these tracks. They can peter out into nothing. But if we keep heading over that way we should hit the main path again."

In fact the track fractured in many places into hundreds of mini-trails where goats had dispersed to seek food among the trees. Tigger could easily have got lost; but Ganesh, with a better sense of the lie of the land, unerringly found where the track resumed. It led mercilessly up and up so that Tigger's breath began to come in gasps and his leg muscles screamed protest. Ganesh, keeping a slow, even pace, did not seem to feel the strain.

Eventually the track rejoined the main path up the valley and by the time the sun had risen well above the peaks they reached a ledge where a spreading tree offered welcome shade. At its foot was a crude stone bench worn smooth by generations of passers-by. Water from a nearby stream trickled through a groove cut into a rock, evidently for the purpose of providing travellers with a drink. But the water dribbled down the face of the rock and Tigger tried with little success to catch some using his hands as a cup.

Ganesh laughed and picked a leaf from the tree. "This is the way to do it," he said, bending the leaf into a funnel and sticking one end into the groove. Clear cold water cascaded from it, a perfect little drinking fountain.

They sat under the tree for a few minutes, safe for a while in this little paradise where they could see anyone approaching before they were seen themselves. The memory of the day's events was oppressive. Tigger said awkwardly: "I'm sorry about your father, Ganesh. I feel we are to blame in a way. If we had not come, he might still be alive."

"If I see Da Silva, I'll kill him," Ganesh said simply.

"We have to get the princess first." Tigger was alarmed that a private vendetta might disrupt the mission. "How far are we from the airstrip?"

"Two hours walk. Maybe less. It may be better to wait a little. People are less likely to come down this path in the late afternoon because they will want to give themselves time to reach the village before nightfall. There'll be nowhere to hide once we get out of these trees."

They made themselves comfortable, hidden among bushes a little uphill from the path and eating some of the food Tigger had brought with him. The shock of his heavy landing had caught up with him and he found himself dozing off.

Ganesh noticed it too. "You sleep a while. I'll keep watch," he said.

The sun had sunk behind the mountain tops by the time Tigger awoke so that their little resting place was in shadow, though nightfall was three hours away. Tigger felt as refreshed as if he had had a good night's sleep. They set off at a good pace and soon reached the edge of the forest. The path took them relentlessly upwards until they crested a ridge, where they were greeted with a sight that stopped Tigger in his tracks. A trick of the topography had brought the entire main valley into view, a giant staircase of slopes and plateaux, ever widening, its sides covered with pine forest punctuated by cultivated terraces, villages, and waterfalls spilling hundreds of feet into the swelling river. A faint haze on the horizon showed where the plains began. Far below them they could just make out the *chung* shop at the river junction. Immediately below them was a waterfall, fed by a stream cutting through a shelf long and flat enough to land an aircraft. "The airstrip," Ganesh said.

To Tigger's relief, it looked deserted. "No sign of any guards," he said. "I'm surprised Da Silva doesn't know about this place."

"Normally it doesn't look like a place where you could land an aircraft. A group of nomads use it as summer pasture for buffalo so there are usually animals wandering about. They must have been moved up the valley, out of the way. In winter this is all deep in snow."

"So let's take a closer look."

They scrambled down the final slope and began walking along a clear strip that ran alongside one bank of the river. The ground sloped upwards slightly, but not dangerously; there were a few barely perceptible undulations but nothing that would upset an aircraft. The sun had almost set by the time they had walked the entire length of the strip.

"It looks OK... Krishna Baba was right," Tigger said.

Ganesh shrugged. "You had to check."

At the end of the runway was a small brick lodge with a corrugated iron roof, presumable a relic of wartime. They sat there and shared food from Tigger's pack while he called up Dougal on the radio.

Dougal's voice came over, faint but reassuring. "I am receiving you. How is the property?"

"You can take over when you like. Perhaps I should do some final checking on legal complications, just to check our rivals aren't in the picture."

"Do if you can. But be careful not to attract attention. Did you see anything of our mutual friend?"

"He apologises for leaving without saying goodbye. He realised that I had gone to the wrong address and came to show me the way. It was a good thing he did."

Tigger gave further details of the "property": the slight slope, the fact that it ran alongside the river, and the best way of approaching it.

Dougal said: "OK. We'll call on you as arranged. I'll

bring a few friends."

"I'll be here."

Tigger switched off and considered his next move. Dougal would arrive "as arranged", their code for sunrise the next day. The timing had been the subject of much discussion. Gosh had favoured flying in just before nightfall and moving in on the village at night; Dougal had felt that moving round the mountains in the dark could prove more dangerous than the guerrillas, who would anyway least expect a daylight raid. The final decision had been postponed until Tigger reported. Evidently, Dougal considered that if Tigger could arrive undetected by day, so could he.

By "friends", Dougal meant soldiers to guard the airstrip and hold the path leading from the village. He had also given Tigger the go-ahead to do a little scouting on his own account. This suited Tigger; it was still only early evening, a near-full moon was rising, and he did not feel inclined to sit around until morning.

Ganesh insisted on going with him. "We don't need to retrace our steps to get near the village," he said. "There's another track that takes us out of this valley direct to the main river, where we can follow the path on the far side. You'll never find the way by yourself."

Tigger began having doubts about the venture as soon as they set off but he could not bring himself to turn back. He knew he was stretching Dougal's go-head to the limit but he was high on adrenalin, and after his short sleep he felt as fresh as if he had just got up. He quickly learned one of the hard lessons of mountains: that heading downwards does not necessarily mean that you have finished with going up. In the massive Himalayas you might have to climb a ridge higher than any British mountain simply to reach the next downward slope.

The ridge they now climbed, opposite the one from which they had approached the airstrip, was not that high but it was very heavy going. The moon lay low, hidden behind

41

the ridge, so there was little light, and the track zig-zagged wildly upwards on a slope only a few degrees off the vertical. Parts of it were little more than a succession of footholds, slippery with the dew of the night. Even more treacherous were little streams that trickled down the slope, turning it into mud. More than once, Tigger had to clutch for a handhold as his foot slipped on a shrub or a root worn smooth by passing feet.

The world lit up as they crested the ridge into full moonlight and they descended steeply towards the big river. Ganesh led the way to a point where it broadened into shallows and they could cross by the use of stepping stones. The path on the far side was substantial enough to take a cart or rough-terrain car, but they still had to walk carefully, hugging the mountainside to reduce the chances of being seen, staying silent, stopping every few seconds to listen for signs of activity ahead.

Tigger's estimation of Ganesh was going up by the hour. Babu's son seemed to have a natural aptitude for the task in hand. Once, he held Tigger back and peered cautiously round a bend. "Take a look but don't show yourself," he whispered. Tigger saw that the path ahead had been cut into a sheer rockface, passing at the far end through a tunnel that looked a likely place for a guard post. But there was no sign of life as they edged forward. Finding the far end of the tunnel deserted, Tigger began to feel more confident: the guerrillas clearly did not expect trouble from this direction.

A quarter-mile further on Ganesh again tugged at Tigger's sleeve. Peering ahead, he could see the flash of water. "It's an old water mill," Ganesh whispered.

"Water mill? It doesn't look big enough."

"Many of the villages around here have one. They're just about big enough to house a grindstone but they offer some shelter and sometimes travellers sleep in them. It might be used as a guard post. The village is two or three hundred yards further on."

The moon had gone behind a cloud and Tigger stared through the darkness at the mill. Was anyone inside? He did not know and he did not relish trying to find out. Ganesh dropped to his knees and without saying anything began to crawl off the path towards the river. Tigger followed him down yet another side trail that led to a series of narrow cultivated terraces. Here they wormed forward, feeling their way with their hands. Rocks, stones and thorns rucked up their clothes and tore at their skin. Tigger, who had forgotten that the world could get so dark, began to feel like a mole burrowing through the night. He was aware only of the feel of the ground – here damp, here sandy, here rock, here cold soft grass – and the sounds, the roar and trickle of water, the whish of the night birds flying, the clicks and whistles of unseen creatures, the rustle and scrape of their own moving bodies, and his own laboured breathing. Somewhere ahead a dog howled, warning of yet another peril: at that time of night, animals were likely to be more alert than men. No sooner had the thought come to Tigger's mind, than a large grunt sounded from nearby. It was only a cow or buffalo calling out in its sleep but it made him jump back with shock, his heart pounding. They had reached a house at the edge of the village.

Ganesh felt about in front of him, then stood up, hugging a wall, tugging Tigger to follow. They edged along the rough stone surface until the wall ended, and they could dimly perceive that they were at the side of a square.

For five minutes, they stood there. An animal, probably a dog, padded across the square but did not see them. Ganesh nudged Tigger and pointed. Straining his eyes, Tigger saw a movement in the shadows on the far side of the square. It was regular, back and forth. A guard. That must be where the princess was being held.

Instinctively, he and Ganesh shrank back as if to sink further into the anonymous night. The sight of the guard seemed little enough justification for all the trouble they had taken to get to the village. Tigger was determined to find out more, and there was a wild hope at the back of his mind that he might be able to effect a rescue by himself. He had not expected to get this far; and now when they had got so close he was determined to make the most of the opportunity.

He cupped his hand over Ganesh's ear and whispered: "You stay here for 30 minutes. If I don't return go back to airstrip. There are two flares in my backpack. Use them to mark the start of the landing strip and light them when the plane comes. Understood?"

"Understood."

Tigger began worming his way round the square. Once he felt a scalding pain in his belly and wriggled desperately to one side, fighting the reflex to jump up. The front of his shirt was wet and he remembered someone saying that there was a hot spring in the village. He had evidently crawled across a channel that took the hot water to the river. By the time he got close to where he estimated that he had seen the guard, he could no longer make out any movement. He waited for several minutes, then heard a cough from nearby. A human cough. A shape moved, and a man who had been sitting down began pacing about again.

Prince Raju had told him of the rough layout of the houses in the village. Built of wood and stone, they had two floors, with animals at ground level and people in the upper floor. He could just make out the edge of the house in front of him, silhouetted against the sky. He was wondering how he could get past the pacing man when the guard decided for him, disappearing round the side of the house. Tigger heard the splash of water, and for all his tenseness, he could not suppress a smile at the strength of human habit that made a man piss furtively even in pitch dark. He took the opportunity to dart forward; his hands located a log slung vertically, with footholds cut into the side to form a crude ladder, and he shinned up it to a balcony that fronted the upper floor.

He felt his way to a door and felt for the latch, waiting for any sound that might cover that of the door opening. When the sound came, it brought further cause for concern. A dog began barking from near the spot where he had left Ganesh, who should have left by now. The dog roused others in the village, and soon there was howling from all directions. Tigger had no chance to worry about Ganesh. He pushed the door, breathing freely as he realised that it was not locked, and closed it behind him as he stepped in. As he paused, trying to see in the darkness, he got his biggest shock of the day. A match flared in front of him and lit a candle. There were three men in the room, lying on mattresses and all looking as startled as he felt. Two had grabbed rifles, which they were pointing at him. The third, holding the candle, was the man he had last seen getting into a Bentley in London.

5   Dougal takes to the river

It had taken some time for Dougal to realise that Ganesh was
no longer in the aircraft after Tigger jumped out. He heard
Ganesh shout something but could not make out what he
said. When the aircraft was safety out of the mountains,
Dougal set the controls on automatic and walked back into
the body of the plane. Whatever had happened to Ganesh,
he decided, he could do nothing about it. He closed the
hatch and was back at Satpur within minutes.

The airport was still under a security blanket; night-shift
workers who had seen the explosion were squatting in the
shade of hangars, waiting for permission to leave. Even so, it
quickly became obvious that the news had leaked out. As a
taxi took him through the city, he saw scrawled in large white
letters on a wall: "British mercenaries go home. Next time it
will be you."

He spent an anxious day planning how to approach the
village if Tigger reported the landing area clear. After all the
fuss about the Spitfires, he decided to use only the Dakota as
he was assured that there was no reason to suppose that it
would be attacked from the air. Gosh would come as co-pilot
and stay with the aircraft to enable a getaway if anything
should happen to Dougal.

"But I shall miss the fun and games, old boy," Gosh protested.

"You may get more fun and games than you care to play.
We've no idea what is going to happened up there. Also you
can liaise with the soldiers. They may want you to collect
reinforcements."

This was a delicate matter. They were to take a dozen

well-armed soldiers to guard the airstrip and cover the approaches, and the Dakota could return to pick up more if necessary. The Solung army, prickly at having foreigners called in to work on its patch, refused to allow them direct control of the troops, who would be commanded by a young captain. Dougal did not like the arrangement but was mollified when the officer turned out to be co-operative and capable.

They took off just before first light the next morning and arrived above the landing zone at dawn. Dougal was relieved to see that two flares had been lit to mark the start of the airstrip; he lined the Dakota up with these and the traveller's lodge Tigger had told him was at the far end. He knew the landing would be tricky because the slight upwards slope of the strip would tend to distort his perception of distance, though it would help the Dakota come to a halt. Nevertheless he got the aircraft down without trouble and immediately turned it round, ready for take off.

Ganesh ran up and told Dougal the bad news. "I think they may have Tigger. We managed to get into the village last night and saw a house under guard. Tigger crawled over to see if he could establish that the princess was there. I haven't seen him since. He told me to come back here if he didn't return. I hung around for as long as I could, but some dogs started howling and I had to get out."

"Thanks, Ganesh. You've done very well. You'd better wait here with the soldiers."

"Excuse me sir, but you will need a guide. I know round here like the back of my hand."

"But you've been up all night. You must be exhausted."

"I slept for an hour. I'm OK but I'm starving. Do you have food?"

The Solungese captain deployed lookouts while Ganesh ate and gave a full account of the previous night's events, using Dougal's satellite images to show the route he and Tigger had taken. "Obviously you landed within their perimeter of defence where they thought they did not need to saturate the place with guards," said Dougal, trying to hide his vexation. "We have to assume Tigger's been captured, which means Da Silva is sure to be on guard. We've lost surprise, and we have two people to rescue instead of one."

"The one direction the guerrillas will not expect us to come from is the river," said Ganesh.

"Why is that?"

"It's too fast and rocky for boats and you can't walk all the way along the banks because at points cliffs drop sheer to the water. But there is a way we could use it. The forests around here are supposed to be protected but a lot of illegal logging goes on. The loggers trim the trees and float the logs downstream. They've been known to strap a couple of logs together to form a raft and ride it downstream. It doesn't happen often because most mountain people can't swim. I spoke to a man who rode the logs and he said it was easier that it looked. You make sure to stay midstream and make for the bank before you hit the rapids. The water is not that deep so you can manoeuvre yourself with poles."

"It sounds mad to me," said Dougal.

"It may sound mad but it has been done. I've always wanted to try it." Ganesh picked up a satellite image and pointed to a place just downriver from the *chung* shop. "I saw some logs stacked here yesterday. There's a clear run from there to just past the village, where there are rapids, but we could pull over to the bank before then."

"We? Are you proposing to go?"

"Sir... you need two people, one at each end, to keep the raft stable. And you need someone to show you the way."

"I can't put your life at risk. What would your parents say?"

"My daddy is dead, sir." Ganesh paused, pointedly.

Dougal had forgotten about Babu, and kicked himself for his tactlessness. "Ganesh I can understand you want to get the people responsible but we have a job to do. We can't

48

have you going on a private campaign of revenge."

"Daddy wanted Sita rescued, too. He would have wanted me to go. So would my mother."

Dougal was not so sure about the last point but Ganesh was no longer a child. "They would certainly be proud of everything you have done in the past day Ganesh. Are you sure this river idea is feasible... I mean, won't the raft be seen from the road and village?"

"The road and village are high above the river. You can't see it for trees most of the way. We'd have to be very unlucky."

Dougal didn't like the plan but he could think of nothing better. They had a stroke of luck when a buffalo herder appeared from the valley below. He had stayed the night in the *chung* shop and reported that this at least was clear of People's Army men.

After a quick council of war with the Solungese captain and Gosh, it was agreed that most of the soldiers would take discreet positions in and around the shop and bridge, covering both routes to the airstrip and serving as a back-up force if one became necessary. Dougal picked up an axe and some rope from contingency supplies they had loaded into the Dakota, and packed weapons and food into waterproof bags.

The weapons included a Sten gun with several magazines for Dougal, and a revolver. Ganesh had learned to fire a rifle in the cadet crops at school and Dougal reluctantly agreed that they should take one for him, as well as a large knife in case they needed to cut any vegetation. "Now be clear Ganesh. I want us all to get out of this alive. I don't want you carrying on a private war," he said.

"Understood, sir."

Then he, Ganesh, and the soldiers set off up the track to the *chung* shop, with one soldier being sent ahead to check for trouble. A disgruntled Gosh was left in charge of the airstrip.

They did not need to make the tortuous detour that Tigger and Ganesh had taken the previous day, and most of the going was downhill, so they arrived at the *chung* shop in little over an hour. The Tibetans were alone, and seemed to think that being taken over by the soldiers was preferable to being at the mercy of the guerrillas. Given the choice of staying or going, they decided to move up to the airstrip until the soldiers left.

Ganesh led Dougal to the stash of logs he had spotted on the riverbank and with the help of two soldiers they lashed three together and levered them into the water. Dougal trimmed a couple of branches to form poles and they were ready to go.

The raft moved slowly when they pushed out from the bank but by the time they reached midstream they were travelling at a fast running pace. The river was broad and relatively shallow at first so that they could touch the bottom with their poles. Dougal relaxed and even felt exhilarated as they sped downriver, but the feeling turned to alarm as they approached a narrow V-shaped gap between two rocky outcrops where the river ran too fast and deep for their poles. They shot through the gap at the mercy of the current and the raft hit a rock as they emerged, nearly throwing them into the water. They fought desperately to stay on board as it swung crazily from side to side but somehow managed to keep hold of the poles and straighten the makeshift vessel; almost as soon as they got it steady, Ganesh called: "Head for the right bank."

To Dougal's surprise this was accomplished quite easily with some judicious prodding, and the raft thudded gently into some gently shelving gravel. Ganesh was laughing. "That was great," he said.

"You have a funny idea of greatness. I thought we were going to come a cropper out there."

Ganesh reckoned that, as much by luck as by judgement, they had landed almost directly below the village though they could not see it through the trees. They pulled the raft onto the bank, unpacked their things from the waterproofs, and began making their way cautiously up the side of the valley from pine tree to pine tree until they could see roofs peeping above a strip of cultivated terraces. A gully promised cover for the final stretch to the village; its sides were choked with vegetation but they managed to clamber upwards along a rock-strewn stream at its base.

Close to the point where they guessed they were at the level of the village, Dougal took advantage of a break in the vegetation to peek over the edge of the gully, but he dropped back immediately in consternation. Only twenty yards away a boy of no more than fifteen was squatting on his haunches, a rifle stretched across his knee, a belt of ammunition slung across his shoulders. It was Dougal's first sight of a People's Army guerrilla.

He had seen enough to realise that the gully crossed the edge of the village and extended beyond towards a road leading up the valley. Dougal gestured to Ganesh to stay quiet and they moved on with even more care, each tiny sound seeming like a thunderclap. When Dougal risked another peek over the edge they were just outside the village and close to the road, which was little more than a substantial path. On the other side was pine forest. There was no-one in sight.

He beckoned Ganesh up and whispered: "Stay here while I make a dash for the trees. You look left, I'll look right. Say OK if it is clear your side. Then I'll move."

Ganesh gave a thumbs-up and Dougal dashed across to the trees when he got the OK. Years of smoking began to tell as he climbed steeply into the forest and a couple of times he had to rest to get his breath back. When he found a good vantage point, he took some binoculars from his bag and carefully scanned the village below. There were few people in sight, apart from a dimly discernible group in a ramshackle teashop and a knot of armed men in the middle of the square, looking at something on the ground. A few moved away, and Dougal could see that a near-naked man was pegged out flat, with arms and legs outstretched, in the full glare of the sun. His body was filthy, but he looked like a white man.

Even as Dougal watched, one of the guerrillas kicked the man in the ribs and walked away laughing. The captive drew up his head in pain, and Dougal saw his face. It was Tigger.

6 What happened to Tigger

When Tigger burst into Da Silva's room it took some seconds for his eyes to adjust to the flickering candlelight. "Nice of you to drop in," said Da Silva, holding the candle forward to take a look at his face. Tigger opened his mouth to reply but instead impulsively blew the candle out and rushed further into the room, guessing that the men would expect him to head for the door. But he collided with someone in the darkness, felt a blow on the back of his head, and blacked out.

He had regained consciousness for some time before he opened his eyes. The world had never felt so cosy. He was a baby, nestling against his mother's breast. He felt woman, smelt woman, and was comforted. When he finally looked up, there was the most beautiful face he had ever seen, lit by a candle. It was the face of an Indian goddess, a goddess of love. Deep brown eyes, soft skin, and gentleness.

She cradled his head in her arms, and her fingers worked over his face, smoothing out the stress. She smiled whispered softly in his ear: "You have been brave. Now be peaceful."

Her voice brought him back to earth. This was not a dream. Indian goddesses, to his knowledge, did not speak English. "Who are you? What is happening?" he asked.

"My name is Sita Sinouk. You were knocked on the head when you tried to get away. I was next door."

In point of fact, Tigger had acted automatically, without any thought of escape; but he did not take up the point. He saw for the first time that there were two village women in the room, squatting in the shadows... even the guerrillas maintained traditional standards of propriety.

"You are the princess?"

She nodded. "What are you doing here?"

The princess smiled as Tigger looked cautiously around. "It's OK. No-one will hear you."

"My name is Tigger Thompson. Prince Raju has sent a group of us to try to rescue you. I'm afraid I've messed things up."

"The prince should not have put you in danger. I asked to be kidnapped."

"You *asked* to be kidnapped?"

"More or less. I did not want to marry Raju. The marriage was arranged. I could not dissuade my parents."

"So you asked the guerrillas to take you away?"

"I would not be so foolish. I asked my brother Laxman to take me. I didn't know he had anything to do with the People's Army. I've only just returned from college in the US. The man you saw in the next room – Da Silva – tricked Laxman and brought me here."

"I know Da Silva. Where is your brother now?"

"I don't know. Da Silva holds sway in this territory. But I do know that Da Silva needs Laxman, because he has a big following, so I'm probably not in any danger. Which is not to say that I want to be here."

"Do you want to be rescued?"

"Not if it means putting lives at risk."

The door opened and Da Silva walked in. Tigger noticed that day was breaking, and thought Dougal must be on his way to the landing strip. He wondered if Ganesh had got back to set up the lights for him.

"So our lovely princess has revived you," said Da Silva. "It was very rude of you to push in like that. You were sick all over me when you blacked out."

"People like you make me sick. I'm allergic to murderers."

"Come now, I'm no killer. I have just been restraining my friends from tearing you to pieces."

"Perhaps you could have shown more restraint yesterday morning. Babu would be alive."

It had not occurred to Tigger that the princess might know Babu. Her face creased with anguish. "Babu? Oh no, they haven't killed Babu!"

"His car was blown up. It was only by a fluke that I did not go with it. Me and two others. An innocent bystander was badly hurt."

"That had nothing to do with me," Da Silva said. "The operation was carried out by an official unit of the People's Army."

"You are detestable," the princess said through her tears. "I know your position among these people. They would not act without you knowing. You murdered Babu just as surely as if you had placed the bomb yourself. Babu was a better man than you will ever be. Tell me, what has the world gained from his death?"

"He was assisting enemies of the people."

"Stop hiding behind slogans, Da Silva. You killed one of the best of people. You can posture all you like but I see through you. You're not trying to improve the lot of the people. You're an opportunist seeking power and you don't care how you get it."

Da Silva's eyes flickered to his guards; evidently, they did not speak English. Tigger sensed that for all the princess was a captive, she dominated her prison.

Evidently noting Da Silva's embarrassment, she said: "Are you worried your bully boys might understand? Afraid that they might realise that you have stuffed their heads with foolishness?"

Now Da Silva was angry. "You think that just because you have had an expensive foreign education that you know better than they do. You live in luxury; they live in poverty. They don't need me or you to tell them that that is wrong. Even your own brother is sickened by it all."

"Laxman is young and sensitive and he cannot accept the

world as it is. He is not fighting a revolution; he is fighting life."

Da Silva gestured towards his guards. "A life in which you are rich and they are poor!"

"A revolution is likely to leave them dead or maimed, and they won't be the only ones. Laxman is in a position to help bring about change without all that."

"Your brother couldn't change a light bulb. All he knows about is flying around in those toy planes of his."

"He'll learn, and so should you. What could a revolution possibly achieve? Thousands of deaths and a country run by people like you, with a worse set of problems than you started with."

"We will have made a society fit for the future."

"You will have replaced one hierarchy by another. And what a hierarchy! Give you power and you will kill all the Babus in Solung because they would make you face how small you are. You are not fit to rule anyone."

Da Silva showed the irritation of a man obliged to rehearse familiar arguments. He and the princess had clearly been through this before. "Stop going on about Babu," he said. "I've had enough of that from your brother. Anyone would think I had plotted to murder the old croak. He got in the way. He had a good life as your family's pet peasant. He was lucky. There are a lot of Babus going hungry because they don't have such good connections. What are you doing to help them? Nothing. Who are you to tell me I am not fit to rule?"

Both Da Silva and the princess seemed to have forgotten Tigger. They glared at each other for a few seconds. Then Da Silva said: "You should have married Raju. At least you could have made some use of your advantages. You could have been queen when his fool of a father died. Without that you are nothing. I told your brother that, when he came up here expecting me to help sort out his family tangles. Your only use now is as a hostage."

That stung. Fresh tears welled in the princess's eyes, and she said: "I would marry a chimpanzee if I thought it would do any good. I don't know how to help Solung. Who am I to be a queen? Unlike you, I don't want to rule this country."

"Perhaps that makes you an ideal candidate," Tigger said.

The conversation had revived nagging questions in his mind about the mysterious Messerschmitts, and why the king had so glibly dismissed the possibility of paying a ransom to rescue Solung's putative future queen. No mention had been made of the princess's brother, nor of the fact that he was a pilot. The king and his son may not have been aware of Laxman's link with Da Silva but they had clearly not told all they knew.

"Ah Tigger... you are still here," said Da Silva. "Surprised that I know your name? I know all about you and your friends. I am sorry to tell you that I shall have to put you through some discomfort. I know your friends are planning to attack this village. You will see that this puts the lives of my friends in some danger. Naturally, I prefer to see you hurt than them. Some people here wanted to torture you for information. I have dissuaded them. Actually, I want to be attacked. This place could hold off an army, and we have ways of getting out of here whenever we choose. My friends have agreed to a compromise. You are to be our bait. You will be pegged out in the square. This gives you a chance to survive. You may live for several days. The square will look normal, but each house is packed with my men. If FitzDougal's reputation is anything to go by, he will not stand by to see you suffer. You will draw him to his death. I have the feeling that he will be easier to beat on the ground than in the air. Apart from anything else, I am in charge down here."

"This is an unexpected kindness. No torture for the guest, just a rack to stretch out on. With such a dull party, no wonder you want a gatecrasher."

Tigger was joking to hide his fear; even so he registered the fact that Da Silva thought an air battle was on the cards, possibly involving Laxman. Two guards frogmarched him out of the room. As he left, he heard the princess say: "Da Silva, if you harm one hair of that young man's head I'll never give you a moment's peace."

"I only wish I could allow him to take you away. It's worse than being married having you here, nagging all the time. I can't even beat you, not without upsetting your precious brother. But I warn you... don't push me too far."

Da Silva strode out to walk beside Tigger. "Watch that woman, Thompson, if you live to get the opportunity. She grabs men by the balls. I daren't put a male guard on her. She'd charm a eunuch into treason."

"You too?"

"Balls I do have, or I wouldn't be here. But I advise you not to be so cheeky if you want to keep yours. You are not going to last long, but I'm sure you'd prefer to die in one piece."

Again, Tigger felt a grudging respect for this man who was about to supervise his torture. He felt foolish at having got himself into this position but he did not feel desperate enough to hate; as they left the house, he heard the sound of aero-engines from up the valley. Dougal was on his way. For better or worse, his fate would be decided soon.

ooo

At first he welcomed the sun. It was cold on the ground, still damp from the night air. As the sun edged over the tops of the mountains, his skin began to tingle with warmth. It was the only pleasant sensation he was to be afforded. He had bruises and scrapes all over his body and a fresh bump on his aching head. He could feel each bump of the hard ground, each little stone pressing into him. His legs, stretched diagonally across pegs, began to ache and itch. Rope chafed his skin. He twisted about, trying in vain to reach a position of minimum discomfort. As the sun got higher, he began to sweat, then burn. He tried to relax into the pain instead of wasting his strength fighting it. While Da

Silva stayed near him, the guerrillas did not treat him badly. But when the leader walked off, a group of them began to taunt him. Someone spat in his face. Villagers kept their children away, but a few slipped off and stood a few yards away, staring. A couple of the kids began to throw stones at him, too small to hurt, but they were shooed back to their homes. Someone kicked him in the ribs but he managed to twist with the impact so that no bone was broken. Eventually, the guerrillas got bored and went to sit in the shade of the houses. Nearby three men lounged in the sparse shade of a tree. Two walked away, and the third slouched over to him. Tiger looked away, expecting a taunt or a blow.

"Tigger!" The voice was familiar. He looked round to see Ganesh.

"Where is the princess?" Ganesh asked.

"In the house with the two soldiers standing under the balcony. Her room is on the right. I walked into the one on the left, straight into the arms of Da Silva. This place has been set up for an ambush. There are guerrillas in all the houses."

"Are there soldiers with princess?"

"Not inside. Da Silva won't trust a man in the same room with her. There are two women acting as chaperones."

Ganesh calmly repeated what he had been told and said: "I'm going to see Dougal." With a rifle slung over his shoulder, he looked indistinguishable from a guerrilla as he ambled off. Tigger settled down for a long wait. The sky had clouded over, which was a relief, and knowing that his friends were close made his discomfort more bearable.

After what seemed like an age he heard the unmistakable roar of an aero-engine, followed by the sound of gunfire and a strange howl that echoed and re-echoed through the valley.

7   The rescue

After seeing Tigger, Dougal had returned quickly to where
he left Ganesh. He had just ducked into the shelter of the
gully when an armoured jeep appeared over the brow of the
hill. At the wheel, driving slowly over the rock-strewn dirt
track, was Da Silva, dressed like an Eastern version of Che
Guevara. To Dougal's astonishment, Ganesh suddenly
jumped out of the ditch and ran towards Da Silva, waving
him to stop. "The boy's a genius," he thought, as he realised
that Da Silva would assume Ganesh was a guerrilla. He eased
his Sten gun into a firing position while Ganesh and Da Silva
conversed in Solungese; Ganesh, pointing urgently in direction of the village, hopped into the passenger seat as if being
given a lift. In an instant he had a knife at Da Silva's throat,
and looked very much as if he was about to use it.

"Don't kill him," Dougal said, bounding into the road.

"FitzDougal," Da Silva said. "You and your men keep in-
terrupting me. Can't I go out for a quiet drive without you
jumping out of the bushes?"

"Look, you swine. The lad holding the knife has every
reason to slit your throat. Your people killed his father yesterday. You have my friend pegged out there. You had better
think of a way to free him, or Ganesh will make sure that you
are very dead."

"I have had the greatest difficulty in persuading my men
from not killing your friend already. They would not allow
me to free him. He is their prisoner."

"Where is the princess?"

"I don't know."

"I don't believe you."

"You are too clever."

Dougal realised that they needed to get the jeep out of sight quickly. "Ganesh, can you drive?" he said.

"Yes, sir."

"There seems to be a track into the trees over there. Take the wheel and see if you can get us out of sight."

Dougal flourished his revolver, fitted with a heavy silencer, and told Da Silva to move over to the passenger seat. He needed little persuading because Ganesh was eyeing him murderously. Within seconds they were parked among the trees behind what looked like a forester's store, and Dougal took stock. Da Silva had furnished the jeep with his usual style: a machine-gun was mounted on the open back, where there were a couple of boxes of ammunition, and bolted above the windscreen was a public-address speaker linked to a microphone resting in a slot next to the driving wheel. It was also equipped with a tow-rope, which they used to tie up Da Silva, first removing his distinctive jacket and Che Guevara beret. The lining of the jacket was used to gag him. Walking round the back of the hut, Dougal saw a footpath that served as a short cut to the village. He could see down into the village, where far more young guerrillas were lounging about than when he had last looked.

"Ganesh, I don't think that lot is going to notice if you walk across there as if you had every right to be here. Try to get a word with Tigger. Find out where the princess is, and come back here."

He breathed a sigh of relief when Ganesh returned and gave Tigger's news. "It's supposed to be a trap, with the guerrillas hiding in the houses," he said. "But they are all hanging about in the square. I guess because he..." – Ganesh jerked a thumb in Da Silva's direction, as if he could not bring himself to speak his name – "... is out of the way."

"I reckoned that too. They're not very disciplined. It's given me an idea."

Dougal got through to Gosh on the radio, taking care that

Da Silva could not hear the conversation, and learned that the army had flown in more troops in a second Dakota; but the soldiers had pulled back from the *chung* shop when they spotted a group of guerrillas approaching with the obvious intention of occupying it. "The captain didn't want to put you at risk by taking them on too early."

"I guess he was right but it's a complication we could do without."

"We have the place surrounded. They won't know what hit them if they do start something."

"Good man. Look, do you have any empty bottles?"

"We can empty some water bottles."

"Right. In about half an hour I want you to take off with a couple of soldiers, fly up out of the valley and swing back to approach the village from the other side. But don't fly over it. Circle round and throw the bottles out of the hatch. They'll make a hell of a racket. Get the soldiers to fire into the air at the same time and make as much noise as they can for a couple of minutes. Then return to the airstrip."

"What about the soldiers at the *chung* shop?"

"Tell the captain that unless he hears otherwise from me, he should attack as soon as he hears firing from the village. After he has secured the shop, he should push as far as can down the path to the village."

Dougal went back to Ganesh. Da Silva was making loud grunting sounds. "Stop that or I am going to have to knock you out," Dougal said.

The grunting stopped.

"Ganesh, in a few minutes, you will hear some howling in the air. When it comes, drive as fast as you can into the square and stop in the centre near Tigger. I'll switch on the public-address system. Pick up the microphone by the driving wheel and shout as loudly as you can that the army is attacking up the valley towards the village. Tell them to head downhill and take up positions in the trees. Act it out a bit. Tell them to keep calm and be sure to take their weapons.

You should hear guns firing from downhill."

Ganesh, who seemed to be a stranger to fear, grinned. Dougal sat in the rear of the jeep, next to the bundle that was Da Silva, ready to man the machine-gun. He wore Da Silva's jacket and cap, so that he would not easily be recognised as a European. After a few tense minutes they heard the howling and the sound of gunfire. As Ganesh put the car into gear Dougal tapped him on the shoulder and said: "You're OK, laddie. Do half as well as you have been doing and we'll get out of this."

ooo

Tigger could not make out what was happening. A jeep screamed to a halt nearby, and a Solungese voice boomed across the square. He could see men running about and thought he heard the rattle of gunfire. The voice kept on, evidently exhorting the men to hurry. The tone was familiar, even if the words were unintelligible. It was Ganesh.

Da Silva's beret appeared in his vision, followed by Dougal's face. Dougal menaced him with a gun and pretended to kick him in the ribs. Tigger writhed as if in agony. His limbs were soon cut free but he had to crawl to the jeep, with Dougal's gun trained on him. Even this effort was too much for his tortured limbs, and Dougal virtually rolled him along, disguising gentle pushes with his foot as kicks.

Guerrillas stopped in their stride and stared, but rushed on as Ganesh shouted orders. The excitement showed in his voice, adding urgency to the orders and fuelling panic amid the confusion. The village was his theatre, the square his stage, and the play hung on his words: if they stopped, the illusion would be shattered; and like any actor, Ganesh had to watch his timing.

One or two guerrillas were already moving towards the jeep when Dougal finally bundled Tigger into the back, on top of Da Silva. Ganesh put down the microphone, pushed in the gearstick, and the jeep roared over to the house where the princess was staying. Luckily, this meant moving away from the bulk of the bewildered guerrillas. The two guards still stood under the balcony. At the edge of the square, guerrillas paused as the rush towards the airstrip flagged.

"Tigger... could you handle a gun?" Dougal whispered.

"I think so."

"Cover the guard on the left. I'll take the one on the right. Don't shoot unless it is clear the game is up."

Ganesh was speaking to the guard in Solungese, obviously telling them to fetch the princess. They began to protest, and there might have been trouble if the princess herself had not taken a hand. She appeared on the balcony looking as chic and calm as if she had just stepped out of a Manhattan restaurant. Boots, slightly bell-bottomed grey jeans, matching blouse and sleeveless cardigan, a bag slung from one shoulder, a shawl folded neatly over the bag. She began berating Ganesh in Solungese as if complaining about being taken away. So real did her anger appear that Tigger thought that she did not know who was in the jeep. But she said in English, so fast that only an accomplished speaker could understand: "I'm coming down. If anyone shoots, don't wait for me. Go."

She climbed down the log ladder, continuing her tirade. The two village women followed her, evidently under the impression that she was being taken to a safer place. If they saw Da Silva's trussed-up body, they might give the game sway. Dougal whispered: "Order those women back, Ganesh."

Ganesh barked an order and the two women started protesting. Lives hung on the foibles of two old women worrying about the propriety of a woman travelling alone with men. The princess began another indignant tirade in Solungese, and walked up to the car as if she were leaving her chaperones under protest.

Dougal jumped into the back and the princess sat in the passenger seat next to Ganesh, slinging her bag on to the floor. She was still closing the door as Ganesh drove off, away from the main body of the guerrillas. She maintained her pose of indignation but whispered: "You have no idea how good it was to hear your voice, Ganesh. It was a priceless seeing all those guerrillas running out of the village."

"Trouble is that their indiscipline cut both ways," Dougal said. "Half of them were running *away* from the gunfire. That means they are in front of us now."

"They've caught on to what's happened," Tigger said, seeing men running back into the square. "Prepare for fireworks."

Ganesh jammed his foot on the accelerator as a bullet kicked up dust near the jeep, then firing seemed to come from everywhere, most of it wild. Dougal fired one quick burst from the machine-gun, and then they were out of sight of the village. A couple of minutes later they saw that a cart had been hastily pulled across the main path; shots rang out and the jeep nearly toppled over as Ganesh skidded round onto a dirt track leading down through trees. The track got narrower the further they went and it was clear they would not be able to drive down it indefinitely. Bullets still whistled through the trees, though they were out of sight of the guerrillas on the road.

Finally the path disappeared altogether and Ganesh began steering wildly between the trees, skidding on dank vegetation. Dougal fired a burst from the machine gun into the trees behind them, more to discourage pursuit that in the expectation of hitting anyone.

Suddenly, they were flying through the air as Ganesh drove straight over a narrow fissure. The jeep began clawing its way up the other side but could not get enough traction and slid slowly back until its back wheels spun in mid-air. The engine stalled as Ganesh gave it a final burst. The jeep would go no further. Nobody dared move. From behind them came the sounds of men approaching cautiously through the trees.

8 Battle at the cliff

Dougal tried to assess the balance of forces that was preventing them from slipping backwards into the gully. "Open all the doors and get ready to jump at the same time. Keep any weapons you have." he said. A few seconds later, when they were ready, he said: "Now!"

The vehicle lurched back as they scrambled out, but the rear end stuck on the far side of the fissure leaving it hanging at a crazy angle. Tigger grabbed the Sten gun and gave the trees a burst of fire as Dougal checked for anything useful that might be retrieved from the jeep.

"What about Da Silva?" said Tigger.

"He'll have to take his chances in the back. I'm not taking the risk of trying to move him. We can't manage a prisoner."

A shot rang out and they saw figures running through the trees; Tigger fired a burst from the Sten to keep their heads down. "Let's go," shouted Dougal and they fled, only to find themselves at the edge of the trees where a cliff plunged sheer into the river. Far above them was the place where the road entered the short tunnel. They could just make out figures setting up a road block.

"Up! Up! Up!" said Dougal, pointing to an outcrop among the trees above them. They were all out of breath by the time they reach it and threw themselves down to the ground. The fissure that had given them so much trouble was now offering a measure of protection because their pursuers would have to cross it within range of their guns.

The princess rolled over and pushed a bundle into Tigger's hands. "Your clothes. They were left in the house when you were taken out."

Not for the first time in the past few hours, Tigger was taken aback by the presence of mind of other people. So intense had been the past few minutes that he had forgotten that he was still dressed only in his underpants.

They sat huddled behind the shelter of the rocks and trees for some minutes, each keeping watch in a different direction. Dougal discovered to his consternation that their radio had been lost in the rush from the jeep and he had no means of contacting Gosh and the soldiers.

Tigger said: "I think the guerrillas are pulling back."

"I guess they think that have all routes out of here covered and there is no point risking their necks trying to winkle us out."

"So where do we go from here?"

"We should try to get as close as we can to that road block. We may have to rush it if the government soldiers don't get here soon."

They edged cautiously uphill until they could clearly see the entrance to the cliff tunnel, where four or five figures crouched behind a crude barrier of pine branches and empty oil drums. "They don't seem to expect an attack from up the valley," whispered Ganesh.

"They think their comrades are holding fort at the *chung* shop. They are going to get a nasty surprise," Dougal said with a confidence he did not feel. There had been no sound of gunfire from that direction, or none that could be heard above the sound of their own little battle.

They waited another hour mostly in silence, the tension rising. Then Tigger said: "Why doesn't the army attack? Perhaps they think we are dead?"

The princess looked subdued now the excitement of the initial escape wore off. "I don't want anyone to die because of me," she said.

"These people are trying to start a war. It isn't your fault."

"It was my fault that I got into their clutches."

"Ssh!" Dougal said. "Watch what is happening up there.

We may have to move." A herd of goats was milling behind the barrier and a couple of the guerrillas had stood up to shoo them over it. If all the guerrillas had broken cover, Dougal would have risked rushing them but he motioned the others to hold their fire. Then came a burst of firing from behind the animals and the guerrillas crumpled to the ground. A group of figures seemed to rise out of the floor of the path, and a flash of understanding came to Dougal.

"It's Gosh, with the soldiers. Run." He headed for the barrier, making no attempt to hide. A few wild shots came from the trees, but Gosh and soldiers had reached the barrier and they kept guerrilla heads down with covering fire.

Tigger, supported by Ganesh, was the last to reach the barrier, which was a terrible sight. Six guerrillas, scarcely out of boyhood, lay dead on a path slippery with blood. Four Solung soldiers had taken position behind the barrier.

Gosh stood among the bodies, unmoved. "Thought you might like us to see you home," he said.

"How come you're here?"

"I joined the soldiers covering the *chung* shop to get closer to the action. The army sent a second Dakota with a co-pilot so there was someone to fly both aircraft out if necessary. When the firing at the village started the guerrillas at the shop high-tailed it up the valley. They must have seen the Dakotas flying over and I guess they thought they were going to be attacked from both sides. We left a guard at the shop and advanced here as quietly as we could so as to maintain surprise. Then a lad came out of the trees with all these goats... and you know the rest. Except that we had to deal with a guard at the other end of the cliff. Messy, like this, I'm afraid. Knife in the back."

"How did you know we'd be here?"

"I saw you leave the village in the jeep from the Dakota and guessed that this would be the most likely place you'd get stuck."

"So it's clear of opposition all the way back to the airstrip?"

"I guess there's a chance someone might take a pot shot from the trees but we have the track covered."

"Where's the captain"

"He's co-ordinating things from the *chung* shop. We're going to pull back to the airstrip now because the army does not want to risk civilian casualties with an assault on the village. Also we're not sure what weaponry they have down there."

Dougal was interrupted by the sound of a revving engine, coming from the direction of where they had left Da Silva.

"They're trying to get that jeep back on the road. That means they'll free Da Silva," Ganesh said bitterly. "They've probably fetched ropes and pulleys from the logging depot."

"More to the point, they'll be able to bring the jeep's machine gun into play," said Dougal. He slapped his side in vexation. "We should have made sure to immobilise it. Now we won't be safe until we're over the crossing at the *chung* shop."

He peered down through the branches of the barrier and said: "Gosh... do you have you any grenades?"

"A couple. The soldiers have more."

"Take a look at that tree." He pointed to earth bank at the side of the road where the roots of a large pine tree stuck out of the earth. "Do you think we could bring that down?"

"You might bring half the cliff down on top of us."

"The cliff is solid rock. It's not going to move but the earth under that tree will. Pound to a penny it would fall down anyway in the next rains."

Gosh grinned. "It's worth a try."

"Tigger, you can't move fast in the state you're in," Dougal said. "You'd better start off now with the princess, and we'll catch you up. You should go too, Ganesh."

"I'd rather stay here. This battle is personal for me."

"It's your choice."

The princess was squatting with her back to the cliff, staring into the middle distance and looking deeply upset. When Tigger approached, she nodded towards the dead guerrillas. "Those boys... they are so young. It all seemed a joke in the village. This is horrible. Horrible."

Tigger, who had been just as horrified at the sight of the bodies, tugged gently at her arm. "At least we aren't the corpses, princess. Come on, we have to go now."

As they set off, the soldiers and Ganesh moved back from the barrier and Dougal lay behind it to give covering fire if necessary. Gosh primed a grenade, lobbed it underarm towards the tree, and threw himself to the ground. Seconds later there was an explosion and some of the bank slid down into the road; but the tree remained standing.

They tried again and at first it seemed that tree would stand firm. Then it fell with an enormous crash, followed by a rumbling crescendo of falling earth. They did not wait to see the effect but raced up the path. The rumbling had stopped by the time they reached the far side of the cliff where they found some minor landslides, caused by material dislodged from above the cliff face, but nothing serious enough to impede them.

"We seem to have brought half the mountain down," Gosh said.

"Then let's make the most of it. We might have blocked the jeep but the guerrillas can still climb over the landslide."

"They won't have it all their own way if they do," said Gosh, nodding towards the well-disciplined Solungese soldiers who were holding back to form a rearguard, one section covering another as they fell back in turns.

There was sporadic firing as they made their way to the airstrip but no shots came anywhere near them. They reached the plateau with just one casualty, a soldier with a glancing wound on the arm. But there was a shock waiting for them. The aircraft were still there. The guards were still there. But there was no sign of Tigger and the princess.

9   Stranded

When Tigger had set off towards the airstrip, his main concern had been to summon the effort needed to drag his battered body up the mountain. He and the princess took what precautions they could, hugging the bank beside the path, and reconnoitering each bend in case there were still guerrillas around. Tigger had told the princess what Dougal planned so they were not immediately alarmed when they heard the grenades explode and the crash of the tree and the landslide. But the sound was followed by a crackling from above them, a rattle of falling stones, and then an awful crashing as a huge boulder came tumbling towards the path. Tigger involuntarily pulled the princess back, and it seemed as if the boulder would miss them. At the last moment it struck a turn of the ground and twisted again. Tigger threw himself backwards, collided with the princess, and they fell to the ground while the boulder struck the path a few feet in front of them and rolled on towards the river. The entire world seemed to cave in as the edge of the path broke away and they fell with it.

The slope was not steep but they slithered down nearly a hundred feet before Tigger jammed his foot into a crevice and come to a halt. The princess slammed into him. Debris had served to lubricate their slide so that they were more shocked than hurt, but the danger was not over. They were perched on a sloping outcrop that plunged sheer to the river just a few yards in front of them, and its surface was covered in pebbles and loose sand. There was solid earth only a few feet above them but when they tried to edge up they started to slip back towards the precipice. "Slowly, slowly," said the princess. "We'll have to clear the loose stuff as we go."

This was not easy. They were lying on their backs and turning round was tricky as the princess had her feet on Tigger's shoulders. They cleared all the loose material to their left, as far as they could, and rolled over in tandem so that they were lying flat on their bellies on the rock held only by the friction of their bodies. The princess had to do most of the clearing work as they edged their way up; Tigger could not look up to see how they were doing because dislodged dust got into his eyes. It was nearly half an hour before they reached safe ground, by which time it was clear from the direction of gunshots that the guerrillas were already between them and the airstrip. Looking down from safe ground, they could see how terrifyingly close they had come to plunging to their deaths. The curve of the slope hid them from the path, but they felt exposed in the open and hurried to some nearby trees.

Tigger had no doubt that they were stuck, at least for the moment. "We'll see what happens after dark. Dougal may wait, or he may leave the soldiers to hold the airstrip and come back with reinforcements in the morning."

The first tinge of sunset had touched the sky, and the surprises were not yet over. There came a series of loud crumps and explosions from the direction of the plateau, followed by the roar of aero engines. Tigger swore softly. "Mortars. I didn't know the guerrillas had them. That's torn it. Dougal will have to go."

"Can they hit the planes in this light?"

"They don't have to. They can do what Dougal did... bring down half the mountain. It wouldn't take much debris on the strip to trap the aircraft."

The Dakota suddenly appeared in the lowering sky, as if it had heard the conversation. The princess laughed.

"What's the joke?" Tigger said.

"All that trouble to get us out, and your friends blow us back again."

72

Tigger smiled. He was curiously pleased to see the aircraft go. There was no pressing danger, because the guerrillas would assume they got away on the aircraft. Suddenly he was free of the fear, violence and bloodshed of the past few hours. There was a beautiful woman in his care, albeit one who seemed perfectly capable of looking after herself; and the need to find food, warmth and rest meant he had no time to dwell on the memory of the corpses on the path, and the question Charlie had raised in London: what was he doing, risking his life for a cause he knew nothing about? The princess squatted next to him, graceful and calm, her face silhouetted against the darkening sky. She said softly: "Let's move closer to the river. In a few minutes, we won't be able to see an inch."

They found a ready-made shelter at the edge of a wide expanse of water-smoothed rocks and pebbles that fringed the river. The ground under an overhanging rock had been cleared to provide a space just big enough for two people. Small rocks were stacked and packed with mud to give extra protection from wind. Straw and pine needles littered the floor. Three blackened stones stood at the entrance to form a pot stand and fireplace.

"Is it someone's home?" asked Tigger.

"It may have been a hermit's refuge at times but it's used by anyone passing by. Mostly sadhus. There are places like this all over the Himalayas and many of them have probably been used for centuries."

"Millennia, even," said Tigger. "I've seen places like this in Europe that have been used since before the last Ice Age."

"Can we risk a fire?"

Tigger thought so. "It's well hidden here and even if someone sees the flame, they probably won't think twice about it. No-one is looking for us, I'm sure."

"You have matches?"

Tigger felt in his pocket. "Yes. I've still got them."

The princess spotted two empty dried-milk tins at the

back of the shelter. "Someone must have left these here, either for their own use or for anyone else stuck out here. I'll wash them in the river and fetch some water. Could you collect some firewood?"

The two tins were standing by the fireplace, full of water, when he returned with armfuls of wood. The princess was nowhere to be seen and he assumed she had gone back to the river to wash. He had a fire going by the time she returned, not from the river but from among the trees.

"I was getting worried about you. It's pitch black out there. How can you see to walk?"

"It's a trick. Imagine your toes are eyes. They see your way, probing on the ground. It's perfectly safe."

Tigger had assumed the princess wanted the water to drink, or for washing. Instead, she performed a minor miracle. From the folds of her cloak she produced mint, mushrooms, and alfalfa leaves she had found growing wild. He was soon presented with mint tea and soup.

"I didn't think princesses would know anything about cooking," he said.

"I cooked for myself at college. I like cooking."

"What did you study?"

"I did an MA in South Asian history in the US. Strange isn't it? Going to the other side of the world to study my own heritage."

"It seems close here... your heritage, I mean. I can imagine all those people who must have sat in this spot through the ages, staring into the fire just like us."

They were silent for a while, tired and deep in their own thoughts, the starlight flashing on the silver river, the whishing branches of the trees behind them, the dark mountains silhouetted against the silver sky. Tigger thought of all the pain and death of the past few hours. Man hurt man but it was a puny vandalism; the crescent moon rose as it always would, the earth still turned, and the living still lived. He looked over at the princess and knew that he could easily

74

become infatuated with her. Watch that woman, Da Silva had warned. Tigger could not stop watching her.

"You make me feel so clumsy," he said. "How can you always be so composed?"

"Sometimes I'm not."

"Like this afternoon?"

"I guess."

The princess did not want to talk about it. She got up and began arranging the straw and pine needles into a bed between the fire and the sloping rock that reflected its heat. "You had better sleep now," she said.

"It will be cold tonight, when the fire goes out."

"The fire will not go out."

"What about you?"

"I am not tired. I have had nothing to do but sleep for days. You've had a hard time. You need to rest. You'll need all your strength tomorrow."

Tigger lay with his face towards the fire, staring into its glow. His last sight of the day was of the princess seated nearby, gazing into the blackness across the river.

ooo

She was still there at dawn, swaying over the glowing fire. Already, she had made mint tea.

"Have you not slept yet?"

"I dozed off a couple of times. I was not tired. Are you up to walking?"

Tigger ached all over. "I'll be OK once I get moving. Do you know this area at all?"

She shook her head. "Ganesh's grandmother lived around here and Babu used to bring us to visit her – Ganesh, Laxman and me – but I can't remember much about the place. I was very young. But a couple of my chaperones hinted at a possible escape route. They were forbidden to talk any more than was necessary in my presence but sometimes they'd chat on the balcony outside my room, knowing that I could hear. One day, one remarked on how disgraceful it was that so few people in the next valley supported the People's Army. A little while later her friend said a foreign hippy had been living like a sadhu over there and there was no knowing what he was up to."

"You think they were trying to tell you something?"

"I'm sure they were."

"By 'sadhu', could she mean a hermit? Krishna Baba, the king's adviser, told us a hermit got the airstrip cleared."

"There are many sadhus up here. I guess you could call some of them hermits. Krishna Baba probably knows all of them. He's lived up here himself."

"You know him?"

"Everyone in Solung knows him. He... " She paused as if deciding not to elaborate, and went on: "The point is that the next day, these same women chatted about a lovely festival in which people from the next valley dress up and walk here via a high pass. They mentioned the beautiful view of the village from the path the visitors used. One joked that it was worth using the high pass now because it was cheaper than the easier route – there was no-one demanding baksheesh."

"By which she meant guerrillas?"

"I guess. It was incredibly brave of them to talk like that, with Da Silva and his men in the room next door. The trouble is, after what happened yesterday he may have posted a guard on the path."

"We'll have to take that chance. He thinks we got away, so he'll be more concerned with soldiers coming into the valley than with people leaving it. He doesn't need to watch every track to monitor army movements. The path we want overlooks the village, so if we head up through the trees vaguely in that direction we'll have a fair chance of hitting it."

The princess was already gathering up their few remaining possessions. "I suspect it won't be as easy as you make it sound but we don't have any other option," she said. "We should get going. The sooner we set off, the sooner we might find some food."

10 Flight out of the valley

All the fears and tensions of the previous day returned as they left their little riverside sanctuary and began the slow cautious climb back to the road. Tigger was under no illusion about the treatment they could expect if they were captured. They would get no mercy after the deaths of the previous day – even the princess could not be sure that her family connections would protect her.

There was no one to be seen on the road and they flitted as quickly as they could into the trees on the far side. Tigger tried not to think about the danger they were in, or the fact that had little idea where they were heading. They made slow progress upwards through the pathless forest, frequently having to fight through undergrowth or find a route across gullies choked with vegetation and boulders. After about an hour they came across a footpath but they had no means of knowing whether it led where they wanted to go – nor even which direction they should take, given the twists and undulations of mountain trails. But instinctively they turned away from the direction of the village and began walking upwards.

The path provided easier going than the forested slope but they were well aware that other people were likely to be using it. They paused frequently to listen out for danger, or to scan the path ahead as a new stretch became visible. One encouraging sign was that it was clearly more than a goat's trail and was unlikely simply to peter out. Soon, it began rising steeply and after a couple of hours they paused to rest at a stream, climbing a little way back into the trees in case anyone should come along the path. Someone did come. They heard laughter and two women appeared wearing colourful shawls, and leaning forward against the weight of straw baskets slung from their heads. They put down their loads and sat on a rock when they reached the stream and began talking. The princess strained to hear what they were saying and then whispered to Tigger: "They are grumbling about the People's Army. They don't like them at all. I'm going down to talk to them. You'd better stay here. There's no sense in letting them know more than they need to know."

The women looked so scared when the princess appeared that Tigger, who was watching from above, feared that they were going to run away. But he was astonished to see them fall to the ground and touch her feet. They stood up and began talking rapidly with her. She called out: "Tigger, you might as well come out now."

When he clambered down she explained that the women were royalists who had seen her when she was young. "They say we are on the right path. The pass is about two hours away and we should descend as far as we can on the far side to avoid getting caught out in the cold heights at night."

"Have they seen anything of the People's Army?"

"There's none between here and the next valley. Not yet anyway. They say that only a few people in this valley support the People's Army and most people in the next are very much against them. But we should not trust anyone because they are all very scared of the guerrillas and might betray us."

The women were insisting on accompanying the princess over the pass and she did not want them risking their lives on her behalf. "That's why I called you down – to show them I had some protection. Also I am doing a deal with them. They're from a family of traders and are moving stock between shops. It's all local-style clothing. I want to get some from them so we will look less conspicuous."

One of the traders, looking at Tigger, said something in Solungese. The princess translated. "She's talking about that hippy. He's living in the next valley."

"Does she know where?"

78

"No. He's staying low to avoid the People's Army."

The two women shared their lunch of spiced potatoes wrapped in chapatis, and gave them each a couple of apples. The People's Army had taken all the cash that the princess and Tigger had been carrying, but she had managed to hide a gold ring, which she swapped for two shawls, some plastic sheeting in case of rain, a skirt and heavy cardigan for herself, and a jacket and cap for Tigger. All chosen with the care that she might have taken in a Knightsbridge emporium, as if the murderous revolutionaries breathing down her neck were of small importance beside the matter of size, shape and colour. The two traders, unlike Tigger, bore this with patience, and indeed took an interest, but they went into a panic when the time came to move on. They began talking rapidly to each other, and then handed the ring back to the princess. She smiled, kissed them both on the cheek, and turned away with tears in her eyes. "They won't take the ring. They don't want to take the risk that the guerrillas will find it on them and they're scared to sell it because people will want to know where they got it. They trust me to pay them later."

"They know you will see them all right."

"If we get away! It's a risk for them in more ways than one and they could have refused to do a deal."

Later the princess said: "I have done absolutely nothing to earn responsibility for these people and I have done nothing to deserve their respect. It makes me feel very small."

ooo

Even in their new clothes they felt worryingly conspicuous when they got to the edge of the pine forest and began a steep climb up the bare mountainside, patched with snow in places that did not catch the sun. At one point they could see the airstrip far across the valley and could make out tiny figures moving across it. "No sign of any aircraft," said Tigger. "I guess the People's Army is making the strip unusable."

When they reached a pile of stones marking the start of the pass, they resisted the temptation to rest, anxious to re-

gain the shelter of the trees on the far side. The path levelled
out for a few hundred yards and then descended steeply into
the next valley, taking them from the shadow of the mountain into the full glare of the sun. The world seemed brighter
in other ways: the going was easier and for no good reason
they felt safer, although twice after reaching the tree line they
had to hide to avoid passers-by. In the late afternoon they
arrived at a point where the path rose precipitously, leaving
the river far below. Tigger's battered body protested with
every step of the climb until they crested a ridge and began
another steep descent that took them to a fork in the path.
The traders had told them about this. They were advised to
take the right fork, which would take them to the other side
of the valley where there were fewer people.

"We'll have to cross the river," Tigger said. "I guess there
must be a way of getting across."

There was. They soon found themselves, hot and exhausted, at the foot of a waterfall where the river plunged
100ft over a cliff. The path extended behind the cascading
water, along the foot of the cliff where pebbles had been
concreted into the rocks to form a flat walking surface wet
from the spray.

"We'll get soaked if we walk across that," Tigger said.

"Then we may as well have a bath," the princess said. To
his astonishment she casually stripped, made a neat pile of
her clothes, and stood at the edge of the path under the cas-
cade, holding her hands out to draw water over her body;
then she dived into a pool scooped out of the river's edge
where the water was deep and placid. It was an exquisite scene, the stuff dreams are made of, yet Tigger hardly dared to
look. He glimpsed the water streaming over her body, a tantalising blur, as he stripped and stepped into a solid sheet of
water that bounced off a rock at the side of the path, knocking him breathless. The heat and the sweat of the day were
gone in an instant, and then he too dived into the pool.

The princess grabbed his hand when they finally left the

water and drew him away from the path to the shelter of some bushes. "Now watch me," she said.

She squatted down and he saw a yellow stream of piss cut diagonally between her legs. It stopped and a turd dropped. Then she jumped back into the pool and washed herself.

Tigger asked as she left the pool: "Why did you do that?"

"Men see me as a body. I show them a body," she said.

To Tigger she seemed to have lapsed suddenly into the girl who not so long ago had been just another name on a school register. She knew the effect she had on men and she both used and resented it, too intelligent to ignore it but too young to accept it; she reacted by being shocking. He began to understand how the princess had come to respond so disastrously to the prospect of her arranged marriage: one side of her wanted to be the Modern Woman; another, as her conversation with Da Silva showed, thought she ought to go through with it. Now there was this element of fractiousness, even childishness, as if she could really expect a hot-blooded man not to be interested sexually when she flaunted herself so beautifully. Yet there was more to her than that: sometimes, she read Tigger too closely for comfort.

She looked uncertain now, and Tigger felt his weight in the relationship. Whatever was going through her head, there was half an invitation in there even if she did not admit it to herself. Or perhaps she was denying something in herself. It was all too complicated. He wanted her but he was damned if he was going to play those games. "I can see you are more than a pretty body, princess," he said. "And I hope you can recognise that men are more than a bundle of lust."

ooo

There would seem to Tigger to be a curious inevitability about their meeting Henry the Hippy. There was no reason to seek him out, no reason to suppose he was the "hermit" mentioned by Krishna Baba. He did not enter their heads as they dried themselves off as best they could, and set off down the valley in search of a safe place to spend the night.

Half an hour down the path they heard the sound of a guitar, and a song sung in English. As one, they turned up a track that seemed to head in the direction of the singer, trying to catch the words echoing off the valley sides:

Saw poverty in happiness,
Saw rich men cry with pain,
Saw princes loved by paupers,
Saw workers lying in state.
There ain't a sum
that makes a man,
No words stem misery.
Bird found the air,
fish found the sea,
we'll find our destiny.
Travel on you roaming kind.
Don't let those sun-cast shadows turn you blind.
It seems so far,
It seems so near.
You quash your hope, you beat your fear

Don't want to be a hero,
don't want to change the world.
Intent to let the movie run
and let my life unfurl.
No human spoil
can buy the oil
to quell the stormy sea.
No wish can earn
the strength to turn
the tides of history.
Travel on you roaming kind.
Don't let those sun-cast shadows turn you blind.
You pull it out,
You put it in.
Some call it life, some call it sin.

Part Two
Travels with Henry

1   Henry zeroes heroes

"So how come you sing one thing and say another?" asked Tigger, drawing closer to the fire.

"What do you mean?"

"You said just now that you always wanted to be a hero and before that you sang that you didn't want to be a hero. We heard you. That's why we turned up here. Was that your own song?"

Henry answered the first question. "Of course I wanted to be a hero as a boy. I guess all kids do, especially if they are born in the middle of a war and stuff their heads with Biggles stories. When I got older I discovered that many of the real-life Biggleses I had idolised had been flying out night after night over Germany mass-bombing innocent people. Killing them by the tens of thousands. So much for heroes."

"The Nazis started the mass bombing," Tigger said. "And the men in the bombers died in their tens of thousands too. They were very brave."

"They were heroic murderers. My dad was one of them. He was killed before I was born. By my mother's account he was a kindly, peaceful man but he became a killer. I understand why and if I'd been in his shoes, I'd probably have done the same. All sides became brutalised by the war. It's happening now with American kids fighting in Vietnam. You remember the My Lai massacre a while back? I wrote a song about that too..."

He picked up his guitar and launched into a sorrowful ballad. Tigger was about to tell him to shut up for all their sakes, when he saw that the princess was as engrossed as

Henry – both apparently oblivious of the danger of attracting unwelcome visitors. He said nothing, at the risk of dying of politeness.

"It's not just the Americans," Henry said when he finished singing. "It's happening in Northern Ireland too. Atrocities on all sides. Heroes have a lot to answer for. Think of all the misery they have caused in the name of fighting for a better world. The world is fine as it is. Left to itself it would carry on happily until kingdom come. It's people who are the problem. We have to sort ourselves out." *

"That's why you are here... sorting yourself out?"

"That was why I was singing that first song you heard. I was reminding myself of why I was here. I was mad at myself for getting involved in all this."

"Henry cleared the airstrip," the princess explained, seeing Tigger's look of surprise. "He's been telling me about it."

"I didn't clear the airstrip. I asked some buffalo herders to do it. They do it every year for a dealer who flies in to pick up charas. They just clear away debris and get their animals out of the way. It's a nice little bonus for them. He's in and out in half an hour."

"What's charas?"

"Dope. Cannabis resin. Pot."

"Is that legal here?"

"It's tolerated. Now and again the police make a show of clamping down, mostly just to collect baksheesh. They'd be hard put to stop the trade. The plant grows wild and it's the biggest earner round here. The locals rely on it. But everyone involved has to keep their heads down, so the dope flights are a big secret."

"How come you know?"

"I get called in to liaise with the herders and translate during charas deals. Unpaid. I don't want to get involved in the

---

* See Appendix 1 for background and Henry's My Lai song *Ballad of a soldier*

trade and it's a way of giving something back."

"Krishna Baba, the king's adviser, told us about you. He didn't say you were English. Do you know him?"

"He's my guru. He used to live up here and knows everything that goes on. He sent a message asking me to get the strip cleared and I guessed why. Everyone knew about the kidnap."

"You took a big risk," the princess said. "You were a hero, despite yourself."

"It didn't seem dangerous at the time. I was already in the area for the charas harvest. Normally it would be well under way by now, but the People's Army has scared off buyers."

"Krishna Baba should not have got you involved. It was my stupid fault getting kidnapped. He should not have put your life at risk on my behalf."

She sounded quite angry. There was something going on with her that Tigger did not quite understand.

"I could have said no," Henry said. "I thought about it, I can tell you. I didn't want to get involved. I'm happy to have helped you, princess, but I was swayed more by the fact that I didn't want the People's Army to gain traction. This country needs to change but the last thing it needs is a civil war."

The princess repeated: "Krishna Baba should not have asked you! He was using you to play power politics. Do you really think you've made civil war less likely by helping me?"

"Perhaps that is a question you should ask yourself. You are the one who was rescued."

She did not want to pursue that line. "I suppose Krishna Baba at least got you to re-engage with life. You can't run away forever."

"Forgive me for saying so, princess, but you are the one who has been running away."

So she had told Henry about the arranged marriage.

The conversation was getting edgy. It was time to change the subject and there was one question Tigger had been bursting to ask. "Tell me, Henry – when exactly was it that you got the airstrip cleared?"

"Just after the kidnap. As soon as I got Babaji's message."

"He told us he sent it three weeks before the kidnap."

"Then he was lying."

"But why? He must have known we would find out."

"He has ways of his own."

"Lying ways?"

"People think he is a fraud so he acts like one. He doesn't care what people think. He has no ego to offend."

"That makes no sense to me."

"Henry is saying Krishna Baba is enlightened... his ego has dissolved," the princess said.

Tigger turned to Henry. "Do you believe that?"

"I don't," said the princess, who had not been asked.

"It's possible," said Henry. "That is why I've been sitting on my bum contemplating my navel."

"He has simply cultivated a few tricks that make people think he is more than he is," the princess said scornfully.

"You really don't like him, do you?" Henry said.

She was silent for a few seconds and then impulsively touched his arm. "Henry, I'm being rotten to you and I shouldn't. I'm afraid your guru isn't my favourite person at the moment. I've known him since I was a child. He was our family priest and I can't take him seriously as more than that. He was nice to me when I was a kid but he supported my parents over Raju and I haven't trusted him since. I think he was trying to use me to get closer to the future king."

"I'm an outsider here but that doesn't ring true to me," Tigger interjected. "Krishna Baba doesn't need your help to get close to Raju. Judging from what I saw of them, they are pretty close already."

The princess sighed. "You may be right. The fact is that I've become suspicious of anyone connected with my family. As it turned out, I couldn't even trust my own brother."

2   Henry gets a shock

Tigger woke the next morning to the sound of Henry spluttering over the day's first bedi. It was well after dawn, and Henry and the princess had already eaten. They had a breakfast of puffed rice and tea ready for him. His muscles felt as if they had been tied into knots. By daylight he could see that their campsite overlooked the main path that followed the river, and he was startled to see someone coming along it. "It's OK. I know him." Henry said. "It's a boy from over the valley. He's come to see me. You two had better get out of sight. It's best he does not know you are here."

They moved up into the trees and lay on a bank where they could see what was happening below them. The boy left after about ten minutes and they returned to find Henry looking paper white. His hand trembled as he handed them tea he had been brewing. "Krishna Baba is dead," he said. "He was assassinated yesterday. Shot in the back. And that is not the even the worst of it. The guerrillas shot five of the herders who cleared the airstrip. It was my fault. It was me who got them involved."

The princess looked almost as shocked as Henry. "If it's anyone's fault it's mine for being so stupid. It's more blood on my hands."

Henry was not listening. "Karma!" he said bitterly. "You dabble in this shit and it blows all over you!"

Tigger said: "Henry, what exactly did the boy tell you?"

"Not much more than I have told you. Some of the People's Army arrived in the village the other side of the river last night and were boasting about the killings. Now the story is all over the valley. You were lucky you came this side of the river or they might have caught you."

"We weren't the only ones to be lucky. We only came up here because we heard you singing. You could have brought half the People's Army here. And then you started singing again, like you were busking in Trafalgar Square."

"True. Too true. I must have been barmy. The danger didn't seem real. It feels too damn real now. They know about me! The bastards must have got it out of the herders. They've issued a proclamation blaming a foreign spy, working in cahoots with his so-called guru Krishna Baba, for the fact that they lost the princess. I'm a marked man."

Tigger could imagine Da Silva at work, blaming the debacle of the escape on everyone but himself.

"The worst of it is that I lied to those herders, or least I didn't tell them the truth. I let them believe it was the usual dope run, a little early because of everything that's going on. They didn't question it. I told them they would be paid a bit more because the PA – the People's Army – was around but I never thought I was putting them in danger. I assumed that the army would take over the airstrip. I've worried since that the PA might question them but I never imagined this."

"How did they know about Krishna Baba?"

"Everyone knows he is my guru and that he has – had – the ear of the king. The herders knew nothing about the rescue. There was no reason for them to get shot."

"It's actual terrorism," Tigger said. "They'll make everyone in the valley too terrified to help us."

"Not everyone. That kid who came today risked his life to warn me. He guessed I'd be up here. If he can guess, so can others. We'd better get out of here fast."

This was the first time Henry had spoken of sticking with them.

"But which way?"

"I can think of only one route we can take and I'm afraid it means a long trek up. The little track that got you here goes right up the side of the valley. It's used by people looking for *dhoop*, a plant used for making incense. It joins a larger track higher up which leads to the pass. I've never been there but I've been told it is easy to find."

"Isn't it an obvious place for the PA to watch out for you?"

Henry was thinking on his feet and took time to answer. "There's a good chance that they are not looking for me. Only a couple of people in this valley know I am here and they won't say anything. I told everyone else I was leaving to get away from the PA. With a bit of luck, now I'm implicated with your lot, they will assume that all three of us got away in the aircraft. We'd better move fast, because sooner or later the PA will get word that we are still in the mountains."

"Is there any reason to suppose that we will be safer the other side of the pass?"

"It's further from the PA base. We'll be seen, of course, but most people won't want to get involved, and there's a chance that we could get down to the main valley and a phone before word reaches the PA. Out here, away from roads and phones, news travels at walking pace."

"Then let's go," said Tigger, standing up decisively.

His legs felt painful and stiff as they set off but his body was adjusting to the terrain and as he got into his stride he found the steep climb up the valley quite easy. The princess looked tired and he guessed the strain of the past few days had caught up with her; but she did not complain. Once on the main path they fell into a routine of regularly pausing, watching and listening, and when they reached the open mountainside beyond the treeline they felt hopelessly conspicuous. Henry had donned a locally-made jacket and cap and tied up his hair up to make him less obviously foreign, but he insisted on carrying his guitar with its battered leatherette case. "It will look like a gun from a distance," he said, when Tigger eyed it doubtfully.

The sun was almost directly overhead when they reached

the pass, where they could see snow-capped peaks stretching in all directions. Henry said: "We had better keep going for a while before we think about lunch. We are very exposed up here and we don't know who might turn up."

"Unfortunately, we do."

The princess, who had been sitting on a rock massaging her feet, pointed downwards.

A group of men was emerging from the tree line, far below. Henry watched them intently for a couple of minutes. "They are not moving. Either they are having a rest or they are setting up a guard post down there. Even if they are coming over the pass we'll have a couple of hours on them if we get a move on."

Their tiredness slipped away as they walked rapidly along the delightfully level crest of the pass, which contoured the mountain for more than a mile, and they broke into a jog when they finally reached the down slope. This was dangerous, because a slip would have meant disaster, but the thought of the guerrillas behind them drove them on. The path took them to one end of a broad pasture dotted with grazing buffalo. Children played outside two crude heavy-canvas tents; nearby a woman cooked over a fire and a man sat on a rock whittling a piece of wood.

"Buffalo herders," whispered Henry. "We could be in trouble if they've heard what happened in the other valley."

"They've seen us. We'll have to brazen it out," said Tigger. "It's best if you talk, Princess. They'll find you less threatening than two foreigners."

The herders greeted them with neither enthusiasm nor obvious ill feeling. Women and children came out of the tents and gathered round as the princess gave a garbled account of recent events. She posed as a respectable woman who had been separated from her husband by the fighting; the "hippies" were kindly escorting her to safety.

"They say we're five hours from the next village," she translated for Tigger's benefit. "I've told them we'll have to rush on to make it before dark."

"Did they believe our story?"

"They know we haven't told them the whole truth. They don't want to know," Henry said. "Let's get out of here. It's bringing me bad memories."

They felt the herders' eyes on them as they walked away. "The good news is that if the herders were right about how far the next village is, whoever was behind us on the path is not likely to cross over today for fear of being caught out in the dark," Tigger said.

"The herders might have been saying that to get rid of us," said the princess.

Tigger, glancing back to take a last look at them, was suddenly overwhelmed by the spectacle of these wild-looking people living in this stupendous landscape. "I feel almost envious of them, cut off from the world up here," he said.

"They lead a tough life. Some of them travel hundreds of miles to get to these pastures," Henry said.

"They look wretchedly poor."

Henry pointed to a lizard scuttling across a stone. "Is that lizard poor?"

"I'd prefer to be a frog. Frogs can live in and out of water. They have the best of both worlds."

"Seriously. That lizard has all the wealth it needs. So do those herders. Poverty doesn't necessarily mean misery. Do you think they are less happy than Mr and Mrs Britain?"

"I think they would prefer to be as well off."

"Would they be happier if they were?"

"What are you saying... that we should forget about poverty and starvation?"

"Those people are not starving."

"They are subsisting. They're one step from starvation."

"They make a living. That makes them better off than a beggar, and a sight more dignified. You are looking at the world and seeing an Oxfam poster. Starvation is a problem to the starving but is not a real problem in the great scheme of things. It's solvable, like all the world's problems. The real problem is getting people to do it."

"By sitting on your backside in the mountains?"

Henry walked in silence for a few paces. "It's as good a way as any. Until people know how to be content with enough, there will always be greed and grasping and fighting over inconsequentials."

"That's a rich man's view."

"I barely have the price of a meal."

"You are playing at being poor. You could go back to England tomorrow and get a job, or live off the fat of the welfare state. It's easy for you to say that we should turn aside from the poor and needy."

"You're twisting my words," said Henry, getting angry. "I'm saying there are deeper problems than starvation. Where there is too little food, some people will die. It's a tragedy but it's a healthy tragedy... nature cures what we don't cure."

They'd all forgotten their fear, and the danger, and the People's Army, and thoughts of what might happen if they were captured. They were talking to think of anything but that. Henry turned round with sudden passion. "Everywhere people are trying to change circumstances. They never look at themselves for the answers... always, they generate conflict. I'd bet more people have died in the name of alleviating poverty in this century than ever died of starvation. It's death by humbug. There has to be another way."

It was a peculiar moment. Tigger sensed a shadow behind Henry's outburst, as if somewhere inside him he felt at a loss. "How can a starving man do anything but try to change his circumstances?" he said. "How can you talk of his tragedy as being healthy? Is this what Krishna Baba was putting into your head?"

Henry stooped in his tracks and his voice became almost a shout. "Look, if it weren't for your lot I would be sitting by my fire giving people food and a chance of some peaceful

94

company. You came here to make war. You are a mercenary, selling death. Who are you to criticise me?"

Tigger had never thought of himself coming to Solung to make war but it was too complicated a point to argue, and he was irritated by a feeling that he was competing with Henry for the princess's approval. They walked on in silence, quickening their pace slightly as if to walk off their anger.

"Bedi break," Henry announced, as they arrived at a little stream. He sat down to gasp over another of his rank little cigars, took out his guitar, and began to play it, trying to calm himself down with his music. From somewhere far away, perhaps from across the valley, carried by the breeze, came the faint sound of a baby crying. Henry stopped to listen. Then he began to sing:

> *Cry baby, cry baby, sigh baby, pity.*
> *See the big people tearing at the earth.*
> *Brothers and sisters born to plenty*
> *and fighting for all that it's worth*
> *in the paradise that gave you birth.*

> *Sleep baby, sleep baby, sleep in your innocence.*
> *Blessed until you grow to understand*
> *the quarrels that blind the blind to Eden,*
> *to the vision of the long-promised land,*
> *to the dream of a ridiculous man.*

> *See baby, see baby, see a world where true love birds*
> *can fly so high as the hours pass like flowers,*
> *Sing baby, sing with the harmony,*
> *with the song of the holy universe*
> *in the paradise that gave you birth*

"That's beautiful," the princess said.

"We are not all born to plenty," said Tigger.

"You think the world has not got enough for all of us?

We live in Eden and we are making it a hell."

"The world I know is not that simple."

"It is too clever for its own good."

Henry flicked away the stub of his bedi, stuffed his guitar back into its case, and strode off without another word.

ooo

They reached that pace that is a blessing for all hikers, when the body finds its rhythm and goes into automatic and the mind goes into a kind of trance, like the space between sleeping and waking, and mile after mile is passed without conscious effort. They knew they were getting close to a village when they came to a little water mill like the one Tigger had seen with Ganesh. Tigger marvelled at its crude but effective engineering: a channel of water drawn from a stream driving wooden paddle blades geared to a grindstone. They followed the mill stream up into the trees, and set up camp out of sight of the road, sitting by a fire while they cooked food they had brought from Henry's. They were all a little subdued. Tigger decided to clear the air. "I'm sorry I threw Krishna Baba at you this afternoon, Henry. I'd forgotten that he'd been killed. I shouldn't have wound you up."

"Tigger, I feel far worse about the herders who were killed. They had done nothing to deserve it. As for Krishna Baba... I don't say he deserved to die but he must have known the danger he was putting them in."

"And the danger he was putting you in," the princess said.

"To be honest, I feel a kind of relief that he is dead. I can be my own person again."

"You were a free agent."

"Not in my head. I thought he was guiding me to some kind of wisdom. Now I have to find my own way."

"You mean you've been thrown back into the world you were trying to avoid."

"Princess, you keep saying that. It's not true. I wasn't trying to avoid the world. I didn't come to this country on any deep spiritual search. I'd left university with my head full of

96

great things. I wanted to be a writer and found myself writing advertising copy for toothpaste. I was bored stiff. I came here looking for excitement, and perhaps for something to write about. And then I met Babaji."

Here Henry mimicked Krishna Baba. "You... Henry... too much thinking. Too much talking. Too many things in your head. You go to mountains. Mountains good. Mountains *shanti*. Mountains peace."

He added bitterly: "Some peace!"

"You didn't need to obey him," Tigger said.

"You know why I got angry with you this afternoon, Tigger? I envy you. You seem to come from a world of certainties, where battles are physical and knowable. I live in a permanent state of confusion. That's why Biggles books fascinated me so much. They took me into a world of clear rights and wrongs, with no doubts or frustrations."

"I can't believe that I am any less confused than you are," Tigger said. "Dougal – my boss – really does live in a world of clear rights and wrongs. That is how he sees things. He's a war hero, too. Like I told you, he's a real-life Biggles."

"You mean FitzDougal – the pilot?"

"You've heard of him?"

"Who hasn't? I should have guessed, the way you were talking. Is he here?"

"He's in Satpur, no doubt wondering what happened to me and the princess."

"I'm impressed. I'm not sure I would have been impressed by the fictional Biggles. Did you know that W.E Johns, who wrote the books, said that he tried to make him the sort of person boys should emulate? At times Biggles kills in cold blood and admits to enjoying it; he is bigoted, racially prejudiced, and when working as a policeman he is not above framing suspects. He's a vicious bastard. Yet this is Johns's conscientiously depicted idea of a proper man."

"He has the attitudes of his time. He'd be a rare man if he didn't. And he has his points. He is loyal. He would risk his life for a friend. He has integrity, in that he only does what he thinks is right. Dougal's like that."

"I'd bet he's done some dodgy things doing what he considers to be right. It's a criminal psychology. Criminals are the most determined of moralists. Swear in front of their women and they will put you in hospital. They'd kill a bank clerk for money, then beat a rapist to death in prison because his crime is beyond their personal pale. They construct a morality to justify their crimes and enable them to feel good about themselves."

Tigger was getting angry again. "Oh come on, Henry! How can you say that about someone you don't even know? Dougal has his faults like everyone else and he wouldn't be above bending the rules to get something done. But he isn't Al Capone. He's a flawed hero, like all heroes, and the world would be a poorer place without people like him. You can't put him on the same level as a criminal."

"I can. And Dougal and you and me and your uncle Harry. We are all from the same stable. We are mad. I'm sure of it. The criminal has his moral code. Johns has his Biggles, his heroic ideal. We are all the same, with our own version of Biggles inside of us, our confused idea of propriety that can lead us to do the most terrible things. We are mad because we don't know what sanity is. That's what I thought Babaji could give me. I thought he could show me sanity."

They were silent for a while, gazing at the glowing core of the fire. The princess came and sat between them. "Krishna Baba was right. You think too much," she told Henry. Then she drew both of them to her, one under each arm, so that they huddled against her like two overgrown babies. For a long time they did not move and Tigger was surprised to find that Henry had soaked the princess's blouse with tears. Still, they stayed close, body with body, heartbeat with heartbeat.

"That is sanity," the princess said, when they finally moved to get some sleep.

3   Terror at the river

They woke the next morning to find a young girl staring at them through the trees. She scuttled down the hill as soon as she saw them and before they could do anything more a woman appeared carrying a bundle of wood. She looked terrified until the princess started speaking in rapid Solungese. Henry whispered to Tigger: "She thought we were from the People's Army. The princess has told her the same story that she told the herders."

The women walked off in the direction of the village and the princess said: "I don't know whether she believed me or not but she's frightened... scared that the People's Army might turn up and scared that we might bring them here. But there are no guerrillas in the village and the people there will know we are here so at least we can walk through without needing to hide."

The village, a cluster of two-storey stone houses, looked eerily deserted when they got there a half-hour later and they had the feeling that eyes were following them from every house. They entered a square where there were neat piles of cannabis plants.

"The harvest has started. They rub the leaves in their hands to collect the resin," Henry whispered, as if he feared a normal voice would sound like a shout in the silence. "In most places they rub it out on the hills where it grows."

The square boasted a single open-fronted shop, and even this looked abandoned, its meagre wares unprotected either by person or glass.

They realised with slight amusement that Henry the self-declared pauper was the only one among them who had any money with him, albeit only a little. He rang the shop's handbell and after some delay a man appeared and with a great show of reluctance sold them rice, lentils, turmeric, chapati flour, matches, tea and biscuits... enough, for the price of a bus fare in London, to keep them going for two or three days. Henry carefully wrapped it all in sealable plastic bags he took from his guitar case. "My little luxury," he said. "You can't get plastic around here and even after the rainy season things can get wet."

They managed to extract a little information from the shopkeeper. He confirmed that this was the only sizeable village on this side of the valley and that it had had no trouble, by which he appeared to mean no People's Army presence. The nearest motorable road, which was also the nearest place they could find a telephone, was a day's walk away in the big valley at the foot of the one they were in.

"He says there are guerrillas in the small town where the valleys meet, and the people here don't want them coming to the village chasing the likes of us," explained the princess.

The news that the People's Army was not in the immediate vicinity lifted their spirits and they began almost to enjoy themselves as they walked down the valley, stopping to drink from streams or to rest under a shady tree, and revelling in the spectacular sweep of the mountainside, the beauty of the flowers peeping from the undergrowth, the ripple and crash of the water, and the kid goats gambolling among the trees. Fighting and death seemed far away, though they were startled at one point to hear a distant roar like an explosion. "Thunder," said Henry, hardly stopping in his tracks.

The main valley suddenly came into view as they rounded a bend in the late afternoon. A truck, looking from this distance like a toy, crawled along a road on the far side of a big river, which was straddled by the town mentioned by the shopkeeper. "I know that place," Henry said. "The two sides of the town are joined by a footbridge. There's no way vehicles can cross."

100

They stood there for a while, sensing that the spell of the day was about to be broken. They had seen no-one for hours, except for a couple of girls herding goats. Now they could see people milling about in the distant town square. The sense of imminent peril returned and suddenly life seemed too precious to be exposed to the slightest risk. Yet they had to cross the river to get away.

A woman was working on a cultivated terrace nearby and they decided to risk talking to her. She looked curiously at the two white men, but otherwise did not seem surprised to see them. The princess, using their familiar cover story, chatted with her for about ten minutes, translating as she went.

"She is very sympathetic and thinks the People Army are terrible. She doesn't think that roaring sound we heard was thunder. It sounded to her like an explosion from down the main valley and she hopes it means the government army is coming to drive out the rebels."

"Has she any suggestions about how we can cross the river?" Tigger asked.

"There's a People's Army guard on the bridge. They are letting people across and she sees no reason why they should stop us."

"Tell her that we are afraid of being held hostage."

The women talked more. Tigger understood one word... *baksheesh*. "Does she want money?" he asked.

"She's OK," said Henry. "She says there is a *chung* shop on the main river bank about a mile up the valley at a confluence with another small tributary. The guy who runs the shop has a boat and ferries people across to save them having to walk down to bridge. Of course he will want money and we have none."

The woman began speaking to Henry, evidently realising that he understood Solungese. "She is a very nice lady, and bright," he said. "She's gathered that we are in trouble. She says there is a turning just down the road on the right that will take us straight to the big river without going into town."

"We should go. She is scared of being seen talking to us," said the princess.

They soon found the side path the woman had spoken of and hid among some trees until shortly before sunset to minimise the chance of being spotted. When they finally set off, the only person they saw before reaching the big river was a child defecating in a field. They walked in silence along the bank, with the lights of the town behind them and the road to safety a tantalising few yards across the water. After a few hundred yards they spotted the lights of the *chung* shop, and hung back in shadows, afraid of showing themselves until they were sure it was safe. The shop was more substantial than the one near the airstrip, with brick walls and a corrugated-iron roof. Outside were a couple of rough-cut wooden tables, with planks thrown across logs serving as chairs. An old sadhu dressed in an extravagance of orange rags and beads sat talking to two young men.

"Matchbox Baba," said Henry.

"The sadhu? You know him?" asked the princess.

"He used to live in the village where you were held prisoner. I guess he must have got out when the People's Army showed up. I heard that they roughed him up a bit."

Tigger was surprised to see Matchbox Baba finish his drink with evident relish and help himself to another. "He's supposed to be a holy man? I wouldn't have thought he would drink."

"He sets himself up as a sadhu, but really he is one of nature's barmen. He used to hang out at a shrine near the village and ran it almost like a pub, except that the customers smoked charas rather than having a beer. I didn't know he liked a drink."

"Why is he called Matchbox Baba?"

"He built a shelter at the shrine with a door made out of a hoarding advertising matches. It made the place look like a matchbox. I don't know what his real name is."

"Can we trust him?" the princess asked.

"There can't be much love lost between him and the guerrillas. But he may recognise you, and he will have no illusions about the risk he would run helping us. You never know what people will do when they are playing those stakes."

The two men drinking with the sadhu got up to leave, and Matchbox took the money for their drinks before they headed away from the hidden watchers along the bank of the tributary. "Matchbox must be minding the shop for the owner," said Henry.

A fat man emerged from the hut, his features indicating Tibetan descent.

"Perhaps that's the owner," whispered Tigger.

"Can't we just slip past the shop and take the boat without asking?" said the princess. "They could get it back from the other side and we could recompense them later."

"We don't know where the boat is and we'd make a hell of a noise trying to find it in the dark," Henry said. "We have to trust someone and Matchbox is as good a bet as any."

"I think the owner is leaving," Tigger said.

The fat man put on his sandals, slung a bundle over his shoulder, and waddled off into the darkness. They waited until he had disappeared, then strolled down to the shop as if nothing was amiss.

"'Enry," exclaimed Matchbox, throwing his arms round Henry's neck. Tigger grinned as Henry's winced at the blast of the sadhu's drink-sodden breath.

Matchbox stepped back, gripping Henry's shoulders and surveying him at arm's length. The sadhu was so cross-eyed it was difficult to know which eye to catch; an enormous brass earring had weighed one ear to a point, giving him an impish air. He spoke in a child-like sing-song: "These... you friends?"

Henry replied in Solungese. Matchbox was not fooled by their cover story. He nodded towards the princess as Henry finished speaking. "Princess Sita. I see her upside." There was fear but no reproach in his voice. In such times, he seemed to say, people must be expected to lie. He fussed about with glasses, while the others sat in silence, waiting for further reaction. Matchbox took another swig of *chung* and called to his god – "Hari Aum" – casting his eyes to the sky as if the emptiness above held the only answers.

The silence in the shop was painful now and the danger felt close and real; from outside through the still evening air came the sound of the rippling river and a soft orchestra of insects, chirruping and cheeping over the insistent worrying of mosquitos. Tigger watched a moth immolate itself in a candle flame. Death struck high and low; only in anticipation, the dread of possibilities, were humans different.

"Baba frightened," Matchbox said at last. Then he burst out: "You men coming... fighting... killing. No good." He added something in Solungese.

Henry translated. "It's all madness."

Tigger had no idea if Matchbox, whose use of the word 'you' was promiscuous, included Henry and himself in 'you men'.

"Mudness," misrepeated Matchbox. "Rice, dahl having... Bas... enough. Baba sitting temple... *Shanti* – peace. Soldiers coming, Baba hurting... mudness. Baba sitting here... 'Enry coming, princess coming..." Matchbox lapsed into Solungese.

"We bring trouble," translated. Henry. "There's food to eat and a bed to lie on – why is everyone at each other's throats?"

"Baba frightened," Matchbox repeated.

Tigger and the princess questioned Matchbox for a few minutes in Solungese. It seemed that the People's Army, fearing a government attack along the valley, had blown up the main road, causing the explosion they had heard and a landslide that would take days to clear.

"So we are cut off?"

"Not by the landslide, unless we are very unlucky. Landslides happen all the time here during the rainy season. In normal times it would not be a big deal. People just walk over them. It just means we won't be able to take a vehicle out of the valley."

"We should still try to get across the river, don't you think? We might be able to find a telephone, or even an army post."

"I guess. But there is another problem. The *chung*-shop owner – that fat Tibetan we saw – has taken his boat across the river. We will have to wait for him to come back."

"Why bother crossing the river? When the boat gets back, can't we just take it all the way downstream out of the valley?" asked the princess.

"It gets very rocky about two miles downstream, which from what Matchbox says is well short of the landslide. A skilled canoeist might get through in good light, but we'd never make it in a heavy boat at night. Also there are no oars. There's a rope across the river to pull the boat across."

"So are we going to have to trust the Tibetan to get us across?"

"Matchbox says he can't be relied on. He's terrified of the guerrillas."

"What about Matchbox?" said Tigger, catching the sadhu's eye and guessing that he understood something of what was being said.

"All he wants is to be left alone," said Henry. "Whatever he does, he is in trouble. If he helps us, he risks getting his balls cut off by the guerrillas. If he does nothing or betrays us, he risks trouble with the government. That's how these revolutionaries work. They force people to take sides."

Matchbox was looking intently at each speaker with his nearest eye, the other hovering in the darkness. He motioned towards the princess. "She rich lady... *prasad* giving."

"*Prasad?*" asked Tigger.

"Holy baksheesh," said Henry, laughing.

He pushed his hand playfully through the sadhu *'s* hair.

"*Prasad.* You old rogue," he said, and then, mimicking the sadhu: "Rice having. Dahl having... *Bas...* enough."

Matchbox laughed. "Baba good man."

The old sadhu would not agree to take them over the river himself but on the promise of future reward he showed them where the boat was moored and told them to hide near there until the owner returned. The mooring was some way from the shop and they would never have found the place themselves.

They found a comfortable spot and settled down to wait, huddled together for warmth as the chill of the night set it. For a few minutes they forgot their peril and Henry talked about the million or so sadhus who wandered the subcontinent, or hung out at shrines and monasteries: magicians, astrologers, medicine men, craftsmen, storytellers; every shade of humanity from rogue to saint. "They are supposed to be ascetics but very few live up to the ideals set for them. Basically, Matchbox is an opportunist. He leads a better life as a sadhu than he would by sweating away in the fields. He sets himself up as a renunciate, but he doesn't really turn his back on the world because he doesn't have much of a world to turn his back on."

"You foreigners always love sadhus because they look so exotic," the princess said. "They're parasites, most of them. They prey on superstition and are tremendous reactionaries. Religious fanatics are as dangerous as political ones in this country."

"Sometimes there is not much difference," said Henry.

"I don't understand how you could take Krishna Baba so seriously," said the princess. "I gave up believing in all his gods almost as soon as I went to big school."

"I don't believe in them, not in a literal sense, and I could never figure out whether he really did either. To me the images and stories of the gods – Greek, Hindu, or whatever – are like communal dreams, oddly meaningful reflections of ourselves and our lives, sometimes crazy, sometimes plain silly, and sometimes profound..."

He was interrupted by shouts coming from the direction of the shop. Their fear flooded back and they gazed hard into the darkness, hearts beating hard.

"People's Army!" whispered Henry. Tigger nodded. There was more shouting and then a piercing scream.

"That's Matchbox," said Tigger, but the scream was so animal that it seemed like the scream of every creature that was ever in terror. "We have to help him."

"There's nothing we can do. If you try to do a Biggles, you'll get us all killed."

For a few awful seconds they waited, longing to flee yet unable to bring themselves to abandon Matchbox. Screams, interspersed by shouts and laughter, rang out again and again. Then a pistol cracked, and the screaming stopped abruptly.

"Jesus, let's get out of here," said Tigger, cursing their indecision. There were torches, dancing in the blackness, coming towards them.

"The river. It's our only chance," Henry said. "Can you swim princess?"

She nodded.

"Keep your clothes and shoes on and take as much of our stuff you can. We'll need it." Henry paused only to pat his guitar goodbye as he shoved it under a bush. The river was only a few steps away and they slipped into it as quietly as they could, wincing with the shock of water so cold it momentarily knocked the breath out of them. Luckily the river at this point was shielded by bushes; they swam primarily to warm their bodies because the current swept them downstream at well over walking speed. Tigger wondered how long they could withstand the cold, until he recalled that some people in Britain made a point of swimming in winter and claimed to enjoy it. After about ten minutes they passed under the bridge at the township, which was mercifully dark;

on the road on the far side of the river they could make out the shapes of trucks and buses held up by the landslide. Tigger trod water to allow the other two to catch up and said: "Should we cross to that side now?"

"Now we're past the town, I think it's best to stay this side," said Henry. "I think I know where we can hide up. Can you stand it in the water for a few more minutes?"

"I think so."

"Princess?"

"OK."

"Just follow me."

About five minutes later he pulled over to the bank where the water was shallow enough for them to stand up in, though the current dragged at their legs. The night air felt warm as they stepped out of the water but they were soon shivering. They were on a scrap of pebbled beach at the base of a gully in a steep cliff. "Thank god. I think we are in the right place. I've never been here but a sadhu pointed it out to me once from across the river," Henry said. He led them to the foot of the gully, where a trickle of a stream flowed over a jumble of boulders. The gully curved so that most of it was hidden from the river. "Climb till we are out of sight. But carefully. Carefully."

They crawled over the rocks, fearful of breaking a limb, until they found a small flat area, littered with pebbles and driftwood, where they could rest. "The place I was told about should be above us but we'd break our necks trying to get up tonight. We'd better try to dry out here," Henry said.

"What is the place?"

"Some kind of temple or shrine. The sadhu said it was special and that I should go there some time. He asked me to be careful who I told about it because if it became too well known it would never be the same again. I don't think he was bullshitting. But we'll find out in the morning."

"If the matches have survived, I think we could risk a fire," said Tigger.

"Cross fingers," said Henry, pulling the box in its plastic bag from his pocket. He grinned. "The bag stayed sealed. They look OK."

"So does the food," said the princess, pulling a pot containing another bag from under her sopping clothes.

The driftwood was bone dry and they quickly built a roaring fire, draping their wet clothes on rocks around it. In contrast to her earlier abandon by the waterfall with Tigger, the princess maintained decorum by carefully holding clothes in front of herself to dry. Soon they were dressed in half-dried clothes, roasting them against the fire, and drinking black tea – fortunately their pots had been packed with the food.

Tigger asked: "Is anyone likely to come here in the morning?"

Henry shook his head. "The only way to get here is by river or by climbing down the gully from the clifftop, which is not something anyone is going to do in a hurry. That's probably why so few people know about the shrine – if it exists. It's certainly why I never got round to checking it out."

They felt safe for the moment, but Matchbox Baba's appalling end cast a shadow over the little gathering. They concluded that the child they saw on the way to the *chung* shop must have put the People's Army on their track, probably quite innocently. Tired though they were, they could not sleep, and they spent the night keeping the fire alive to get their clothes dry and cook a stodgy meal of rice and lentils.

At first light they put the fire out for fear the smoke would give them away, and began to climb the gully. It was not easy. There was a hint of a path: a foothold flattened out here, a small bed of pebbles there, traces of centuries of footfalls on boulders. But the gully was so choked with vegetation that it took them a full hour to climb 200 feet and they nearly missed the place they were seeking. Tigger spotted a channel carved into the rock, almost hidden behind a shrub, and when he went closer to investigate he was confronted by a sight for which the word magical might have been invented.

4 The princess tells her story

It looked like a little courtyard jutting from the cliff, protected from falling rocks and debris by the slope of the rock above. A ledge formed by some quirk of geology had been flattened out with pebbles and packed earth; at one end stood a peepal tree, its roots buried in cracks in the rocks, with stones arranged at its foot to form a seat; next to it was a patch of alfalfa, doubtless descended from plants grown there by someone long in the past. A small stone wall had been built along the open edge of the ledge. The channel Tigger had spotted fed water from the ravine to a little drinking fountain shaped like a lion's head, and on via a second channel to an ornate pool that overflowed down the cliff via a culvert in the wall.

A path leading from the ravine to the ledge had largely broken away but there was just enough left to provide precarious access. Only when they got on to the ledge did they realise that a small temple was set into the rock, its entrance adorned with sensuous carvings of deities, male and buxom female. Inside, at the centre of a cave the size of a small bathroom and barely tall enough to stand up in, was a large stud-shaped object. "Shiva lingham," said Henry, for Tigger's benefit. "The centrepiece of all Shiva shrines."

The princess was ecstatic. "A cave temple! I never knew there was one in these parts. Nobody knows, I am sure. No-one except people like your sadhu, or I would have heard about it."

Henry pointed to the damaged path. "I guess access was blocked by a landslide at some point. The blockage must have been washed away over the years but by that time the

110

temple had been largely forgotten. I guess people who did know about it kept quiet because it was useful to have a refuge. There have been a lot of turbulent times around here."

The temple faced south, away from the valley they had just left and across foothills to the plains. "There's safety over there," said Tigger.

"Oh, we're safe enough here!" said the princess. "I can't get over this place. It's so lovely."

They summoned up energy enough to lay out their remaining wet things to dry in the sun, and were asleep almost as soon as they lay down to rest. They woke when the midday sun drove them to the shade of the peepal tree where they built a fire and cooked yet another meal of dahl, rice and alfalfa. Haute cuisine it was not but it was good body fuel. Tigger, who had been a little surprised at Henry's purchases up in the valley, now appreciated how many meals could be made from a relatively small amount of rice and lentils. By the time they had finished eating they had decided to go no further that day. They were too exhausted, even after their sleep.

"I know more or less where we are," Henry said, as they gazed out across the foothills. "There is another motorable road in the valley on the far side of the ridge above us. I'd guess it is not far away, a few hours walk at most. But it is in notorious dacoit territory."

"Dacoits are bandits," explained the princess, seeing Tigger's puzzled expression.

"Popular bandits, among the locals at least. They are seen as Robin Hood figures," Henry said. "They keep the locals sweet because they need their support. They're brutal, if the papers are to be believed – but so, probably, was Robin Hood, if he ever existed. Many landlords behave so badly towards the poor people working the land that it's not surprising that some see dacoitry as their only option."

"Or revolution," said Tigger.

"You think the People's Army is right in trying to overthrow my family?" the princess asked sharply.

"I didn't say that. Even Prince Raju says there is a lot wrong with Solung."

"I hate to think what could happen if Solung blew up," Henry said. "The trouble could easily spread to India. Naxalbari is not far away over the border."

"Naxalbari?"

"It's a village where there was an uprising a few years back. It spawned a murderous Maoist movement that has been gaining strength in many parts of India. Or rather it spawned several movements. Naxalite has become a general word for any violent opposition in India. Any opposition at all, in some places."

"Not just in India," the princess said. "Some people refer to the People's Army as Naxalite. Da Silva certainly does."

"Prince Raju told Dougal that he feared the People's Army might join with Indian revolutionaries and spark a revolution right across the sub-continent."

Henry shook his head. "I can't see that happening. The Naxalites are too fragmented."

"What's of more concern to us right now is what is going on over the other side of that ridge," Tigger said. "Does the People's Army have a presence over there?"

"I'd say they'd steer clear of it. There are easier places to operate. Why take on armed dacoits when you can bully defenceless villagers to get your way?"

"Are the dacoits that dangerous? We have no money. Why should they molest us?"

"If they realise who the princess is..."

The princess frowned. "Sita. Sita. My name is Sita. Please don't keep calling me princess as if I am something special."

"Princess suits you," Tigger said, impulsively. "You *are* something special."

"I mean it, Tigger," she said, smiling. "Apart from anything else, calling me princess at the wrong time could be dangerous. It's very unlikely that the dacoits would recognise me by sight. My parents always kept my picture out of the papers."

"The pr...Sita's right," said Henry said. "We have to be careful what we say. But we also have to face the fact that we stand out a mile, the three of us, and the People's Army knows we are on the loose. They might put the word out to the dacoits to watch out for us. We can't trust anyone, least of all a load of bandits. The more I think about it, the more I think it is best if you stay here Sita, while one of us goes for help. There's enough food to last a couple of days. No-one is going to come here."

"I'll set off in the morning," said Tigger.

"Tigger, you know it is going to have to be me. You don't know the area. You don't speak the language. And, if push comes to shove and I need help, there are a couple of people around here who owe me."

"I don't want you to go risking your neck for me," the princess said defiantly.

"Don't bother your head on that score," Henry said grimly. "It's my best chance of getting out alive too."

ooo

Over dinner that night, the princess spoke for the first time in detail about her life and how she came to be kidnapped. "I feel so stupid about it now but at the time I didn't know what else to do. You have to understand that I'm like a stranger in my own country. I've lived longer in the West than I have in Solung. I was sent to boarding school in England when I was ten, and went to college in the US when I was 18. I love my parents but they are very traditional. To them a girl's duty, her sole purpose, is to get married, have children and look after their families. And marriages are arranged, of course. For a long time I could not understand why my parents sent me abroad to be educated. It seemed out of character for them. I've since learned that the king persuaded them. He has no daughters and I was always a favourite of his. I'm fond of him too. He's a sweetie."

113

"He managed to rub Dougal up the wrong way," Tigger said.

"He does that to people sometimes. He puts on this old duffer act but he is much more worldly than my parents, and much cleverer than the people around him."

"Prince Raju said much the same thing."

"Did he?" The princess sounded surprised. "I hardly know Raju, though I was engaged to him when I was eight. He was thirteen. I was sent away because the king thought he would need an educated wife, which is pretty enlightened by Solung standards. But neither the king nor my parents understood how much being abroad would change me. I had to step back centuries when I came back to Solung."

"How long ago was that?"

"Only a few weeks ago. I've been back on holidays but that's not the same as coming to live and make my way here. I came back absolutely determined that I was not going to marry a man I hardly knew. I hadn't seen Raju for years. I was going to break off the engagement, and that was that. But I was greeted by my mother telling me how delighted she was that the marriage date had been set by the astrologers. That's how things work here. I felt like a breeding mare being prepared for a prize stud. I pleaded with my parents at least to get the wedding postponed. I begged them. I cried myself dry but they wouldn't listen. Actually it was worse than that: the idea was so outrageous that they couldn't even bring themselves to think about it."

The princess was fighting back tears. "They are probably worried sick about me now. They are not bad people. They thought they were doing what was best for me. They don't understand that the world was changed."

"How did Laxman get involved?"

"He was the only person around I could talk to about it. He went to school in England too, and so he is not locked into Solung thinking. He's a year older than Ganesh but he always seemed to me to be young for his age. He wasn't interested in going to college. All he wanted to do was fly. He spent most of his time at our uncle's flying club."

"The one with the Messerschmitts?"

"I've no idea. I don't go to my uncle's."

Clearly the princess had no interest in aircraft.

"What about Laxman's politics?"

"That's a new thing. About a year ago he got involved in a protest about some poor girl who got raped. It was all dreadful and nothing got settled but he became very popular with the poorer people, especially in our area. Solung is very tribal still and they really treat him as a prince. I think it went to his head a bit. He's very sophisticated on the surface but he has this naïve streak, like a teenager. He thinks that being able to see everything that is wrong in the world is the same as knowing what to do about it. I was very glad to see that he was engaging with the world... that he cared. I thought he would grow up. I never dreamed he was mixed up with the RMP."

"That's the political wing of the People's Army?"

"So it seems."

"When did you find out?"

"Everything came to a head when I threatened to run away. My parents actually set a guard on me. They said it was for my own protection but of course I knew the real reason. Laxman was furious and said he would help me get away. It was very easy. I went out riding with two guards. I made an excuse to dismount at a certain place and two young men stepped out from some trees and fired guns in the air. All three horses bolted, as I knew they would."

She smiled at the recollection. "The guards managed to stay on their horses but they were being thrown about at all angles. It would have been funny if the situation had not been so serious. I was worried for a moment that they might be injured. A car drew up and the young men bundled me into it.

The lingham seemed to come from the very earth
(see page 122)

"That was the only odd thing at the time. They pushed me in rather than letting me get in. I thought I was just running away but they seemed deliberately to make it look like a kidnap."

"They were People's Army?"

"They were, but I didn't realise that. Laxman was with them. He said a friend of his had a place where I could hide out for a couple of days. We drove for about an hour and stopped at some kind of lodge to meet up with his friend, who turned out to be Da Silva. Laxman was obviously in awe of him and presented him to me like he was a celebrity, as if he expected me to be impressed. There was an odd atmosphere and I began to feel very uneasy."

"Did Laxman tell you anything about Da Silva?"

"No. He'd been very cagey about his politics. He knew that I didn't like a lot of what goes on in Solung but he feared, with good reason, that I would not approve of him going anywhere near the People's Army. My guess is that Da Silva persuaded Laxman to try to get me involved by arranging a meeting with him, and that they saw my escape as a good opportunity. Da Silva is certainly conceited enough to believe that he could talk me into revolution, especially if he put me under an obligation to him by helping me get away. Laxman thought I would be as captivated by Da Silva as he was. I'm making Laxman sound stupid but he isn't. He's kind. He is charming, dashing even, and very clever when he applies himself. He knows a lot about subjects he is interested in. But he's an innocent. There is a level at which he doesn't understand the world. He was oblivious of the danger he was putting me into... handing his own sister over to the most dangerous man in the country."

"What do you mean, handing you over?" Tigger asked.

"In effect, that's what he did. I'm not sure that Da Silva intended to kidnap me at first. I was an asset and he was keeping his options open on the best way to capitalise on me. If I had been friendly, I might have proved more useful to him as an ally like my brother. But I didn't trust him and when he began talking about taking me to his place in the mountains to hide out, I said thanks very much but I'd rather make my way over the border to India until things died down. When I picked up my bag to leave, his men blocked my way. Laxman took Da Silva's side at first, saying I was being silly, but finally he insisted that I should be allowed to go if I wanted to and said that he would take me anywhere I wanted to go. Da Silva launched into a tirade about how I might betray the revolution, that I knew too much about the link between Laxman's movement and the People's Army. It was silly because I didn't even know Laxman had a movement. I'm completely out of touch with what has been going on in Solung."

"But Da Silva was right, from his point of view. Letting you go would have been risky," Tigger said.

"All the more reason why Laxman should not have got me involved. He and Da Silva had a furious row in which Laxman threatened to withdraw his support and Da Silva threatened to haul him before what he called a revolutionary court for compromising the organisation. I was frogmarched out to the car while two other men restrained Laxman."

"Has Laxman split with Da Silva now?"

"So far as I understand, no. He would certainly have put me in danger if he had because they would not harm me for fear of alienating him entirely. But he believes in it all, and as you have pointed out Da Silva could legitimately claim that I was being held, in relative comfort, as a security risk."

"You also made a good hostage."

"Exactly. I was an insurance policy."

"Against Laxman's defection?"

"That or any other situation in which I might be used as a bargaining chip."

Tigger suddenly realised that the princess might not know about the ransom note. "You know Da Silva was asking half a million pounds for your release?"

118

She was shocked into silence for a few seconds. "I didn't know that. No."

"In retrospect it was a little odd. For one thing there was no deadline on the demand..."

"Da Silva must have been keeping his options open. He probably saw the ransom demand as a way of making my disappearance look like an ordinary kidnap. If he was offered money, he could decide what to do from there."

"The other odd thing was that the reasons Raju gave us for not paying the ransom seemed... not wrong exactly, but a little heartless. It was government policy not to pay up and the king could not be seen to favour you."

The princess pursed her lips. "I am glad I didn't know that when I was in Da Silva's hands."

"It makes sense if the king knew that your brother was in effect guarantor for your safety, at least in the short term. Do you think he knew of Laxman's involvement?"

"What do you think? You have spoken to him."

"I always had the feeling that he and his son were holding something back."

The princess shook her head. "I don't know what to do. I can't stay here for ever and I can't face going back to my parents. I've burned my bridges as far as marrying Raju is concerned. And what am I going to say if they start questioning me about Laxman? He could be in big, big trouble. I wish there was a way to get away for a while to let things cool down."

They sat in silence for a few moments, staring into the fire. Then Henry asked: "Can you get hold of any money? Say a few hundred pounds?"

"I've got it in the bank, for sure."

"I can't promise anything, princess. I am not going to put any of our lives at risk just to save you embarrassment. If I find a phone quickly I'll use it to summon help, which means almost certainly that you will have to go straight to Solung. Otherwise, I'll head for Uttarprayag, the nearest big town. Someone I know flies in and out of a village near there regularly and there's a fair chance that he will be there. He would probably fly you out for a price... or for a favour if he knows who you are."

"Who is it?"

"You are going to have to keep quiet about him if I tell you. He is the dealer who does dope runs to the airstrip Tigger used. There's virtually an open border with India – all the international security is done at Satpur airport – and he can fly in and out without being checked."

"India would suit me fine."

Tigger said ruefully: "I don't know what Dougal will say if I turn up in Satpur minus a princess."

"You won't be minus a princess. I'll ring my parents and tell them I'm OK and how wonderful you have both been."

"Steady on, princess," said Henry. "Save your congratulations. We haven't got out of this yet."

5   The temple of love

Tigger watched Henry go early the next morning with mixed feelings. He would rather have got moving himself but he could not deny the wisdom of remaining at the temple with the princess and it would be pleasant to be alone with her for a while. He was already half way in love but he did not care to inspect his feelings. He accepted the closeness he felt with her as a natural consequence of what they had been through together. In other ways, the gulf between them was such that he never seriously considered getting involved with her.

The atmosphere between them changed after Henry left, as if a barrier had been removed. Tigger could not take his eyes off her as she bustled about washing her things and cooking. She refused his help. "Make the most of this... it may not last. This is the nearest I have ever been to living like ordinary Solungese women live, and have done for centuries. I want to see what it is like. I'm enjoying it. Besides, I've nothing else to do."

She had set up a little kitchen by the campfire, everything in its place, and cooked lentilburgers and chapatis. The pots she cleaned with tough grass, using clean ash from the fire as an abrasive. "You seem to know what you are doing," Tigger said.

"I saw women do this as a kid."

"I've camped out with a lot of men, and none of them would have set this place up quite like you have. Women do things differently."

"That might be a reflection of the kind of men you hang out with. I know men who are precious about everything they do and women who are complete sluts in the home."

"You get all sorts in both sexes. But women are born different, I am sure of it. They have different interests, different priorities. For one thing, most women fancy men."

"You are a classic warrior. Is that in your genes, or is it your idea of what a man should be?"

"I'm hardly a warrior. If I were, I would have joined the air force. Like your brother, I just wanted to fly. My parents died in a car crash when I was 14. I inherited a little money from them and spent it on flying lessons as soon as I was old enough. Got a job at an air museum where my dad had worked and flew a lot of old aircraft. That's how I met Dougal, flying Spitfires in a film."

"You've got involved in a mini-war here."

"I couldn't resist the chance of an adventure. I suppose that's down to my genes, but reading boy's own stories as a kid probably had a lot to do with it too. Henry wasn't the only one to read Biggles. I came here like every young fool of a boy who ever ran off to war. I had no idea what I was getting into. For all I knew you could have been the wicked witch in the hands of the good fairies."

Tigger became acutely aware that he was staring at the princess, fascinated by her sure, capable movements. When she began washing her body, dressed only in a long tee-shirt, he moved away in discomfiture, taking their stump of a candle to look inside the little temple. The timeless images stirred him: the inscrutable faces of the gods, the stylised eroticism of their couplings, and inside the cave the starkest sexual image of all: the lingham, a waist-high stone phallus.

Now, for the first time, he appreciated the power of the ancient symbol. The lingham seemed to come from the very earth. Looking closer, he saw that it *was* the earth: the lingham and much of the temple interior had been sculpted out of the cliff. With the princess so deliciously close outside, and the awesome images, Tigger had never felt so affected by a place. It seemed to draw its peculiar feeling from the centre of the earth and touch upon the source of life.

It was cold in the cave and Tigger moved outside to sit in the sun, still gazing into the temple. After a few minutes, the princess came and stood behind him.

"It's beautiful," he said, for the sake of saying something.

"So are you," she said, sitting next to him.

Tigger, taken aback yet again, changed the subject. "Did you see that the lingham is carved out of the cave floor?"

"So is the yoni."

"The yoni?"

"People only ever speak of the lingham, the phallic symbol. Even Henry did. It's a man's world. Look at the base of the lingham."

The base was surrounded by a raised channel, like a miniature moat, with a funnel at the front. Tigger had taken it to be a simple embellishment.

"The lingham is set into the yoni, the vagina," said the princess. "Complete, it is not a male symbol, it is male and female, the creative interplay of all dualities. It is nought and one, nothing and something, masculine and feminine. It's the primordial mating. And look... within the yoni is a channel. It's the river of life."

Tigger thought of the guerrilla boys, dead on the path, and of Babu's blazing corpse, and of the screams of Matchbox Baba. "The lingham seems to breed nothing but violence. Perhaps it is time we started noticing the yoni," he said.

The princess ran a finger down his cheek. "You are funny," she said.

Tigger turned and touched her cheek, and he knew that the unthinkable was going to happen. Their lips met and they leaned backwards, and the princess's dress slipped up, inviting, and there was a fumbling, and lingham met luscious yoni. It was an animal mating, a quiver and it was over, but there was no sense of disappointment. There had been no need of foreplay, and both of them knew that that first entry had been a foreplay in itself, a discharge of urgency. There was plenty of time before Henry would arrive back. "The phallus has its points," the princess said.

All morning they lay in each other's arms, discovering their bodies, tuning in; and talking, learning about each other in the way only lovers can.

"Do you feel all right about this... I mean, in a temple?" Tigger asked.

The princess giggled and put a finger on his chest. "It's a bit late to think about that."

"It seems so disrespectful... of other peoples' beliefs. But not a desecration. This place has got into me. All these images... I feel they are blessing us."

"Of course they are blessing us. This is a temple of love."

"People made love here?"

"I wouldn't be surprised. Sex is a perfectly natural pleasure of life. This temple celebrates life... it celebrates sex. Some people in this country are embarrassed by places like this. They even deny that the lingham-yoni is a sexual symbol."

"What went on here?"

"One day someone will probably earn a PhD trying to find out. It's an oddity for this area but carvings like this can be found in temples far to the south of here. There are still temples in India where childless women go for a fertility rite that consists of being impregnated by a priest. And some temples are virtually a cover for prostitution. These are extremes, though. Hinduism today is generally coy about sex but that has not always been the case."

Her mood seemed to change and she gave a little shiver. "I think that's why I feel so strange about being here," she said, as if the thought had just occurred to her.

"What do you mean?"

The princess sat up so that her naked body was lit by the dappled light from the peepal tree, as perfect as the women carved in stone. "I'll tell you about it," she said. "But you must promise to keep it a secret. You must promise to keep

124

this a secret, too... about us, here." She waved her hand vaguely round the temple. "Promise?"

There was that little girl in her again. "I promise," Tigger said.

"No-one must know about us making love... especially here."

"Sita, you needn't worry. I won't tell anyone."

"I am worried. Are you familiar with the Ramayana?"

"Isn't it an Indian folk story?"

"It's a collection of stories about King Rama and his wife Sita. She's the ideal wife of Hindu folklore, so you can see my parents' thinking when they named me after her. She's what they wanted me to be. They didn't reckon on me being like her in another way. The Sita of the Ramayana is kidnapped. To cut a very long story short, Rama rescues her. There's all manner of death and destruction, then the big question is: what was Sita up to when she was in the clutches of her kidnapper?"

"You mean was there any hanky-panky?"

"Right. So how do you think Rama resolves the question?"

"He asks Sita."

"He sticks her on a bonfire and burns her. An ordeal by fire. As a matter of detail Sita volunteers for it, but Rama does nothing to stop her. The idea is that she will survive if she is innocent."

"Nobody is going to do that to you."

"The fire just comes in a different form these days."

"Double standards don't. I bet no-one asked Rama who he'd been screwing."

The princess laughed. "It's no joke, Tigger. I'm terrified of getting involved in a scandal, and I'm afraid that at times I've been rather foolish in risking one."

It was Tigger's turn to laugh. The princess caught his eye, looked down at her nakedness, and gave a rueful smile. Tigger said: "Look, I promise to keep my mouth shut. Tell me

125

why you feel so strange about being here."

"There is another tradition that is about as far from chaste little Sita as you can get. It's the polar opposite of the tradition Krishna Baba followed, which is all about asceticism and meditation and self-control. It's called Tantra, and I got involved in it when I was in the US. I thought I'd turned my back on it when returned to Solung. But... it is almost scary that I have landed up here. There is probably no other place like this in all of Solung, and it's the very embodiment of Tantra. I've been thrown right back into it."

She was silent for a few seconds, as if struggling with her thoughts. Suddenly, astonishingly, she was in tears. "I have to tell you about it, Tigger. I have to tell someone. I couldn't even tell Laxman."

The sun was getting lower and they were in shadow. The princess put on her shawl, and Tigger drew her to him. She said: "I was all jolly hockeysticks, an absolute innocent, when I left school in England to go to America. When I got to college there, I was utterly shocked at how the girls carried on, boasting about how many men they had taken to bed. Of course a lot of men came on to me but I really wasn't interested. I suppose Sita was my Biggles, the ideal I was born to. I expected to go home a virgin and marry Raju. Then I fell in love with an American professor. He had an Indian guru and he was into Tantra."

"He taught you about it?"

"His version of it, or his guru's. I'd always associated Tantra with those pretty pictures called mandalas. You've probably seen posters of them on sale in London even if you don't know what they are."

"I've heard of Tantric sex."

The princess waved her hand at the temple carvings. "This is it, set in stone. The male figure is Shiva, who is usually depicted as a kind of patron god of ascetics, the embodiment of what some people call the right-hand path to wisdom. The images here are left-hand path. They are Tantric.

126

They are the lingham-yoni in human form. They show Shiva making love with his wife Parvati, also known as Devi or Shakti. They are Shiva-Shakti, the interplay of male and female energy."

"So are most pop songs. Where does it get you?"

"The power of sex. The ascetic tries to step back from sexual desire, to objectify it, to stop identifying with it in order to attain mystic realisation. The tantrika tries to harness sex, to lose the ego in the act of making love. It is not a doctrine. It is a technique."

"It sounds like a pretty wild chat-up line to me."

"Well, it worked on me. My professor put it rather better than I have."

"You tried it out?"

"Of course."

"And you found God?"

"Not that I noticed. But we had a lot of fun trying."

"That doesn't sound like enough to reduce you to tears."

"My professor was more than enough. Tantra is not something to be trifled with. The tradition includes some dangerous ideas, such as the ritual breaking of taboos. Having sex outside marriage, eating forbidden food... that sort of thing. There's a list of five, as I recall, and not all of them are outrageous by modern standards. The principle is more interesting than the detail. The professor saw it as an early form of psychotherapy... a way of reaching a new understanding of yourself by breaking through all the stuff that is put into your head as a child."

"That's called growing up, isn't it?"

"Grown-ups don't throw off their upbringing. Look at you in the temple this morning. You looked so sweet, moping around, trying to play the gentleman. You wouldn't make a move because Biggles didn't do that sort of thing. It wasn't you holding back; it was Biggles."

"It was civilisation. It was good sexual manners."

The princess kissed him on the cheek. "Like I said, you

were so sweet. But civilisation warps as much as it refines. It packs our minds with stuff that we act out without being aware of it. My professor believed taboo breaking was an ancient way of forcing someone to become aware of all these habitual attitudes. You might not reject them all as a result but you arrived at a new integrity."

"So what did that mean in practice?"

"They – the guru and his followers – related all this to psychotherapeutic techniques like encounter groups, in which there were essentially no rules of behaviour. It was a modern form of taboo breaking."

"Did you do that?"

"I didn't get involved in the groups. There were too many people involved, too much risk of a scandal. Anyway, coming from my background, having a tempestuous love affair in a foreign country was about as taboo as I could get."

"I have to be honest, princess. To me, it all sounds self-indulgent and, like you said, dangerous."

"That is just what it was, Tigger, at least as far as my professor was concerned. Tantra is a supposed to be an exploration, not a license for depravity. It is a path that should be trodden with great care. It has a murky history full of charlatan magicians and dirty old babas exploiting young women. But I thought it had a streak of the divine. And I was in love for the first time in my life."

The tears were coming back again. Tigger asked gently: "Were you being exploited?"

"I'm a grown woman. I'm responsible for my actions. I don't think it was all nonsense – at least it was something worth exploring. My professor believed in what he was doing but he was fooling himself, using Tantra to justify the unacceptable. Far from becoming more aware of the roots of his behaviour, he simply rejected conventional ideas of right and wrong. I thought, when I was in love with him, that this was a way of challenging me to look at my own values. But just as I was coming to the end of my time in the US, happily after I

128

had got my thesis in, I found out that he was married with two kids. I was horrified."

"He dropped you?"

"Far from it. It wasn't rejection that hurt me. It was not the fact that he had lied, or had not told me the whole truth. It was the fact that he wanted to leave his wife and kids and go away with me. I lost all respect for him. I could not respect a man who would do that, certainly not in the way he talked about it. He seemed to think that in the modern world of contraception and sexual freedom, women should expect their men to leave and their children to be left fatherless. This was a man I had loved. I was devastated, and that was the state of mind I was in when I came back to Solung."

Tigger held her and they were silent. Then the princess said: "Tigger, whatever happens now I shall never forget these past couple of days with you and Henry. You've given me my life back, the two of you. I mean that."

Tigger stayed silent. There was too much in her words for him to process, and perhaps something he did not want to process. The hint of a goodbye.

ooo

Henry was back in the morning, earlier than expected, and the atmosphere in the little sanctuary changed almost immediately. They were both delighted to see him but Tigger quickly realised that the princess did not want Henry to know what had been going on. She was still affectionate but she was affectionate to them both. All reserve had dropped and she treated them as if they were her own brothers.

Henry breezed in carrying milk, eggs, and fresh bread. "We have got to get going," he said smiling. "The princess's... er Sita's... car awaits. She has a plane to catch. But first... breakfast."

They cooked and ate while he told his story. Getting to the top of the cliff had not been easy but he had done it in just over an hour; two hours after that he reached a road on the far side of the ridge. "The first vehicle that came along was a country bus. Absolutely packed. People spilling out of the windows. But it stopped, assuming I wanted a ride. I said I had no money and had to get to Uttarprayag and the people on the bus clubbed together for the ticket and crammed me in. It was a very slow bus, stopping everywhere, and took about two hours to do 20 miles but it got me there. Alexis, my friend, was in town and is happy to help. He's agreed to fly Sita to some place within striking distance of Calcutta for nothing. Though I'm sure he'd be happy to get a present when you sort yourself out, Sita."

Tigger asked: "Isn't he worried about getting the wrong side of the People's Army?"

"It is getting too hot around here for him anyway. The guerrillas are trying to muscle in on the dope trade but he doesn't want to deal with them. For one thing he would have to do the dirty on his friends in the valley and for another the People's Army will use the money to buy guns. He doesn't feel good about that and he wants out. There are a lot of other places he can do business."

"Did you say you have a car?"

"I exaggerate. A car would be too conspicuous. We have a lift on a truck going up the valley to pick up some stuff. The trucker won't be expecting you – he thinks I am doing a charas run for Alexis. I'll tell him I've just bumped into you and offered you a lift. We have to meet him on the road on his way back in about four hours. He'll wait if we are delayed. He won't get paid otherwise."

They made good progress up the cliff, as Henry had already found the optimal route. At the top was a substantial path leading right out to the plains but after about a quarter-mile Henry led them down a side track. Two hours later they came to the road, where the truck was already waiting. The owner, sitting in the front next to his driver, looked suspiciously at Tigger and the princess. Henry said something in Solungese and the man spat on the ground, then motioned them with bad grace to a bench behind him that doubled as bed space and accommodation for paying passengers. Tigger, still worried about the People's Army, was relieved to note that their seats were largely hidden from the road.

"I had to double his money but I expected that," Henry said as they drove off. He spoke rapidly, in case the trucker understood English. "Now listen carefully. The truck is going to drive to the edge of the airfield and the aircraft will taxi over, supposedly to pick up its cargo of charas. There will be some dodgy people around so I want to avoid Sita being seen. As I get out, you follow as if we are stretching our legs. Keep out of sight behind the aircraft. Jump in as soon as you can, Sita. Keep your goodbyes short. We don't want more trouble from the trucker."

Tigger asked: "What are you going to do when you get to India, Sita?"

"I'll lay low with friends near Calcutta but I don't want to get them into trouble by using their address. You can write to me c/o the poste restante at the main post office in Calcutta using my family name S. Sinouk. But I'll be out of town, keeping my head down. I'm unlikely to be able to pick up messages for a while – perhaps three or four weeks."

No contact for weeks. They sat in silence for nearly an hour as Tigger digested this disturbing news and the truck trundled on. The airstrip turned out to be a long stretch of hardened earth at the edge of a village. At the far end, they could see a small aircraft near a cluster of buildings. "A Cessna," whispered Tigger. As Henry had predicted it began taxi-ing over when they stopped. He delayed getting out until it was close, so that it swung round in front of them as the princess climbed from the truck. Tigger, who had vaguely imagined Alexis as a dashing young man, was surprised to see that the pilot was plump, middle-aged and balding. The Princess kissed Henry and Tigger on the cheek, hugged them briefly, and whispered: "I love you both. I'll write."

Then she was gone.

6   In the hands of the dacoits

Tigger had expected to feel bereft and he did; but as they
stood by the truck watching the Cessna take off, he had an
overwhelming feeling of relief and elation. They had done
it... the princess was free. He became aware that Henry, talking rapidly in Solungese, was arguing with the truck owner as
he paid him off from a wad of notes supplied by Alexis. Finally the trucker got into the vehicle and drove off.

"He refused to take us on into town," Henry said. "He
says he does not know what is going on but it is not what I
paid him for and he is worried that it will bring him trouble.
He doesn't want to be seen with us. I can't say I blame him.
We can get a bus from the village but we're going to have to
brazen things out."

The heat of the plains had felt pleasant at first after the
mountain cool but it became oppressive as they walked in
the full blaze of the sun towards the village half a mile away
across the airstrip. Cows, evidently held back to enable the
aircraft to take off, were beginning to wander across and the
smell of burning dung drifted over from village cooking fires.
Henry talked as they walked. "We will probably meet Bikash, who is the strong man around here. He's a dacoit but
Alexis pays him protection money for using this airstrip."

"I hope Alexis hasn't got any drugs on the aircraft. It
would be dreadful if the princess got caught in a drug run."

"There's none around at the moment because of the difficulty of getting it out of the mountains. Bikash has been
told I went to pick some up. There's no knowing how he will
react if he suspects what's been going on. If anyone asks I am
going to say you'd been walking in the mountains and

hitched a lift with me when you got to the road."

Villagers stared at them curiously as they got close to the buildings and by the time they reached the far end they had a trail of children following them. A group of men sat in a bamboo shelter where a fat woman in a saree squatted next to a fire stewing a saucepan of tea. In the centre of the group was a large man wearing white cotton trousers and a waistcoat that showed off a powerfully muscled torso.

"Hi, Bikash," said Henry.

"'Enry... who your friend?"

Henry said something in Solungese and Bikash turned to Tigger. "Walking, eh? You watch out. Many bad men here."

"I have no money for them to steal."

"Sadhu, huh? *Brahmacharya*, eh?" Bikash winked and laughed. His courtiers – for so they appeared – laughed dutifully.

"*Brahmacharya*... celibate," Henry explained. Was this a sly reference to the fact that they had had a young woman with them? Had the princess been spotted? The question crossed both their minds.

Bikash went on: "Nettive pless?"

Tigger was baffled for a moment. Then he mentally translated. "My native place? I come from London."

"You want chai? "

"I'd love some," said Tigger.

Bikash clapped his hands to get the woman's attention and ordered tea. Then he said: "London... I know London. Buckingham Pless, Waterloo Steshun. Queen."

"You've been to London?" asked Tigger.

"I read books. Bikash good reading. You see princess?"

Tigger's heart missed a beat. "Princess? Who?"

Bikash laughed. "You and 'Enry talk to Bikash, eh? Come."

He stood up, motioning his henchmen to remain where they were, and led them a few yards away to a stone seat at the base of a shady tree. He spoke to Henry in Solungese.

"Bikash says a princess escaped from the guerrillas in the next valley," Henry translated. "She was with a man. Did you hear anything about it?"

"I stay clear of guerrillas... nasty, rough people," said Tigger.

"Woman get on plane," said Bikash.

Henry replied in broken English, for fear that he and Tigger would get their stories confused. "No woman... man. Hippy... long hair. Alexis friend."

"I like Alexis friends. Why no come see me?"

"Man buy charas. He afraid you steal. I tell him you good man. He say no-one here good man."

To Tigger's surprise, Bikash roared with laughter. "Your friend right. No good men here. But Alexis friend – no trouble. Alexis bring too much money. No steal. Good business."

The fat woman came up with a tray of teas. Bikash took his without a word of thanks. "You nem?" he asked Tigger.

"Tigger."

"Teeger. I tell you... king good."

The conversation was getting difficult to follow. "You like the king?"

"King good. People's Army bad. Here Bikash king. I tell this man, kees my arse, he kees my arse. Guerrillas... dogs." Bikash spat into the dust.

Bikash reverted to Solungese and his voice rose almost to a shout.

Henry translated. "Bikash is angry that Alexis didn't tell him that he was flying the princess out. He would have charged Alexis more if he had known. Only the boundless goodness of his heart, and his respect for Alexis, prevented him from blocking the take off and ransoming the princess himself."

"Why does he kept talking about a princess? We know nothing about her," said Tigger.

"I told him that. He's not buying it. He thinks that she

was with us."

More men had arrived at the shelter, crowding round the entrance, staring at them, Tigger saw with alarm that they carried what looked like country-made shotguns. "My men," said Bikash, seeing Tigger looking at them. "Bad men."

Again, the conversation lapsed into Solungese. Henry speed-talked a translation so Bikash would not understand his comments: "He's dropping hints about holding us to ransom, but I'm sure that is bluster. He daren't hold us or he would have held the princess, who is much more valuable. He doesn't want his boat rocked, and messing with foreigners or the princess could invite trouble from outside his little world. I'm wondering why he moved us out of earshot of his men. I think he has some other agenda, something he didn't want them to hear."

Bikash spoke again in Solungese.

"He's asking if there is a reward for information about the guerrillas. He knows something and he wants us to help him get money for it in return for letting us go."

"What kind of information?"

Bikash started speaking rapidly in Solungese.

Henry translated. "It's about arms. Bikash says the People's Army is getting a shipment soon. He can find out where and when, and he'll let us know. If he gets paid."

"Why doesn't he approach the government himself?"

"That's not a simple matter for an outlaw. You're the nearest to the government he can get. He sees you as a foreign mercenary in its pay. He thinks you *want* the information."

"No doubt the King would. What's to stop the authorities simply arresting and interrogating him?"

"If he has useful information, wouldn't they would want to keep him in place as an informer? Anyway, if an arrest was that easy, he would already be in jail. He'd take to the hills and they'd end up without him or the information. It's not worth the risk. He only wants 5,000 rupees... that's less than 700 dollars."

"So why doesn't he ask for more?"

"I'd say he'd give the information for free if he thought it would help defeat Da Silva. The People's Army must be as much a threat to him as the government is. Perhaps more so. It's stronger than he is, and it probably undermines his support among the lower-caste poor. Why settle for crumbs from the table of a self-styled Robin Hood when you can have a revolution?"

"How does he propose to keep in contact?"

Henry again conferred with Bikash.

"He wants one of us to come back with some money."

Tigger shook his head. "I don't want to mess with this. I've no idea what's going on here and I don't want to get any more involved. For all we know the government may already have the information he is trying to sell. Tell him we will check it out when we get back. He can call me at the airbase and we'll take it from there. In the meantime, how are we going to get out of here?"

Again Henry and Bikash spoke in Solungese. Again Henry speed-talked a translation. "He's agreed to that. He'll also give us a number where we can leave a message – perhaps the one he uses to liaise with Alexis. He seems quite keen on a deal. Maybe, with Da Silva breathing down his neck, he is hoping to square himself with the government. There has been talk of an amnesty for dacoits willing to go straight. The bad news is that everyone seems to have known that the princess was in the area with two foreigners. Bikash says we could hit trouble if we walk out of here by ourselves, so he is proposing to take us to the nearest railway station in a truck. I think we are going to have to trust him."

ooo

If Bikash was making money out of his villainy, he was not spending it on vehicles. His truck, a brightly painted, locally made wooden body stuck on a standard chassis, had seen better days, The tyres were worn paper smooth, one side window was broken, none of the instruments worked, and the electric horn had been replaced by a large, painted bulb-horn next to the driver's window. Tigger and Henry were hidden under sacking in the open back. Four men pushed the truck to start it, then clambered into the back, placing shotguns on the floor. Bikash climbed into the front, next to the driver, and two more men crammed in after him.

The truck stopped after they had been chugging along for about half an hour, and Tigger and Henry were invited into the cab. Apparently, the danger area was behind them. The cab was hot, with the engine cowling sticking up close to the driver, but a cool breeze came through the open window. Tigger felt cheerful, as if he were going on a holiday trip.

Bikash was in an expansive mood, wanting to talk; but conversation was almost impossible over the noise of the engine and it did not sparkle.

"Bikash helping king. You telling," Bikash shouted.

"You loyal man. Very good," Tigger shouted foolishly. They said nothing for a few minutes.

"Guerrillas killing Bikash if they catch," said Bikash, miming his throat being cut.

"Guerrillas... bad," shouted Tigger.

"Rellwey stetion... half a mile," shouted Bikash.

The truck was slowing down already, as if the driver could not trust himself to pull up in time. His brakes were soon put to the test. The truck rounded a curve and they saw a bullock cart slung across the road 30 yards ahead. The driver slammed on his brakes and the truck shuddered to a halt. Even before it had stopped, Bikash screamed: "Get out!"

They never knew what he had seen. Tigger and Henry, who were nearest the door, tumbled out into the road as a series of explosions rang in their ears. They were crouching down in a ditch before Tigger realised that he was hearing gunshots. The noise continued for fully a minute and then ceased abruptly.

Tigger raised his head to find two men standing over him grinning, rifles slung under their arms. Bikash's body was sprawled half in and half out of the cab, his chest a mess of blood. His men lay on the road in pathetic, bloody heaps. Only one was alive, bent double over the wall of a culvert, whimpering. A man stepped out of the bushes and casually shot him in the head.

Strolling down the road came a man wielding an umbrella like a walking stick. His black hair hung to his shoulders and his pockmarked face sported a carefully waxed handlebar moustache; he wore a green velvet jacket with brass buttons; a pistol and ornate knife were stuck into a cummerbund at his waist, above voluminous pantaloons.

Henry was the final surprise. White faced, tears streaming down his face, he ran up to the newcomer and screamed: "You murderer! You bloody murderer! What did you do that for?"

Tigger did not have the release of anger. He looked at the bodies around him and was sick at the feet of the gunman

7   The dacoit hunter

"Vermin," said the man. "These men were dacoits. They died as they lived. If you had seen women they raped, mothers weeping for dead sons and husbands, fathers with no-one to tend their fields when they are old... then you would not cry."

Henry was clenching and unclenching his fists in frustration. "Come," the stranger said, inclining his head towards a narrow path that led away from the road. He walked off with not a glance behind, flanked by two men carrying rifles at the slope. Too shocked to argue, Henry and Tigger followed, keeping a few yards behind so that they could talk in comfort. About 20 heavily-armed men materialised from the bushes by the roadside and fell in behind them.

"Who is he?" asked Tigger.

"I can't remember his name – he's known by his initials, – but I've seen his picture in the papers. He's notorious for this sort of thing. These men are vigilantes, so we are safe – I think."

"What do you mean, vigilantes?"

"They live on the other side of the river that marks the dacoit territory. The dacoits slip over the river, raid the farms and villages over there, then return to their own territory where the police can't or won't follow them. It's like tribal warfare with a bit of caste war thrown in. The character in front is a Rajput, a member of a warrior clan that spread up from India. He's backed by property owners and also by of some of the poor who believe he protects them. He forms vigilante patrols to chase the dacoits over the river and into their own territory. If he catches or kills a known dacoit he gets a bounty. By all accounts he is just as bad as they are, and has what amounts to a private army. He is reputed to be responsible for scores of deaths."

"I suppose the government can't do anything about it."

"Our friend *is* the government. At least, he is a member of parliament. Anyway, what can the government say when its own forces can't control the dacoits? Even if a dacoit is arrested, the chances are that he will get off. People are too terrified to testify, and many officials can be bribed to secure his release. That's why the police and vigilantes feel free to shoot to kill."

"The police do take action then?"

"Of course. But there is undermanning and corruption at all levels. Our friend here got charged with murder and the case was thrown out of court. He has too many friends in high places."

Henry shook his head, as if to get rid of unpleasant thoughts, and lit a bedi.

"There's a constant struggle going on between the land-owners and peasants in the countryside. So many people are involved across the subcontinent that if they were concentrated in one place you would call it a war. Yet it is so dispersed that it is like background noise. Each incident gets no more than a mention in the papers if it is noticed at all. The landowners don't have it all their own way. There's the violent opposition of the Naxalites and in places peasants have grabbed land, sometimes legally, sometimes not. But they are at a disadvantage when it comes to the law. There are interminable arguments over who owns what land. Records are complex and chaotic, and court cases can drag on for years. Even if a peasant is granted ownership of land, as often as not he cannot farm it. The landlord will simply drive him off, or start legal proceedings he cannot afford to fight. Much of the country is at peace but where it's bad it can be very bad indeed. There's crop looting, intimidation, assassination, and people owing allegiance to their most effective protectors. There's a caste war, a crime war, and a festering revolution going on all at the same time. And that's before you get to the intercommunal stuff between Moslems and Hindus."

"You sound like an advert for the People's Army."

"What do you want – what happened in China? Mao Tse Tung and his Great Leap Forward? Do you know how many people died in that? Do you know how many people died in the revolution that preceded it? This place is a mess but at least it didn't go through all that."

They had reached the river, where an assortment of rowing boats was waiting. Henry and Tigger had to get into separate boats. Tigger tried to rest his mind by gazing at the scenery as they made their way slowly downriver past boys washing buffalo and women washing pots and clothes. Barren muddy banks dipped here and there to reveal paddy fields, oxen, ploughs, and peasants at work – just a few of the passive masses of the subcontinent. All the killings, the wars, the rapes, the kings and princes, the empires, the philosophies, the corruption, the politics, seemed to have crashed over these people like a stormy ocean on rocks leaving them unchanged. Who ruled them was of little importance compared with the need for food, the land to grow it, the seeds to plant, and a home to live in and raise children who could bring comfort and security to old age. Or so it seemed from a distance. Tigger scolded himself for allowing the beauty of the scene to seduce him into sentimentality. The countryside was both beauty and beast, and the beast had just killed eight men.

The boats headed for a jetty on the far bank, where Tigger and Henry were shown into the back of a Land Rover. The Rajput sat in the front, next to the driver, and the rest of his contingent clambered into a truck.

"You know me?" asked the Rajput, turning to face them.

"I know your face," Henry said.

"I am NRJ. NRJ Singh. I hunt dacoits."

"So we saw," Tigger said. "Those men were helping us.

The king will be very angry with you."

"King will be pleased. Dacoits were armed. They were going to kill you," NRJ said in fluent English, dropping articles in the South Asian manner.

"They were taking us to the railway station."

"They were taking you outside their territory so they would not be blamed for your death."

"They were taking us to catch a train to Satpur."

"That's what they told you. Why were they carrying guns? They were going to kill you."

"They were armed to protect us from other dacoits." The discussion was futile. Tigger realised that NRJ was simply establishing the story he would tell the authorities.

"You don't know these people like I do. They are animals. You can never trust them. Never!"

NRJ banged the seat in emphasis.

"How did you know we would be there?"

"I have spies. They said dacoits take you away to kill you. Where is princess?"

So he did not know everything. "She is safe. How did you know about the princess? "

"How could I not know? It was in all the papers yesterday. There are many foreign news people in Satpur waiting to see if you will come."

"That explains how Bikash knew," Tigger said.

"Which of you is Mr Thompson?"

"I am. This is Henry..." Tigger realised that he did not know Henry's surname.

"We must go to Satpur. I will take you. We will speak to king. We will tell him good news."

The idea of Satpur suddenly lost its appeal to Tigger. He did not want to face reporters, and certainly not with NRJ, who was obviously out to capture some glory and ingratiate himself with the king. He asked: "Where are we going now?"

"To my house. We can eat. I want to hear your story. You are very brave man."

142

"I would not be here but for Henry and the princess," Tigger said. "We got out together."

Henry had sat tight-lipped throughout the conversation. When the Land Rover stopped, and NRJ got out to pay some of his men, he muttered: "I don't want to go to Satpur. If those reporters get my name and picture I'll be a marked man. I'll never be able to walk around Solung again. Even India will be dangerous."

"Do you think I want to face them?" said Tigger.

They fell silent when NRJ returned, and a few minutes later the Land Rover turned into the drive of a large bungalow. "My home," NRJ announced. He snapped orders in Solungese to servants who opened the vehicle's doors. "These people will show you to shower rooms," he said. "Do you want clean clothes?"

"You have any?"

NRJ snapped his fingers and issued orders to a maid, who rushed off.

Tigger said: "Can we telephone from here?"

"Later. Exchange is broken down."

Having had experience of telephones in Satpur, Tigger knew that this was not unlikely; nevertheless, NRJ was probably lying. He wanted a triumphal entry into Satpur bearing good tidings.

Tigger took a blissful shower but he could not wash away the memory of the murdered dacoits. "I feel almost as if I betrayed them," he told Henry, as they dressed in crisp white cotton suits provided by the maid.

"The worst of it is that there is damn all we can do about it."

"We could get NRJ charged with murder."

"He would get off. How can we prove Bikash was helping us? Even if we could, NRJ could still say he was acting in good faith and didn't want to risk our lives. He obviously isn't worried. He didn't even hang around to give a story to the police."

"We'll have to go to Satpur, Henry. Both of us. They will expect you to make a statement about the killings. I don't want to go there any more than you do but we can drive straight to the base where Dougal is, and steer clear of reporters. NRJ won't be averse to going into town by himself. He'll make an entry like a conquering hero."

"What's the point of making a statement? Nothing will happen."

"Bikash was no angel but you owe it to him and his people to put the truth on record, even if it is not acted upon."

"I'm sick of it all. Everything I have been through in Solung has blown up in my face in the past few days. First the herdsmen getting killed, and Krishna Baba, then Matchbox Baba and now Bikash and his men. It screams evil, but I know it's the way of the world. And I hate... I hate that bastard NRJ more than I've ever hated anyone. He should be strung up."

The man he had been hating and hanging fussed into the room and invited them to food on the veranda. Apart from three armed guards wandering about the garden, they could not have wished for a more relaxing scene. A cow lolled soulfully under a banyan tree at the centre of a lawn in front of them. A gardener pottered among flower beds. The veranda was framed by bougainvillea flowers wafting in a gentle breeze. The table, brilliant white in the reflected sunlight, was laid with stainless-steel plates, bowls of rice and a selection of spicy dishes.

Henry did not touch the food and stared sullenly into the middle distance.

"Your friend does not say much," said NRJ.

"He doesn't like you," said Tigger.

"And you?"

"I am polite."

"Those men were killers. Everyone is better off for their deaths. I saved your lives. Why do you hate me?"

"Don't go through that again," Henry burst out. "That

144

scene on the road was disgusting. If you really wanted to help people here you would do something about the poverty that surrounds you. Perhaps then there would not be so many dacoits. I know about you, NRJ. You style yourself as a dacoit hunter but you have a very fluid idea of who is a dacoit. You and your men act as enforcers for the high-caste landlords. You are fighting a caste war."

"Me fighting caste war? What are dacoits doing? They kill small farmers who come to me and my friends for protection. It is we, not dacoits, who give food to poor in times of drought. Poor are our subjects... how can we be enemies?"

"Most of them are too scared to be anyone's enemy. That's why the dacoits get respect. They stand up to the likes of you. You are as bad as they are. You are all killers."

"I use same methods but to different end. Dacoits are like Naxalites... they want to grab land and property. I want to stop them. They want to decide with their guns. I stop them with guns. They fight in shadows, I fight in open."

"Can you blame them for wanting to seize the land? The high castes lay claim to it all. They have subjugated people for centuries."

"Then why do people here support me? I won my seat in parliament with 10,000 votes."

"I won't ask you what methods you used to get them."

"Nobody makes a fuss when communists or dacoits intimidate voters. Nobody notices when dacoits kill farmers. But as soon as dacoit is killed, everyone calls it caste atrocity. If government can't protect us, we have to protect ourselves."

"I despair," Henry said, shaking his head. "I watched you today, NRJ, walking among those bodies like you were starring in a movie. You loved it. It'll serve you right if the People's Army move into Bikash's area, right on your doorstep, with you first on their target list. You'll deserve all you get."

Henry did not wait for a reply. He got up from the table and squatted on the veranda steps, his chin resting on his clenched fists. NRJ gazed after him open-mouthed.

"Just get us to Satpur," Tigger said wearily.

NRJ stalked back into the bungalow and Tigger sat next to Henry, who was squatting with his head in his hands.

"You shouldn't let the world hurt you so," Tigger said.

"It's not the world... it's me. Who am I to judge NRJ? I can't tell him anything. I have death on my hands. I don't have any answers. And when I start questioning, I end up sounding like just another politician."

8   The king asks a favour

They did not go straight to Satpur. By threatening to denounce NRJ in front of the world's press, they persuaded him to drop them at Dougal's airfield base. NRJ went to the capital alone, still claiming he had saved their lives. Their arrival was an anti-climax as the princess had already been in touch and Dougal was expecting them. He, too, was all in favour of keeping their faces out of the papers. "It's safer that way. We can't do the same for Ganesh. He's become a national hero and he deserves to be. We couldn't have pulled this off without him."

Tigger and Henry stood before him like boys brought before the headmaster. "Ganesh probably saved my life," said Tigger. "And so did Henry here. The princess and I couldn't have got away without him."

"You did a good job, both of you. But in my day when we went rescuing we came back with the goods. We didn't let them go gallivanting off like it was holiday time."

"The princess is a free agent. She was offered a lift and she took it. What do you expect us to do – tie her up?"

Dougal sat back and gazed steadily at each of them in turn. "Women," he said eventually, raising his eyes to the ceiling. "They can't resist creating complications. I know there has been something going on that I don't know about and right at this moment I don't want to know. I've been tearing my hair out for days wondering what happened to you Tigger. We didn't know if you were dead or recaptured, and we daren't give any indication that you were missing for fear of alerting the People's Army that you were at large."

"NRJ told us it was in the papers yesterday," Tigger said.

He realised with a shock that Dougal had been badly shaken by his disappearance, and this was the nearest he would get to admitting it. Charlie had been right: Dougal wasn't as tough as he made out. He was trying to sound cool but he looked worn out.

"We put the word out as soon we discovered that the guerrillas were looking for you," Dougal said. "That was how we knew you were alive. It was the first good news we'd had since we sprung the princess. It was bad news for some poor wretch in that valley you were in, though. Apparently the People's Army murdered him trying to find out where you were. Do you know anything about it?"

"Unfortunately, yes. Matchbox Baba. We heard it happen. How did you get to know?"

"The whole valley knew about it. I guess the guerrillas wanted people to know, to make them too terrified to help you. The police will want to question you about it."

"Not now, I hope," Henry said. "I'm absolutely bushed. I was up half the night and we've had a hell of a day."

"Tomorrow will be fine. I'll hold the police off."

"Is there anywhere I can sleep here?"

"You don't need to stay here. The princess has booked you into a hotel. I'll get our driver to take you. You'll need to be fresh tomorrow. The king wants to see you both."

Dougal rang a bell and ordered a car to be ready. Gosh appeared as Henry was walking out of the door and looked at him with unconcealed amusement. "Hi Tigger," he said, as if Tigger had just arrived for work. "Who's the hippy?"

"He's been helping Tigger," Dougal said.

"What's he doing in Solung? Looking for drugs?"

"His guru was here," Tigger said, irritated.

"Beats me what these people think they are going to learn out here," Gosh said. "The place is a shambles."

ooo

Henry was woken the next morning by the hotel manager, who presented him with a new guitar, flown by special deliv-

148

ery from Singapore, and an envelope containing $1,000. They came with a telegram, sent from Calcutta, which read: "Replacement for the guitar you lost. Money a gift from grateful me. Please use to tide you over till you decide what to do next. Perhaps you could show Tigger more of Solung and India, and maybe visit me? I'll be in touch. Love Sita"

He showed the message to Tigger, who called in soon after breakfast. Tigger felt a pang of jealousy, though he too had had a telegram with a similar disturbingly vague invitation. "She doesn't say where she is," he said.

"She can't say. Not if she wants to keep her people off her back. She'll assume her telegrams will be intercepted."

They spent the day giving formal statements about the events of the past few days and learned that the princess had arranged for payments to be made discreetly to the traders who had given them things on credit. Both Tigger and Henry were at a loss, for different reasons. "I don't want to be paid for what I did but I'll take the money as a loan," Henry said. "The princess has me sussed. I've been knocked sideways by all this. I have no idea what to do now."

Tigger could not stop thinking about the princess, though wherever she was he suspected that she was already out of his reach. He did not need to answer any awkward questions about Laxman; the princess had already talked to her family by phone about his role, depicting him as having been duped by a notorious revolutionary while trying to help her. The king, in conversation with Dougal, played down Laxman's revolutionary links but he took the young prince's flying activities seriously enough to persuade Dougal to extend his company's contract by taking on the task of building a small fully-equipped air force around the four Spitfires. Dougal agreed only after conferring with Solung intelligence officers, who assured him that other Messerschmitt pilots at Laxman's flying club were politically as far from Da Silva's revolutionaries as it was possible to get. Laxman himself seemed to have moved towards the political centre since his sister's kidnap by becoming friendlier with Solung's Communist Party, the main opposition to the ruling nationalists, which despite its name was more like a European-style democratic socialist party. He was busy organising his followers into youth cadres similar to ones set up by the communists.

One of Dougal's tasks would be to train four pilots, including Ganesh, to fly the Spitfires. But three candidates had yet to be chosen, and they would first go to a flying school in India; in the meantime Dougal would arrange the purchase of ammunition and spares, organise ground crews and get them trained up to military standard. The aircraft had already been fitted with modern radios. Surprisingly, in the light of Dougal's reluctance to get involved in a potential civil war, he had undertaken to provide temporary air cover against an unspecified threat. Tigger stopped short of questioning him on the point when Dougal said, even more surprisingly: "Gosh and I can cope here. Business is slack back in London and you've been through a lot in the past few days. Why not take a break and grab the chance to look at Solung? Perhaps drop down into India. Take your time."

ooo

"There's something going on," Tigger confided to Henry. "It's not like Dougal to suggest a holiday, especially when he is paying me."

"It does chime suspiciously well with the princess's invitation," Henry said. "Do they think we might lead them to the princess?"

"It wouldn't be like Dougal to agree to have spies set on us. Maybe he really does think a break will do me good."

The suspected plot thickened the next day, when Henry and Tigger had an audience with the king. Henry, his hair tied up in a bun, was dressed in a tropical white suit borrowed from Gosh. They were ushered into a small room, where the king sat alone behind a large desk.

He stood up as they entered. "Great show, chaps. Great show," he said. "I've got a couple of gongs here for you...

150

nonsense, of course, but they give you something to boast about, eh? Something to show the grandchildren? Gather you don't want a song and dance with the press, so we'll have to do it here. Now stand up straight... we have to do this with a touch of ceremony."

Tigger smiled as Henry straightened marginally from the slouch he had affected in his unfamiliar clothing, as if trying to disown it. The king solemnly pinned a large, blue-ribboned medal on each of their chests. "The Grand Order of the Heroes of Solung. It's not the best-known medal in the world but it is the only one I've got. Pretty, eh?" said the king. "Now sit down, if you will. I want a word with you."

They sat in two armchairs while the king turned his back on them and looked out of the window. "You understand that we can't charge NRJ, don't you?" he said over his shoulder. "The fellow's a bad egg and a fool but he'd run us a merry dance in the courts. The fact is that Bikash and the other men he killed, or most of them, had a price on their heads."

"You mean he'll collect a bounty?" said Tigger, horrified.

"Blood money!" exclaimed Henry.

"A reward," corrected the king. "That's the main reason he does it. I can hardly give him a reward with one hand and throw him in jail with the other."

"But, er, Your Highness," said Henry, almost choking on his principles, "if you will forgive me for saying so you will drive people into the arms of the People's Army. Many see Bikash as a hero because he stood up to the likes of NRJ. They also know Bikash was a criminal who deserved punishment. If he had got a proper trial they would have respected the justice of it, even if they didn't like it. Killing someone in cold blood is not justice."

"The way things are it's the only justice there is. Bikash would certainly have fought back and killed if he had had the chance. What about justice for his victims, have you thought about that?"

Henry was silent. The king turned and sat down opposite them. "I know you are right," he said. "I know how things ought to be. But I can't turn this country round on a six-pence and I've worn myself out trying. That's another reason I can't come down on NRJ: I don't want a bad press over this. I want as fair a wind as possible for the princess because I want her to marry my son and be queen one day."

Tigger was amazed. It had not occurred to either of them that the king, who surely knew the kidnap was not what it seemed, would want the wedding to go ahead. The old fox had switched the silly-ass pose off like a light bulb and he had stage-managed this scene perfectly.

"We want what's best for the princess," Tigger said.

"What about what is best for the country, eh? I know a lot more about Princess Sita than you think. I have to. She may be a young woman to you, but to me she is an affair of state. She's a spirited girl; she's a rebel. I respect that. I don't want a mouse behind the throne. Sita knows Solung. She knows the larger world. Raju is a good boy, a studious boy, but he has no imagination. He needs a push in the right direction now and again... just the job for a good woman."

"The princess does not want to marry Raju," Tigger said.

"She hardly knows the boy – how can she tell?"

They were silent, nonplussed. The king continued: "Do you know what the alternative is? Raju's wife has to come from a certain set of families, and to have been born at a time approved by the astrologers. I have no control over these matters. There are only about five women in the entire country who would qualify. One of them is Sita and the other four... well, I am sure they are fine girls but they have no knowledge of the world. Their outlook is medieval."

Henry said: "With respect, sir, you can't expect the princess to martyr herself because the prince can't find a suitable wife."

"You talk like I'm going to burn her at the stake. There are far worse fates than marrying my gentle son. Some people have to die for their country, don't you know? That's what I call martyrdom."

"Raju is not the country."

"Pray to God that he's the future of it. What would you have to replace him... a government run by the someone with the mentality of NRJ? The only way either his lot or the communists could get into power would be by civil war. There is just a chance that, with good leadership, Solung could stumble into stability and prosperity without that. Sita has a brother with the communists and her roots in the establishment. She doesn't want to be queen which means she is less likely to cling on to power if it is not in the interests of the country. She is a bright girl. She is in a perfect position to hold the country together."

Tigger marvelled that Solung could reduce a modern ideological battle to a medieval family affair in which even a revolutionary could be a political asset. It explained Laxman's apparent immunity from trouble.

The king continued: "I'm told you are going into India. I want you to take a message to her."

They hadn't decided they were going to India. It seemed they were being gently pushed there.

"We don't know where the princess is," Tigger said.

"She'll find you," the king said.

"Why us?" Henry said.

"She'll talk to you. She won't talk to her family about these matters."

Tigger asked: "What do you want us to say?"

"Her country needs her. Is that dramatic enough? She'll be among those hippies in Goa, I expect. Tell her she can have her play time. If she can't be good, then for God's sake be careful. There is no great hurry. She'll tire of that kind of life. She was not born to it. I want her back when she has had her fling. I don't expect promises. I just want her to give Raju a chance."

"Aren't you scared of a scandal?" Tigger asked curiously.

"Of course, but if it happens it happens. Sita has got the sense to be able to turn it to her advantage... the hippy queen, that sort of thing. She could be the most sensational ambassador this country has ever had."

"Queen, did you say?"

"This is absolutely between you two, me and Sita. If she marries Raju I shall abdicate, so that I can nurse them through their first days. I'm not going to last much longer. The old ticker is giving up. One last thing: has either of you boys fallen for her?"

"She is difficult to resist," Tigger said evasively.

"Splendid... then you are just the chap to go and see her. You can both get it out of your systems." The king thought for a few seconds. "Let Sita stew by herself down there for a while. Why don't you both stay in Solung for a few days... take a walk in the countryside. Henry knows the place; he can show you round. Take a look at everyday life. It might help you to understand Sita's position."

"I'll think about it," Tigger said.

The king grinned. "Now, my dear fellows, I have work to do. Drop in and see me if you return to Satpur. And mum's the word, eh?"

ooo

"It's a bit hard on you, isn't it?" Henry spoke as the door closed behind them.

"On me?"

"You're smitten. I know the signs. And I saw you and Sita canoodling when I was climbing back to the temple."

"She wants it to be a secret."

"Then a secret it is."

"I've gained a medal but I have a suspicion I've lost a lover. What worth is young Tigger beside the fate of nations?"

"Well, I have to admit that the king is a man in a million. Most men in this country would try to squash the princess flat. Not just the men either. It's not uncommon for girls to be killed for doing what she has done."

154

Prince Raju was waiting for them in the palace courtyard. Tigger looked at him with a new curiosity and an immediate sympathy. He looked upset and Tigger realised that it could not be easy for him to put up with the princess's caprices.

The prince opened the conversation by giving them the news from the mountains, where the People's Army had dispersed to avoid an expected assault by the army. "They'll be back," the prince predicted ruefully. "Trying to get the People's Army out of the valleys is like squeezing water out of a sponge. Take the pressure off and back it comes."

After revealing that compensation would be paid to the families of the murdered herders, Raju moved to what was clearly the real reason for his approach: "You are going to India, aren't you?"

"So everyone tells us. Your dad wants us to take a message to Sita," Tigger said. "We don't know where she is but if we do see her, do you want us to give her a message?"

"You can tell her that I understand. I am caught between East and West, too. I too am expected to marry a stranger. We're in the same boat."

ooo

The foreign journalists hanging out in Satpur, frustrated at not having a rescued princess to present to the world, were beginning to ask questions that might soon have them looking for Tigger and Henry. It was time to get out of town. First, Tigger went to the airbase to see Ganesh, who had just returned to Satpur following his father's funeral. Physically he still looked as if he had stepped off a school playing field, but he was more self-assured and brushed aside all thanks for his help. "Tigger, I was doing it for myself. I'd have done anything to get at the people who killed daddy. I shouldn't say it, but I wish I'd killed Da Silva when I had the chance."

"It was as well you didn't. We might not be here now," Tigger said. "Have you flown one of the Spits yet?"

"Maybe next week. Dougal wants me to do a few more hours in the trainer at the flying school."

155

"Had you flown much before?"

"I've been flying since I was 17. I worked as a mechanic with daddy in exchange for flying time. Laxman came with me once and then began taking lessons himself. Then he took to hanging out at his uncle's flying club."

"Did you fall out?"

"Not fall out. We moved apart. I wasn't made welcome at the club, though Laxman encouraged me to go there. Then he started spending a lot of time with political people. I did not like some of his friends. And now..."

"Something's changed?"

"Tigger, I know I am not supposed to know but some things can't be kept secret. Everyone knows that Laxman is mixed up with the people who were holding the princess. I am sure he would not have done anything to harm her. But those people killed my father. If he sticks with them, how can I feel good about him? We've been friends since we were boys but the way things are... I try not to think about it. I'm flying every moment that I can, all expenses paid by the government. I can't believe my luck."

"It's not luck, Ganesh. You've earned it. And the government needs you. So far as I can see you are the nearest it has to an air force."

"You and Henry are taking a holiday in India?"

"As you say, some things can't be kept a secret. It seems everyone in Solung knew we were going to India before we did."

"Send my love to the princess if you see her. Tell her I thought it was first class the way she played along when we got her out of the village. She is a brave lady. People say she may marry Prince Raju. I hope she does. He'll be king one day and she'd make a great queen."

9 Tigger tags along

Tigger's inclination was to get as near as possible to the princess as soon as possible but he didn't know where she was and she had effectively cut herself off for three or four weeks. He did not care to wonder why. Henry did not want to go to India immediately. "I should drop in at Krishna Baba's ashram, to pay my respects. After that I just want to take to the road for a while, walking. I need to clear my head. You can come if you like – it's the best way to get to know the country – but if you prefer to go and see some of the tourist sights, I could meet up with you later in India."

"I'm happy to string along. But are you sure it's a good idea to stay in Solung? The People's Army may be looking for us still."

"If everyone thinks we are going to India, the People's Army will think so too. No-one will know what is going on out in the sticks. Anyway, we won't be any safer in India than here. Revolutionaries don't respect borders."

If Tigger's politeness had held sway, they would never have managed to board the clapped-out bus on which they left town. There was already a crowd waiting when they arrived at the bus station half an hour early. Women in sarees squatted with babies and toddlers amid baskets of vegetables and mysterious sacks and bundles strewn over the betel-stained paving. Occasionally, one of the women would add more stains, spitting out the red betel juice from between stained teeth. Old men sat patiently smoking bedis, the odour mixing with that of human and animal dung, urine, and the rich smell of burning cow pats. Young men strutted self-consciously in bright shirts and sharp trousers country-made in styles badly copied from Bollywood movies.

The crowd rushed to the bus as soon it arrived, and there was a struggle as people trying to get off fought through those trying to get on. One old lady, cursing shrilly, was pushed to the ground, but managed to get up, apparently unharmed. Others from the crowd threw bags through the open bus windows to claim seats; a couple of young men climbed in through the windows. The bus had become a seething mass of life, like a tin of maggots, and in the middle of it was Henry. He rushed forward and managed to hold back the passengers trying to board until most of the people on the bus had got off. By the time he and Tigger got through the bus door, all but two seats had already been claimed via the windows. "You've done this before," Tigger remarked as they sat down.

"Most of the time, I take one look at the battle and decide to walk."

The bus was now packed well beyond comfortable capacity. Standing passengers jammed into every space so that the conductor had to force the door shut. They sat baking for five minutes while the driver took tea, after which he got into his seat with the aplomb of an orchestra conductor taking the stand. The engine was started and the bus rattled and roared off in the direction from which it had come. It stopped every mile or so, and each stop meant a major readjustment as people got off or on; the crush did not prevent the conductor from forcing his way up and down the bus to collect fares, sweat streaming down his face.

"It's the story of modern India, this bus – packed way beyond capacity yet somehow it creaks along," Henry said. "At Independence in 1947 the population was just under 350 million. Twenty-five years later it's approaching double that and it's expected to top a billion around the millennium. The same thing is happening here in Solung."

"I've heard say there is still enough food to feed everyone."

158

"Having enough food is not the same as having the capacity to feed everyone. The food doesn't get to everyone, and not everyone can afford to buy it. Development can't keep pace with the increasing numbers. The infrastructure can't cope, the social structures can't cope, and neither can the economy. The result is widespread poverty and it's likely to be that way for decades. People talk about the population explosion as if it is a problem of the future. It is already a catastrophe."

"I'd bet most of the hungry people are glad that they were born. You said yourself that poverty does not necessarily mean unhappiness. You can't wish people's lives away. It's not a catastrophe by their lights."

"Their lives are not a catastrophe; their poverty is. And it's the poor who are swelling the population. It is the poor, not the rich, who have the big families. The richer the place gets the more paupers it gets."

The bus dropped them at a dusty market place, where a young girl scooped up buffalo and cow pats from the road. Nearby, an entire wall was taken up by discs of dung, stuck on to dry for use as fuel. They walked to Krishna Baba's ashram, which consisted of a collection of guest rooms clustered around a small temple at the edge of town. Tigger was relieved to see that the disciples included a few westerners, so that he and Henry did not stand out. The atmosphere was funereal, with people queuing to prostrate themselves in front of a large picture of the guru, which had been set up on his favourite chair on a dais and garlanded with flowers. Henry sat cross-legged behind the crowd for a few minutes watching; Tigger squatted uncomfortably next to him, feeling like a stranger at a funeral. Finally Henry stood up and said: "Enough. Let's go."

As they walked away, Tigger said: "How on earth did you end up here, with Krishna Baba?"

"Lots of people were coming to see him. I was curious."

They sat down at a small chai shop and ordered tea.

Henry said: "Did you ever think that the way we look at human affairs is primitive... that people in two hundred or two thousand years' time will look back at us and think how naïve we were?"

"I think that now. Look at the way I blundered into this country not knowing a thing about the place."

"That was just lack of knowledge. I mean naïve in the way we understand ourselves and our affairs. Think of it: civilisation has only been going about ten thousand years, probably less. That's only 150 lifetimes – the number of people at a small party. That's not a lot of time to figure it all out."

"Did you think Krishna Baba had figured it out?"

"I didn't expect him to understand any more than anyone else. He wasn't teaching political science or social psychology. I thought he might show me a different state of being, a transcendental awareness, enlightenment."

"Did he?"

"I hardly touched on the methods that are supposed to achieve it. Now I don't suppose I ever shall. Maybe the princess is right. Maybe Babaji had latched on to an ancient con trick to gain power over people. Maybe enlightenment, or whatever you care to call it, is a fiction. It's not a matter of reason: you can achieve it, so they say, but you can't prove it."

"I can't get into all that stuff. I was raised an atheist but I had Christianity rammed down my throat at school. You can't argue with the love and kindness bit, but the rest was a load of nonsense so far as I was concerned."

"Christianity works for some people. Good luck to them if it makes them happy and they don't warp it into something harmful."

"Oh come on Henry! All that stuff about the Holy Ghost and the angels!"

"It's like my grandmother. She's good hearted, she's part of the family and I love her, but she's done things that she shouldn't have done, she has her corners, and she talks rubbish half the time. That's the Christianity I was brought up with. I grant that some takes on it are pretty nasty. But how can you not love all those beautiful old English churches, dripping with the history of the communities they have served for centuries? And the wonderful music – even some of the fairy tales? I can still get a spiritual lift from a service because it takes me onto another plane. Sometimes I sit in one and I let the sound and ritual take me over, and I'm away in a manger with sweet gentle Jesus and for the love of God I want to believe, I really want to believe. Then I listen to what they are saying and, like you..."

"It's nonsense!"

"It's a beautifully tattered relic of the Roman empire. A state religion gone to seed. The trouble with religions is that they have given God a bad name. It's got to the point where you can't mention the word in polite society. It's the new taboo."

"Perhaps that's because it doesn't make any sense."

"Religions don't make sense. They are yesterday's under-standing. God makes sense."

Tigger was incredulous. "You really believe in God!"

"I know God exists. I define God as existing."

"Henry, for heaven's sake! How can you define God?"

"God is everything science describes and everything it can't describe, including you and me experiencing the world. God is everything known and unknown, everything seen and unseen. God is what we are and what we came from. No other word is big enough. All descriptions are descriptions of God."

"You are simply saying that God is existence."

"And the rest! I'm a pantheist. It's pantheism, as I see it. Your experience of existence is the only thing you can say with certainty about God. It is God manifest. How you con-ceive of God beyond that hardly matters because you can't know the full truth. You will always be wrong. What matters is your relationship to God, to life."

"I don't see where that gets you."

"It means you can discuss what God is or is not without pointless arguments about whether God exists. There is no conflict with science because science is simply another description of God. If you think science is a sufficient description, that's fine: you have a clockwork God. But God still gives you a context for your life. That is something people had in the past. That's what we lost with the triumph of science. People threw God away when they threw away their religions. They uprooted themselves. God puts people in their place."

Tigger shook his head. "I don't need putting in my place. I know where I am. I'm sitting here. I'm an atheist. I don't need a God..."

"The living Earth does. Humanity does. Do you think we would put their future at risk if we gave them half the respect that people in this country give to idols? The Earth is sacred. The universe is sacred. Life with a capital L is sacred and preserving it for as long as possible is a sacred duty. The human world needs a fundamental change of perspective or it will die."

"Is this the stuff Babaji was teaching you?"

"Babaji taught spirituality, which has little or nothing to do with beliefs. If he heard me talking like this he would have laughed and told me to shut up and do some meditation."

Henry stopped talking suddenly and gazed across the chai shop where a woman stewed sweet tea in an aluminium pot over a wood fire. "I'm ranting," he said, shaking his head. "I've had all this bubbling in my head in the mountains and now I can't stop talking about it."

They walked out of town until they found a small stream and camped beside it, hidden from the road, scrabbling together enough sticks to build a fire and cook a meal. Henry played his new guitar as they sat under the stars next to the last flickering flames of the fire. After a few minutes, he said:

"A few weeks before I left England, I went to a debate between a scientist specialising in evolution and a bible-thumper who believed God created the world. There was no real debate: the scientist just plonked a dinosaur bone on the table in front of him and hardly needed to say more; his opponent's arguments were puerile. But the odd thing was I couldn't see it as a victory for science."

"You think God created the world?"

"Of course not. Creationism is a non-answer to a nonsensical question. What got me was that the scientist spoke as if by explaining evolution he was explaining everything. He had described a fundamental mechanism of life, for sure, but he seemed to think he had seen off God. Even more irritating, even though I saw myself as an atheist, was the fact that his opponent couldn't put up a better argument for God. So what should he have said? I've thought about it a lot since coming to Solung. Scientists are like the proverbial blind men trying to describe an elephant: each feels a different part – a foot, a trunk, an ear, a tail, or whatever – and none of them comes close to describing the animal. Yet nothing they say about the animal is untrue. Science and God are not incompatible. I tried to write down the least I could say about God that was consistent with science and it came out as a nursery rhyme."

Henry began to sing:

> Oh mama, dear mama,
> tell me what do I see
> in the campfire at night
> by the quiet moonlit stream?
> All the blaze and the glory
> is it just chemistry?
> Oh riddle me ri,
> Oh riddle me ree.
>
> Oh papa, dear papa,

tell me what do I see
in the bright stars at night
through the dark whispering trees?
Is the mystery and wonder
just astronomy?
Oh riddle me ri
O riddle me ree

Oh my love, she's my starlight,
She is beauty to me.
When I look in her eyes
tell me what do I see?
Is this feeling inside me
just biology?
Oh riddle me ri
Oh riddle me ree.

I'm your mama and your papa,
I am all that you see,
I am all that you hear,
I am all that we be.
All your science and learning
is just theology.
I am riddle me ri,
I am riddle me ree.

ooo

For the next few days they tramped from village to village, sleeping among sadhus in the courtyards of temples, or in schoolrooms that small communities set aside for the use of visitors, or in the open countryside. To encounter a village was like encountering a person. Each had a sameness in form: at least one little general store and a chai shop; at least one shade tree with a little dais at its base where people sat and chatted through the hottest hours of the day; communal wells or pumps where the women and girls gathered with their brass pots to fetch water; houses arranged in position and style according to the status or caste of the occupants, from brick buildings for government officials to mud huts for paupers. As often as not there was an artificial lake known as a "tank", where people bathed, and animals drank, and clothes were washed. Yet each village was different, with its own communal personality: some rich, some poor; some friendly, some suspicious; some clean, some dirty, some very dirty indeed, with villagers defecating next to the water they drank or washed in.

The roads between the villages were narrow and lined with gnarled trees, with orange and white flashes painted on their lower trunks. Carts and the occasional lorry rumbled past; less frequently came an Indian-made Ambassador car, the only make available in the country. Now and then, they would see a tribe of monkeys playing in the trees; lizards scuttled to safety as they passed; the croaking of frogs announced nearby water. On either side of the road was the eternal patchwork of tiny fields. During the rainy season, the monsoon watered the land at its whim. For the rest of the year, the people were dependent on how much the land could catch and hold of the water flowing from the mountains. Each little caprice of the water's journey across millions of square miles of the plain spelled fortune or misfortune for the farmer. It flowed through countless channels and undulations, or filtered up from the water table. Where the rivers blessed the earth, there was security and growth throughout the year; where the river was fickle with its blessings, there was insecurity; where the river did not bless, there was desert. The blessings could be counted on the landscape: greenery on watered land, dry crops on drier land, and patches of arid earth. "Look at those fields and you see why the great rivers are held as holy," Henry said. "You can also see how they are desecrated."

Such a small matter, it had seemed, the logs on the river by the village where the princess had been held, logs like the ones Dougal and Ganesh had used for their makeshift boat.

Corrupt officials turned a blind eye to indiscriminate felling on the mountain slopes to feed the increasing demand from the swelling population for wood for fuel and timber. For untold centuries, the trees had held back the water so that it flowed down to the plain even during the dry season; the trees also helped to anchor the earth that clung precariously to the mountain slopes. Now the fertile plains were prone to flash floods and drought and the rivers were silting up with mountain spoil.

"People are fighting it," Henry said. "But it is just one example of the way we are looting the earth. One little sacrilege among many. And you ask me why we need God."

"To punish us for our sins?"

"If you step under the wheels of a bus are you punished for your foolishness?"

They had reached the outskirts of a village where there was a small shrine, its entrance blocked by an iron grille. "Take a look in there," Henry said.

Inside was a statuette of a flower-bedecked four-armed goddess of ghastly beauty: shiny black with pert breasts, a bright red tongue sticking out between gleaming teeth. She wore a necklace of skulls and a girdle of severed arms. One left hand held a bloody sword, the other a severed head; one right hand was held in blessing, the other in a gesture signifying "fear not".

"One image of God," Henry said. "Kali, the mother and destroyer, the giver of life and death, pleasure and pain, fortune and misfortune. To accept Kali is to accept life – and people in this area are taught from childhood to worship her. Kali can't countenance imbalance. She cures it with her sword. Sometimes her sword is called war, sometimes famine, sometimes disease. She's also the goddess of time, and time settles all."

10   Dog Baba

The next day they met Dog Baba. Their first sight of him was an orange speck in the distance. A good quarter-mile away he was waving to them as if they were old friends. Closer still, it became clear that neither of them had seen him before. Such details did not reduce Dog Baba's bonhomie. "'Ippies... *accha*... good," he bellowed from a range of thirty yards.

This affability was not his only idiosyncrasy. He kept stopping in his tracks for a few seconds and it became clear that these pauses were dictated by his companion... a sharp-nosed dog, distinguishable from a million other street dogs of the subcontinent only by the fact that it looked well-fed and wore a necklace of bells, with a garland of bedraggled jasmine flowers. When the dog was in front of Dog Baba, the sadhu walked. When it fell behind, he turned towards it and waited.

The dog matched the sadhu's friendliness with interest. It threw itself at Tigger and Henry in turn, yelping with enthusiasm.

"Dharma... 'ippies liking," said Dog Baba. "Dharma good dog. Dharma no like bad men."

He flourished a conical hashish pipe the size of a beer bottle. "We chillum smoking," he announced.

Tigger eyed the massive chillum with some trepidation. Without waiting for a reply, Dog Baba had spread a cloth at the side of the road and sat down on it.

"You... charas having?" he asked.

They had none. Dog Baba's face fell. Then he produced a large black lump from the folds of his orange loincloth, cut

167

a piece off it, and began stoking the chillum. Ten minutes later the world was a different place: the clicking of insects, the cries of birds, the scampering of unseen creatures, had become a symphony; the spread of fields, the gnarled roadside trees, the wisps of white on the blue of the sky took on a Van Gogh glow, as if their existence was somehow amplified.

The dog lay stretched out with its head in the sadhu's lap. "Dharma, charas no needing," said Dog Baba, laughing. "Dharma always flying."

"Like his master," said Henry.

"Me master... no. Dharma my master."

This was a point Dog Baba clearly reached with all strangers. He began a little performance. From another fold in his clothes, which like a magician's sleeve seemed to be an endless source of wonders, he produced a tiny bell and tinkled it. The dog sat on its haunches. Dog Baba walked round it three times, chanting and ringing the bell; then three times in the opposite direction. He produced a scrap of paper containing red powder which he used to make a mark on the dog's forehead. He made a similar mark on Tigger and Henry, who could do nothing but play along with the curious charade. The sadhu then knelt in front of the dog, touching its paws in the traditional mark of devotion, and muttering what were presumably prayers. Finally, he placed two little bowls in front of the dog; in one he placed a scrap of stale chapati, in the other, water from a can hanging at his waist. Throughout the performance, the dog had not moved. Now it ate and drank.

"Puja," said Dog Baba, as he sat back and prepared another chillum.

"An act of worship," translated Henry.

"He's worshipping the dog?" asked Tigger incredulously.

"Dog... Bhagwan," said Dog Baba.

"Bhagwan... God," explained Henry.

They sat by the roadside for another hour, while Dog Baba stoked chillum after chillum. Men stopped and sat down forming a circle around which the chillum passed. Women stood behind them, giggling and talking about the strangers. One of the newcomers produced a chillum full of *ganja*. Dog Baba, having gathered his audience, began to tell his story, much embellished with mime and expression. He was in Solung to join a *mela*, a religious festival near Satpur where thousands of sadhu*s* would gather. He wanted for nothing. God provided all. Some years previously, in the days before he was Dog Baba, he had been on a pilgrimage in the mountains heading for one of the sources of the holy Ganges. He had taken a circuitous route, far from the usual pilgrim trails, and far from any villages, when the dog had entered his life. It was trotting along, quite alone, for all the world as if it were itself on a pilgrimage. (Here Dog Baba mimicked the dog, padding with his hands and putting his head jauntily from side to side). The dog had simply tagged along with him. As they drew close to the temple at the holy source, Dog Baba fell and broke a leg. (Here a wince of pain, a gesture to the leg that had been injured, a gasp of sympathy from the audience). He could not move; he thought he must die. He was high, high up on the mountainside, where few men trod. The dog came up to him and licked him, then walked away. Dog Baba was very sad; he felt that his only friend had abandoned him; he meditated upon Krishna, and sought to prepare his soul for its departure from the Dog Baba body. For many hours he lay there, sometimes passing out from the pain. Then he heard barking and the sound of a man's voice. (A sad face breaks into joy). The dog had returned. It had gone to the temple and barked and barked. Even though dogs are low creatures and unclean, something about it had impressed a priest at the temple. He followed the dog, not knowing why, and saved Dog Baba's life. It was a miracle. (A shake of the head; the audience wonders).

Dog Baba recalled the last great journey of the five Pandava brothers, heroes of the holy *Mahabharata* saga. Four of

169

the brothers died on the journey until only the eldest, the flawless Yudhisthira, was left.... plus a little dog that had followed him all the way. The king of the gods himself arrived in a glowing chariot to take Yudhisthira to heaven. But Yudhisthira refused to enter without his faithful little companion. He said: "All the acts that have earned me heaven would be set to nought if I behaved without compassion towards this dog."

Thus Yudhisthira proved his perfection. The dog changed its form and became his own father, Dharma, who announced that his son had passed the final test to enter heaven.

Just as Yudhisthira's dog had proved to be the vehicle for a great soul, so must Dog Baba's faithful companion have come in this lowly form as a guide for true seekers of wisdom. For was not God revealed in the High and the Low? And anyone who had been to school knew that the English word dog was God spelled backwards. So Dog Baba had called his companion Dharma, after that great holy dog; and from that day to this he had never walked in front of the dog, so as always to keep in sight his dharma, his duty of righteousness and his never-ceasing quest for enlightenment.

"Your dharma depends on who you are," whispered Henry, who had been translating this charade for Tigger. "Righteous behaviour for a soldier, say, is different from that for a princess."

"Or a sadhu, presumably," said Tigger.

The unswerving seeker of wisdom touched Tigger and Henry for some rupees and set off cheerfully down the road to the next village, where someone had already promised him a meal.

"That story about the dog saving him," asked Tigger, as they watched the sadhu depart. "Do you think it is true?"

"Gimmicks get babas fed," Henry said. "Dog Baba is half sadhu, half showman. Melas like the one he is going to are like a circus... babas on beds of nails; babas who contort, babas who never sit or lie down, babas who don't talk, babas who babble gibberish, hustling babas, and some quite considerable men. Dog Baba has more to him than a lot of them. He's a walking moral tale."

"But how can anyone take him seriously, worshipping a dog? It's crazy."

"It's sublime."

"Dog worship?"

"How you see God is not important. Any image that moves you is fine, because God is in everything."

"Even devil worship?"

"That's not worship. It's sickness."

"I can't see the point of worshipping anything."

"It's a transcendence. It takes you out of yourself, forcing you to recognise that you are part of a wider reality. I'd say anything that helps you love and respect that has to be healthy."

"But it doesn't do that. What about all the wars fought in the name of religion?"

"Religion, not worship. Worship is an act of love. Religions are an instrument of earthly power. State power. Priestly power. For better and worse. They can be a comfort and joy; but they can also be a torment."

They were silent for a while, still sitting where Dog Baba had left them. Finally, Tigger said: "It's all too much of a nonsense. I don't think you'll ever catch me rushing to the nearest temple."

11   The revolutionaries

It was past mid-afternoon when Tigger and Henry finally got up from the roadside. The weather was changing: the first pink hint of sunset lit up massed clouds that rolled across the horizon. Soon, clouds covered the entire sky; the air grew sticky and heavy, rumbling with unease, sliced by dry lightning. They were not far from the next village and found the shelter of a chai shop just in time to escape a drenching. The pastel tones of sunset gave way to a neon glow from lightning that was now almost continuous, sparking spectrums across the billowing clouds. The heat was oppressive and when the rain finally began, it was as if the air itself had started to sweat and the wind rushed to the cooling water like a sigh of relief.

It was still raining when they awoke after an uncomfortable night under the dripping awning of the chai shop, and they were glad to be offered a lift in a truck to a more substantial village where they found a colonial-era resthouse where rooms could be rented. It rained all day, with only brief intervals when the clouds broke, and they were happy to stay indoors and browse the yellowing paperbacks left by previous visitors. They emerged the next day to find that the dusty roads and fields had turned to mud, with puddles in places reaching the proportions of a flood.

There had not been a whiff of danger since they left Satpur and they felt none as they set out to explore the village, not even when they turned into a square dominated by a two-storey building sporting a red flag. As they walked past a man sitting on the porch, smartly dressed in a crisp pyjama suit, invited them over to talk.

"It's an RMP office – People's Army politicos," whispered Henry. Tigger's heart missed a beat as other men, dressed more casually in shirts over baggy *dhotis*, emerged on to the porch and stared at them. But the atmosphere was friendly, in the manner of a hundred similar encounters they had had with curious inhabitants of villages where strangers were a valued entertainment.

They were ushered into a cramped office and seated like exhibits for the RMP workers who jammed the room to take a look at them. On the wall was a picture of Marx, garlanded like a Hindu household god.

"We believe in Marx," said the man in the suit, seeing Tigger looking at the picture. He seemed to be the manager.

"You Communist Party?" said Tigger, feigning ignorance and lapsing automatically into broken English.

"We Revolutionary Marxist Party. No Communist Party. Different."

"How you different from Communist Party? "

"We want blood," said the man.

With a better command of English he might have expressed himself more gently; as it was, he could hardly have sounded more chilling. Tigger looked at the friendly faces around him and tried to imagine them in the heat of a revolution, brutalised and pitiless.

"Chai?" The RMP leader said, snapping his fingers. One of the workers scuttled off to fetch tea; revolution apparently did not extend to the relationship between master and servant. "You know East Germany?"

Tigger had visited the grim Soviet zone of Berlin, in the East German republic set up by the Russians at the end of the Second World War, and had found it less than inspiring; but this was not the time to say so. Henry had shown him examples of the ponderous English-language propaganda distributed across the subcontinent by Russia as an "act of friendship"; evidently it had impressed some people more than similar material put out by the Americans.

"East Germany, communist, good. West Germany, capitalist, bad," said the man.

"West Germany rich," Tigger said. Despite the friendliness he had a feeling that they were being checked out.

"Rich exploiting poor. East Germany no exploiting. East Germany stronger than West Germany," said the man.

On a wall poster behind him, written in English, were the words: "The RMP, as a workers' party and toiling peoples' mass party, derives its historic justification from a correct scientific assessment of the realities of the present-day economic and political situation of the country and is therefore incapable of being refuted by revisionist sophistry."

They sat with the men for ten minutes, drinking tea and making polite conversation, and were given an English-language leaflet, almost opaque with jargon, attacking the mainstream Communist Party for advocating reforms "within the framework of bourgeois democracy" that would leave power in capitalist hands. The party aimed to organise "workers and other sections of the toiling masses" to seize the power of the state for a truly socialist transformation.

"It's an open call for insurrection," said Tigger in astonishment, as they left. "Even in England you could get arrested for putting something like that about. What puzzles me is how a marketing man like Da Silva could get involved with an organisation churning out such turgid propaganda. You would think he would at least get them to make it more intelligible."

"Maybe it works better as it is, like a half-understood litany that becomes imprinted on the brain. It's policy as scripture: mysterious in its language, absolute in its authority."

Henry revealed that the RMP men, unaware that he understood their language, had spoken of them mockingly in Solungese as two dumb but harmless hippies. Reassured, they continued their walk and found that the village was more extensive than it had seemed at first, boasting a couple of government buildings and a police station. The rains had been a disaster for some villagers, destroying their crops.

174

"Jump!" shouted Henry
(see page 187)

Too much rain was as bad as too little.

On their way back to the resthouse, the RMP leader emerged suddenly from a side turning with a group of his followers and said angrily: "You are spies."

"We are tourists," Henry said.

"We know who you are. I ring party leader in Satpur. You fight People's Army in the mountains."

"We are on holiday," Tigger said, truthfully. He noticed with relief that a uniformed policeman stood at the edge of the group. His relief was short-lived. A voice whispered in his ear: "You come."

His arms were grabbed from behind and he was frog-marched away by two men. Two others were bringing Henry along. Villagers stared as they walked past and it seemed that if they were in danger, it was a very public one. A trail of RMP supporters followed them, jeering. Someone spat at Tigger.

"Keep cool," Henry said. "I think we have been picked up by plain-clothes police."

So it proved. Their captors said nothing but led them to a police cell and locked them in. The crowd stayed outside, still shouting.

After a few minutes they were taken to another room, where they found all the things from their room carefully laid out on a table. Still the policemen said little, but their manner was now deferential. After a couple of minutes, the local police chief entered and apologised for their treatment.

"We had to move fast – those people would have beaten you up, or worse," he said. "Naturally, I'd already had you checked out. This is a sensitive area and I have to be on the lookout for agitators. We have been instructed to give you protection and any help you require."

"That's good to know," said Tigger.

The policeman spoke with the drawl of an expensive education. His manner was respectful, but Tigger sensed that he was angry at the complications they had caused. Tigger tried to imagine his private face: the way he dealt with sus-pects in anonymous back rooms, and how caught up he might be in the web of corruption and brutality for which the police force was notorious and from which it was difficult for any man to remain disentangled.

"We collected your stuff from your room because it would be unsafe for you to go back there," the policeman said, in a tone expressing more explanation than apology. "I'd advise you to leave the district as soon as possible. Even with a permanent police guard I could not guarantee your safety. If you have any pressing reason to be here…"

Tigger answered the implied question. "We are on holi-day."

"Of course, of course." The police chief did not sound convinced.

"We have been wandering around for days without a breath of trouble," Henry said.

"In this part of Solung you have only to turn a corner to move from safety to danger. We are close to the border here. We get smugglers, gun runners, agitators, guerrillas, and criminals passing through. On top of that the RMP is concentrated here. We have to be careful."

He spoke as if compelled to explain why a cultured, ca-pable man such as himself was in charge of such an out-of-the-way place. Tigger was curious about how an organisation like the RMP was allowed to operate unmolested. "Why did you take us in, instead of moving against the RMP? In our country they could have been charged with threatening be-haviour."

The policeman fiddled with some papers on his desk. He did not relish having to explain himself to two foreigners who had the ear of the king.

"Why don't you ask the government to send me a few hundred more men?" he said.

Tigger regretted not having phrased his question more mildly. He decided to play the official role the policeman assumed of him. "I did not wish to imply that you should have arrested those men. I just wanted to know how you see the position."

"How can I arrest half the village for the sake of two foreigners? Citizens are entitled to challenge anyone they regard as foreign agents. As far as the people here are concerned you *are* foreign agents. The RMP are a law unto themselves in this area. They hold the real power and they will keep holding it until the government decides to crush them – if it ever does."

"Are you afraid of them?"

"Everyone here is afraid of them, even their supporters. Personally, I don't understand why the government tolerates them. But I am a policeman, not a politician. It is not required of me to understand."

"Maybe the king does not want to make martyrs of them," said Henry.

"Martyrs of *them*?" said the police chief angrily. "What about me, and my wife and children, and my men and their families? What about the people who would die if that lot ran loose? What about those martyrs?"

"This is just one small area of Solung," Henry said. "The situation is not so bad in most of the country."

"It would not take much for the trouble to spread."

The police chief began to pace the room, thwacking his thigh with his swagger stick. "I'm sick of people in the city, people who have never been to this place, telling me what I should do and should not do. They have no idea what is going on here and they don't have to live with the results of their nonsense."

The police chief caught Tigger's eye and looked uncomfortable. "I'm not against the king," he added hastily. "I am sure he is trying to do what is best for the country. My concern is the safety of this area, and of my men and our families. We are not safe here. I keep my ears close to the ground and if I hear a rumble I shall run, and I don't mind who knows it. I'm a four-hour drive from the nearest army base, and the People's Army could overrun me any time it chooses."

The policeman paused, to let his words sink in. "I'm not a coward. I'll fight when there is reason to. My own view is that the government should crush them now, before they get any stronger. I'll do my duty here as long as I can. But I'm not going to stay around to get cut up if the government does not give me sufficient protection."

"You want us to tell Satpur that?" Tigger said.

"I've told them. I'm not afraid to speak my mind. They say sending troops here would be regarded as a provocation. They'll only send troops in *after* there has been trouble. What's the point of that? But tell them by all means. They might believe you."

They slept that night at the police station and the next morning they were bundled into a police Land Rover to take them to the nearest railway junction a two-hour drive away. "Make no mistake... you will be watched. You must get far away from here as soon as possible," the police chief said.

"This is just what I didn't want to happen," Henry muttered. "I can't move about freely without going in fear of my life."

A large cow lay placidly in by the ticket window at the railway station, where they were handed first-class tickets to Calcutta. "Looks like we're being told to go to India," said Tigger, who was not averse to being closer to the princess.

"I won't give in to these people," Henry said obstinately. "Let's get on the train as if we're going to Calcutta, then jump off at a small station when no-one is looking."

They were both stressed from the events of the previous day and Tigger was getting angry. "This isn't a game we are playing, Henry. You know what they did to Matchbox Baba. Do you want that to happen to you?"

Henry was silent for a few seconds. "So let's decide when we're on the train."

They were a couple of hours early for the train and two policemen, armed with vintage Lee Enfield rifles, guarded them as they waited. If there were dangerous eyes watching, they might have been any among scores of people waiting for trains amid a confusion of bedrolls, cooking pots, kerosene stoves, playing children, squatting sadhus, goats, cows, *paan* stalls, newspaper sellers, beggars, rickshaw wallahs touting for custom, and porters with bright red waistcoats. Film music blared from chai stalls and radios. Muddy children in rags proffered titbits of spiced batter, or sold chai poured from large teapots into throwaway earthenware cups. Each train that arrived was an iron majesty belching steam, smoke and fire; the urchins ran alongside it touting for custom even before it came to a halt. One glance at the carriages was enough to make Tigger doubly glad to be travelling first class. Third-class carriages had people jammed into every conceivable space: five or six on seats designed for three, with more standing in corridors and lying on luggage racks.

Even on the train, Tigger and Henry found that they were effectively under guard. They had been booked into a compartment with two army officers, next to a carriage full of armed soldiers returning from leave.

Henry remained morose and Tigger sensed that his troubles went deeper than irritation. He said no more about leaving the train and Tigger did not raise the subject. The soldiers got off when they reached the Indian border, where formalities took more than an hour. India looked little different from Solung. "At least we are out of terrorist territory," said Tigger.

"Don't you believe it. Remember this is Bengal, birthplace of the Naxalites, blood brothers of the People's Army. But you were right about Solung. I feel safer here, if not actually safe. The worst of it is that the RMP are justified in seeing us as enemies. We have been acting as government agents, whether we like it or not. That policeman was giving us a report, not holding a conversation. Power is a dirty

180

business in this part of the world and I don't like to be associated with it."

"Can power ever be clean?"

"I don't know," Henry said. "And I don't know if avoiding it can, either."

ooo

Tigger had other things on his mind; he had written one brief letter to the princess, tortured in its restraint, telling her they were heading for Calcutta and that she could contact them via the poste restante there. He had put her out of his mind as far as possible over the past few days, but now that there was a prospect of seeing her he could not stop thinking about her. He lapsed into silence, aghast at the power of his infatuation with a woman he hardly knew and who he sensed would bring him trouble. Only when they pulled into Calcutta's Sealdah station was he dragged out of his reverie; and barely two minutes later she was thrust back into his mind again. Splashed across the front page of a London newspaper on sale at a news-stand was the headline: FIRST PICTURE OF KIDNAP MYSTERY PRINCESS. Under it was a photograph of the princess stepping into a taxi outside the Calcutta general post office.

12   Condemned to death

They sat in a chai shop to read the paper, which was dated the previous day. The picture had been taken the day before that, and the caption declared that this was the princess who had mysteriously vanished after being rescued by a team led by the pilot-adventurer Edward FitzDougal. Nobody had known what she looked like because her family refused to release pictures, and there had been much speculation about why she had avoided publicity after her dramatic escape. There had even been rumours that she had been killed. The picture revealed that not only was she very much alive, but she was also very beautiful. The "mystery" of her disappearance remained, because she had refused to answer questions and sped off in the taxi. In fact the picture did not do justice to her looks because she had managed to hide most of her face behind a headscarf.

Tigger's inclination was to rush straight to the GPO to look for messages but Henry urged caution. "That story poses almost as many questions as it answers," he said. "How come there was a photographer there at that particular time who knew what she looked like? It's a professional shot taken with a good camera. There are import restrictions on cameras here which makes them thin on the ground."

"It could have been taken by a tourist."

"A tourist who knew the princess by sight? I don't think so. They must have been watching the post office."

"But we and the princess were the only people who knew about the poste--restante arrangement."

"There was that truck owner and his driver. The ones who took us to Alexis's aircraft."

"They didn't seem to understand English."

"Everyone here knows some English words because they have been adopted into the language. They would have understood Calcutta and post office. That would be enough for anyone who knew about the poste-restante system. Those truckers probably boasted about picking up the princess and found themselves being questioned by the People's Army."

"It still doesn't make sense. Why would the People's Army want the princess's picture splashed over the papers?"

"Whatever the reason, we have to assume that they are still watching the poste restante to see who turns up." Henry thumped the table in exasperation. "Damn. Damn. Damn. It was bad enough not being able to walk around Solung in safety. Now I have got to on my guard even in India."

"Maybe we are being paranoid. Why would Da Silva's men want to pursue us down here?"

"Those RMP guys weren't exactly friendly. We are going to have to take care."

They decided that they had no option but to check their mailboxes, and feeling rather foolish, they adopted some B-movie tactics to see if they were being followed. First Tigger sat in a café and watched the GPO as Henry checked his mail, then Tigger checked while Henry waited. They saw nothing suspicious. There was no letter for Henry and two addressed to Tigger – both, to his chagrin, beginning "Darling Henry and Tigger."

The first and earliest invited them to join her at a friend's place near Calcutta. The second read: "I've just been photographed outside the GPO and I'm afraid someone must have been watching out for me. It is very worrying. I don't know why they are still interested in me. Da Silva may have a spy at the post office reading my mail, so ignore my previous message because I will have to leave the place I have been staying. I won't tell the people there where I am going, because I don't want to get them involved. Sorry if I am sounding panicky but it was very scary when that photographer jumped up out of the blue. I'm being careful what I write in case the wrong people get to read this message."

The princess wrote that a friend called Betty at the British Deputy High Commission in Calcutta would pass on messages. She gave no surname for Betty and the letter concluded: "I am heading out now but will tell Betty when I've found somewhere else to stay. Please come and see me if you get a chance. But take care. You may be in danger too. Lots of love to you both. Sita."

Tigger did not know whether to feel relieved that the princess had contacted them, disappointed that he would not see her immediately, or distraught that she wrote more like a friend than a lover. She had every reason to be fearful, but could Da Silva's influence really extend to the mail system?

"It's not impossible," Henry said. "There are sure to be Naxalite supporters in Calcutta so she is right to be wary but there is no obvious sign of tampering on the letters. Whatever, it looks like we are stuck here until we hear from her."

No question of Henry going off by himself then, Tigger thought wryly. The princess had got both of them following her around like dogs. Henry's only comment on the matter was: "What was it that Dougal was saying about women and complications?"

ooo

Calcutta, Henry observed, was like an exaggeration of all the best and worst of India. Nobody knew for sure how many people lived here: there were simply too many in too much chaos to count. More flooded in daily from rural Bengal and neighbouring states, and their numbers had been swollen by refugees who stayed on after the recent war in what was then called East Pakistan and was now the independent state of Bangladesh. The poor immigrants slept on the streets, or rented bed space in crowded rooms, and if they were lucky enough to get work, they sent remittances to their families back home. In parts you could hardly move without being accosted by streetwise beggars: children with Oxfam faces thrust forward by their parents to sob and cry hungry before scuttling off giggling to play in the gutter; haggard faces haunting the doors of restaurants, so that you could not forget that the price of your meal could feed a family for a week; an outstretched hand at the exit of a shop, your own hand still heavy with change. Among beggars, deformity was an asset: it drew sympathy or its sister guilt, feelings that could bring in *paise*... money. So to walk the streets was to be confronted with stumps of arms and legs, club feet, leprous skin, mangled hands, humped backs, sightless eyes – or apparently sightless, for beggars were not above feigning blindness, or nurturing sores carefully highlighted by red antiseptic. Some, reputedly, were not above deforming their own children.

There was no pleasure in generosity: if you gave much, you might be asked for more, or hounded down the street by a horde of beggars crying "*paise, paise*" like a litany of conscience, and they would not leave off for half a mile, not even after you turned and cursed them, or begged them to go away. To live in Calcutta you had to become detached, like doctors, so that the misfortune of others did not overwhelm you. Tourists got the worst of the beggars because they were foreigners and did not understand. Old hands learned that charity had to be targeted and discreet.

The beggars were merely the public face of misfortune, and not generally the worst: the weakest had no energy to beg. People and families cracked up in the squalor and tensions of the *bustees*, the shanty settlements that spread like a fungus over every scrap of waste land. Many other people were living in genteel poverty, maintaining the appearance of a tolerable living standard by making every *paise* count. Most touching of the street people were those who had made a step up from begging: the old man touting a jar of boiled sweets, selling them off singly at five paise apiece; street traders who spent every waking and sleeping hour next to little piles of farm produce or a few plastic trinkets; rickshaw wallahs who slept curled up in their hand-drawn vehicles, far away from their home villages and families. Wherever there was a chance or work or profit, there was someone exploiting it: boot boys, gofers, carters, scribes filling in government forms for the illiterate, hustlers, bottle collectors, paan stalls, cigarette sellers, cane-juice sellers.

The city bore itself like a run-down house occupied by squatters who would not take responsibility for its maintenance. The paint was peeling, the roof leaked, the toilets were clogged, the services erratic, but somehow it remained intact and homely. It was a dirty city, its century-old sewers long overloaded, so that human excreta polluted the streets along with rubbish left to rot. Consequently there was much sickness. For the poor, sickness could spell catastrophe: a job lost, a hoping for the best. Free medical care was available, but the public hospitals were packed like football grounds, and doctors could spare little time for niceties. Hospitals could do nothing to satisfy the most commonly needed remedy... good food. It was this hard side of Calcutta that struck visitors most forcefully, because it was so visible. Yet Calcutta was also a cultured city, rejoicing its own rich literature and musical traditions, and for people with money it could be an agreeable place to live. There were mansions and clubs for the rich and almost anyone with a reasonable income employed servants, giving them a class of luxury unknown to most people in Western cities. Even these menial jobs were a big step up from beggary.

Tigger and Henry, reluctant to announce their presence by registering at a big hotel, put up at a Buddhist resthouse near Calcutta University, amid streets lined with stalls selling second-hand books. Never did a place look more like a backdrop for a revolution. Walls were scrawled with political slogans, many of the shops specialised in political tracts, and the floors above them were dotted with cramped, dusty offices of this workers' party and that. The city seemed to be in continual political ferment. It was a Saturday, and they would not be able to contact the princess's friend until her office opened on the Monday. Tigger took the opportunity to check-call Dougal, a little fearful that some emergency might require his return to Solung. But Dougal reported that the king wanted Tigger to stay in India. "It seems that I am being paid to have a holiday with the girl I love in order to persuade her to marry someone else," Tigger remarked to Henry later. He was joking of course: how could he be in love with someone he had known only for a few days?

ooo

They might have known something was amiss two days later when a rickshaw wallah waiting at the kerbside outside the resthouse offered them a reasonable price to take them to the British High Commission. They were so relieved at avoiding the customary ritual of haggling, in which the most generous of intentions and the best of tempers could founder on a rickshaw man's wilder ambitions, that they mounted his vehicle without a second thought – 'mounted' being the operative word, as passengers on these hand-drawn people carts were perched well above the people jamming the sun-baked streets. Henry noticed that the rickshaw was not taking the quickest route and his immediate reaction was that this explained the reasonable fare: the man had mistaken their destination. Even as he leaned forward to speak, the rickshaw wallah turned off the main road into a cul-de-sac and an Ambassador car pulled in behind them, blocking the way out. "Jump!" shouted Henry.

The rickshaw was still moving and Tigger nearly fell over when his feet touched the ground. In the moment it took to regain his balance, he took in the scene: the rickshaw wallah straining to a halt; a blank wall in front of them, tenement buildings on either side, the car behind, and a sneering Da Silva in the front passenger seat. Henry was trying in vain to open a door on one of the tenements. Tigger rushed down the other side of the alley, looking in vain for an exit. Da Silva had not bothered to get out of his seat. He did not even pick up his gun, which lay prominently on the dashboard.

The two friends were trapped, and he knew it.

"Thought you'd prefer a lift to riding in that uncomfortable machine," he called from the open car door. Tigger felt sick. He had been carefree only seconds before; now he was in deadly danger. He and Henry squeezed into the tiny Ambassador as meekly as if they were indeed being offered a lift. There was little else they could do. There were two other men in the car with Da Silva: the driver, and a man in the back seat holding a revolver.

Da Silva covered his own gun with a handkerchief, and the driver reversed out of the alley. The most sinister aspect of the drive that followed was that no effort was made to prevent Tigger or Henry from seeing where they were going. It did not augur well for a long life. They drove out of the city centre and through suburbs of *bustees* and crumbling tenements.

Da Silva spent most of the journey going through the contents of their pockets. He found a leaflet about travelling to Bombay that Tigger had picked up at a travel agency over the weekend when they were checking out options. Bombay was a likely destination or staging post for anyone heading south.

"You were planning to go to Bombay? Why were you going to Bombay?"

"We're going to see a man who wants to make a film about the princess," Tigger said.

"With me cast as villain, no doubt." It was clear Da Silva rather liked the idea.

"No doubt it could be arranged."

"It's a bit soon to begin a film. The story is not over yet. The heroes are going to come to a sticky end."

"The script is still being written."

"Has anyone been mentioned for my part?"

Tigger realised with astonishment that this was a serious question, and that Da Silva believed the story about the film: his vanity was such that he *wanted* to believe it.

188

Henry named a well-known Indian film star.

"He is fat and foolish. I could do better myself."

Da Silva was probably right on that count, Tigger thought. He seemed to conduct his business as if he were in a movie; dressed in a well-cut tropical suit, he looked as cool as if he were a Calcutta magnate off to a conference.

They were taken to a bungalow at the edge of town and locked into a small room containing only two mattresses on a concrete floor. There was no window; the only air inlet was a tiny grating above the door. Da Silva warned: "You will have no chance of escape. A guard will be posted outside."

"What are you going to do with us?" Henry asked.

"You will be questioned in the morning."

It was not yet midday. The next few hours were spent in terrible anticipation of what the questioning might consist of. Henry was remarkably calm. He said loudly, in case their cell had been bugged: "I guess our one consolation is that we cannot be forced into betraying any secrets because we have no secrets to betray."

They examined the room for any possibility of escape. The walls were of brick but the mortar was of poor quality and would have succumbed to the most primitive of implements. But there was nothing they could use; the guard had even removed the single light bulb from the room.

They slept little that night. The next morning a breakfast of spiced chapatis was thrust through their door; half an hour later Da Silva arrived with two armed guards. They stood behind him while he questioned them for more than an hour, making no sign that they understood what was being said. Da Silva seemed particularly interested in how long Dougal intended to stay in Solung. And what was Tigger doing wandering around with a spy posing as a hippy? How much did they know of the People's Army plans? Did the army plan an offensive? The most persistent questions were about Bombay. Were they perhaps going there to buy armaments for Dougal?"

"I'm a hippy, not a gun runner," Henry said.

"Even better. I've always wanted to shoot a hippy. I despise hippies... idle rich kids pontificating about peace and love while half the world fights for survival."

"I am not rich."

"You live off the fat of a country that grew rich by exploiting poor countries like mine."

"You think you don't exploit the poor? The rich exploit their labour; you exploit their hope."

"I give them hope. What have you got to offer – the platitudes of that rogue Krishna Baba? I know all about your association with him."

"I know all about your association with his murder."

"He was an enemy of the people, conspiring with the king. We did you a favour getting rid of him. Why you idiots come out here looking for God I don't know. There's no peace and love in religion here. Do you know how many Hindus and Muslims died killing each other when you British ran away from this country? Thousands, in Calcutta alone! It's still going on. Hindus killing Sikhs. Sikhs killing Hindus. Muslims killing Hindus. Hindus killing Muslims. Religion is a major factor in holding this place back."

"On that, at least, I couldn't agree with you more," Henry said emphatically.

Tigger affected surprise. "Let me get this straight... I had you both down as religious cranks."

Da Silva was surprised. "Me?"

"Back in London... You saluted the God in Dougal. It took me aback... I didn't know he had one."

Da Silva laughed. "I was trying to annoy him. How else was I going to get him to come? "

"You wanted him to come?"

"He is famous. There would be no point in killing some anonymous Solung pilot. No-one would notice. I have my image to consider."

"But you told Dougal not to come."

190

"He is like a mule. He'll do anything but what you tell him to do. Like your mule of a friend here, slagging off religion as soon as his guru dies."

"I was slagging off religious bigotry."

"That's the stuff! Krishna Baba must have seen you coming. He did well for himself, getting fools like you to fall at his feet. He should have called me in on the marketing side. We could have done charter flights for suckers from the States. Ten dollars a platitude."

"Platitudes are undervalued. All great truths are platitudes."

"Good point! A hundred dollars a shot, then. It's the only way a platitude is going to feed a hungry baby."

"I can't see that killing off poor old Babu was any help to anyone," Tigger said.

"Babu was a mistake. He was not important enough to be a target. The attack was designed to kill your friend FitzDougal. It was a promotion."

"A promotion? What do you mean?"

"A publicity stunt. To put the People's Army on the world stage and attract backers and recruits. The kidnap of an obscure princess in a country few people have heard of was not going to get the newswires humming. We needed to get a celebrity involved. It didn't work out quite as we expected but we got our publicity and we are still getting it."

"By snatching pictures of the princess?"

"Neat, wasn't it? Nice picture in the papers. Actually we hadn't expected that little bonus. The main reason we were watching the post office was to catch you. You were sure to come sniffing after her like dogs after a bitch on heat. We are going to kill you, of course."

They had expected something like this, but they were still shocked into silence. Finally Tigger said: "Can I ask why?"

"Losing the princess was not good for our reputation. People need to see that no-one can cross us and get away with it. We would have killed the princess too but I'm afraid that would have caused trouble in the ranks."

"You mean with her brother?"

"Laxman has too many qualms to make a good revolutionary. Anyway you make better victims than the princess. People don't like women being murdered but they'll be happy to see us kill a couple of foreign spies. We'll make sure your deaths don't go unnoticed. It's a pity in a way. We might have been able to do a deal over that film. Perhaps you could give me the number of your contact in Bombay?"

Henry was too angry to banter. "How can you obsess about some stupid film when you are up to your ears in mayhem and murder?" he said.

Da Silva jabbed him sharply in the stomach. "Don't be cheeky, hippy. Let the grown-ups talk. This is a serious business we're discussing."

Henry had doubled up in pain, unable to reply. Tigger said: "You're saying show business is serious?"

"Revolutions are show business. They feed on propaganda. Propaganda is show business."

"And killing us is show business?"

"Exactly. It's taken a long time but I think you are beginning to understand. Now listen to me carefully. I have some business to attend to so I'm going to leave you to talk things over with your hippy friend. You have told me nothing yet that I did not know already, except for the business of the film. You had better come up with something useful to tell me when I come back or life is going to become uncomfortable for you. You have the choice of an easy death or a very, very painful one. I want to know how long Dougal plans to stay in Solung, and anything you know about this film."

Da Silva turned abruptly and left the room, motioning the guards to follow him. They heard the lock click and they were alone.

13   Brother in arms

Da Silva's interest in how long Dougal would be in Solung had puzzled Tigger because he had assumed that their work there was virtually over. Whatever the reason, it seemed beyond his concern now. "I'm sorry to get you into this," he told Henry.

"It's not your fault."

"Don't tell me. It's your karma."

"Shit," Henry said, kicking a mattress. "I'm too young to die."

Desperately they searched the room yet again for any way out but there was none. Henry called the guard, in the hope that a visit to the toilet might provide some kind of implement to tackle the mortar in the walls. The guard did not answer and they heard a car driving from the bungalow – presumably Da Silva was off on his business. Henry called again, and this time the guard replied. There followed a lengthy conversation in Bengali, which was close enough to Solungese for Henry to understand. Finally, he reported: "It's no good. Da Silva has left instructions that we should not leave the room until he returns. The guard does not know how long he will be away."

He slumped on to a mattress in dejection.

They spent the next couple of hours concocting a story about the fictitious film project, but they had little hope that it would gain them time. Their discussion was interrupted by the sound of a car drawing up outside the bungalow followed by the sound of voices. They heard a barked order, and steps approached down the corridor.

"It must be Da Silva," said Tigger, his despair sounding in

193

his voice. The door opened and two young men with pistols in their belts stepped into the room; behind them the room guard was grovelling to a young man immaculately dressed in a linen suit. He looked vaguely familiar, but he was not Da Silva.

"I've come to take you away for further questioning," he said in perfect English.

Flanked by the two gunmen, they were led to yet another of the ubiquitous Ambassador cars. The driver, still at the wheel, pointed a pistol at Tigger and Henry as they crammed into the back of the car with a gunman on either side.

A fat man bustled out of the house shouting "Sir, Sir!" and began importuning the man in the suit for money to repair the roof. The stranger turned to the car and shouted to the two prisoners: "Don't even think of trying to escape. These men have orders to shoot."

Turning to the fat man he said: "I can't deal with it now."

"But *sahib*, there are holes in the roof. When it rains..."

"Patch the holes as best you can. I'll get them dealt with as soon as I can."

As the stranger had guessed, Tigger had indeed been weighing up his chances of making a fight of it in the car rather than simply to submit to execution. But there was another surprise as they began to move off. The stranger kept looking ahead but said: "That was a tricky moment. I was afraid you were going to try to make a bolt for it. Just sit still and look frightened and I think we might get out of this. Which of you is Tigger?"

They were pulling out of the bungalow's driveway now. "I am," said Tigger, who was beginning to understand what was happening.

"You must be Henry," said the man, turning to Henry. "Allow me to introduce myself..."

"I know who you are," Tigger said. "You're the princess's brother Laxman. You look just like her."

Laxman smiled. "The men sitting next to you are my

friends. It is better that you do not know their names. They speak very little English."

Henry said: "I have lost track of the plot. Could someone tell me what is going on?"

"You rescued my sister from Da Silva. I rescued you. It was the least I could do. I promised Sita that I would not let Da Silva harm you." Laxman paused as an Ambassador car appeared ahead of them, coming towards them. "But I am afraid we are not quite out of the woods."

The car shot passed them and they saw Da Silva's startled face staring at them. His car screeched to a halt behind them. "He's turning to come after us," said Tigger.

Laxman said: "I'm damned if I am going to run away from him. We'll have to let him have his little tantrum."

They drove on without changing speed and Da Silva's car screamed past and skewed to a halt in front of them. Laxman wound down his window as Da Silva got out and stormed over shouting: "What the hell do you think you are doing?"

"I was collecting my guests."

"They are prisoners of the People's Army."

"They were your personal prisoners. You have no authority to take them. The agreement was that you should take no further action of this kind without consulting me."

"I am entitled to use my initiative when you are not around."

"But I am around, and these men are under my protection."

"Do you know who that Tigger Thomson is? He flies Spitfires. He's a very experienced pilot. He could be the death of you."

"Da Silva, you should be very careful about what you are saying."

"And you should be very careful about what you are doing. You could screw everything up."

"You have screwed up, Da Silva. Three times, by my count. You betrayed my trust by kidnapping my sister, you messed even that up, and now you are shooting your mouth off when you shouldn't."

"All the more reason why those two should die. They know too much. I demand that you hand them over. The men in the car behind me are armed."

"You are not that stupid, Da Silva. There are guns trained on you now. If any shooting starts, you can be sure that you will be the first to die. I advise you to get into your car and return to the house."

Da Silva was shaking with fury and began screaming abuse. The only words that registered with Tigger were: "I'll get those two, one way or another." The young prince calmly wound up his window and nodded to the driver, who swung the Ambassador past Da Silva's car and drove sedately on. Da Silva was still standing in the road glaring after them when they turned a corner and he passed out of view.

The tension in the car seemed to switch off when it was clear that they were not being pursued. Laxman and his three friends began discussing what had happened in Solungese, with much laughter. Seconds before they had looked like hardened gunmen; now they were behaving like four lads on a Saturday-night jaunt. As they chatted, Tigger's mind raced to process everything that he had heard. How could he be any danger to Laxman, and what was it that he and Henry knew too much about?

Close to the city centre Laxman dropped his friends off and took the wheel. "It is best if you get out of town," he told Tigger and Henry. "I have a place you can go to. Show me where you were staying. We'd better pick your stuff up before Da Silva gets it into his head to stake you out again."

ooo

It was too late to call the High Commission for news of the princess and, still a little wary of Laxman, they did not mention the fact that they were expecting a message. Darkness had fallen by the time they left the city, weaving their way among cyclists, people, bullock carts, and trucks on unlit country roads. It was an unnerving business; few of the vehicles had lights, and those that did rarely had a full set working so that it was hard to get an impression of their size; trucks with single lights looked like motorcycles; unlit cars and carts loomed out of the darkness as if out of nowhere. Laxman drove well, with none of the suicidal recklessness of so many drivers in a country where the law of the road was barely enforced. He warned as they set off: "You will understand that there are some matters we cannot talk about."

Tigger said: "There are some matters I don't even want to think about. I don't expect you to tell me but I cannot imagine why Da Silva thought I could be a danger to you. I came out here to help rescue your sister and as far as I am concerned that job is done."

"But you are still under contract to the Solung government?"

"I'm under contract to my boss," Tigger stopped short, suddenly aware that anything more he said on the matter might be useful to the People's Army. He also realised that he did not actually know what he was signed up for. He continued lamely: "I suppose I mean that I see you as a friend."

"Tigger, there are times when even friends have to fight. It is better that we keep some things to ourselves."

Conversation was awkward at first, not least because among the forbidden subjects were the interests that Tigger and Laxman had in common: flying and aircraft. Yet Laxman obviously wanted to talk and gradually they got a fuller idea of what was going on with him. He had had a long letter from his sister singing the praises of Tigger and Henry. "She said she would never forgive me if anything happened to you, and I have to tell you it nearly did. You were very lucky to escape when the RMP cornered you in that village."

"You know about that?"

"I heard. I don't know whether you realised it but the policeman who stepped in probably saved your lives. I could not have done anything for you there. It is Da Silva territory, an RMP stronghold."

"You are not RMP?"

Laxman did not answer for several seconds. Then he said: "The RMP and its military wing, the People's Army, are Da Silva's babies. I have kept my people at a distance because I felt that I should take responsibility for them. Most are from an area my family has ruled for centuries. They follow me as much as they follow my politics. And many members of the People's Army also trust me more than they trust Da Silva. So I have a lot of support. That's why he daren't cross me today."

"But he has crossed you! He kidnapped your sister!"

Laxman smiled ruefully. "I suppose Sita has told you the story. He completely wrong-footed me on that, I confess. It never crossed my mind that he would push me that far. But the thing was, none of us expected it – including Da Silva. He hadn't planned to kidnap her, I'm sure. It was a spur-of-the-moment thing after she said she wanted to go her own way. He took that personally and he was trying to save face. Also he sees everyone in terms of how he can use them. He hadn't worked out how he would use Sita but he knew for sure that she was going to be of no use to him if she walked out."

"She would also be a security risk."

"That's the story Da Silva put out within the movement, because of course people thought he had done the dirty on me. But Sita couldn't at that stage have told the intelligence people any more than they knew already. I'm well aware that they keep tabs on me. When I saw Da Silva after the kidnap he claimed that he had been trying to force me to make a choice between my family and the revolution, to get me to commit, but I'm sure he thought that up afterwards."

"Nevertheless you chose the revolution."

"I chose to do what I could for my sister without compromising it. I got someone to tip Prince Raju off about where she was. I was in agony. I'd have died if anything had happened to her but I couldn't get her out myself without taking on half the People's Army. So I am doubly indebted to you. You saved my sister and you helped me."

"Does Da Silva know you tipped off Raju?"

"I doubt it, but that would not stop him from accusing me of it. He will blame anyone but himself."

Henry said: "I would not trust him further than I could throw him. He'd kill you the moment he had no further use for you if he thought you were standing in his way."

Laxman's grip tightened on the steering wheel. "I have no illusions on that score. Da Silva wants to use me to help him gain power. If we succeed he will try to kill me. He wants to be the Mao Tse Tung of Solung, or even of India."

Tigger said: "Honestly, it is beyond me why you still have anything to do with him after what he did with Sita."

"Obviously, I've asked myself that many times. But I have to put the country before my own private grievances. The sad fact is that it is people like Da Silva who make change happen. I couldn't do it on my own."

"Because you are not ruthless enough?"

Laxman looked uncomfortable. "I'm sorry but I am saying more than I should. Do you mind if we change the subject?"

But it was the prince himself who kept returning to the subject. The more he spoke, the clearer it became that he was deeply troubled and caught up in something that was going out of his control. He began to tell his life story as he drove through the darkness of the moonless early evening.

"I loved school. I didn't think I would, being sent abroad to cold old England. I hated it at first. I mean here I am treated like... well, like a prince. Everything is done for me. Suddenly I was at a boarding school in a wet English October. A new boy. No servants. No doting parents. The lowest of the low. But by the time I left... maybe I am being nostalgic, but everything was so safe, so easy going, so good hearted. If anything was wrong, there was someone trying to do something about it... do you know what I mean? And I liked being just like everyone else. Of course some people sucked up to me because I was a prince but they weren't people who mattered to me. People go on about the class system in England but it's nothing to what happens here."

Tigger prompted: "Your sister said you refused to go to college."

"I wasn't ready to go. Ganesh got me into flying. We were friends from when we were kids. His family has worked for us for generations but his dad trained as an aircraft mechanic with the RAF during the war and while I was growing up he was working at a small flying school. Ganesh worked there for a while in exchange for lessons."

Laxman stopped talking and Tigger realised with astonishment that he was close to tears. "I did some lessons and when I got the basics my uncle Sanjeev invited me to try one of his aircraft. He said I could fly at his club any time I liked for the cost of the fuel. I invited Ganesh over but it got very awkward..."

"Because of his caste?" asked Henry.

Laxman nodded. "Ganesh comes from a family of servants. If he had not been a friend of mine the ... other club members... would not have let him near the place. But even when he was with me it was very uncomfortable for him. He stopped coming. I felt bad but I still had to keep using my uncle's place because by that time I was responsible for the aircraft there. My uncle more or less gave them to me."

Tigger noted a slight hesitation when Laxman spoke of the club members. He asked: "How did you feel about the people who froze Ganesh out?"

Laxman shook his head. "I can't tell you any more about that," he said awkwardly. "It was awful but nothing like as bad as what happened later when Ganesh's daddy was blown up." Laxman was wiping his eyes and for a moment it seemed as if he would have to stop driving. "I have never felt so bad in all my life," he said. "Babu was like a second father to me. I had no idea that Da Silva's men were going to do something like that."

Henry leaned forward from the back seat. "You knew the People's Army had declared war on the state. People die in wars."

"People die here all the time. Innocent people," Laxman said with sudden passion. "Do you know how I got involved with all this? After I got back from England a young girl was found hanged in a village near where I live. She had been gang raped and no-one knew whether she had hanged herself in shame or whether she was murdered. People in the village knew who had raped her. The police knew who had raped her. In fact there was strong suspicion that a policeman was involved. But she was low caste and no-one cared. Or rather no-one with any power cared. There was no investigation. No-one was charged. I tried to intervene but there was nothing I could do about it. You say the People's Army has declared war on the state. It seems to me that the state has declared war on the people."

Tigger said: "Do you think Da Silva's lot would do any better?"

"I'm not one of them, Tigger. I can't even read that stuff they churn out. I do know that they were the only people who took an interest in the fate of that poor girl and people like her. And I know that they want to tear down the whole rotten edifice of this society and start again."

He spoke as if the world's problems could be swept away like a pile of rubbish. Tigger was reminded of the princess the day she stripped off in the mountains: one minute the complete grown-up, the next like a glowering teenager. But he said nothing, content to let her brother tell his story.

"I didn't plan to get involved," Laxman said. "Some of my friends were interested in politics. I went along to meetings and demonstrations and I got asked to speak. Then Da Silva offered me a position as a commander in the People's Army."

201

Henry said: "Because you were a prince?"

"Of course. There was no other reason. He was trying to use me. There's nothing wrong with that. All kinds of charities and other organisations try to get people like me involved for the same reason."

"Didn't you think you were being manipulated?"

"It did not seem like that at the time. I was very impressed by Da Silva. I'd never met anyone quite like him before. But I turned down his offer. The People's Army is an illegal organisation and I did not want to put myself, and more importantly my followers, outside the law, at least until I was sure that it was necessary. The offer did make me think that I might as well use my position to do some good. I set up my own organisation, or at least my friends did. I never dreamed it would take off as much as it did. Suddenly I found myself with a following of – well, I am not going to tell you how many. A lot of people. Almost all of them from my home area. It was mostly because I spoke out about that poor girl. They joined the movement because they thought I had influence and they trusted me to fight for their interests. Da Silva encouraged me to set up youth cadres, which I envisaged as something a bit like the Boy Scouts. But under his influence it became more militaristic, with weapons training. That's what I mean about him making things happen. Left to myself I would never have pushed things that far. Now he talks of my people as if they are part of the People's Army. But I am their commander, not him, and numerically we are bigger."

Tigger noted that this description of Laxman's youth cadres was rather more worrying than that provided by Solung intelligence officers. Either they did not know what was going on, or they were deliberately playing down the prince's activities to keep Dougal on board.

Henry asked. "Do you think that was another reason for the kidnap, that you were becoming too powerful? That Da Silva wanted to cut you down to size?"

"There may have been an element of that. As I said, I don't think Da Silva thought it all through beforehand. I handed my sister to him, idiot that I am, and he played the situation for everything he could get. Eventually he used the kidnap to publicise the cause, and in that respect I suppose you could say it was a success. But far from cutting me down to size he actually increased support for me in the movement because people didn't like what he had done. On top of that he was made to look a fool. That is why he is so angry with you two."

"But he is still powerful?"

"The strange thing is that Sita's escape has strengthened his position. She'd become more trouble than she was worth politically and he couldn't kill her off without turning me and most of the country against him. And keeping her prisoner made him look weak because, whatever he said, it looked as if he was holding her hostage to keep me onside. Now everyone – my people and his – can know for sure that I am committed."

They were coming close to their destination. Laxman slowed down, looking for his turning, then drove down a narrow crumbling road that required all his concentration to negotiate. Half an hour later they were in a small fishing village, gazing over the sea of the Bay of Bengal. Part of the village had been given over to bougainvillea-fringed bungalows, most of them serving as retreats for wealthy people from Calcutta. Laxman turned into the driveway of one of these and announced: "This is my uncle Sanjeev's holiday home."

Two servants emerged to take their bags and a third ushered them into a large drawing room with plush armchairs. As Laxman bustled out to check arrangements, Tigger was startled by the sight of an ageing photograph displayed prominently on a sideboard. It showed a man shaking hands with Adolf Hitler.

14   The man who treated with Hitler

"Subhas Chandra Bose, better known as Netaji, the beloved leader," said Henry. "Depending on your point of view, a Nazi fellow-traveller, or a brave patriotic fighter for freedom."

"Or both," said Laxman, catching the end of the conversation as he entered the room.

"The greatest Indian of the twentieth century, bar none," said an older man who walked in behind him.

"This is my Uncle Sanjeev," said Laxman, looking a little uncomfortable. "I thought he was still in Solung."

"Too hot! Too hot! I needed some sea air!" Sanjeev, wearing a *lungi* and an unbuttoned white shirt damp with sweat, looked as if he still needed some air as he puffed red-faced across the room and sank with evident relief into an armchair. He had a thin moustache and short grey hair and looked the far side of 70, though Tigger guessed that he had aged beyond his years.

"Uncle, this is Tigger and Henry. They are the Englishmen who helped Ganesh and FitzDougal rescue Sita."

Sanjeev showed no interest in shaking hands. "English, eh? You English never understood Netaji – you hated him because he wouldn't bow down to you. You'd have strung him up if you could have found an excuse. You'd have strung me up too if you thought you could get away with it."

"I don't think Tigger and Henry would have been old enough to hang you, uncle." Laxman said.

"Nothing personal," said Sanjeev. "I've nothing against the English, so long as they stop trying to run other people's countries."

"Uncle fought with the Indian National Army, the INA, against the British in World War Two," Laxman said, by way of explanation.

"The Indian National Army? I thought India fought on our side," said Tigger.

The conversation over the next two hours turned Tigger's view of the Second World War upside down, with Britain cast as a villain. Subhash Bose, one-time mayor of Calcutta, had spent most of the 1920s and 1930s as a leading militant in the agitation against British rule in India, clashing with the pacifist Mahatma Gandhi over his campaign of passive resistance. At the start of Hitler's war in 1939, Bose escaped house arrest and fled to Stalin's Russia, which he believed might support an uprising in India. After finding little enthusiasm for his cause in Moscow, he tried his luck in Germany, where Hitler allowed him to form a small Indian Legion recruited from prisoners of war and Indian residents of Germany. Bose was given the title Netaji, or "respected leader", which to opponents had a sinister resonance with Hitler's title Der Fuhrer – "The Leader".

"Strangely enough, Hitler had admirers in India as far back as the thirties," Henry said.

Tigger looked quizzically at Sanjeev. "What did Bose think he was doing, dealing with a man who regarded Indians as subhuman?"

Sanjeev retorted angrily: "Who are you English to criticise Hitler? You tried to rule half the world and showed no respect for the people of India."

"Britain has a lot to answer for, Sanjeev," Henry said. "We've certainly done a lot we should be ashamed of in India. But Indians can hardly claim to be better than us on the matter of showing people respect. You don't show respect for each other. Just look at the way lower castes are treated. To this day Hitler strikes a chord with some Indians because Nazi views on race chime with caste and anti-Moslem prejudice."

"They are a very small minority, Henry," protested Laxman, casting another uncomfortable glance at his uncle. "You're making it sound like India is about to stoke up the gas chambers."

"Pfff... all that stuff about killing Jews has been exaggerated," Sanjeev said. "Whatever happened, Netaji couldn't have known about it. And what to say? Such things happen in wartime. Do you think the English always behaved like gentlemen?"

"We did not set up extermination camps," said Tigger, becoming angry.

"We killed by incompetence and neglect," Henry said. "It's reckoned that more than two million people died in the Bengal famine of 1943."

Tigger was silent for a second. "I don't know about that. Perhaps I should. But I'm sure it wasn't death by design. You can't equate 1940s Britain with the Nazis. Even in the Empire, Britain promoted the rule of law."

"Englishmen's law. When it suited Englishmen," harmony

"They locked us up if they thought we would cause trouble. I know what I am talking about. I was in the English army for two years."

Sanjeev had been serving as a lieutenant in the British Indian Army in the Malay peninsula when the Japanese attacked in late 1941. After the fall of Singapore, the Japanese gave captured Indian soldiers the choice of prisoner-of-war camp or enlisting in the newly-formed INA to join them in what was presented as a fight to free India. Bose was brought over from Germany to lead the INA, which eventually numbered around 40,000 – including Sanjeev.

"Bose surely couldn't have had any illusions about how the Japanese would have treated India if they had succeeded in getting here," Tigger said. "Japan had been on the rampage in China since the late thirties."

"We would have taken to the countryside and fought for

206

our freedom, if necessary," Sanjeev said. "In the meantime our attitude was that 'my enemy's enemy is my friend'. We weren't the only ones playing that game. The English and Americans were happy to ally with Stalin when he was fighting Hitler."

"Stalin ended up taking over half of Europe," said Tigger. "That's what comes of flirting with the devil."

"To us, the English were devils."

"If you felt like that, why did you join the British Indian Army in the first place?"

"I was young and I wanted to play soldiers. I grew up very quickly when the Japanese first attacked and the English ran, I can tell you. A lot of my friends were killed. I thought why should I die for a country that subjugated my own?"

"But your country was Solung. Solung was not India."

"India in those days was not the entity it is now," Henry said. "It was jumble of states and statelets subject in one way or another to the British. Most of them were subsumed into what became India and Pakistan when the British left."

"But not Solung, more's the pity," said Sanjeev. "The father of the present king kept his kingdom by licking English arses. In fact he thought the sun shone out of their arses. So does his son, the present king."

"Whereas Netaji preferred Hitler?"

Tigger's acid tone was lost on Sanjeev. "Netaji respected a strong leader."

"A fuhrer?"

"He thought India needed a strong leader. In my opinion it still does."

Sanjeev's eyes flicked to Laxman, who said: "Uncle... please don't start that."

His uncle ignored him. "If Netaji had lived, this country would not be in the mess it is in now. A democracy is all very well in a developed country but it is no good in a place where most people can't even write their own name and everyone is pulling in different directions. Netaji would have pulled India together, and there would have been no non-sense about keeping Solung out of it. There are times when a country needs someone like that. You should understand that, Laxman."

"Uncle, please stop." Laxman's tone was more insistent now. It was clear that he was not merely embarrassed by the opinions of his uncle; he was under pressure to adopt them.

Tigger thought it better to steer the conversation to safer ground for a while. "Was Netaji killed in the war?"

Sanjeev told how Bose died in a Japanese plane that crashed in Taiwan three days after the end of the war. Japan's attempted invasion of India had failed and its forces, including the INA, were driven back through Burma with enormous losses by Allied troops including a large number of Indians. The British regarded INA soldiers as traitors and court martialled some of the officers after the war. San-jeev recounted with pride how the authorities were forced to back down after a public outcry and mutinies among British Indian forces. "The INA may have lost on the battlefield but we were a political success," he said. "We made the British realise they could no longer hold on to India. They could not even trust their own Indian Army to support them."

"I'd say they could hardly trust the British Army," Henry said. "British conscripts had just spent five years fighting one kind of oppression – why would they risk their lives prop-ping up another? They wanted to go home. Everyone in Britain was sick of war. In fact the British and Indians alike were in too much of a rush to end British rule. A lot of peo-ple died in communal violence as a result."

"You got out, that was the main thing, and it couldn't happen fast enough so far as I was concerned," Sanjeev said, lifting himself out of his armchair. "It was all a long time ago. What matters now is that people seize the moment like Netaji did. It makes no difference to me – my time is coming to a close. Look at me. I am tired already. I need to sleep. But Laxman here..."

"Uncle... please," said Laxman.

"He knows how I feel," said Sanjeev, turning to Tigger and Henry. "I wish you gentlemen good night. And no hard feelings, eh?"

He shook hands awkwardly and left.

ooo

"I'm afraid uncle has a thing about the English," Laxman said. "He had a very bad time after he was captured at the end of the war. They treated him with contempt because he had changed sides. He's never forgiven them."

"That I can understand. It's his politics that worry me," said Tigger. "I can't respect anyone who sees Adolf Hitler as a role model."

"The idolising of Subhas Chandra Bose is almost as disturbing," Henry said. "There are people who see him as a saint. Many believe his death was faked and that he is living somewhere ready to return when India needs him again. His history has become sanitised, as if people in this country need to see him as Mr Right fighting Evil."

"Every country does that," said Tigger. "The British sanitise their view of the Empire. The Americans sanctify the bunch of tax-dodgers, turncoats, smugglers and slave owners who founded the United States."

"Sanctifying Bose is dangerous because it sanitises Hitler in the eyes of young Indians," Henry said. "You get Hindu nationalists who revere Hitler, and goosestep like fascists, and get involved in some very dirty racial politics."

Laxman said: "They are a small minority. Most Indians see Bose simply as a brave man who fought people he saw as his country's enemies, which is true. They see uncle and his INA comrades as heroes."

"I'd say India's freedom was won as much by the two-and-a-half million Indians who for whatever reason volunteered to fight the Nazis and Japanese militarists. They were the real power in India after the war. Britain could not have fought them even if it had wanted to. But I can see why Bose appeals to your Indian Biggles: he took on the British militarily. Far more manly than soppy old Gandhi."

Laxman was puzzled. "Biggles? You mean the pilot in the books?"

"It's Henry's little joke," said Tigger. "Biggles is the name he gives to every man's sense of manhood, the hero he aspires to be."

"I read Biggles books at school. I used to dream about flying Spitfires. I've still never flown one. The king wouldn't take his out of the crates for me."

"And now you are flying Messerschmitts?"

They were on forbidden ground again but Laxman seemed not to notice. He wanted to explain himself. "I haven't turned Nazi, if that's what you mean. Look, my uncle's an old man and he may be a little crazy as a result of what he went through during the war. I'm the nearest to a son that he has got and he is trying to live his dreams through me. He wants me to carry on where Netaji left off. It's ridiculous, but that is the way he thinks."

"Is that why he gave you the Messerschmitts?"

Laxman did not answer directly. "He heard that I had got involved with the People's Army and was very excited. It was like old times for him."

"But the People's Army are Maoist. Sanjeev does not sound like a communist."

"Well, as Da Silva said, Sanjeev wouldn't know Karl Marx from the Marx Brothers. Bose saw himself as a socialist and that's good enough for my uncle. He asked to meet Da Silva and was very taken with him. Da Silva is very clever at telling people what they want to hear. He gave Sanjeev a vision of using an uprising in Solung to spark a revolution in India during which a strong leader could emerge and pull the country together."

"Netaji reborn," remarked Henry, drily. "And, I wonder who would be the new beloved leader?"

"You can guess what Da Silva thinks. My uncle's fantasy

is to put me up there. As I said, it is ridiculous. I mean me and my friends have an agenda... we want to end corruption and casteism, spread education, and raise living standards. We want to force through change. But I don't want to run a country. I wouldn't know how. I wouldn't want Da Silva to run the country either – he and the RMP hardliners will have to be reined in some time. But all that is lost on Sanjeev. He got carried away in the course of the talk with Da Silva and offered the People's Army the use of his aircraft."

"The Messerschmitts?"

"Yes. Only he didn't want to give them directly. He signed them over to me – partly, I think, to distance himself in case of trouble, but mostly to commit me to the cause. He wanted me in up to my neck. So I found myself with an own air force."

"But what on earth can you do with four MEs?"

"I... I can't tell you."

"You shouldn't be telling us any of this, Laxman. You are talking treason."

Laxman shrugged. "What difference does it make? I'm sure the king knows most of what's been going on."

"What did Sanjeev think when the princess was kidnapped?"

"What do you think? His reaction was much like mine. We were implicated by association and could not do much about it. Sanjeev never trusted Da Silva anyway, or he says he didn't. He sees himself as using Da Silva, just as Da Silva thinks he's using my uncle."

"Doesn't Sanjeev have any qualms about trying to bring down the king? The king is his brother-in-law, isn't he?"

"Half brother-in-law. The queen is my uncle's half sister. Sanjeev hates the king. He won't admit it but he does. He resents the fact that he went through hell in Malaya and Burma while the present king and his father sat out the war in comfort and got through Independence with their kingdom intact. I'm sure he bought the MEs out of spite when the king bought his war-surplus Spits."

"How much did Ganesh know about this? Was that the real reason why he didn't use your uncle's club?"

"It was the reason I didn't push him to stay. I did not want to get him into trouble."

"But other members froze him out because he was low born. That doesn't sound like communism," Henry said.

Laxman looked very uncomfortable. "Other pilots at the club think a lot like my uncle and treat him like a hero. They belong to some Hindu nationalist group. I suspect that Sanjeev does too but he has never let on to me. I fly with them but I keep my distance politically. That is why my uncle keeps carping on at me."

"Are they serious about trying to take power in India?"

"I think only Sanjeev is crazy enough to think they could. They have common cause with Da Silva in that they want to destabilise Solung. If India takes over Solung as a result, they become part of the greater Hindu nation which is what they want. Otherwise they plan to gain power in Solung on the back of the People's Army and then invite India in. Revolutions make strange bedfellows. Sometimes I think they just want a fight. They have these classic fighting machines in prime condition, and they want to use them in earnest."

Something in his tone prompted Tigger to ask: "Do you feel like that?"

"If I'm honest, yes. Part of me does. You must feel the same deep down."

"You mean with the Spits? I wouldn't risk my neck for the thrill of the fight, if that's what you mean," Tigger said.

"Sometimes destiny puts you in a position where you have to fight."

"So does foolishness," Henry said.

"I hope you are not feeling the hand of fate now, Laxman."

"I never planned to be in the position I'm in. It just happened."

There was silence for a few seconds as this sank in. Then Henry said: "It happened that you landed among a bunch of quasi-fascists. Does Da Silva know about the politics of these people?"

"He doesn't care, any more than he cares about my politics. Da Silva only cares about power. We'll fight for him and as far as he is concerned that is all that matters – at least for now."

The sophisticated young man who had rescued them in Calcutta only hours before suddenly looked like a lost little boy.

Tigger said: "It sounds like a case of 'create mayhem and then fight for the spoils'. It's a murky business and I don't like to see you involved in it, Laxman – especially when you start talking about being destined to fight. You are a free agent. You have a choice. If I were you, I'd get out as quickly as I could."

Laxman shrugged. "It's too late for that. I have all these people relying on me. They got into this business because of me. I can't let them down. I have to make sure that they get something out of all this."

ooo

They were all too keyed up to sleep. A crescent moon rose, giving them enough light to walk down to the beach and along the shore, past a line of fishing boats drawn up on to the sand along the edge of the village. They talked as they walked, trying to persuade Laxman to extricate himself from Da Silva, but it was impossible to penetrate his peculiar mix of fatalism, naivety and sophistication. The changes he wanted to see were laudable but he showed no clear idea of how he would bring them about, and he had an alarming faith in his ability, with the help of his friends, to outwit the ruthless machinations of Da Silva and the RMP.

Some way into the conversation, unaware of Tigger's keen interest in seeing the princess, he announced as a by-the-way that she knew they were at Sanjeev's house.

213

"She's been in touch?" said Tigger in surprise.

"We keep in touch via her friend Betty at the High Commission. Betty had a message for you both to contact me when you got to Calcutta, but I guess you didn't get it."

"We were on our way to see her when Da Silva grabbed us."

"It was Sita's idea to bring you here. She can't stand Sanjeev, but it was as good a place as any to get you out of the reach of Da Silva. He doesn't know about this place. So far as Sita knows, I have simply brought you here as arranged. She doesn't know that you were Da Silva's prisoners."

"Where is she?"

"I don't know and I don't want to know. I don't want to know where you go either. It's better that way to avoid the slightest chance of me putting any of you at risk. Your safest bet would be to leave the country. I can't guarantee you protection. I shall be too busy watching my own back."

This was the first hint he had given that he might be endangered by having helped them.

"Can we call Sita?"

"I don't have a number. There's no phone here, anyway. The lines don't stretch this far. I guess she'll be in contact."

By the time they turned back and headed for the house, dawn was painting the sea pink and people from the village were out preparing nets and boats for the day's fishing.

15 Back with the princess

Tigger fell asleep almost as soon as he lay down on his bed and it seemed only seconds later when a boy servant shook him awake and said: "Sahib, your car has come."

"My car? I don't have a car."

"It's outside," said the boy. Tigger peered out of a window to see a Sikh smoking a bedi in the driver's seat of a dilapidated, black-and-yellow Ambassador taxi parked outside. "Sita sent it," said Laxman, coming into the room. "That's Harjinder at the wheel. Our family has used him for years. We call him Harry."

"Where is he taking us?"

"I haven't asked. Wherever you want to go, I guess. There's no hurry. Harry is used to waiting. He gets paid by the day. Have some breakfast and get your things together."

Tigger did hurry, galvanised by the possibility of seeing the princess. But it was still only 9am and Henry, bleary eyed from lack of sleep, took his time so that it was noon before they were ready to leave. Sanjeev had still not made an appearance.

As they about to get into the car Laxman said: "Tigger, I guess you will have to go back to Solung at some point?"

"I suppose so but as far as I am concerned my job there is done. Dougal will be winding up his work soon. We can't stay out here for ever."

"Well, I wish you would stay away from Solung."

"What do you mean?"

"I don't want us to end up on opposite sides."

"I think you should get as far away from Da Silva as you can. But that doesn't mean I am about to fight you over it."

"You do what you have to do, Tigger," Laxman said enigmatically. "Whatever happens, don't feel bad about it."

Tigger stared at him for a few seconds then said: "It makes me uneasy hearing you talk like this. I have no intention of doing anything I might feel bad about. We're friends, right?"

"That's what worries me. Go, Tigger. I hope we meet again in happier times."

Tigger, who was under the impression that this was a happy time, got into the car. As they drove off, he saw Laxman staring after them looking utterly forlorn.

"Laxman sahib, many troubles," Harry said. "Princess Sita, she is very worried."

The mention of the princess made Tigger realise that they had no idea where they were going. "Where is the princess? Are we going to see her?"

"One minute, sahib." Harry pulled over to the side of the road and stopped, then produced an envelope from the glove compartment. "The princess say give you this after leaving house."

He handed the envelope to Henry, who was next to him in the front seat; Henry gave it to Tigger, knowing his sensitivity about the princess. It read:

"Darling Tigger and Henry, So sorry I missed you in Calcutta. I'm heading south to Goa for a few days – my English friend is lending me her beach house there. I'd love you to come down if you can. I don't think it is safe for you in Calcutta. Better to fly from Bhubaneshwar Airport. Harry will drive you there. He has two sets of open air tickets. You only have to book your flights. Please use them. I'm feeling a little scared and alone after what happened in Calcutta – you probably know by now that someone took my picture. They must have been watching out for me. You will be doing me a great favour by coming. Telegram your ETA to the address Harry will give you and I'll have a car waiting at the airport. I won't meet you because I don't want to risk being recognised. Don't know whether you have seen the papers but

that picture has been splashed all over them – supposed mystery of supposedly missing princess. First in the English press and then here in India. Luckily the photo does not give a good view of my face but I don't want to take chances. I dread to think of what nonsense the papers would write if I were photographed with you. And I don't want Da Silva to know where we are. He's dangerous.

If you can't make it down to Goa, feel free to ask Harry to take you anywhere you want to go. But I'd really love to see you. Lots of love. Sita."

Tigger was becoming used to the way she treated them both as equals in her affections but he was struck for the first time just how isolated she must feel returning to the subcontinent after spending most of her life abroad; all her friends seemed to be foreigners. "She wants us to meet her in Goa," he said, handing the letter to Henry.

"You going to see princess. Good," said Harry. "Princess is very nice lady. Very pretty. Not good for her to be by herself. Too many bad men."

ooo

Dougal said much the same thing when Tigger called him to tell him of their escape and of what he had learned from Da Silva. "You'd better find the princess and stick with her," he said. "And that comes from the king. The girl could be in danger."

Tigger revealed as little as possible of what Laxman had said, afraid of incriminating the young prince, but he felt honour bound to tell Dougal about his meeting with Sanjeev and the hints of a possible air battle. "Laxman won't be doing much flying for a while," Dougal said. "The king has blocked fuel supplies to that flying club he uses."

ooo

They arrived at Goa's Dabolim Airport two days later, after a frustrating journey involving two flights and tedious waits at airports. A taxi was waiting for them as promised, and they drove for half an hour until the driver stopped outside a chai shop in a small village, announcing that this was where he had been told to take them. "That's fine," said Tigger, guessing that the princess did not want him to know where they were staying.

As the taxi drove off, a young man emerged from the chai shop and said: "Mr Tigger and Mr Henry? Welcome to Chapora village. I am Patrick, the landlady's son. I've come to show you to your house."

Patrick led them through the village, passing several westerners scantily clad in the eclectic mix of Indian clothes favoured by hippies. Nobody took the slightest notice of Tigger and Henry. A short walk across paddy fields brought them to another part of the village where Patrick led them to a red-tiled bungalow set a few yards back from a palm-fringed beach. There was no furniture, except for a made-up bed in each of two rooms, and a table with two chairs in what Patrick described as a kitchen, though it contained no obvious means of cooking food. The windows had wooden shutters instead of glass. Almost as soon as Patrick had left via the back door, there was a knock on the front door and the princess burst in, flinging her arms round each of them in turn. "I can't tell you how glad I am to see you," she said. "Wait until Patrick's out of sight and we can go next door and talk in more comfort."

The house a few yards away was almost identical on the outside but the princess had made it more homely with wall hangings, and matting and cushions to sit on. There were three chairs at the kitchen table, with a Primus stove that the princess stoked up expertly to make tea. She explained: "Betty, my friend in Calcutta, hired this place for a few weeks but she couldn't get down herself. She booked the house next door for you for fear of a scandal if I was discovered sharing a house with two men. It's cheap – the monthly rent is less than you'd pay for night's stay at a Bombay hotel."

"That's how the hippies can afford to stay here," said Henry.

"Not for very much longer, I'd say. This place will be full of tourist hotels in a few years. I didn't realise until I got here that this was a crazy place for me to hide. I stick out more than you do. Indian women don't holiday alone, and they certainly don't hang out with Western hippies. The hippies are all walking about naked on the beaches but if I did it there would be outrage. This may be 1972 but it's 1872 in attitude as far as Indian women are concerned."

"I'm sure the papers would love to get a picture of you cavorting on the beaches in the altogether," said Henry.

"My parents would die of shame. But I'd look just as conspicuous wearing clothes. I daren't draw attention to myself so I stay off the beaches altogether during the day."

"If the worse comes to the worst and the papers get on to you, you can say that we are your bodyguards. It's true, more or less," said Tigger.

"I certainly feel a lot safer with you here. I've been quite nervous being down here by myself after what happened in Calcutta. This house is very isolated at night. Betty would never have agreed to let me use this place if she had known I would be here alone. I have to confess that I told her I would meet up with you at Sanjeev's place before coming here. I wanted you to meet Laxman and I thought he would talk more freely if I wasn't with you. I hoped you would talk some sense into him. He was keen to meet you, so I arranged for him to pick you up and take you to Sanjeev's when you made contact."

"It didn't quite work out like that," Tigger said, and recounted the story of their kidnap and rescue.

The princess was shocked into silence. "God, is this never going to stop?" she said eventually. "I'm very relieved Laxman got you away but now I'm worried about him. I hope he hasn't pushed Da Silva too far."

"He seemed confident that he could keep him in check."

"Did you get much of a chance to speak to him?"

"We had a long talk with him but I don't think we had

much effect. He talks as if his life is on a railway track that will only take him in one direction."

They spent the rest of the afternoon sipping iced drinks fetched from a makeshift stall on the beach, and recounting their conversations with Laxman and his uncle. At the mention of Sanjeev, the princess frowned. "Sanjeev has always been a troublemaker. He created a lot of ill feeling in the family after the war when he accused some of them of being British collaborators, as if being a Japanese collaborator was any better. But people see him as a war hero and he plays the part to the hilt. Laxman hero-worshipped him as a kid. He knows better now but he's still attached to his uncle – I think because he knows he is the only one of us that Sanjeev is at all close to. It would be sad if Sanjeev weren't so dangerous."

Sunset was falling when Henry stood up and said: "It's like a gathering of the clans in Goa around this time. There'll be people here I know. If you don't mind I'm going to take a quick look round to see who is here."

The princess gave him a canny look and said: "This is your holiday, Henry. Do as you wish."

ooo

Tigger suggested a walk on the beach in the fading light. The sun was a blazing orb on a golden ocean as they stepped on to the deserted sand and walked in silence along the water's edge. Tigger wanted to hold the princess but she kept her distance, as if touching him would release too much. After some time she said: "Why did Henry leave?"

"I guess he thought we had something to sort out. He knows what happened between us in the mountains."

"You told him? You promised..."

"I didn't tell him. He saw us canoodling as he was climbing back down to us. He's cool. He won't say anything."

They came to a palm-covered promontory at the edge of the beach, and stood gazing at the darkening waters. "There's something we haven't told you," Tigger said. "We

220

have messages for you from Prince Raju and the king. The prince asked us to tell you that he understands what you are going through..."

"I know, and I have treated him so badly. He sent me a lovely letter through Betty, saying he was willing to forget the past and start afresh if I was. But he didn't want to marry me if I did not think I could commit myself to making it work. It was a shock to me, I can tell you. I thought I had burned my boats to far as he was concerned. It was sweet of Raju to write, though I suspect his father prodded him into it."

"He sounded pretty genuine when he spoke to us. Did you reply?"

"I asked him to give me a little more time, but he'd already offered that in his letter. I was running away from a decision just like I ran away from you when we got out of the mountains."

"You were running away from me?"

"And everything else. My parents. Life. But I needed you too, Tigger. I can't tell you how much. It's hard to explain. That time with you and Henry... it was the first time since I'd been back when I felt I wasn't taking on the world by myself, when I was with people I could trust who cared about things I cared about."

"And now you have to go places where you can't take us?"

"I don't *have* to do anything, except make a choice."

"In the mountains, you spoke as if you already had made a choice. You didn't want to marry Raju."

"I didn't want to be forced into it and I didn't feel ready for it after everything that had happened in America. Apart from the upset of breaking up with that wretched professor, I'd lost faith in my own judgement. Who was I to take on the role of a future queen? The thought of having to deal with all those people hanging round the king..."

She gave a little shudder. "But now... I am so worried about Laxman. I am afraid he is going to do something silly.

Perhaps if I had more sway over what happens in Solung, and if I offered to work with him for change... maybe he might cut off from Da Silva. But it's not fair on Raju to marry him for the sake of my brother. Nor on the country, for that matter."

"The country's good and Laxman's good are not necessarily mutually exclusive. Laxman's aims seemed quite sensible. The trouble is that he believes the only way to achieve them is a revolution."

"I'm terrified he is going to tip the country into some ghastly conflict that will last years, and get himself killed into the bargain."

"I should give you the king's message. He made us promise not to tell anyone else and said you should keep quiet about it too. He says he will abdicate if you marry Raju. You'd be queen."

The princess was shocked into silence for a few seconds. "What on earth was he thinking of? Is he trying to bribe me with a crown?"

"Sita, I don't think he meant it like that. He doesn't expect to live very long. He hinted at some kind of heart trouble."

"He always talks like that, as if he is going to peg out at any moment. It's another way of manipulating people."

"Whatever. I'm sure he really is concerned about the future of Solung. The odd thing was that he said we would find you here. I don't know how on earth he knew."

"I told him once that I wanted to run away to Goa and be a hippy. I was joking but he must have seen that it was half true. I envied the hippies for their freedom. I still do. Even more so after what you have just told me."

"You don't want to be queen?"

She shrugged. "Look at me, practically a prisoner in my own house. I can't be free and I knew it before I come here. I only said that to the king because I was trying to shock him out of his expectations. He was treating me as if I was already

222

his daughter-in-law. But he is not shockable. You wouldn't think so, to meet him. But he isn't."

"You can say that again. He shocked me. I've never known anyone be so matter of fact about things other people get worked up about. He said that you should take your time and get everything out of your system. His actual words were: 'If she can't be good, tell her to be careful.'"

The princess gave a wry smile. "He told *you* to tell me that?"

"After I more or less admitted that I was in love with you."

She fell silent, staring at the sea. After a while she said: "Tigger, a few days together and a few hours of dalliance is not love."

"It's not much of an exchange for a kingdom, that's for sure."

She stayed silent, turning her head away from him. Tigger thought for a moment that he had offended her. "I'm sorry, I didn't mean to sound bitter," he said. Then he caught sight of her face and saw that tears were pouring down her cheeks. When he went to comfort her, she flinched. "It's me who should say sorry," she said, pulling herself away. "Please, Tigger... Let's just walk."

They clambered with some difficulty over a shadowy promontory to the next beach and walked in silence on the wet sand where the water welled up over their bare feet. Finally she said: "I've been so silly, behaving like a little girl. I thought that if I could get you and Henry down here it would be like it was in the mountains. You know... we would be good companions."

"No dalliance?"

"Now you are here it seems so complicated. It's like... I can't escape my position in life."

"I guess Henry would say it's your karma."

"Funny, isn't it? A small word with such a big meaning."

"So is love."

There was another pause. Then the princess said: "That time we spent in the temple together... It seemed so unreal after we left. Henry turned up and we carried on as if nothing had happened."

"Because you wanted it to be kept a secret. We didn't know that Henry had seen us."

"I almost kept it a secret from myself. I shut it away in my head like an old dream. I've been so stupid. I've hurt you and that was the last thing I wanted to do."

"Sometimes I wonder what would have happened if it had been me that went for help and Henry had stayed with you in the temple."

"I don't know, Tigger, if I am honest. I'm not sure anything would have happened if it hadn't been for that place. I am not superstitious but it felt so strange being cast adrift there at that time. All those beautiful, primal images of sex and fertility cried out for me to make love to you."

"And I thought it was me...."

The princess stopped in her tracks. "Tigger, of course it was you. It still is. Don't you understand? I daren't make love to you because I love you too much. I don't trust myself to leave you when I should. I don't trust myself to make the right decisions when you are around. And I don't want to hurt you any more than I have already."

"I'm prepared to take that risk."

The princess turned to face him and looked into his eyes. She was close now and he was viscerally aware of her body, almost as if they were touching. "Tigger, if I have to go, I have to go. No recriminations. No regrets. You promise?"

"I promise," he said, but she hardly heard because she had buried herself in his arms.

16 Cocooned in paradise

Henry was one of thousands of young Westerners who had been travelling to India since the early sixties, at the dawn of the age of mass recreational travel when anywhere east of Greece seemed gloriously exotic. It did not take them long to discover Goa, where many became latter-day Lotus Eaters, seduced into a life of narcotic ease in a paradise where their money could last at least ten times longer than it would back home. Some eked out their savings by bringing small amounts of charas down from the Himalayas, a jaunt that could land them in jail if they got caught. Criminal types dealing in large quantities gave Goa a darker edge. So did junkies, hooked on harder stuff, and kids who drove themselves crazy smoking supercharged chillums or taking too many psychedelics. For the most part, though, the visitors were harmless, indulging a fashion for a romanticised Hinduism that took them wandering far from Goa around a country that to their foreign eyes looked like an endlessly fascinating living museum. Some, like Henry, went eccentrically native.

In the late autumn, after the charas harvest, many of the wanderers gravitated back to Goa for what became an extended party lasting well into the new year. Their numbers were swelled by holidaymakers on short stays, attracted from all over the world by Goa's growing reputation. By the time Tigger and Henry arrived, Goa's coastal villages were becoming more crowded by the day. The newcomers were of many different shades, making the princess less conspicuous, and she began to lose her fear of being recognised, especially as the newspapers seemed to have forgotten about her. She was still wary of being seen on the beach in daytime, and when she was out and about she kept her face hidden behind sunglasses and judiciously tilted sunhats. She and Tigger retreated into a world of their own, reading and wandering around the Goan villages and markets by day, and returning for a swim at sunset and an evening spent cooking and talking alone. When local people called, as they did regularly to hawk pastries and drinks, Tigger kept out of sight to reduce the chance of a scandal. It was impossible to feel seriously threatened for long in beautiful Goa. Tigger pushed aside nagging thoughts that Da Silva might still want them killed to restore his credibility, and that he and Henry might be in more danger than the princess if word got out about their whereabouts.

Tigger called Dougal from the nearby capital Panjim for his regular check-in, and was relieved to be told to stay where he was. Henry opined: "I reckon that king is playing a very long game."

Henry accepted without comment the fact that Tigger stayed in the princess's house and for a few days he ran a considerable establishment of his own at the other building, where people gathered to cook communal meals and play music. He took up with an old girlfriend but after a couple of nights she had gone. "I needed to be by myself," he explained, without elaboration. Tigger, who had got to know his friend's moods, sensed that something was troubling him but he was too absorbed in the princess to pay much attention. One evening Henry came round and sang some of his old songs, and talked about the young people who flocked to Goa. "Most of them see it as a glorified holiday camp and a lot of very nasty things go on. But a lot of the kids really do come to India looking for God. They come here looking for something we seem to have lost in the West."

The princess asked: "Did you find it here?"

"I think I did," Henry said. "But I don't know what to do with it."

The princess's troubles surfaced at night. Once, lying in Tigger's arms, she said: "You know those first days when we were together in the mountains... I was in such a strange state of mind. I had this sense of boundless freedom, as if I were escaping from my past as much as from Da Silva. You must

226

have thought me very odd after what happened at the water-fall."

"To be honest it seemed a little childish."

"It was babyish," corrected the princess. "Literally. Like a baby pooing on the carpet. I don't quite know what came over me. I did it and then came out with that stuff about men. I guess the resentment was real but it was really just a rationalisation."

"I don't know how much weight people give to Freud these days, but he would have loved it."

"It was very Freudian. A forbidden act to spite my parents. But that too is a rationalisation. I just did it. Now, it seems almost as if I was going back to the beginning of my life to start all over again. Especially because of what happened later. That temple has haunted me ever since. I can't get it out of my mind. It was so weird arriving there at that moment in my life. And what happened between us... it felt like a rite of passage, as if the temple had drawn us into a Tantric ritual."

"The sex?"

"The taboo breaking. The confrontation with everything I had been taught to become. Everything I had shrunk from in the US."

"But you said you did not feel bad about what we did."

"I didn't feel bad about what you felt bad about."

"It didn't seem right... even in a temple of love."

"As a matter of detail we were *outside* the temple. But you have your demons. I have mine. I could hardly have gone further off the straight and narrow by Solung standards... a deflowered princess, a runaway bride, a putative queen, making love in the open air to a casteless foreigner she had only just met."

"If that's Tantra, it's the flavour of the age. Everyone is going through it. It seems to me as if all our old values are being turned upside down, if only to see what is underneath."

"The ground has shifted, that's why. The Pill, the dole and education have changed the underpinnings of relationships utterly in the space of just a few years. Mainly in the West, but it is going to happen here. Women have control over when they get pregnant, they can get good jobs, and in places like Britain they can even get state aid to raise children on their own. They don't need men like they used to – not financially, anyway. Husbands are an optional extra, nice if you can get a good one."

"I wouldn't want to bring a child up on the dole."

"Tell that to a single mother out here. You wouldn't want to bring up a child *without* the dole, with no prospect of work, and everyone treating you like a slut. Mothers here are at the mercy of men willing to support them, and that was the case with most mothers everywhere just a few years back. People say that attitudes are changing and that we are rejecting the old ways. Actually life is changing, and we are just trying to catch up."

"It's not just in sexual matters. Look at you and Henry... you've been westernised and he's been easternised. The world is shrinking. Everyone's ideas are being thrown up into the air. Mine certainly have since I came here."

The princess went quiet for a few seconds. Then she said: "It doesn't mean you reject all the ideas you were born to. You might find a new respect for some of them. That's what the temple crystallised for me. Not at the time. It's been working on me. My opinions haven't changed on some things. I still don't believe my parents should have the right to force me to marry someone. And I certainly don't need an astrologer to tell me when I am ready to be queen."

"So what do you respect?"

"It sounds old fashioned but I think it is the idea of duty."

"Duty to do what?"

"Duty in marriage, for a start. Marriage is about much more than you and me here in bed. This is playtime. This is dalliance. Marriage is a formal acceptance of responsibility...

228

for your husband or wife, and most of all for any children you may have."

She hesitated, as if unsure how Tigger would take what she was about to say. Then she said it: "And in my case I feel I have a duty to my country."

Tigger thought of Dog Baba, with his aim always to have an eye on his dharma, his personal path of duty and right-eousness. Was that what she was getting at, her English losing the breadth of the Indian word? What was her idea of the dharma of a princess? He didn't ask because he didn't want to hear what she might say in reply.

It could not go on. Tigger knew that. They had cocooned themselves from the world and they couldn't bring themselves to break out. They knew in their hearts that the world would soon burst in and make the decision for them.

ooo

"Alexis the pilot is in Goa," said Henry. "I haven't seen him but he has been asking people if they have seen me. He's been staying a couple of beaches up from here."

"Shall we go and visit?" said the princess.

Henry shook his head. "He's gone off on business for a few days. I just hope he hasn't said anything about us. He knows how to keep his mouth shut but he'd be off his guard down here. If he heard I was here, he might let something slip."

"We've been keeping our heads down," said Tigger.

"Not enough, you can bet on that. The villagers don't miss much and neither do the hippies. This place is a gossip mill. I don't think you have been recognised yet, Sita, or we'd have heard. But if Alexis gave the slightest hint that you might be the so-called missing princess, you can bet that all Goa would know it as a certainty within a day."

"Perhaps it's time for me to get back to Solung," the princess said. "I've got to get my life back together and I've been worrying that I am putting you two in danger. If Da Silva learns that we are here he is more likely to come gunning for you than me."

"If the word had got out that you were here, this place would be crawling with press people and cameramen," Henry said.

Tigger smiled, despite his concern. Henry's flashes of media savvy, a relic of his time in an ad agency in London, still seemed incongruous in a man he had known only as a fugitive hippy hermit.

"The fact remains that I am putting you at risk," the princess said.

"We chose to come here," Henry said. "It was our choice. But I may as well tell you now. I'll be leaving soon. I have agreed to play a couple of songs at the full moon party in a couple of days. After that I'll go to Bombay and fly back to England. It's time I plugged back into the world again."

Tigger was surprised at how saddened he was at the news. He had got used to having Henry around. "What's brought this on?" he asked.

"Laxman, funnily enough. That night we were arguing with him... I kept wondering who I was to hold him to account. I didn't agree with him but at least he is engaging with the world, trying to do his bit. I love this place and I have learned a lot here but it's time I went home and got on with life."

"What are you going to do?" he asked.

"Who knows? Play music. Write. Maybe study. Get a job, even."

The princess ran forward impulsively and hugged him. "I am so glad Henry. I shall be sorry to see you go but you'd be wasting your life hanging out here. Do you think it is safe to stay? Don't you think we should go immediately?"

"We'll be OK for a couple of days. Even if word gets out that you are here we'll know soon enough to be able to get away before Da Silva can do anything about it."

Tigger did not argue. He did not want to think about leaving because he knew what it would mean. He did not want to part from the princess. But Sita was no longer avoiding the subject. Later that day over lunch she asked Henry: "Supposing I did get involved in Solung... do you think I could do any good? What do you think could be done with the place?"

"How should I know, Sita? I know little or nothing about the economy. You couldn't change the country overnight, that's for sure, and trying to get anything done would be a long and probably thankless task. Ultimately it would be for you and the Solungese to decide."

"You must have some ideas. It's good to get the view of an outsider who knows the place."

"I've been accused of having tunnel vision about population but you asked me for my opinion and that is what I'd focus on. Solung's social problems would be much more manageable if you could bring down the birth rate. If you pushed the issue in the right way I think you could get wide support."

"But birth control is not going to solve all the ills of Solung!"

"It is a good focus. Educated women raising children in a healthy environment don't have large families. That's a fact. So to address birth control properly you'd have to tackle all Solung's running sores: poor education, gross inequality, malnutrition, poor sanitation, and public health in general. As usual the biggest problem is not what to do, but getting people to do it. The awful thing is that Laxman was right about Da Silva. It is people like him who precipitate change."

17   The dream of a ridiculous man

Henry's imminent departure had brought them all closer together again. The next evening, as they sat on the beach, the princess asked him to sing the song he had played after they left the buffalo herders in the mountains. "I love that song. What is it called?" she asked after he had finished.

"The dream of a ridiculous man."

"Who is the ridiculous man... your guru?"

Henry laughed. "Not unless you call Dostoevsky a guru. It's the title of a story he wrote about a man who has a vision of a world in which people live in peace and harmony."

"He sounds like a hippy," Tigger said.

"A hippy with a heavy dose of Judeo-Christianity. It's a vision of the fabled time before Adam and Eve discovered sin and were expelled from Eden, when people loved each other like brothers and sisters. I don't know whether Dostoevsky believed such an age really existed."

"Do you?"

"It exists now. Where would the world be without love and lovers, and children, and mums and dads, and homes, and kindness, and beauty, and toleration? It's everything that holds us together – everything that makes life worth living."

This was the sort of talk that irritated Tigger. "That's not the real world," he said. "The real world has hate and greed and ugliness and oppression and conflict and everything that tears people apart and makes life hard."

"It still has love. Love is there all the time, buried by the quarrelling. People get so caught up in the world that they lose sight of what is most important in their lives. Dostoevsky's dreamer decides to spend his life reminding them, telling them about his vision. Of course, they think he is crazy."

232

"They're right," Tigger said. "All he is saying is that the world would be a better place if people were nice to each other."

"That doesn't make it untrue, or not worth considering. It's an also-true. However horrible the situation, however irreconcilable the argument, however terrible the conflict, it is always also true. The dreamer's world is always there as a possibility worth striving for. The ridiculous man believes people are capable of developing wisdom and he is always there to say so."

"What use is that when you are faced with someone utterly ruthless like Da Silva? Or, come to that, like Laxman, who sees a war as the only way to right the wrongs of the world?"

"I'm not a pacifist, Tigger. Sometimes you have to fight because you make things worse by not fighting. Confronting the likes of Da Silva, perhaps there is no option. Laxman is a harder call because he means well. He is a good man attracted by war. It excites him and gives a purpose to his life, and it reduces complex problems to a matter of death or glory. He thinks he is addressing Solung's problems; actually he is likely to make them worse."

The princess asked: "Did you say that to him?"

"Tigger and me both. We spent a whole night telling him. He insists that revolution is the only possible route to change. His main worry talking to us seemed to be that he might end up having to fight Tigger."

"Oh my God!" said the princess, burying her face in her hands. "You never told me that, Tigger."

"Because it is not going to happen. And platitudes wouldn't help, even if it did. They won't stop a bullet."

"Tigger, you are so cynical sometimes," the princess said. "What hope is there if no-one talks love and peace? It seems to me that Dostoevsky's dreamer is the only sane man in a mad world."

"And people think he is crazy! They ignore him."

"Crazy people can be very powerful, especially when they

are truthful and loving. I believe in the power of love. You have such a jaundiced view of people, Tigger. I still believe most people are fundamentally good, despite what we have been through in the past few weeks."

"Sita, your brother is fundamentally good. It doesn't stop him from making bad decisions."

Henry steered the conversation away from the painful subject of Laxman. "I have to say I agree with Tigger. There is no point trying to love-bomb people like Da Silva. They will simply exploit your naivety."

"There's a lot to be said for hell," Tigger said. "It must have terrified a lot of people into behaving themselves. I mean in the past when people believed – *really* believed – that sinners roasted in hellfire..."

"That's one idea we certainly won't be importing from the West," the princess said. "There's enough hell on earth without bringing the afterlife into it."

"You have the Law of Karma. Arguably, that's even worse an idea. It's pernicious," Henry said.

"But you're always going on about karma!" said Tigger.

"The word karma, not what's called the Law of Karma, as if it is a fact of life like gravity. The Law of Karma insists that wrongdoers will *always* get their comeuppance, in a future life if not this one. It pretends that life is fair."

"There's no justice in it, that's for sure," said the princess. "I have done nothing to deserve being born a princess."

"And nobody deserves to be born poor. Life is not fair and karma is a much meatier word if you accept the fact. It becomes a matter of luck and choice, like a game of cards. Your karma at any moment is the sum of the hands you have been dealt and the consequences of what you did with them. But according to the Law of Karma, luck does not come into it. If someone is born poor, they have only themselves to blame. They must have done something wrong in a past life. This is what makes the law pernicious. It's the lie underpinning the caste system."

234

"I am trapped in it. I can't un-princess myself."

"That's your karma. I wouldn't complain about it."

A pair of Goan pigs, famous for using toilets as feeding troughs, chose this point to emerge briefly from the palms fringing the beach. Henry laughed. "Look at those two. We live the life of Riley while they eat our shit. Nature has no justice. Nature has no right or wrong."

The princess gave a little shiver. "You make it all sound so bleak. It would be such a comfort to believe in a God who loves us and looks after us, and punishes the wicked, and lays down wise laws."

"God does lay down the law. We lay it down. We create our own justice. Our law is God's law. We are part of God."

"I don't think of God like that," the princess said. "Sometimes I get the feeling that God exists, but only as a separate, all powerful being."

"Because you think of God as a person. Most people do. It makes God easier to relate to. When you start thinking about what God might be, language breaks down. It can't even cope with science, so how can it encompass God?"

"You've lost me."

"How do you describe an electron? It is both mass and energy, thing and event, particle and wave, there and not there. Language relates to the world at a human scale. In the sub-atomic world there is nothing so simple as a 'thing'."

"I didn't do much science," the princess said.

"No matter. What do you mean by saying God is separate? The word relates to the physical world – this thing is separate from that, this person is separate from that. But God is neither a thing nor a person. God is something else, beyond language. You think of God as being separate yet the feeling is within you. God is both separate and not separate. You can't know what God is. All you know is what is going on inside your head, including your perceptions of the world and God. And that too is part of God. Everything and every nothing is a manifestation of God."

"You are imagining God," Tigger said.

"You are imagining yourself. You make yourself up as you go along. That is how you function. God is part of your imaginary landscape. God is part of you."

"We're hardly godlike," said the princess. "We get so many things wrong."

"We learn from our mistakes, generation after generation. Not perfectly, but these are hard lessons and we are still children. It seems clear to me that we are part of something much, much bigger than ourselves. We are tiny components of a process that has lasted billions of years. We are our universe becoming conscious of itself. We are the eyes of God."

Tiger turned his eyes up in mock exasperation. "You are ranting again, Henry."

Henry ignored him. "I feel it in my bones. Probably we are not the only intelligent life in the universe. Just possibly we are. Just possibly our joy is God's joy and our pain is God's pain. Just possibly, if we don't learn to live together and preserve life on this planet then we will not only be killing ourselves, we will be killing God."

He caught Tigger's eye and grinned. "OK... I'm ranting. But after what we've been through recently I feel like screaming from the rooftops. It hit me suddenly this morning, when I woke up and saw the beauty of the world, and thought how good it was to be alive. And then I thought of what happened to us in Calcutta. It seems so unreal now. That creep Da Silva was going to kill us and take all this away from us in the name of some piffling ideology..."

"You flatter him," said the princess. "He's not fighting for an ideology. He's in it for himself. He is fighting for power."

"So. Even worse. He is exploiting the ideology of his followers, and together they are trying to bully and manipulate everyone else – including their enemies, including me – into war. I feel like everyone who has ever been dragged into a conflict they don't want because other people have ideas they are willing to kill for. There's too much of it going on, and it's all so bloody petty in the great scheme of things." He picked up his guitar and sang:

> Did you ever get the feeling that life
> is a butterfly, a'flutter by?
> And this ever-bleeding trouble and strife
> goes on and on I don't know why.
> Such faith in hope they show
> who go expecting all their dreams.
> Such dice with death they throw
> just for some high-faluting scheme.
> I won't believe it till it's come.
> Ain't gonna miss it when I'm gone
>
> People pitting sitting shitting little only people
> who get up and run and have their say,
> setting up a learning earning yearning operation
> that goes on despite they fade away.
> I hear the breath of wind,
> I see the wave upon the sea.
> I watch the murmuring crowd go shuffling by,
> sometimes it seems
> a cavalcade, a shade, a low
> fashion parade, a passing show
>
> Ain't easy living, hard to decide
> the time to fight and the time to let lie
> when you're donkey for a carrot so wise
> it's moved on before you can finalise
> How grand the warriors stand
> behind the emblems on their shields
> How proud their guns speak loudly
> puking hate on martyr fields
> A way of death, a way of life
> A bloody-minded travail rife.

People pitting sitting shitting little only people
who get up and run and have their say,
setting up a learning earning yearning operation
that goes on despite they fade away.
I hear the breath of wind,
I see the wave upon the sea.
I watch the murmuring crowd go shuffling by,
sometimes it seems
a cavalcade, a shade, a low
fashion parade, a passing show.

ooo

"For a peace-and-love hippy you write an awful lot about war," observed Tigger when Henry finished singing.

"Hippy talk of peace is only another way of talking about war. How can anyone of our age ignore it, when our fathers and grandfathers were sent out to kill and die in wars? It could have happened to us, like the kids dying on both sides in Vietnam right now. The world wars never stopped. They fragmented into smaller wars, just as terrible for anyone involved, but for the rest of us they have become background noise, something to watch on TV. War has become normal, like bad weather that you hope won't come your way." [*]

"But what to do? You can't just abolish war."

"We could do a lot more to constrain it. We could stop feeding it with weapons, for a start."

"Easy to say. Harder to do."

"But not impossible. As usual the big problem is us. We don't have the will or the wisdom as a species to do it. There are no easy answers because military power shapes the human world and probably always will. But change is possible. The world can change and most importantly we can change. We can grow up. That is the dream of the ridiculous man."

---

[*] See Appendix 2.

18   A goodbye party

Full-moon parties had become a tradition among the foreign visitors in Goa. For most of them it was a novelty to find their lives affected by the moon, and to discover just how dark and light the world could get at night. The romance of the moon was lost to the modern world, her light outshone by electricity, her mysterious beauty outraged by lenses that revealed every intimate crevice. In Goa visitors could see as their ancestors had seen the inscrutable fiery objects that made day and night: the sun forceful and masculine; the moon comforting and feminine, revealing herself as coyly as a virgin each month until finally wondrously naked, in a glorious counterpoint to the cycle of human fertility. The full moon bathed the beaches in gentle light, opening them for the night.

It was a cheerful day, leading up to the party. Westerners lazed about in expectation of a long night; the Goans prepared food and drinks they would sell to the privileged foreigners. Even the pot flip-outs were infected with the sense of occasion, their usual manic solemnity breaking down amid the good humour around then. Henry spent much of the day away from the house jamming with one of the visiting bands. The princess for the first time mixed freely with the other visitors, unafraid of being recognised, in what Tigger took to be a signal that she too would soon move on.

The party was financed by a whip-round among the visitor aristocracy of film stars, pop stars and rich dealers. A stage was raised on the beach and generators hired to power an amplification system for bands who had brought their equipment over from Europe. By sunset, the party area was already surrounded by little food stalls. Alcoholic drinks were on sale at cafes, but the parties were not generally drunken occasions. There were other ways of getting high.

"I'm going to dance all night," said Henry, when he arrived back to prepare for the party. His one-time girlfriend, a blonde English girl called Sue, had reappeared.

"You've been booked to sing," she reminded him.

"Very late on. I've got a few hours yet," he said.

The mood could not have been more different from the previous day. Old friends and new acquaintances of Henry's dropped in, guitars and drums appeared, and the house rang with music. They were not yet on the beach and the party had already begun. Their mood changed shortly before sunset when a friend of Sue's, who had been staring at the princess, approached her and said: "Excuse me, but I have to ask. You're not that princess who is in the papers?"

Tigger, who was standing next to the princess, tried to cloak his shock in sarcasm. "She's the Queen of Sheba, actually. I didn't know the papers knew she was here."

"Sheba? Where is Sheba? I think the papers said she was Indian," the girl said. Then, turning to the princess: "You're not really a queen, are you?"

The princess smiled. "Tigger was joking. No, I'm not a queen and I am not Indian, I'm afraid. Nothing so exciting. Why did you think I might be a princess? Do I look like her? I only ask because someone else asked me the same question. Has this just been in the papers?"

"I don't know about the Indian papers. I saw it in an English paper carried by someone who had just flown in. There was a headline saying 'Kidnap princess seen in Goa', and I asked to read it. It was just a snippet about that princess who went missing after being kidnapped. It said she'd been seen hanging out here with hippies. There was no picture. It was probably bullshit. They make these things up, the papers."

"Why did you think I was her?"

"You look Indian. It's not often you see an Indian wom-

240

an hanging out with Westerners in Goa."

"Well, I'm sorry to disappoint you," the princess said, smiling.

"I've always wanted to meet a princess."

"She's a princess to me," said Tigger, putting his arm round her. He wondered if it was the girl or the paper that had got her nationality wrong.

"Cool," said the girl vaguely, and wandered off.

It was some minutes before Henry could be prised away from his friends to be told about the news report. He didn't think it was Da Silva's work. "He would have arranged pictures. My guess is that Alexis opened his mouth in a bar somewhere. There are a lot of press people out here. Alexis wouldn't know he'd be putting us in danger."

"That's the question – are we in danger?"

"We have to assume that Da Silva will pick up the story. That leaves the question of whether we matter enough for him to chase us to the ends of the earth."

"Or whether it is politic for him to chase us," said Tigger. "He may not want to push Laxman too far."

The princess said: "I don't want to put you two in danger for a moment longer. I think we should leave now."

"I'm leaving tomorrow anyway. This is a goodbye party so far as I am concerned and I don't intend to miss it."

"I can't see any problem with staying here tonight," Tigger said. It may be full moon but the light won't be good enough for anyone to find us in the crowd. We can make our decision in the morning."

"We go in the morning, then," the princess said.

ooo

They had no need to look for the party when they finally left the house. The music drew them on. They passed through a perimeter of stalls, through an inner circle of people crouching in groups sitting round camp fires, and on to the dance area around the band. The gentle breeze could not dispel the pervasive odour of charas, and there was the electric at-

mosphere that comes with the mixture of a crowd and psychedelics. The colours of the day had turned to silver and
grey and people no more than a few yards away were reduced to silhouettes.

The night passed quickly, though Tigger did little but sit
talking and listening to the music, getting up occasionally to
dance. He had a feeling that a season in his life was coming
to a close but he tried not think about it. The thought of the
princess's future was too painful to dwell on.

Henry, wearing only a *lungi* and a loose, open shirt,
mounted the stage just before dawn and sang a couple of the
songs that had become familiar over the past weeks. As the
sun peeped over the trees lining the beach he sang one that
was new to Tigger:

We were born when the fire of a gazillion suns burst
And the stuff of uncounted worlds like ours dispersed
Energy takes substance, substance takes form
Tell me brother where are you in the primordial storm?
Wind blow
River flow
Synergy
Ecstasy
Now is eternity

We grew up in the ocean, we crawled on to land.
And we saw and we felt and we tried to understand
Living is the atom, dying is the cell
Tell me sister where are you in the primordial hell?
Wind blow
River flow
Synergy
Ecstasy
Now is eternity

The present... the only moment that is forever. Was sanity

there, free of the past, poised for the future? Here by the womb of the ocean, Tigger saw his friend's vision of the enormity of God manifest: the sea turning pink as the world turned from night to day; fishermen walking along the edge of breakers with their nets to begin their work; and on a cliff far above them, a girl dancing wildly, silhouetted against the dawn sky as the band played on. Henry was still singing:

We tamed nature with our poison,
we killed men with our care.
We saw death in our victory,
we filled Eden with despair.
Beyond sense is the object,
beyond thought is the seen.
Tell me brother where are you in the primordial dream?
Wind blow
River flow
Synergy
Ecstasy
Now is eternity

The sun was higher now, a golden orb above the palm trees. God's light shining on wayward humans, people who could both love beauty and desecrate it with their cruelty and foolish greed. God's light shone because it had to, and all tears were God's tears, and all joy was God's joy.

"You're crying," said the princess. Tigger saw the love in her eyes, but he knew that he was losing her. "This is sanity," she had said in the mountains as she embraced them. If sanity was love, what was loss of love? Was that the source of the world's madness?

"How will you feel, marrying a man you do not love?"

"I shall marry a man I *can* love, if he still wants me. Raju is a good man. All good men are lovable," she said.

They did not hear the shot. It was lost in the music and the wind and the sighing of the ocean. They heard screaming

from people close to the stage and saw Henry collapse to the
ground.

Part Three
Showdown in Solung

1   Death and recall

For the first time Tigger saw why the king had been so insistent that the princess was the best choice for his son. There had been a glimpse in the speed and efficiency with which she had meted out thanks and rewards after escaping the mountains. Now she became a bundle of energy. She ordered an ambulance to take a badly injured Henry to a private clinic in Panjim, arranged for a specialist to fly down from Bombay, contacted the British and Solung authorities to put them in the picture, and even rang Henry's sister in Dorking. To head off awkward questions from the press, she booked separate rooms for herself and Tigger at a hotel in Panjim. Reporters and TV crews arrived with suspicious alacrity and had clearly been tipped off about a link between the shooting and the missing princess. Tired of running away, she held a press conference in the hotel lobby where she fielded questions with grace and discretion. Fortunately, reporters had already questioned Henry's friend Sue, who had described herself as his girlfriend, which put paid to any suggestion of a scandalous relationship between the princess and the shot man. The princess described Henry as an old friend who had arranged security for her while she was recovering from her kidnap ordeal. She could see no reason why this should get him shot. Her evident distress over the shooting softened the questioning and she gave reporters enough of a story to satisfy their editors, at least for that day.

Henry had been hit in the lung but was lucky to get first aid from a former US army medic who had experience of dealing with gunshot wounds in Vietnam. He was also lucky in that the gunman had used a low-calibre rifle more suited to target shooting than assassination; and the bullet had missed his shirt and hit bare flesh, leaving a clean wound. But his survival was by no means guaranteed – and nor was Tigger's, with the gunman on the loose. His one consolation was that the amateurish assassination betrayed the limits of Da Silva's capabilities.

Sick with anger and shock over the shooting, he tried to call Dougal to update him but the line to Solung had gone down; instead he sent a telegram with the hotel phone number and a message to call. The initial police investigation was desultory but it gathered pace with arrival of the press. Tigger had to make a lengthy statement describing the background to the shooting, including the story of their capture and escape in Calcutta. The policeman who laboriously transcribed his statement did not ask why they had not reported their abduction at the time it happened. So as not to incriminate Laxman, Tigger explained their escape vaguely as the result of a dispute between People's Army factions. Both he and the policeman knew that they were going through a necessary formality and that there was no chance of the gunman being caught. Whoever pulled the trigger, there was little doubt who had ordered the shooting.

Tigger, alone for the first time in days, slept little that night and returned to Chapora early the next day to pick up Henry's things – minus his guitar, which some opportunist had stolen on the beach after the murder. He called in at the clinic, where Henry lay unconscious awaiting an operation, then returned to the hotel to see the princess's lovely face splashed over the freshly delivered London papers. There was also a terse message from Dougal: "Call immediately."

Remarkably he got a call through straight away from his hotel room. Dougal sounded stressed. "Tigger, I need you back now."

"Haven't you heard? Henry's been shot."

"He's not the only casualty. Gosh was killed yesterday."

"Jesus!" Tigger went silent for a few seconds, struggling to think of an appropriate response. Then he said: "I'm sorry Dougal. How did it happen?"

"I'll tell you when you get here. There's been a series of tit-for-tat killings. You had better watch out."

"You don't need to tell me that. I was only a few yards from Henry when he was shot."

"How's he doing?"

"He's alive. That's about all I know at the moment. I don't like to leave him."

"Tigger, you are needed here."

"It could take me a couple of days to get to Solung – even assuming I can get flights."

"We've sorted that out. You're booked on a flight leaving from Bombay at 7pm tomorrow. We couldn't find a connecting flight from Goa, so you may have to take a taxi through the night. But be on that 7pm flight."

There was another shock when Tigger went to the princess's room to break the news. "There's been a series of killings in Solung," she said before he had a chance to speak.

"I know. Gosh is dead."

"So is Sanjeev!"

"Sanjeev! Why would Da Silva kill him?"

"He didn't. It was the nationalists."

"But Sanjeev was a nationalist."

"A Hindu nationalist. He wanted Solung to be part of a Hindu India. Solung nationalists want to stay independent."

"I remember now. Sanjeev wanted India to take the Solung over, or Laxman to take over India – or both, so far as I could figure out. Even Laxman thought he was crazy."

"I am sorry about your friend Gosh."

"I'm sorrier about Henry. Gosh was a soldier. It was his job to die and he knew it. He'd killed a lot of men in his time. Strictly in the line of duty, of course, but it didn't bother him. He wasn't the most sensitive of men."

"You didn't like him?"

"He was a good man to have on your side. Dougal and he were close but they'd been through a lot together. Dougal sounded quite upset. How did you find out about Sanjeev?"

The princess looked uncomfortable. "Raju told me. I rang him this morning."

She had contacted the prince! Tigger knew this would happen at some point but it was still absurdly hurtful. He said with affected nonchalance: "Did you agree anything?"

"I told him that I can't leave here until Henry's condition is more stable. Sue, Henry's girlfriend, has to go back to London. I'll get him up to Calcutta as soon as I can. He can be treated under guard at the hospital in Calcutta that my family uses. Raju says he will meet me in Calcutta."

By tacit consent they switched subjects. There was a lot of news from Solung. Word had got out that Laxman had thrown his lot in with the rebels, and somehow he had got fuel enough to fly Sanjeev's aircraft to a newly cleared airstrip below the village where the princess had been held, which had been reoccupied in force by the People's Army. The Solung nationalists saw this as evidence of Sanjeev's complicity with the rebels. He was assassinated, then Gosh was killed, followed by two RMP stalwarts and a couple of Solung nationalist MPs. The king had declared a state of emergency, imposed a curfew on Satpur, and outlawed the RMP, many members of which had been arrested. A considerable cache of arms had been seized. Parliament was suspended and the king was running the country with the aid of a council of trusted MPs. Indian troops had been placed on standby on the Solung border, ostensibly to prevent trouble spilling over.

"Jesus Christ... what have I got myself into?" Tigger said.

Just hours ago, he reflected ruefully, he had been sitting blissfully on a beach.

ooo

The princess double-checked flights to Bombay while he

packed and managed to get him one for that evening, thanks to a cancellation; this meant he had to leave the hotel almost immediately. He persuaded her not to see him off at the airport to avoid the press, though his biggest fear was of losing his composure in front of the cameras when parting from her. As he picked up his bags to go, she said: "I'm so sorry, Tigger. I wish..."

He interrupted her. "We both wish Henry was safe and well. I'm not sorry about anything else. No regrets, no recriminations... remember?"

"Promise me you won't let Dougal push you into getting involved in any fighting."

"If Henry doesn't pull through, I'd happily wring Da Silva's neck. Apart from that I promise you that the last thing I want to do is get involved in any more bloodshed."

"There is just too much to say."

"Then don't try. Perhaps I'll see you in Solung."

She flung her arms round him, her tears wetting his neck. "Princess, I have to go," he said, pushing her gently away.

He was out of the door before she could protest and sneaked out of the back of the hotel to avoid the press. He could not sleep on the flight to Bombay and there was no rest even when he arrived. An agent of the ISB, the Indian Security Bureau, led him to a side room and questioned him aggressively about why he was "fleeing" from Goa.

Tigger faced the questioning with weary resignation but as it dragged on he feared that he might miss his flight, or even that he might be detained indefinitely. But after a couple of hours he was told he was free to go. The agent shook his hand as he left and said: "Sorry about the grilling. I had to do it. Pay my respects to Squadron Leader FitzDougal. He was a hero of mine when I was a boy. From what I hear, he could do with some help now."

Even in India, Dougal was famous.

2 A row with Dougal

Lovelorn and sick of death and danger, Tigger did not want to be in Solung. The army jeep with two armed guards that met him at the airport was welcome for the security it promised, but it was a reminder of the fact that he could no longer wander freely around the country. He did not belong here and yet here he was risking his life for... for what? He did not believe in the promises of the People's Army or the chancy strategy of Laxman, but neither could he put much faith in the ramshackle medieval regime they were trying to bring down. The place was a mess, and he had no idea what should be done with it, and it was not his business anyway. Solung was for the Solungese to sort out. On top of that it was cold and raining.

Dougal, waiting on the veranda of his official bungalow, greeted him with rare warmth. "Good to see you, Tigger."

"Sorry to hear about Gosh."

The truth was that he felt sorry for Dougal, who looked older and more stressed than Tigger had ever seen him.

"He was a fool and a bore at times but he was a good friend and I'll miss him," Dougal said.

His voice was shaking.

Look after him, Charlie had said. Tigger had done little about that, hardly giving Dougal a thought when he and the princess went missing in the mountains, probably dead amid who-knew-what horrors, and it must have seemed that the mission had been a complete disaster. But you couldn't pile on the commiseration with a man like Dougal. Tigger said lamely: "How did it happen?"

"He was found dead in a street. Stab wounds. The body

of a Solungese man with a broken neck was found nearby."

Gosh had been proud of his prowess at unarmed combat.

"People's Army, I suppose," Tigger said.

"We're not clear about that. Gosh may have been throwing his weight about. You know what he was like. It's been edgy in town for a while, so we hadn't been going there much. Just a few agitators causing trouble, but enough to create an atmosphere. And we've become quite a focus for PA propaganda. Foreign mercenaries interfering in Solung affairs – that sort of thing. Even so, most people are friendly. Gosh was going crazy kicking his heels at the airfield and took off into Satpur for the evening. I guess he had a couple of drinks. According to the police, a crowd laid into him after he thumped some guy who called him a CIA poodle. The PA claimed responsibility but it may have been just a street fight. We simply don't know."

The tremor had gone from Dougal's voice. It was back to business.

"I haven't seen anything in the papers about the killing," Tigger said.

"It's been kept quiet. You know about Sanjeev? He was the first to go."

"The princess told me."

"His death has been all over the papers here. Seems he was quite a character. A lot of people revered him for fighting us during the war but clearly he had enemies too."

"He was certainly a character – a little crazy from what he went through in the war, according to Laxman. It can't have been an easy time for him. He was an interesting man but I can't say I took to him. I certainly didn't like his politics."

This was the first opportunity Tigger had had to discuss with Dougal in full the conversations he had had with Laxman and Sanjeev. He felt uncomfortable about giving all the details, as if he were sneaking on a friend, but with lives at stake this was no time to indulge schoolboy qualms.

In turn, Dougal filled him in on what had been happening in Solung. Tigger had set off a chain of events with his report on what Bikash had said about an arms cache. Officials were sent to placate the dacoit's village and chase up the lead. They discovered that a large cache of arms, donated by a maverick oil power, had been hidden in the valleys in the area where the princess had been held. Truckloads had been driven to the foothills and taken up into the mountains by donkey trains. The area was supposed to have been surrounded by government troops but there were too many paths to cover – and, Dougal suspected, too many people who could be bribed to turn a blind eye.

Only a tiny part of the cache had been found before the onset of winter made operations almost impossible in the area. "Personally I think the army pulled back too far. They control the main valley but the guerrillas are back in the mountainsides," Dougal said.

"What about the MEs? Why can't they be impounded?"

"Because the army would have to fight its way in. Anyway Laxman has done nothing wrong overtly to justify an action like that, and he stopped flying after his fuel supply was blocked. The king didn't want to outlaw him because it would make reconciliation more difficult. No-one noticed that the People's Army had adapted a stretch of road for use as an airstrip, down valley from where the princess was held. The work was disguised as a logging operation. A few days ago Laxman and his friends suddenly upped and flew the MEs there. He must have had a stash of fuel."

"You have to hand it to Da Silva. He doesn't hang about."

"He used machinery stolen from the logging companies and the work was done by people who knew what they were doing. He's getting professional advice from somewhere. Probably the Chinese. The MEs are well protected in enclosures cut into the mountain, and reinforced by logs. They would be very hard to hit without a guided missile."

"Have you seen the MEs?"

"We took off when Laxman did his little flit but he had landed before we got half way to the mountains. After that we haven't gone near them. Our task is done if they stay on the ground, and frankly we have not been ready to take them on in the air. Actually, I don't see why the People's Army bothers with the MEs. They are more of a liability than an asset to a guerrilla army because of the problems of guarding, fuelling and maintaining them on the ground."

"It makes perfect sense to me, now I know Da Silva better," said Tigger. "He is a marketing man selling a revolution – and, I suspect, himself – to an international audience. He told me once: 'Revolution is show business. It feeds on propaganda. Propaganda is show business.' I remember his words precisely because they explained so much. Look at the way he orchestrated coverage of the princess's kidnap. Now he is staging a replay of one of the most famous air battles in history. Spitfires versus Messerschmitts starring the celebrated Squadron-Leader FitzDougal. The press and TV people will love it."

"A bloody flying circus, in other words," said Dougal bitterly. "TV crews have already been nosing around the valleys and they've been pestering me for interviews. I refuse to talk to them. Do you think Laxman knows what Da Silva plans?"

"I am sure he has a good idea. He kept hinting that we might end up in a fight, like it was a fixture in a football league. He's idealistic and thoughtful but at some level I think it is a game to him."

"Sounds like a description of you when you tried to talk me into taking this job."

"Fool that I was."

"The king seems to think Laxman is the key to averting a war. You may understand more about that than I do."

"He does seem to be semi-detached from the People's Army. Da Silva manipulated him into accepting military training for his youth cadres but they remain separate under Laxman's command. I guess the king hopes the princess will

255

be able to persuade her brother against war. That is probably one reason why he wants her to marry Raju. It would give Laxman the prospect of power and influence through his sister. It's medieval – power broking by marriage."

"I thought he wanted you and her to get hitched in the hope that Laxman would baulk at fighting his own brother-in-law. He seemed mighty keen to keep you down in India with her, paying you to take a holiday in the sun while Gosh and me slogged away up here."

This pleasing possibility had not occurred to Tigger. "I only wish that were true. The king is a subtle man and he knew perfectly well what he was doing when he sent me to her. He may have been backing both horses but I think he had a pretty shrewd idea which one would win."

Dougal gave him a long hard look. "Whatever has been happening with her, I hope you've sorted it out..."

"Lay off, Dougal... there is no problem with the princess. With Laxman, yes. That stuff about persuading him against war is wishful thinking. He's gone too far to pull out."

"Then it looks like we are in for a battle."

Tigger shook his head. "Do we have to do this, Dougal? We contracted to rescue the princess. She is free. We contracted to train up some pilots; you have been training them. It's their fight, surely."

Tigger could see Dougal did not like this line of questioning but he answered reasonably enough. "We are contracted to provide air cover until the pilots are trained. They've only just started at flying school in India and have no more than a few hours flying between them. Not one of them has flown a Spit. Except Ganesh. He is good. He's been flying a lot."

"So with Gosh gone that makes three of us. Laxman's got four planes and four pilots."

"We took on far worse odds many times in the war. And Laxman has no radar. He's flying blind."

"I'm flying blind at the moment, Dougal. What about my contract? I never signed up to fight a war."

Dougal's face clouded. "Are you in this or not?"

"If I'm going to put my life on the line, I want to get the position straight. Rescuing the princess was a jaunt. This looks more like war against a people I have nothing particular against. Laxman saved my life, remember."

"Ganesh saved your life, too. If it weren't for him you would be sun-dried meat."

"But fighting, possibly killing, someone who saved me... I can't do it."

Dougal thumped the table in exasperation. "Tigger, it was you who wanted to come out here. You were perfectly aware that we could get involved in something like this. It's a bit late for you to start having cold feet."

"I haven't got cold feet."

"Then what's all this croaking about contracts? "

Dougal seemed a lifetime away, like an ageing father estranged by a changing world.

"Perhaps I've grown up a little."

"You've been a sight too close to that hippy friend of yours... all peace and love at a safe distance from the battle."

"He risked his life helping me get out of the mountains."

"He grabbed his chance of getting in with the king."

"That's not fair, Dougal."

"Then what's all this about? Do you want the guerrillas to win?"

"I can't get enthusiastic about the government either. Not enough to risk my neck for it. And I am not sure that it is necessary for us to fight. Surely we can put that airstrip out of action in some way."

"It's not that easy. An airstrip can easily be patched up, when you have bulldozers. And without doubt bombing it would entail killing innocent villagers. We'd bring down half the mountainside. It's cleaner if we tackle the MEs in the air. That's what we're being paid for."

"I can't understand why you agreed to provide air cover. We'd done what we'd come to do. We could have got out."

"We had to stay on here under the old contract. We'd agreed to provide training."

"Training, but not combat. You didn't have to take this on. The war has been over for a quarter of a century and you are still finding battles to fight. Don't you ever ask yourself why? You must like it!"

"Tigger, you don't know what you are talking about. You can't have the slightest idea of what it is like to fight a war. I wouldn't wish it on my worst enemy."

"I can't think of any other reason why you'd let yourself in for this. Unless it was a chance to get back to the glory days. Spitfires bashing Messerschmitts. Dougal flies again."

For a moment, Dougal was speechless. "You impertinent little whelp! If this were a proper military unit, I'd have you put on a charge for speaking to me like that. I've given my word to help out here, and I'm not going back on it. Those skunks of terrorists killed Babu, remember. They probably killed Gosh. They shot your hippy friend. Do you want to let them get away with that?

"Laxman would never have harmed Henry or Babu, and it's Laxman I would be fighting. Since I came to Solung I've seen more than a dozen people killed, directly or indirectly because of my actions. I'm sick of it."

"No more than I am. But when I start something, I see it through."

The anger had gone out of Dougal's voice; he looked hurt and fed up. It was hopeless. Tigger knew that he could not back out. He had already let Charlie down, letting his mouth run away with him. He couldn't let Dougal down too.

"I'm sorry, Dougal. The truth is I am mad at myself. You are right. I've only myself to blame. I wanted to come. I was like a schoolkid looking for adventure. Now I don't want to fight, but I don't want *not* to fight..."

"Well, if you want to back out..."

"I'd better put some flying in," Tigger said, feeling sick to his soul.

3   The princess makes an offer

The Spitfire, which had once seemed so romantic to Tigger, now looked vicious, standing on the tarmac with its twin cannon and four machine guns checked and oiled for action. The boy in him still saw it as a beautiful machine; the reluctant warrior saw its ugly purpose as a flying gun platform, and the Battle of Britain that made it famous as just a local episode in a grubby global struggle between different styles of tyranny. The Western Allies had claimed the moral high ground but Britain retained its preposterous empire and the US had its black underclass and unacknowledged imperialism. And what of the German boys who had flown their Messerschmitts against Britain? Were they to blame for what they did, or was it the society that moulded them? They had been indoctrinated from boyhood more comprehensively than Biggles books could ever mould the likes of Tigger. Did all societies hone their boys for war? Were boys born to fight? Was that why he was preparing for battle?

Tigger's doubts could not suppress the thrill he felt as he approached the Spitfire that had been assigned to him. He checked it automatically for faults, worried that Babu's death might have led to poor maintenance. But Dougal had not been idle in the past few weeks: wartime comrades of Babu's had been conscripted and with Ganesh's help they had been able to train up ground crews. Each man had been given responsibility for a small section of the machine, so that even though crews were larger than normal, they were more efficient than could have been hoped for in the time. "The new radios are the same as the ones fitted into Laxman's Messerschmitts," said Ganesh, as he watched Tigger get into the

259

cockpit. "Sanjeev got them in a job lot and sold four to the king before all this trouble blew up. We can hear Laxman's people talking if we switch to their channels."

"That means they can hear us too."

"I think Dougal is doing something about that."

Ganesh had rarely been parted from the Spitfires while Tigger was away. When he was not flying, he was working on them, and when he was not working on them he slept next to them. Tigger remembered his courage and intelligence and he was glad they were on the same side.

"The Spit's looking good, Ganesh. Thanks for looking after her."

"Good to see you back, Tigger. We need you."

Again Tigger regretted his clash with Dougal. He knew that he could never have left Ganesh and Dougal to fight the Messerschmitts, two against four.

The tiny cockpit of the Spitfire felt claustrophobic, with an oppressive smell of glycol coolant and high-octane petrol. The high, long nose made direct forward vision impossible until the tail lifted up on take off, and to reach the runway he had to tack from side to side so that he could see where he was going. Once in the air, he calmed with the exhilaration of flying, and there was a binary simplicity about the firing button on the control column: you either fired or you didn't. If he had to fight there would be no time or room for doubts.

The control tower at Satpur airport had been alerted to warn him of any strange aircraft but he made a point of trying to get into the habit of scanning the skies visually because it could make the difference between life and death. He did not want to invite trouble so he headed away from the mountains, with their hidden MEs, and put the Spitfire through some aerobatics, relieved to find that his skills seemed little affected by his lack of practice. Spectacular manoeuvres would be of little use in battle but they gave him confidence.

Back on the ground Tigger persuaded Ganesh to join him for a meal at one of Satpur's better restaurants. The lad still looked young enough to be at school, but he was a celebrity in the city after his part in the princess's rescue. Tigger was aware that people's eyes followed them as they were ushered to the best seat in the restaurant.

Ganesh listened in silence as Tigger told him how upset Laxman had been over Babu's murder; he also relayed Laxman's explanation of why he had allowed Ganesh to be frozen out of Sanjeev's flying club.

"I knew there was a reason and I knew he would not have killed daddy. Laxman was my friend," Ganesh said. "But I find it hard to forgive him for staying in league with that bastard Da Silva."

"How do you feel about fighting him?"

"His parents were a second mother and father to me. How could I feel good about robbing them of a son? Laxman is doing what he thinks is right. I am doing what I think is right. If that means we have to fight, then so be it."

"Are you sure?"

Ganesh shrugged. "If we had killed Da Silva when we had the chance, your friend Henry might be dining with us now without a wound in his chest. There is no knowing what will happen if we don't stop these people now."

ooo

Dougal had called Tigger back from Goa because he feared the killing of Gosh might signal an imminent air attack; but days passed without incident. The king decided to let the rebels stew in their valleys for a few days and they showed no inclination to break out. The Messerschmitts stayed grounded and Dougal guessed that Laxman was finding it difficult to get aviation fuel through the army blockade. But it was a nerve-racking time: the Spitfires had to be either in the air or ready for take off at all times, and their pilots had to remain nearby in case of an attack. Laxman's airstrip was hidden from radar by the mountains but army observers could spot any aircraft taking off within seconds and the Messerschmitts would take upwards of half an hour to reach Satpur, tracked by radar most of the way. So they were unlikely to be taken by surprise.

Henry was making rapid progress thanks to the immediate medical attention he had received, doubtless assisted by the fact that he could no longer smoke his lung-busting bedis; and as promised, the princess had flown him to a private hospital in Calcutta. From there she reported regularly on his condition in notes that to Tigger's eyes were hurtfully free of endearments, an omission for which she apologised obliquely with a cryptic reference to the need for security. Considering that her love life was a matter of state concern, it was not impossible that their correspondence would be intercepted.

Then, out of the blue, she rang him at the airfield. "Tigger, I can't say much on an open line but that matter we talked about... I've made my decision. I'm going ahead with it."

"You mean I should congratulate you?"

"It's not certain. We have to get approval... but yes."

Tigger, feeling like his heart had hit his boots, was shocked into silence. In his mind he had given the princess up long ago, but he still ached for her.

"Are you upset?" she asked.

He avoided the question. "It's stressful here. We're on standby all the time, in case of an attack."

"Tigger, you said you wouldn't get involved."

"I couldn't leave Ganesh and Dougal to take... that lot ... on alone."

He could hardly credit what he was saying. Here he was talking to his former lover about fighting to the death with her brother.

"I hope to God it won't be necessary. That's the other thing I rang you about, Tigger. I need to ask you a big favour. I want you to fly to Calcutta tomorrow."

"Sita, I'm on standby. Laxman could attack at any minute."

262

"Tigger, trust me. Come here tomorrow. Please."

"But Dougal...."

"The king will sort Dougal out."

"Well if Dougal gives the OK..."

"He will. You're booked on the midday flight. You'll be met at the airport by someone showing a British High Commission identity."

"Right."

"And listen... everything I have told you – *everything* – is an absolute secret."

"Right."

"And Tigger... I'm looking forward to seeing you."

"Right."

Reduced to monosyllables, because he could not trust himself to say more, he put the phone down.

ooo

Tigger assumed vaguely that the princess's friend Betty from the High Commission, whom he had never met, would be waiting for him at the airport. But he was greeted by a military-looking man with a pronounced London accent, who bundled him into one of the ubiquitous Ambassador taxis and chatted away as if he was a travel agent introducing the city to a new client. Tigger realised for the first time that the High Commission's interest in the princess's affairs extended beyond the personal; someone there was keeping a close eye on what was happening in Solung. It occurred to Tigger that this was probably why Dougal agreed to extend his contract to provide air cover in Solung: the British government must have asked him to. Tigger felt a stab of resentment that Dougal hadn't told him, then chided himself for jumping to conclusions. He resolved to say nothing on the subject unless Dougal volunteered information. This was no time to get into another argument.

The taxi stopped at a large hotel in the city centre, where the stranger led him past the reception desk and through to the back of the building where a car with a European driver was waiting. "Sorry about all this malarkey," the stranger whispered as he motioned Tigger to take a seat. "We can't be too careful. I am going to slip off now. There's someone here who will take you the rest of the way."

A figure slipped out of the shadows and got into the car beside Tigger. It was the princess. She kissed him briefly on the cheek and whispered: "Thanks for coming."

"Where are we going?"

The driver obviously knew because he drove off without a word. "It's not far," said the princess.

For a full minute they sat in silence as the car negotiated the heaving Calcutta streets. The princess looked as beautiful as ever, her face half hidden by a headscarf, caught in the flickering light from the paraffin lamps of the shops and street stalls, Tigger saw her eyes well up with tears, and her hand slipped into his and gave a gentle squeeze as the car pulled into the drive of a dilapidated hotel with shuttered windows that looked as if they had not been painted since the days of the Raj. She took out a mirror and dabbed at her eyes to clear them and led Tigger into the hotel and through to a lounge where she ordered tea.

"Can you please tell me what this is all about?" he asked.

"We're going to see Laxman."

"Laxman?"

"He's here. Or he should be by now. But I want to talk to you first."

"About Prince Raju?"

"Partly, yes. I couldn't say much on the phone."

"It didn't take you long to sort things out with him."

"Raju's been in Calcutta for a few days. He's been very sweet – like his father, but without the buffoonery. We've been very open with each other. He's had his girls and he knows I've had boyfriends."

"You told him about us?"

"We haven't been *that* open. He doesn't want to know. It's best that way. I'd like you to be friends with him when this has all blown over. I'd like *us* to be friends."

Tigger did not want to think about her and Raju. "That's not what you brought me here to tell me," he said.

"It's one reason. I've missed you and I've been very worried about you. And I couldn't tell you about Raju properly on the phone."

They stopped talking as a waiter came over with a tray of teas. "So what about Laxman?" asked Tigger when he was out of earshot.

"I contacted him because I wanted to talk to him, to try to persuade him to do a deal to avoid a civil war. But he was under siege in the mountains and it was risky for him to get out. It's risky for him here too because the Indian intelligence services are looking for him. He said he didn't want to run the gauntlet of all that just to get another lecture from me."

"He must realise that if you become queen he could push through reforms far more effectively than by starting a war."

"Tigger, you mustn't say a word about me becoming queen. So far as I know you and Henry are the only people the king has said anything to about abdication. It might have been a whim of the moment for him. And remember he told you to tell no-one but me. I've never mentioned the possibility to Raju and I am perfectly sure the idea has never entered his head."

"But even as Prince Raju's wife..."

"Laxman doesn't know about Raju yet and obviously I am hoping that it might sway him. I can't make him any promises but I know Raju wants to see reforms in Solung too. Of course I couldn't say that in a letter. Our engagement has not been announced yet."

"A letter? You've been writing to Laxman?"

"Crazy isn't it? Life goes on even in revolutions. I managed to get one call to him when he dropped in on our parents. But after that it was letters. The postal service is still working in the valley."

"You still haven't explained what I am supposed to be doing here."

"I haven't explained because I don't know. Laxman finally agreed to meet me, but only on condition that you were here too. I was worried that it was a trap to get you killed."

"Laxman wouldn't use you to kill me, surely?"

"Someone forging his letters might. Betty's friend George at the High Commission, the man who met you at the airport, was very helpful and got the handwriting checked out and it seems genuine. He suggested that I choose this place to meet because it is run by the aunt of my old *ayah* – my nursemaid – and I could refer to it in a way that only Laxman would understand."

"I think there is more to George than meets the eye."

"I'm sure of it. He has people staking out all the rooms here but one. That's the one we're going to now. Laxman is waiting for us there."

ooo

It may have been a trick of the light but Laxman looked older than he had seemed only a few weeks before. He jumped up nervously when they entered the room but greeted them warmly, kissing his sister on the cheek and shaking Tigger's hand.

"It's good to see you, Tigger."

"Glad to see you too. I wish it could have been in better circumstances."

"I am sorry about Henry. How is he?"

The princess broke in.

"Tigger hasn't had a chance to visit him yet. He's as well as can be expected for someone who has been shot in the chest."

"He is not going to die?"

"He's walking around already, but no thanks to your friend Da Silva. He was very lucky. An American doctor who was on the beach knew about gunshot wounds and did all the right things."

266

"That shooting was none of my doing, you know that. I warned him that it would be dangerous to stay in India."

"Is that why you asked me to be here, to tell me that?" Tigger asked.

"I asked you here because I am here, which means I can't fly in Solung. If you are here you are not in Solung and can't fly, which evens things up. Also I trusted you not to lead me into a trap."

"Do you mean to say that you don't you trust me ... you don't trust your own sister?" the princess asked angrily.

"Sita, your letters could have been forged. I'm running a big risk being here. The intelligence people in India want to question me, and Da Silva is breathing down my neck. He doesn't know I'm seeing you but he suspects that I want to do some kind of a deal."

"Do you?" Tigger asked.

"I wish I could persuade you to stay out of Solung. This is not your fight. You and Henry should have gone back to England."

"I couldn't leave Dougal and Ganesh to fight alone."

"That's the other thing I wanted to say. I want Ganesh left out of this. He is too young."

"He was man enough to get me and the princess out of the clutches of Da Silva."

"His family has suffered enough. I don't want him involved."

"He is a member of the Solung armed forces. He is under orders. I have no control over him."

"You could nobble his aircraft. I could make sure one of my aircraft was grounded in return."

"This isn't a game, Laxman," Tigger said in exasperation.

The princess was seething. "Laxman, the best way you can protect Ganesh is by stopping this unnecessary war. You are not just putting Ganesh's life in danger, you will be risking hundreds and even thousands of lives, not to mention your own."

"Is this all you have called me here for, Sita? I told you I did not want another lecture. If the People's Army does not act now, Solung will go bumbling along like it has been for centuries. I tried changing things peacefully when that poor girl got killed and nothing happened. Absolutely nothing changed."

"You got a lot of support."

"From people who have no power."

"I shall have power. You could work with me."

Laxman stared at her in astonishment.

"What do you mean?"

"I'm going to marry Prince Raju."

Laxman was shocked into silence. Finally he said: "I can't believe what I have just heard. Tell me I got it wrong."

"I'm going to marry Raju."

"Sita, you can't do this."

"I can and I am."

"After all we did to get you out of it! After all you said! Who was it who said she would never marry a man she didn't want? Who was it who was going to set an example to all the other young women in Solung being forced into marriages?"

"They were your words not mine. You always want to glorify everything. I didn't want to be forced into a marriage, that was all. I wasn't ready for it. I will be able to do far more for young women in Solung this way than by running away from Raju. He wants to change things as much as you do."

"By shutting down parliament! What kind of change is that?"

"Whose fault is that? It was you and your friends who forced the king to impose martial law. But the suspension of parliament does give us a chance to push through some reforms. That's what I wanted to tell you. You could do a lot more by stopping this war and working with Raju and me."

"Sita, Raju is what I am fighting! He represents everything that is wrong with Solung. It cannot be right for people like him – people like us – to be born to rule others. It is certainly not right when it results in a society as corrupt and oppressive as the one in Solung. You can't cure corruption by becoming part of the corruption."

"Raju is not corrupt. I am not corrupt."

Again Laxman was reduced to silence, staring at his sister. Tigger too stayed quiet, feeling like an intruder in a family argument.

Then Laxman said: "You're doing this for me, aren't you? You are marrying that man to try to persuade me against doing what I know must be done!"

"Of course I want to stop you ruining your life and plunging Solung into war. How could I not? How could I possibly want to see you and Tigger – two of the people I love most in the world – fighting each other to the death?"

"So you admit it! You are marrying a man you don't love out of some crazy idea that it will somehow save me. It is not going to work Sita. Forget it. Tell Raju to forget it. Get on with your own life and stop trying to run mine."

"How do you know how I feel? Raju is a fine man. He is a lovely man."

"You are not marrying out of love."

"I am marrying *for* love. I am marrying someone I can grow to love, like women in this country have done for centuries. How many women here or anywhere else in the world really know the man they marry on their wedding day?"

"They stand a sight better chance of a good life if they are already in love. Why don't you marry Tigger, if you love him so much?"

Laxman threw the line out to make a point, but from his tone it was clear that he was oblivious of the effect it would have on Tigger and his sister. Tigger saw the innocence of a man torn between ancient and modern attitudes: it had never entered Laxman's head that his high-born sister might have consorted with a casteless foreigner.

The princess covered her embarrassment well.

"I love you. I love Tigger. I love Henry. I love lots of people. But there is only one man I want to marry and that is Raju."

"To try to stop your brother from doing what he knows he has to do..."

"That is not the only reason Laxman. What else am I going to do with my life? We had no choice about the position we were born to. We don't deserve the power it gave us but we have a duty to use it as well as we can. I can use it by marrying the future king of my country and helping him to transform it, to get rid of the injustice and oppression that we both hate. How else would I get the opportunity to do that?"

"By joining the revolution! Do you think I am not using my position as a prince? My people follow me because of who I am, because of the power of my birth."

"You are using it destructively."

"I'm destroying things that need to be destroyed. You are destroying yourself. You are destroying your life. You are prostituting yourself!"

"How dare you say that to me, Laxman!"

"What else do you call it... selling yourself to a man for power? I don't buy this noble sacrifice stuff. Don't kid yourself you are doing it for me because it is not going to work."

The princess was in tears. "Who said anything about sacrifice?"

Laxman looked at his watch. "It's no good Sita. We are not going to agree on this and I have to go."

"Please Laxman, please don't do this." She touched his arm but he pulled himself away.

"You tried, Sita. I'll grant you that. If it makes you feel any better, nothing you could say could stop me now. It's gone too far. I couldn't turn back, even if I wanted to."

"Neither can I," said the princess.

Laxman was out of the room before either of them could say more. Tigger put his arms round the princess and she sobbed on his chest. "Why did he have to be so horrible?"

270

she said.

"He didn't mean those things. He wasn't really arguing with you. He was trying to persuade himself. He's backed himself into a corner and he can't get out."

"You think that's what I have done too, don't you? You think Laxman is right about me and Raju."

"I don't think you are prostituting yourself, if that's what you mean."

"You know what I mean. About why I am marrying Raju."

"Only you know the truth of that."

"Then believe me. It's what I want Tigger."

Tigger pushed her gently away. "Sita, I have to go."

"You're not going to see Henry?"

"I can't. I'll have to take the first plane back. I can't risk Laxman getting back before I do."

"Tigger you're not going to fight? I can't bear it. You'll kill each other. You can't do this!"

"And what if I don't? How am I going to feel if Ganesh gets killed outnumbered two-to-one fighting against Laxman?"

"And how am I going to feel if Laxman kills you – or you kill him?"

"You did all you could to stop it. Laxman's made his choice. I've made mine. You won't need to blame yourself. Give my love to Henry. I miss him. I wish he was around."

"He will be. I am sure of that."

ooo

The meeting with the princess had been painful but Tigger had other things on his mind on the short flight to Solung. It seemed highly unlikely that Laxman had gone to Calcutta solely to see his sister; he would have needed a very good reason for the visit to avoid arousing Da Silva's suspicions. Tigger remembered the king's clampdown on supplies of aviation fuel. If Laxman had been sorting out new supplies, his little air force could be back in the air very soon. It was not a comfortable thought, forcing Tigger to confront the enormity of what was unfolding; fear gnawed at the pit of his stomach.

His spirits lifted after he landed at Solung. An army jeep was waiting for him as usual to escort him to the airfield. Sitting in the front passenger seat was Dougal, and in the back sat a familiar plump figure still sporting the clothes and pale skin of London.

"Charlie," cried Tigger. "What are you doing here?"

Dougal's old sidekick eased himself over to make room for Tigger. "I've just got off the plane. Couldn't leave you chaps in the lurch, could I?"

"Charlie wouldn't let a friend down," Dougal said pointedly.

Tigger ignored the barb. He felt desperately sorry for Charlie, who had wanted nothing more than a quiet life and would have felt under pressure to join them after the death of Gosh; he felt even sorrier for Charlie's wife, who had to sit alone and wait. Their son and daughter had grown up and left home. But Tigger had to admit that he also felt relieved. Charlie might lighten Dougal's moods, which had become increasingly dark and unpredictable, and he would even up the numbers. If Laxman did push them to a fight, it was going to be four against four.

ooo

4   The Song of God

Tigger had rushed back to Solung to another fretful anti-climax. He spent the next week waiting on standby, with a daily routine of training flights with Charlie, Dougal and Ganesh. After two days Laxman's aircraft began to show up on Satpur's radar screen, making brief flights close to their mountain base. Clearly Laxman had found a fuel supply and was keeping his pilots in trim. Dougal, in consultation with the king, decided to maintain the diminishing hope of avoiding all-out war by not taking them on unless they made a move towards the capital.

Then, suddenly, Satpur was flooded with press and TV people. The ostensible reason was the announcement of the engagement of the king's son to Princess Sita, who after hitting the news in Goa had been redubbed the 'hippy princess' by the headline writers – another example, Tigger thought ruefully, of the old king's prescience. But a prospective royal marriage and a possible civil war, in a country that few people could place on a map, would not normally generate so much attention. Someone had been feeding journalists with more headline-worthy information about a split between the princess and her brother, with a hint that it was connected with her kidnap and the immediate prospect of Battle of Britain hero FitzDougal reprising his role leading Spitfires against Messerschmitts. It was war as show business, and Tigger knew Da Silva would not have been stirring up the interest unless something was about to happen.

The media influx created another kind of crisis, because Solung was not equipped to deal with it. Someone was needed who understood the Western media and could explain the situation to them, and the princess knew of only one person who both fitted the bill and was immediately available. Tigger laughed when Henry arrived at his door early in the morning with his hair cut short and dressed in the same suit Gosh had lent him to see the king. "That's a fine way to greet a man who's just come back from the dead," Henry said.

"You're supposed to be in Calcutta recovering."

"I'm still trying to recover. It's been a big shock. I haven't had a haircut in years."

"Never mind that. What about your wound?"

Henry winced as he sat down. "Hurting but healing."

Tigger ordered breakfast for two to be brought to the room. It was a huge relief to have someone around he could talk to freely. Dougal resisted any discussion of their situation that went beyond practicalities, Charlie always deferred to Dougal, and though Tigger had had many long talks with Ganesh he did not want to burden the lad with his concerns.

Henry had a few of those too. "I can't quite credit what's happening to me. What the hell am I doing here?"

"What *are* you doing here?"

"I've got a job. Media relations. It's the princess's idea. I don't know what I am supposed to tell these people. From what I gather, they are convinced that you and Dougal are about to fight Laxman. I'm an old-fashioned peace-and-love hippy. I don't want to promote a war."

"Then promote the peace. You'd be doing me a favour. I don't want to fight. And I certainly don't want to fight someone who saved my life."

Henry smiled.

"Why are you smiling? My life is on the line here. I don't see anything to smile about."

"It was what you said. It was not funny funny. It was funny curious. Remember, when we first met you told me that you felt like you had walked into a Biggles book? Just now you sounded like you had walked into the Bhagavad Gita. I've been reading it while I was recuperating. Do you know it?"

"I've heard of it. No more."

"It's the most famous part of the Mahabharata, the saga that includes that story Dog Baba told about a dog at the gates of paradise. But it is not a story. It's a conversation between the warrior Arjuna and his charioteer Krishna."

"Krishna, the god?"

"Right. Arjuna's predicament is very like yours. He is a kind of ancient Biggles – a model warrior – and he is about to fight a battle in which he has friends on both sides. The Gita starts with him saying: 'I don't want to fight.' He doesn't want to kill his pals. Just like you said just now."

"And what does Krishna say?"

"He tells him to fight. Arjuna is a kshatriya, a princely member of the warrior caste. Fighting is what warriors do. If he refuses to fight in a righteous war he is denying his purpose in life. It is contrary to his dharma."

"And killing is not?"

"It is of no account in the great scheme of things, according to Krishna. Dying is just a matter of souls swapping bodies."

"As someone who may be about to die in battle, I have to say I don't find that argument persuasive."

"No more do I. You have to see it in context. Think of the knights of medieval Europe – a load of warlords and their henchmen fighting for power, land, glory and wealth, while subscribing to lofty chivalric ideals."

"We may be slaughtering, raping and pillaging but by God we are doing it honourably..."

"Exactly. Not so far from how some people think today."

"I guess chivalry must have provided some restraint."

"Restraint in the way knights treated each other, maybe. I doubt if it did much for the plebs. It gave the church some sway over the knights by holding them to moral account. The Gita is many hundreds of years older but in a similar way it prettifies the behaviour of warring lords, at least in their own eyes, and promotes the slippery spiritual authority of priests. That's a modern perspective, of course. The writer or writers would not have seen themselves as doing that. Bhagavad Gita means Song of God. It is a spiritual how-to manual, not a political manifesto. It describes various paths to enlightenment, and in addressing Arjuna's dilemma it sets a model for making any decision."

"Is it still relevant?"

"It wouldn't have inspired centuries of study if it had nothing to say. A traditional Hindu would read it very differently from me, but it speaks to us all because the issues it addresses are with us still. We still have to make decisions, and the dharma, the proper role, of a warrior is still open to discussion. And that's without touching on the God stuff."

Henry hadn't been back two minutes and it was as if he had never left. He was ranting again, but Tigger didn't mind. It seemed unreal to be sitting there waiting for battle while discussing the warring philosophy of long-dead people, but it took his mind from his fear.

"I guess a good soldier is one who fights as cleanly as he can in a righteous cause," he said. "I've been brooding about that sitting here waiting to fight. I envy those first Spitfire pilots who fought in the Battle of Britain; at least they had no reason to doubt what they were risking their lives for."

"Britain was hardly right by the lights of people like Sanjeev. Neither side was clean."

"Even Sanjeev would grant that Britain was entitled to defend itself from attack."

"The Gita is concerned less with the reasons for the fight than with the problem of how to stay clean in a messy world – a world that demands answers to problems with no perfect solutions, or no solutions at all beyond those offered by time. Some of it is hard to relate to: stuff about caste purity and observing religious rites – the kind of ethnic baggage carried by all religious texts. And Krishna tells Arjuna how to clear his karma to escape the cycle of death and rebirth, which means little if you don't believe in all that."

"Do you?"

"Not literally. It makes sense if you see reincarnation as a metaphor for human generations. You don't have to look far to see countries struggling to free themselves from the past – often from stuff that exists only in people's heads. A civil war could blight Solung for decades, even centuries."

"I don't need the Gita to tell me that."

"It's not always obvious to the people affected. Karma at least gives us a word for it."

"It's still just a word. We already have the idea."

"Words shape our thinking, and our thinking needs re-shaping. We're still behaving much as we did ten thousand years ago. It's as if we have learned nothing over the generations, nothing from our mistakes. We read the lessons but we don't change the way we think. If those old modes of thought aren't karma to be cleared, I don't know what is."

"I wish my karma would clear me out of all this."

"The Gita would be with you on that one, but it's a long hard road to enlightenment," Henry said, smiling. "You can take comfort from the fact that the Gita is comfortable with the paradox of your situation."

"Paradox?"

"You and Laxman fight on different sides, yet you may both further the cause of Solung. The revolution is providing the impetus for reform, yet it is probably best defeated."

"So what are you saying... that Laxman and I are both right? That's a fine proposition to stake my life on!"

"You can both *believe* that you are right but you can't know what is for the best. You can only make a judgement. You can't possibly know the full results of your actions because life is too complicated to predict. Kurukshetra, the battlefield of the Gita..."

"Was it a real battle? I mean is this history as legend, like Homer and Troy?"

"It probably stems from a real battle in the distant past. The Gita has distilled it into something else. Kurukshetra symbolises existence itself and its eternal play of dualities. It is leela, the play of the gods. Our dilemmas are just part of that game. We cannot resolve it... it resolves itself like the river resolves itself into the ocean. No-one knows what is really going on. Only time will tell."

"Henry, does this sort of stuff go on in your head all the time? How on earth do you get to make any decision?"

"I used to wonder that myself. I couldn't believe in anything. In the past few weeks I've had to face the obvious fact that we *have* to make choices. Even not making a choice is a choice. That's why I've been rereading the Gita. I thought it might help me to choose well."

Henry paused.

"And? Did it help? What does it say?"

"You really want me to go on? I could witter on all day."

"I can believe it. But we don't have all day. Give me enough for breakfast."

"Some of it is too much for breakfast. It gets obscure. One thing the Gita talks of is discrimination, the ability to distinguish the real from the unreal."

"I have no problem doing that."

"Not in the way Krishna means. He tells Arjuna that the battle is not important because it is not real. We poor blind unenlightened creatures mistake the world as perceived by the senses for the underlying reality – we mistake the waves for the ocean. And we delude ourselves into thinking that our ego, the image of the self constructed by the mind, is the perceiver. By meditating we can discover our soul, the inviolate watcher within, which is part of a universal soul."

"Well, that's a lot of use to me now, isn't it? What am I supposed to do if Laxman comes at me in a Messerschmitt? Call him on the radio and ask him to give me a couple of seconds to meditate before he attacks? Maybe then my body wouldn't feel so real when he shoots me down in flames?"

"Arjuna has a similar reaction, though he is rather more polite about it. He is talking to a god, remember. Krishna tells him that people of action can take a different path to

278

wisdom. Just as the ascetic strives to dissociate his inner self from the cravings of his body, so the warrior can act without any personal investment in the results of his actions. Win or lose, death or glory, it's of no importance."

"Kipling said that. *If you can meet with triumph and disaster, and treat those two impostors just the same...*"

"I doubt if Kipling saw himself as spouting the Gita, but it catches the gist. So does a coach who advises a sportsman to focus on his game. It's a dissolving of the self in action. More interesting to me is the act of decision. Krishna is talking about a profound spiritual detachment, a selflessness that can be brought to any decision. Arjuna does not want to kill his friends. That is a reason for not wanting to fight; it is no justification for not fighting if the battle is righteous."

"I wouldn't be here if I did not believe that. Are you saying that I am profoundly detached?"

"I'd say that you are profoundly normal. Most people would agree with you in principle, but how many would actually fight? They would refuse, and then come up with an excuse to massage their self-esteem. People, all of us, do that sort of thing all the time. We might oppose a tax rise because it will cost us money, for instance, then invent grander reasons to allow us to feel good about it."

Tigger was getting exasperated. "Henry, people have to see things from a personal point of view. It doesn't mean they don't have a wider perspective. It is the way the world operates."

"And don't you think it is rather primitive? Is it the way the world *should* operate? Should we not at least value detachment so that it becomes part of the political discourse?"

"But why? Why is it important?"

"Because we are wrecking the earth, perhaps? Because we refuse to see what we don't want to see? Because we are squandering the world's resources? Because we are poisoning the world for profit? Because we rarely look beyond the needs of our own times? The health of the living world should be as fundamental to the way we think and act as the health of our own children. It is far more important than our own short trivial lives. We are blinded by our selfishness! Don't you think that people of the future – and I hope and trust that there will be people in the future – don't you think that they will be shocked at our naivety?"

"My only concern at this moment is the question of whether my short life is about to be cut shorter, and I can tell you it isn't trivial to me. I don't know about being blinded by selfishness. The only reason I'm sitting here waiting to risk my neck is that I don't want to let my friends down."

"I'd bet that is why most soldiers don't cut and run. But I don't believe it's the only reason you have not backed out. You would never have agreed to fight on Da Silva's side."

"I don't know that I am on the side of good, either. I'm sure Sita and Raju will start off with the best of intentions but they will probably end up presiding over yet another dodgy regime."

"They will have to make compromises, but you know Sita enough to know that her heart is in the right place."

"And to help her I have to fight to the death a man I count as a friend. Nothing you have said can make me feel better about that."

"There you go again. That's just what Arjuna says."

"And?"

"Krishna says you can't go wrong if you act out of love of God. Like that old hymn: *Teach me, my God and king, in all things thee to see, and what I do in anything, to do it as for thee.*"

"I know that hymn from school and it has nothing to do with war. You make it sound like a creed for a holy warrior... a warrior who kills in the name of God."

"You mean the warrior who kids himself that he knows what God wants? Not much detachment there! The hymn is talking about *any* action. So is Krishna. Sometimes a warrior has to kill. If he can't do that out of love and respect for life,

280

then he shouldn't do it at all."

Tigger's exasperation was turning to anger. He was angry because he was tired of being held to have a duty to address other people's problems, and he was tired of killings, and he was tired of being afraid. He was angry because he had lost the princess and the euphoria of Goa. He was angry with Henry, not least because Henry was there to be anger with.

"Listen to yourself, Henry, talking about killing as an act of love! Sometimes I think you could talk yourself into anything. You're full of chapter and verse. You are just like all the warmongers and politicians, spouting fine words while others do the killing and dying."

Henry gazed out of the window towards the distant mountains, trying to regain his composure. Finally he said: "This is my Kurukshetra too, Tigger, and it has already nearly cost me my life. I didn't need to come back to Solung. I could have gone back home to safety. I could have sat there and pontificated about what was happening here, and let this country go to hell. Would that have made me any more righteous? Doing nothing can kill as surely as a bullet."

"But what happened to all your talk of peace? What happened to the dream of the ridiculous man?"

"He is still dreaming. Peace is still possible."

Tigger's anger had subsided almost as suddenly as it had come. He was thinking of the battle that he knew in his bones was imminent. "I'm sorry, Henry," he said. "The fact of the matter is that I don't want to die, and when I think about what might happen I am terrified. I can't stop thinking about it with all this waiting. I wish we could love it all away. I wish I could pray to God and be comforted. I wish I could love God. I just can't see any God to love."

"You loved your parents didn't you?"

"Of course."

"God gave birth to you and nurtured you as much as they did. Why can't you love God?"

"I can't talk to God."

"Of course you can. You do. I've heard you. You say 'Thank God!' Or 'Jesus Christ!'"

"They are just expressions. Exclamations."

"They are a kind of prayer. You are relating to God."

"It's meaningless. God doesn't relate to me. God can't talk to me."

"Not to argue the point, nor can dogs. You can love a dog."

"Dogs give something back."

"It's a different kind of relationship. So is your relationship with God."

"But I can't love your God. I can't love a definition."

"Because you can't see the poetry for the words. It's like you are seeing a loved one as a collection of organs – heart, liver, lungs – and not as a totality, the person. When you talk to the princess, you don't see yourself as talking to a kidney."

"God is not a person. You said it yourself."

"A ship is not a woman but that does not stop sailors speaking of her as one. People of old had no problem seeing God as a person. The Gita sees God in the form of Krishna. Christians see Jesus as the son of God. You can personify God any way you want. God can be father and mother to you, beloved and loving. You have orphaned yourself."

There was a knock on the door and a servant called: "Sahib, time for your meeting."

Tigger thanked him and stood up. He had a curious feeling that this was a moment he would remember all his life: the early-morning sun slanting through the windows, the mist lifting off the distant mountains, the remains of a breakfast on the table, and Henry sitting there all earnestness.

Henry said: "I've got to go too. I have to see Raju."

He paused as they moved out and said: "Tigger... you love life, or you would not want to hang on to it. If you love life, you love God. God is life."

5 The propaganda war

Tigger strolled across the airfield to a hut where a young captain gave them daily briefings on the military situation. The meeting usually amounted to an extension of breakfast as the officer had little to report and spent half an hour chatting with the airmen over cups of tea. Or rather Tigger, Dougal, Charlie and the captain chatted; Tigger noticed that Ganesh tended to stay quiet when Solungese officers were present and seemed far more at ease when he was alone with the Englishmen. Caste and class attitudes still ran deep in Solung. Today's meeting was different. First Tigger announced the news of Henry's appointment, which was greeted with incredulity by Dougal, who could not bring himself to say his name. "That hippy friend of yours? What are they playing at?"

"Dougal, I can't see what you have against him. He got me and the princess out of the mountains, remember? He knows Solung better than any of us. He speaks the language."

"He needs a good haircut! My God, if he had been in my squadron I'd have soon knocked him into shape."

"The princess *is* knocking him into shape. He's had a haircut and he is wearing a suit. He has even got a job. What are you complaining about?"

For what seemed to Tigger to be the first time in weeks, Dougal laughed. "Well if she can get that hippy off his backside maybe she really is capable of turning this country around."

The mood changed as a phone in a corridor outside the room rang. It was Charlie's wife, who had heard on the news that trouble was brewing; somehow, she had hit lucky with Solung's creaking telephone system. The other three pilots could hear him through the thin wall as he tried to reassure her. Charlie talking to his wife sounded nothing like Charlie talking to them. "Darling, I'm going to be OK," the old pilot was saying. "I'm sure nothing is going to happen. Give my love to the kids and tell them not to worry."

Dougal rose suddenly and looked out of the window. Tigger caught a glimpse of his face, reflected on the pane, and felt a pang of sympathy. Dougal looked lonely. He had no wife or children waiting for him at home, and he had lost his father, mother and only brother while still a lad. According to Charlie, Dougal could have taken his pick of any number of beautiful women as a glamorous fighter pilot during the war, but he fell for one who dumped him for a fellow officer. He risked his life daily in the air but never again risked his heart on a woman. His old comrades were the nearest he had to a family. Tigger suspected that Dougal was fretting about Charlie as much as Charlie's wife was, but he would do everything he could not to show it.

Charlie ended his call with evident relief as their Solungese liaison officer arrived, accompanied by a colonel from the Solung intelligence service. They had serious news. Agents had reported that the People's Army planned to launch a number of co-ordinated attacks on police stations and army posts across the country. It was not known when the attacks would happen but they would be triggered by some kind of action in the mountains where the arms cache was located.

"We think Da Silva will try to push us into a costly attack there, tying down the army and weakening its ability to defend the countryside," the colonel said.

Dougal, back to his usual no-nonsense self, asked: "Can't you just hold back... keep the fighters bottled up in the valleys?"

"It's springtime. The snows are melting. The passes are

clearing. The guerrillas control most of the high ground in the area so they can move in and out of the valleys almost at will. We think most of their arms have been stuck in the high ground because of the winter snow. The thaw will allow them to start distributing weapons around the country – presumably for these attacks. Of course we have set up road blocks on all the routes out, and we have banned night-time traffic in the area, but the best we can do is make movement harder for the guerrillas. And small groups of soldiers guarding lonely roads make good terrorist targets in themselves."

"Surely you should move in as soon as possible then?"

"Not if Da Silva is about to make a move. For political reasons we would rather react to that than take pre-emptive action."

"So you can't be accused of starting a war?"

"Partly that. But there is also the matter of the princess's brother Laxman. His men are not People's Army and they have yet to be involved in actual fighting."

"They are the ones concentrated in the valley?"

"They're the bulk of the forces there. We're still hoping to split them from the People's Army. If we attack they will be forced to commit to Da Silva. Our reading is that Da Silva wants them to hold the line while his men spirit away the arms, giving him full control of the weapons. He has his hardcore loyalists up there with him, his Praetorian Guard. They've been trained by professionals and they know what they are doing."

"Laxman is not stupid enough to let Da Silva outmanoeuvre him that easily," Tigger put in.

"He probably figures he has enough support to keep Da Silva in check," the colonel said. "But he has not yet committed an outright act of war..."

"And the princess cannot bring herself to start a war against her own brother?" said Tigger.

He felt the smack of a shell hitting his machine
– see page 301

"I didn't say that. The king runs the country."

Dougal gave a snort of impatience. "Like the king appointed that hippy to talk to the press. I'd bet that young woman runs rings round the king. She seems to run rings round every man she comes into contact with."

He gave Tigger a sour look.

"I'm lost," said Charlie. "You chaps have been here longer than me and you have a better idea of what is going on. I take it that we are still waiting for Da Silva to make a move. Am I right?"

"You've got it," Dougal said.

"That move could involve Laxman's aircraft," the colonel said. "If the aircraft start attacking us we will be forced to attack the valley where the airstrip is, unless you neutralise them. Are you confident that you can take on Laxman?"

"You understand that we can't get involved in any ground war? We will not go shooting up the guerrillas. Our contract only covers dealing with the aircraft."

"Understood," said the colonel.

"That leaves only two circumstances in which we will act: if Laxman starts attacking your forces from the air, or if he attacks us directly. We have observers and radar tracking every move the MEs make so Laxman would be hard put to take us by surprise in a direct attack. Charlie has brought some scrambler sets over from London so the radar people can talk to us without the other side eavesdropping. We'll know where Laxman is, where he is going and how high he is. That gives us an advantage. Doubtless Laxman will have spotters on the ground but they will be able to report little more than when we take off and land. My guess is that he will try to draw us into a fight near the mountains where the radar is less effective. In any event we should get the better of them."

Tigger, looking at their faces around the table, wasn't so sure. He was confident that he and Ganesh were at least the equal of any pilot Laxman could put up. None of them

287

could match the combat experience of Dougal and Charlie but the veteran pilots were showing their age. God only knew what was happening with Dougal, and Charlie was unfit, worried about his wife, and battle weary. Overall, Tigger decided, the two sides were probably evenly matched. Their fate would be decided largely by luck and strategy; but Dougal was right in that their access to advanced radar gave them a strategic edge.

Charlie could not hide his lack of enthusiasm. "I still find it hard to see what is at stake here," he said. "I mean supposing we all got shot down, what difference would it make? Four rogue Messerschmitts are not going to be very much help in the long term to a guerrilla army. They would have to commit a lot of people just to defend the airstrip."

"That was my view at first but I've been thinking about it," Dougal said. "If they have fuel dumps placed strategically around the country they could lead the army a merry dance for a while at least, hopping around using roads as temporary airstrips."

"Da Silva thinks internationally," the colonel said. "He wants to draw India into the conflict. He hopes that if Laxman wins control of the air over Solung, India might send in its forces – ostensibly to restore order."

"Ostensibly?"

"Many high-up people in India believe Solung should be part of their country. An invasion could turn into an annexation."

"That is certainly what Laxman's pilots want," Tigger said.

"Crazy old Sanjeev's flying playmates... we know about them." The colonel's voice was heavy with distaste.

"Laxman himself is not interested in India," Tigger said. "He sees his little air force as a means of furthering the revolution in Solung."

Charlie looked bewildered. "But his pilots and Da Silva both want India to invade?"

"For different reasons," the colonel said. "Da Silva wants

to spread his revolution into India, where there is already a strong Naxalite movement. The pilots want to be part of what they see as a greater Hindu nation. If India invades, their job will be done so far as they are concerned. In fact we suspect that they may be in cahoots with sympathetic elements in the Indian government and military."

"If Solung is that unstable, is annexation such a bad idea?"

"It would be a disaster," the colonel said. "There would be huge opposition here. The king could hardly declare war on India, so people would flock to the People's Army to fight the invaders. The conflict could go on for years."

"And that can be avoided if we defeat Laxman?"

"If only it were that simple. The battle is attracting world attention to Da Silva's revolution and it shows his fellow travellers in India that he is in earnest. On top of that, if Laxman is killed, he will have no significant rival for power."

Charlie have Dougal a despairing look. "So it's win-win for Da Silva?"

Ganesh broke his silence. "To my mind, the real importance of the aircraft is up here." He tapped his head. "These people who follow Laxman, and many of those in the People's Army... they are my people. They come from my area. I know them. They are country people. Good people but uneducated and superstitious. Most have never seen an aircraft close up. Most have probably never set eyes on a foreigner. To see their noble prince, their champion, take to the air in this flying machine to fight a famous foreigner will be to them like something out of the stories of the gods. If Laxman wins, it will be as if the gods are on their side. If he loses, they will lose heart."

"You are too modest, Ganesh," the colonel said unexpectedly. "You are a hero to the young people of Solung. If Squadron Leader FitzDougal will forgive me for saying so, you are more respected here than he is. The people will see the battle as between your way and Laxman's way. But I agree that the psychological effect of the battle could be critical. I think it could settle the future of this country."

ooo

A few hours later, they were in the Spitfires. It was close to sunset, a time Dougal calculated to be the least likely for Laxman to attack, as he would be reluctant to risk a tricky landing in the mountains at night. They flew in the once-famous finger-four formation, the aircraft forming roughly the same relative positions as the tips of the fingers of the right hand. Dougal flew in front, with Charlie to his left, slightly below. Dougal's job was to navigate and watch the space ahead; Charlie's was to watch for aircraft coming out of the sun.... a task that would take all his experience, for it required a knack many fighter pilots never lived long enough to acquire. Tigger followed Dougal, slightly above and to the right; and Ganesh, higher still, took up the rear. The positions were devised to give maximum cover and visibility. In theory, Charlie and Ganesh – the wingmen – were supposed to stick through thick and thin to the aircraft in front, providing cover while the other two attacked. In practice, the two-pair formation was likely to break up in a melee.

In his filming days, Tigger had had to study fighter tactics, and had carried out many mock fights. Most battles were decided by initial position: height gave an advantage, pilots contriving to dive out of the blinding sun and pull up under the opposing aircraft from behind. The Messerschmitt and Spitfire were about evenly matched: the ME could climb higher and dive faster, but the Spitfire had a tighter turn. This was important when under attack – a pilot had to break away at the last moment, when his attacker was about to fire. If he turned fast enough, he might bring his attacker under fire; if he did not, he might be dead.

It was this breaking manoeuvre that the four pilots practised, Dougal calling the commands by radio. There was an obscene beauty in the deadly choreography, the aircraft wheeling with balletic perfection. Tigger felt a sudden guilty exhilaration by the prospect of battle. Even now, Laxman's aircraft could emerge at any moment from the mountains. The chance was not great, but it added urgency to the routine of constantly scanning the sky.

Henry was waiting in their messroom at the airstrip when they landed, to ask if they could attend a press conference the following morning. "I'm not going to speak to that pack of jackals," Dougal said. "I came here to fight, not to talk."

"I'd rather not speak to them either," said Charlie.

"And Tigger can't leave this base in daylight," Dougal said. "Neither can Ganesh. We may have to take off at any minute."

"We're holding the conference on the base. The film people want to get a shot of the aircraft."

"I don't want those people crawling all over this place."

Henry would not be browbeaten. "I've checked the bona fide of everyone who will come. If you don't get a good press over this, you'll have lost the battle before you start. We have word that Da Silva has crews filming the MEs."

"Then Tigger and Ganesh can do the talking. You want handsome young men, not doddery old fogeys like me and Charlie. I'll have nothing to do with it," said Dougal, collecting his papers. Charlie followed him out the room, throwing an apologetic look at Henry.

Ganesh laughed. "It will be a change for me to have someone else doing the talking. I had to face the press by myself after word got out that the princess had been rescued. Dougal refused to have anything to do with them."

"Henry, did you have to land me in this?" Tigger said with some asperity after Ganesh left.

"Believe it or not it wasn't my idea."

"The princess?"

"Think again. Higher."

"Raju?"

"Higher."

"The king?"

"The same."

"You've seen the king?"

"He was at the meeting. He asked me what you thought about my new job. I told him what you said."

"Me? What did I say?"

"That I should promote peace, not war. The king thought it was a great idea." Henry mimicked the king. "I think you chaps make a great team. You should both talk to these newspaper and TV wallahs. Ganesh too, so they can see the kind of splendid young man Solung can produce."

"Nothing about Dougal and Charlie?"

"He knew Dougal wouldn't do it. Like Ganesh said, he has always refused. It's not in his contract."

"It's not in mine either."

"Come on, Tigger. You are putting your life on the line for this; you don't want it all to be for nothing. You know Da Silva sees the air war primarily as a propaganda exercise. He's put a lot of effort into getting media attention. If we play this right it could all backfire on him."

"How? What are we supposed to say?"

"That's what I asked the king. He said he didn't care." Henry lapsed into his king's voice. "You chaps can say what you like. Shake the place up a bit, eh what?"

"That's no help."

"Just be yourself. You don't want this war. You want what is best for Solung."

"You said yourself... I can't know what is best."

"But you know what's for the worst, and that's what you have to try to put over. War has to be an option of last resort. Most of these news people don't give a damn about Solung. They will be interested only in you and Ganesh, because they want an exciting story and they know you are about to fight for your lives. We have to use that interest as a way of getting people our side. That's the point of letting the media loose on you. At some point, when the time seems right, I'll announce that the king is to abdicate in favour of

292

his son and that Raju is drawing up a program of reforms."

"What reforms?"

"They can't write a manifesto in five minutes. But if Laxman does not do anything too rash he could play a part in drafting it. Raju is offering an amnesty for fighters who agree to give up their arms. Only where there is clear evidence of murder will anyone face charges, but they will be dealt with leniently if they give themselves up."

"You say Raju is drawing up the reforms. What about Sita?"

"You should know. She is not one to hold back and we can be damn sure she will be conscientious about it. I think the old king is half in love with her. He treats her like a favourite daughter. The prince is well meaning but I don't think he has a clue what to do. He's obviously in love with Sita too but that is not the only reason he is marrying her. He knows that she has more nous than he does. He needs her."

"And so, I guess, does Solung," Tigger said forlornly.

"It's true, Tigger. I've been talking to people around Satpur and the atmosphere has completely changed. A few months ago all this 'hippy princess' stuff would have caused so much outrage that she would hardly have dared to show her face here. But she has put Solung on the map, and people like that, and everyone loves a wedding. Young people see her as breath of fresh air and the fact that she has opted for a traditional marriage has mollified even the old conservatives, who are beginning to see that they face a choice between modernisation and civil war. She's being seen as the only person with a hope of holding the country together."

ooo

The first respect in which Henry was wrong about the news conference was that the reporters became as interested in him as in Tigger and Ganesh, and not just because of his remarkable transformation from rootless hippy to official spokesman for the king. Henry began by flourishing a piece of paper and announcing: "I'm going to begin with a statement." Clearing his throat, he read out: "It is better to die honourably than to live in shame. I hail your pure soul, my son, and mourn your body riddled with the bullets of the oppressors. As long as blood flows through my veins, I shall never forget the brave words you spoke in support of toilers' rights and the deprived classes. I am happy that by sacrificing your life, you have made more people aware of the rightfulness of your path. Your father does not grieve your martyrdom. Honoured be your memory, and the memory of other proud young men of the People's Army, who have sacrificed their lives for their ideology. They have fought to relieve the misery of the people. They have suffered the persecution of the oppressors. Their names shall live for ever."

Tigger was as surprised as anybody. "What on earth is that?" he asked.

"Propaganda. It was found in the pocket of a student arrested for rioting. He claimed that it was written by the father of one of the unfortunate guerrillas who got killed when the princess escaped. But later he admitted writing it himself with the aim of circulating it. I think it is very touching."

"Why did you read it out?" one of the journalists asked.

"Because it is a state of mind some of the kids in this country have got themselves into. I don't want to see them waste their lives starting a needless war."

"They're hardly starting a war. There's been one simmering away here for months," said one reporter. "I understand Ganesh only just managed to escape with his life when he rescued the princess."

"It wasn't just me. It was Henry and Tigger who finally got her out," Ganesh said.

This was the story the media wanted to hear. The air battle would be a story if it happened but it had supposedly been about to happen for so long that no-one really expected that it would. The saga of how Henry and Tigger met and escaped with the princess might be old news, but no-one had heard it before and it was good enough to be going on with.

Gradually it was coaxed out of them. Then an English reporter said: "It's like something out of Biggles."

"That's what you've came for today, isn't it... a Biggles story?" Henry said.

There was a brief interlude while Biggles was explained to the non-British people present.

"Spitfires, Messerschmitts... what do you expect?" the journalist said.

"Just understand that there is more at stake here than Tigger and Ganesh risking their innocent young necks. You can help Solung. Dramatise it, by all means. Write your Biggles stories. But please make the point that war is the last thing Solung needs. This is a country struggling for stability, justice and prosperity. There are poor people here but they are not all unhappy and starving. There are rich people here but they are not all evil. There are people longing for what they haven't got, and people living in fear for what they have got. There's the makings of a lot of trouble. But Raju and the lovely Sita will be rulers soon and they are full of good intentions. Tigger and I are backing them because we believe that they can help this country leave the twentieth century a sight healthier than when it entered it. Biggles has had his day. We need a new kind of hero, a hero who can address the real problems of this world. The problems that can't be solved with guns."

"What the hell are those Spitfires doing here, then?" asked an American. "They look lethal to me."

"So we hope we won't need to use them."

The American asked: "Tigger, are you a new kind of hero?"

"I'm a pretty poor class of one. I came here to rescue a princess, and she ended up rescuing me. I don't want to fight. I don't want to kill. And, frankly, I'm afraid."

"If you do fight, I'd say that makes you more of a hero."

"Not in the way Henry means. He thinks we idolise the wrong people."

"And what do you think?"

"He has a point."

Henry interjected: "Did you ever wonder what we would do with ourselves if all the conflicts in the world were miraculously resolved, and there was nothing more to discover, no more rivers to cross, no more mountains to climb? You can bet some fool would start trouble out of sheer boredom. Real heroes are people who can cherish life in all its mundanity. They are the wise. They are the ones who keep it all going."

"Not an idiot like me who goes out looking for excitement and blunders into a war," Tigger said.

"But why are you fighting? This is not your country..."

Tigger did not mention the flash of excitement he had felt the previous day at the prospect of battle, nor the feeling that if he backed out he would spend the rest of his life wondering what he had missed. But what he did say was true enough. "Sometimes, unfortunately, fools like me are needed. I've stumbled into a position in which I can affect who controls the air over Solung, and maybe, just maybe, flip the balance between peace and all-out war. I can't turn my back on that. I don't want to see this country tear itself apart."

ooo

The second respect in which Henry was wrong about the news conference was that he did not get to announce the king's plan to abdicate, nor Raju's proposed amnesty and programme of reforms. Tigger's little speech was interrupted by the sound of an explosion from the direction the airport's control tower. A klaxon sounded and a voice came over a loudspeaker: "Scramble, scramble, scramble!"

Scramble they all did. The cameramen grabbed their equipment; the reporters ran to the door, Tigger and Ganesh raced to their Spitfires, Dougal and Charlie raced out of their rooms. Cameras were set up and focussed in the time it took the pilots to leap into their cockpits, Within two minutes they were taking off under the eyes of the whole world.

296

6   Dougal's last dogfight

There was a nauseous feeling in the pit of Tigger's stomach as he pressed the starter and the engine roared into life. Despite having been standing under shade, the cockpit was stiflingly hot. Tigger left the cover open during take-off, revelling in the rush of cooling air.

As soon as he was off the ground, he felt completely calm, concentrating on routine tasks: retracting the undercarriage, correcting trim, sliding the hood closed. The Spitfire was climbing steadily, the single propeller clawing at the atmosphere, its four blades twisting automatically with airspeed so as to deliver maximum thrust from an engine with the power of thirty family cars to a frame as trim and light as a racing yacht.

Tigger had realised, even as he ran to the aircraft, that Da Silva's men must have knocked out the radar that had been the Spitfire pilots' one big advantage. He was surprised to note that Dougal was leading them away from the mountains, and thus presumably away from Laxman. On reflection, he saw that this made sense: the Spitfires would have a chance to gain height before turning to meet the MEs. If Laxman headed straight for the airstrip, sacrificing height for speed in the hope of pouncing on them just after take-off, the Spitfires would have an opportunity to catch him at a disadvantage. It was perfectly possible for the aircraft to miss each other altogether in the open sky, though a clash might still occur when either side decided to return to base. It was a cat-and-mouse game, with each side trying to manoeuvre into the position of playing the cat.

Dougal was careful not to overtax the antique engines;

nevertheless, they were already at 15,000 feet after just five minutes in the air, when he wheeled the formation round on a course that would put them between the airstrip and the sun.

After all the waiting and talking, Tigger felt a kind of exultation at being finally committed to action. He could see the mountains ahead, their dusty green lower slopes shimmering in the heat haze, their snow-white crowns laced with wisps of cloud. Never had he felt so full of life, yet so close to death. Was it for this feeling that some men took so gladly to war? He viewed the world with a kind of nostalgia: the wonderful fact of existence spread out before him, as touching as an old familiar song. Almost involuntarily he prayed: "Oh God, please let me live." But he knew God's answer, and it was the same for all beings: this is your life, and death is its price."

A spasm of fear clutched at his stomach and was gone, leaving an unfathomable exhilaration as he heard Charlie's voice come over the radio: "Bandits. Seven o'clock high."

Laxman had outguessed Dougal. He too had flown a dog-leg course, climbing steadily, and he had taken off from four thousand feet higher than the Spitfires. He was coming out of the sun, but he had not achieved complete surprise. Charlie was too old a hand to be caught napping.

"I see them," Dougal said, but he did not alter course. Tigger's heart was pounding, as if trying to hurry along each agonising second. Snatching a look round, he could see the Messerschmitts clearly outlined in the sky behind him and could almost feel their sights lined up on his back.

"Break right, now!"

Tigger was turning even before Dougal completed the order. He bunched in his seat to take the g-force as the aircraft twisted around and up. Dougal had not lost his sense of timing and the Messerschmitts seemed to have been thrown into disarray.

Tigger found one right in his sight as he straightened out. The pilot, unaware that Tigger was so close, was pulling out of his dive. Tigger could see the oil stains on the aircraft's wings. Grasping the spade-grip of the control column he pressed his firing button in a short burst. The Spitfire shuddered and dropped speed with the recoil as the two cannon and four machine guns in its wings opened up with devastating effect. Tigger saw his shells strike home and the aircraft exploded in a ball of yellow flame and thick black smoke.

It had all happened so quickly and easily that Tigger was disoriented for a few seconds. Glancing round, the only aircraft he could see was a Spitfire, spinning to earth. Dougal's voice came over the radio, shouting urgently: "Break, Tigger!"

Again, he pulled the Spitfire round in a tight turn. He felt the smack of a shell hitting his machine and saw a Messerschmitt turning with him, trying to line up to open fire. Suddenly, it flipped on to its back and smoke poured from its engine. The pilot jettisoned his cockpit cover and dropped out.

"Two down," Dougal said, as he pulled his Spitfire alongside.

Utterly bewildered, Tigger wondered how Dougal could keep track of what was going on. "Where are the others?"

"Charlie's down. Ganesh followed an ME in a dive. He's a plucky little beggar but he won't catch it. Laxman followed him down. He may be in trouble."

They had drifted away from the airstrip and were now heading back, away from the sun.

"What happened?" Tigger asked.

"Keep your eyes peeled for any sign of Ganesh. I'll watch the sun." There was a tone in Dougal's voice which Tigger had never heard before, as if violent emotions were fighting for release.

Tigger repeated: "What happened? "

"Charlie didn't pull out of the break. I think he must have blacked out. The leading ME got him... the one with the red-painted nose. I guess it was your friend Laxman..."

There was a heavy stress on the 'your friend'.

Dougal continued: "I went for Laxman but he dived. Then I noticed the ME on your tail."

"Thanks for shaking him off. What do we do now?"

"Follow me. I guess Laxman will collect his pal and try again."

Even though Satpur radar was out of action, they still had the scrambler radio link which could provide reports from observers on the ground. Through this they discovered that the Messerschmitts had not returned to base. Observers had seen four aircraft crash... and two parachutes. No-one could have survived the aircraft Tigger hit; that meant one other probable fatality.

"Charlie's dead," Dougal said.

"It might be Ganesh."

"It's Charlie. I know it."

Dougal seemed to be speaking to himself. "It's best this way. Ganesh is young and useful. Charlie couldn't have wished for a better way to go. Pity he didn't take one of the bastards with him."

Tigger was becoming alarmed. There was a crazed edge to Dougal's voice. They were skirting the mountains now, well above the snowline. The stark, silent, solid peaks added to the eeriness of stalking two unseen aircraft in the vastness of the empty sky.

Dougal began rambling over the radio like a man demented. "Charlie was a good wingman. Never let you down. He was the best. Stuck to your tail like a limpet. Never missed a thing."

"Dougal, I can't concentrate. Please don't talk so much."

They had been talking over the new scrambler link; suddenly Dougal's voice came over the other radio, the one like those installed on the MEs. They had kept the receive channel open to eavesdrop in case Laxman broke radio silence – in fact at one point before Dougal began raving Tigger thought he had heard Laxman's voice, barely audible over

300

the engine noise. Now Laxman would be able to hear everything Dougal said.

He was still rambling. "Don't worry Tigger. They are not going to get away... I was shooting down Messerschmitts before they were born... They can hear me now, and hear me good. I want the skunks to know what's coming to them... Laxman... I know you're out there but you won't get away from me. We've got a score to settle. You wouldn't be so keen to launch a war if you'd seen what I've seen. You need a lesson and you're going to get it."

The radio was silent for a few seconds, then Dougal shouted: "Laxman... hear me good. I'm pulling south straight towards the airport at Satpur. If you want to fight, you know where I'll be."

Tigger noticed the 'I'. Dougal had lost his grip and in his mind he was alone against the world. When his Spitfire turned south, Tigger had no option but to follow. He struggled to keep his position behind Dougal and at the same time watch for danger from the direction of the sun shining fiercely through the thin air. He tipped his wing occasionally, trying to block the glare. Somewhere in that direction would be Laxman's aircraft.

Dougal's world was shattered, Tigger saw that now. He was a flying anachronism, a real-life Biggles getting old. He was an effective man, a considerable man, even an astute man within his field of focus. But he was yesterday's man, a hero of commemoration days, the diminishing ranks of old comrades, and schoolboys. Tigger had grown up. Gosh was dead. Now it seemed that faithful old Charlie was dead.

The thought brought Tigger's focus back to present dangers. The pilots had spent hours discussing tactics and he ran through the options. The limited range of both the ME and the Spitfire meant that they would have to refuel in around half an hour, and would be vulnerable to attack when they were landing.

Neither side could afford to hang around over the opposing airfield if they wanted to retain enough fuel to return to base. But Laxman would be more likely to take the risk in order to settle the battle before Satpur had a chance to lash up some radar coverage. So, half-crazed though he sounded, Dougal was only challenging Laxman to meet them where the remaining MEs were most likely to be anyway.

The Spitfires were above the airstrip now, with its ants of humans standing strangely still, all eyes at the sky. Tigger caught the glint of zoom lenses, and automatically checked again in the direction of the sun. Was that a twinkle or two, slightly offset from the blinding glare... the tell-tale reflection from the canopies of two Messerschmitts?

"Bandits... one o'clock high."

"I've got them." Dougal's voice was calmer.

No last-second break this time. The two Spitfires swung round and headed up to meet the attack. The Messerschmitts were not far above. Within seconds, they grew from dots to clear silhouettes... the aircraft were closing at a speed of more than six hundred miles an hour. Tigger and Dougal were flying abreast now, and so were the two aircraft in front. It was man against man. Time seemed to slow down, as well it might, because at one mile apart the aircraft were just 10 seconds from collision. At a distance of 1,000 yards, Tigger fired a short burst, more in an attempt to unnerve the other pilot than in the hope of hitting the tiny target presented by the slim fuselage and thin wings of the Messerschmitt in front of him. At 300 yards he registered the aircraft's red-painted nose: it was Laxman's, and they were a second apart. Tigger could see its guns flashing.

The Messerschmitt's nose lifted as its belly passed vulnerable as a baby over the Spitfire's guns. Then it was gone. To Tigger's right, a Spitfire and Messerschmitt collided with an explosion that sounded even above the roar of Tigger's engine. Dougal had fought his last battle.

Since his first warning burst, Tigger had not fired a single shot. His aircraft seemed to be the only one in the air. He scanned the sky for a few seconds, and on an impulse shouted into his microphone: "Laxman!"

He considered that Laxman had been listening on the Spitfire's frequency, or he would not have taken up Dougal's challenge. But there was no reply.

Tigger persevered: "Laxman. I couldn't shoot. I don't want to kill you. I don't want to fight you. Can't you see that it is all over?"

There was silence for a few moments, then he heard Laxman's voice: "Is it just you and me left, Tigger?"

"No, it's not. There's millions of us left. It's not the end of the world."

"Why didn't you fire at me?"

Tigger hadn't thought about it. But he said: "Do you need me to tell you? You're a better man alive than dead."

It was almost like speaking to someone from the dead, for there was neither sight nor sound of Laxman's aircraft. Laxman said: "What else is there left to do but to fight? "

"We can talk. If you want to fight, we can fight tomorrow. But hear this. The king is abdicating. Raju will be king and your sister will be queen. They plan to offer an amnesty to your people if you give up fighting. They are drawing up a program of reform. They need your help. There is no need for this war. I'll keep this radio channel open. Let's see if we can sort something out. There's been too much killing today. Agreed?"

The reply was faint. Either Laxman was finding it difficult to speak, or his aircraft had flown into a radio shadow.

"I'll call you back in three hours," Tigger said.

ooo

There was a restrained cheer from the waiting newsmen and ground crew as Tigger landed and switched off his engine. Someone had persuaded or bribed a technician to pipe the radio to the public-address system so that everyone had followed the conversations that had taken place in the air. Tigger was in no mood to answer questions, especially after learning that Charlie was confirmed dead, and Henry whisked him away by jeep to the peace of the pilot's sleeping quarters.

The sight of the two dead pilots' things brought tears to Tigger's eyes: they had been father and uncle to him. "Dougal lost it," he told Henry miserably. "He just rammed the ME."

Henry had to leave to field questions from the media and the princess was on the line before he was out of the door. "Tigger, I can't thank you enough for what you did. I nearly died when you and Laxman were fighting it out up there."

"So did I," said Tigger.

"I'm sorry about your friend Charlie..."

"Princess, I appreciate you calling but I can't talk about it now. I'm still reeling."

"I'll call in a while," she said.

The intelligence colonel came with news of Ganesh. Piecing together information from radio traffic and reports from the ground it seemed that, as Dougal had said, Laxman had gone after Ganesh as he chased the fourth ME. Ganesh was seen to bale out. Nothing had been heard from him since.

7   Ganesh takes the lead

Ganesh's experience at the start of the dogfight had been much like Tigger's. More by luck than judgement after the break he found himself on the tail of a Messerschmitt, but unlike Tigger he was not given an easy shot. The ME dived and turned and weaved in a bid to get out of the way or get a shot at its attacker; Ganesh stuck to the chase with such concentration that he had no idea where the others were, or of how far he had travelled. But his hours of training with Dougal paid off in that he automatically scanned the skies for other possible attackers.

He spotted a second ME diving on him from behind and broke right just as it fired a burst at him; as he tightened his turn in an attempt to get a shot at his new attacker he saw for an instant the face of the pilot looking at him. It was Laxman. A voice came over the radio. "Break Ganesh! For God's sake break!"

Again he pulled the Spitfire round but it was too late. The ME he had been chasing had looped round and was diving on him; he felt shells strike his machine and smoke began pouring from the engine. With great difficulty he swung the canopy back and pushed himself out of the machine. Only after his parachute opened did he realise that the warning voice had been Laxman's.

Dangling serenely from his parachute he saw his beloved Spitfire skid over the side of a mountain and bury itself into trees. There was no sign of the two MEs.

He landed at the edge of a paddy field, close to where the mountains rose from plain, and quickly bundled up his parachute before making his way to a nearby road. Here he began to feel a little uneasy. From the air he had seen people working in the fields but there was no-one in sight now. It dawned on him that they might be hiding, scared to be seen with him. He must be in territory controlled by the rebels.

He heard the sound of an engine and a country bus appeared coming towards him. There was nowhere for him to hide, and the people on the bus must have seen him, so he thought he might as well flag it down in the hope of getting a ride to safety. Even before it had stopped he knew there was no chance of that. The bus was full of armed young men in peasant clothes; some looked as young as 15. One on the front seat formed his hand into the form of a pistol and pretended to shoot him. He was in the hands of the rebels, evidently on their way to reinforce the fighters in the mountains.

They made it clear he was a prisoner, motioning him to get on the bus, but they were not unfriendly and indeed were clearly in awe of him – Ganesh was still surprised at how famous he was in Solung. They were Laxman followers from Ganesh's own area and they knew exactly what had been happening. Or almost.

"Prince Laxman shot you down," one said in Solungese.

"It wasn't Laxman, it was his friend," Ganesh said in the same language.

"Did Prince Laxman try to warn you? I'm sure it was him. Did he try to save you?" asked one of the group, who looked a little older and seemed to be in charge. Speaking in good English, he introduced himself as Ravi.

"I think he did. But he had just tried to shoot me down," Ganesh said.

There was a transistor radio in the bus and the boys – even Ganesh could not think of most of them as men – had been listening to it before they picked him up. Now they turned the volume up and Ganesh realised that the national station was broadcasting the aircraft's radio traffic live, with commentary during the silences. He heard Dougal's crazed challenge and the bus stopped so that everyone could hear what would happen next. The tension in the bus grew in the minutes leading up to the final clash. Clearly, the entire country would be listening: the people in the villages, in the towns, even out in the fields, and the fighters waiting nervously in the mountains for an expected army attack. They heard the explosion as Dougal rammed the Messerschmitt, and Tigger's voice telling Laxman that he did not want to kill him, and then his rushed announcement of the abdication, the amnesty, and the offer of co-operation over reform. The boys on the bus, who spoke only schoolroom English, kept asking. "What is he saying? What is he saying?" Ravi left Ganesh to explain, presumably in the hope of gleaning more information himself. His charges were political innocents and of course they had no idea of the princess's attempt to negotiate with Laxman in the run-up to the battle. The latest offer sounded to them as if Laxman was being offered everything he could have wished for. The mood lightened and became almost festive as the bus started moving again.

"Maybe there will be no war. Maybe we can be friends," Ravi said to Ganesh.

"You think Laxman will accept?"

Ravi shrugged. "Who knows? We will trust his judgement, whatever he decides. But the People's Army won't like it if he does accept. They are not interested in deals. They want to overthrow the king. At least, their leaders do."

They passed through a couple of small villages without stopping and then turned down a dirt road, when the boys became quiet and tense. They were coming close to what could soon be a battle zone.

Ravi stood up and addressed the bus: "There's a PA checkpoint ahead and we need to take care. You all heard what happened in the air today. Prince Laxman wanted Ganesh's life saved. We should respect that. Leave me to do the talking. Keep quiet and keep your guns out of sight unless there's trouble."

"I thought you and the PA were supposed to be allies,"

said Ganesh.

"That does not mean we are friends. They can't be trusted – look at the way they kidnapped Princess Sita. And they try to order us about. Some of them are OK, but Da Silva has collected a lot of hard cases around him up at the base and the ones at this checkpoint are bastards. If they find out that we have picked you up they will demand that we hand you over them. That would not be good for you."

Ravi mimed a cut throat. "We'll take you to Prince Laxman. You helped his sister. He will protect you."

The checkpoint was manned by three older men armed with Kalashnikovs. Ravi stood at the passenger door to speak to them. They made no attempt to check the bus.

"Heard anything? Any idea what's happening?" one of the men asked,

"The villagers said there's been an air battle but they did not know anything more," Ravi said.

"We heard a crash and I thought I heard some firing," the man said.

"We wouldn't hear a thing over the noise of this old boneshaker. Anything been happening here?"

"The word is that the army is closing in. You'd better leave that bus here and walk the rest."

"I have orders to leave it where the footpath starts."

"I am telling you to leave the bus here." The man unslung his rifle.

Rifles appeared at the open windows of the bus.

"Comrade, we do not take orders from the PA," Ravi said. "If you want to run away you'll have to do it on foot."

The guerrilla spat on the ground, and put his rifle back on his shoulder. "Who said anything about running away?"

"If your commander has a use for this bus, he should ask my officer. You know the form."

Ravi slapped the side of the bus and they drove on. "There's something funny going on," he said in English as resumed his seat next to Ganesh. "Those guys were in radio touch with their commander. They knew more than they let on. They were sounding us out. That's why I didn't want to tell them how much we knew. That deal your friend talked about on the radio may have caused ructions."

"Why did they want the bus?"

"They wouldn't have tried to commandeer it without orders. I wouldn't put it past the PA to corner all the transport in case they have to run for it when the army attacks."

Ganesh said nothing about the possibility of the PA wanting to corner the arms cache. He knew from his briefings that the army was primed to attack once Laxman had committed an act of war but he was surprised the Ravi seemed so sure. "Do you think the army is going to attack?" he said.

"You tell me. We've all been ordered into the mountains, so we assume an attack is expected."

"I'm surprised you can drive around like this. I thought the army had this area bottled up."

"It can't cover all the mountain paths but there are only a few roads out of the area and it guards those. We would know immediately if they were moving into our patch."

"But these lads can still get in and out?"

"You'd need a million men to seal off this area completely. We've been around here for weeks. It's cold up in the mountains at night and we don't have enough warm clothing, so we spend as much time as we can down here in the warmth."

The bus rumbled on for another couple of miles until the track petered out into a footpath going into the foothills. The driver parked it behind some trees, on a patch of ground that had clearly been used before for the same purpose. When everyone was off the bus, Ravi ordered the driver to move it further into the trees where it was not immediately visible.

"That'll make it little harder for the PA to find if they decide to take it," he confided to Ganesh in English.

He detailed two men to scout ahead of the group and told the others in Solungese: "We've got a long walk ahead of us. Keep your eyes peeled and your ears open. Your life might depend on it."

As they set off up the hill Ganesh thought what a crazy battle he had been through, with two of the participants trying not to kill someone they were supposed to be fighting. And now he had fallen among the enemy he was being treated almost like a friend; he was not given a gun, but neither was he being treated like a prisoner. He thought briefly of making a run for it down the steep forested slopes at the side of the path, but rejected the idea. He had a feeling he would be of more use staying with Laxman's men. He also had a feeling that Ravi thought so, too.

ooo

It was still only early afternoon when the three-hour deadline for a call from Laxman passed, and the Solung army was put on standby for action at dawn the next day. Tigger tried calling Laxman on the frequency they had used but there was no reply. He realised on reflection that his spur-of-of-the-moment deadline did not mean much as he had said he would keep the channel open; he sat in his room, while the intelligence colonel and his aide monitored the radio in an adjacent room. The princess was listening in too, at her new apartment at the palace.

Tigger learned, to his relief, that she had already spoken to Charlie's devastated wife who had accidentally heard her husband's death reported live on the radio in faraway England. That was one dreadful task he did not have to face immediately. He felt profoundly depressed. Four people, including Dougal and Charlie, had been killed and yet nothing had been decided. In terms of body-count and downed aircraft the battle had been a draw, assuming Ganesh had survived; the Spitfires could be said to have won a military victory because Laxman's little air force had been neutralised; but the political effect was incalculable because it would not be hard for Da Silva the skilled marketing man to present the result as a rebel victory.

It had been Henry's decision not to cut off the live broadcast of the radio traffic during the battle; he felt that people would not be so keen to get involved in war if they were confronted with what it entailed. What had vindicated his decision was Tigger's unscripted outburst, which gave the offer of an amnesty and reform more prominence than it would ever have had if Henry had had a chance to make his formal announcement. But in truth there was little more in the offer than the princess had offered Laxman in Calcutta before the battle.

"The difference is that the offer came from your heart, Tigger. You don't want any more killing. People will respond to that," Henry said, when he popped into the room between fielding questions from the media.

"Laxman turned it down before," Tigger said miserably.

"But now his sister is practically queen. He will be as close to power as it is possible to get. And your appeal was not just to Laxman. The whole world heard it. He can't just slide out of it. He'll have to come up with some damn good reasons for turning it down."

A little later, the princess rang. "Laxman didn't call."

It was a statement, not a question.

"There's still time."

"The army is going in early tomorrow. It's out of my hands. They need to stop all those arms being dispersed."

"Will they hold back if Laxman calls now?"

"Maybe. The generals are losing patience. They say we shouldn't risk the country for the sake of my brother."

"It's for sake of peace, too."

"Generals don't think like that. Ours don't, anyway. I think they would quite like a war."

"I think maybe I did before I found myself in one."

"Tigger, I feel dreadful. You must be feeling so alone. I wish there was something I could do."

Tigger had never wanted the comfort of a woman's body so much.

"You must be feeling pretty wretched yourself, not knowing what's happening with your brother," he said.

"And Ganesh. His mother is with us here, waiting for news. She's frantic with worry. And Tigger... she is convinced she heard Laxman warning him on the radio. I heard him too."

"Princess, I don't want to be unkind but sometimes you hear what you want to hear. But you can tell his mother from me that if anyone can get themselves out of trouble, Ganesh can. I wouldn't put anything past that young man."

ooo

He had been climbing for more than three hours and it was still only 4pm, with the day stretching behind him for what seemed like a year. The little column that had started with no more than 20 men was now more than 150 strong, the numbers swollen by men joining it from side tracks. It was clear that Ravi was higher in the command structure than Ganesh had assumed, for the newcomers all deferred to him; some recognised Ganesh, but they seemed to take his presence for granted.

There was little talk, and then only when people joined the column, but invariably it was about the recent air battle, the terms of the deal on offer, and the prospects for peace. Ganesh was impressed by the discipline and organisation of the group: this was no rag-tag mob; they had clearly been trained and each man carried a weapon, with a blanket that doubled as a cloak, wrapped in a plastic groundsheet – not much to keep out the damp mountain cold of the night, but better than the thin plainsmen clothes that they wore. They came to a hamlet where 100 more men were waiting. Ganesh heard Ravi asking them why they had not dispersed to their positions. There were whispered conversations and glances in his direction. Then Ravi came over to Ganesh and said: "They want you to explain the government offer."

Ganesh knew quite a lot about it, having discussed little else over supper with Tigger and Henry the previous evening, and he found himself facing intense questioning. It became clear that the division between the People Army and Laxman's men was not clear cut; some of the men present appeared to be delegates from PA units who had come to talk to Ravi as the highest-ranking Laxman fighter around. The tricky point was the amnesty.

"I'm not the government," Ganesh said. "I can't tell you anything for sure. I understand there will be an amnesty for anyone who has not committed murder; if there is evidence of murder the person concerned will get a fair trial and if they surrender voluntarily they will be treated leniently."

"What about Prince Laxman? Didn't he shoot a plane down?"

"We don't know what happened. I can testify that he tried to save me."

"Will he accept the offer?"

"You'll have to ask him."

"We can't," said Ravi, in English at his side. "That's what these men have come to tell us. Da Silva called Prince Laxman and two of his commanders to a conference after he landed. They seem to be virtually prisoners at the base. The PA men here say they've been told Laxman is going to be executed for betraying the revolution, but that could be just a rumour. They think Da Silva is trying to stop him doing a deal with the government and they're not happy about it."

"Just their units?"

"They only speak for their units. We don't know how many would agree."

"We have to get the prince out," Ganesh said.

"But if we start fighting among ourselves, the government army could seize the chance to launch an attack. We risk being caught between them and Da Silva's hardliners."

"That is what Da Silva is counting on. He wants the army to attack. It will destroy the chance of a deal and force your people to fight for their lives while he gets rid of the prince and slips away with your reserve of arms. With Laxman out of the way, he's gambling that what's left of the rebel forces will rally round him as the strongest leader. They probably wouldn't have much option."

"So what do you think we should do?" Ravi asked.

"Where were you headed right now?"

"The airstrip. It's guarded by our people. Laxman refused to trust the PA to do the job. All the other men are being sent to various pre-planned locations. They have to report by code word over the radio when they are in place."

"I suggest that they pretend to take up their positions as ordered, sending the code word at the appropriate times, but collect at the airstrip, keeping as low a profile as possible. We can work out a full plan of attack in the meantime."

"But what about the army? "

"I suppose Laxman's aircraft is at the airstrip?"

"Of course."

"I could try using his radio to get them to hold back but that would alert Da Silva."

"Your aircraft is actually nearer. Our guys said it crashed about a mile from here."

"It must be in pieces."

"It hit the trees at an angle and the wings took a lot of the impact. A lot of the body is intact. The radio might work."

"There's a scrambler set on it. It would be best to use that. If you get a couple guys to lead me to the crash, I could see you up at the airstrip."

Such was the power of celebrity and connections. These bewildered men did not need to be told Ganesh's story; they knew him to be brave and resourceful; he was one of them but he was also close to that rarefied elite who controlled Solung, including, however ambiguously, Prince Laxman. If anyone among them could sort things out, he could. In the space of a few minutes he had been transformed from their prisoner to their leader.

"We should move at once, before it gets dark," he said.

ooo

314

Tigger too was getting worried about Ganesh. He had been reluctant to fly over the crash area to look for him for fear destroying any chance of peace by provoking another dog-fight; now there was barely an hour to sunset and if he was going to go it would have to be now. He was about to make a move when a signals sergeant monitoring the radio next door called: "Message for you to switch on the scrambler, sir!"

"Then switch it on, dammit!"

They had not expected anyone to use the scrambler. As soon as it was switched on Ganesh's voice came through, faint but clear. "Tigger, are you there?"

"Are you OK?"

"I'm fine. It's very important that the army holds back its attack. Things are moving here. It could make them worse."

"Where are you?"

"I'm with some of Laxman's men. Da Silva is holding him prisoner, with two commanders, and threatening to execute him. We're going to try to get him out but we can't do that if the army is shooting at our backs."

"Can't you let the army do it?"

"It's too difficult politically, and anyway we'd never sort it out in time. We couldn't even contact all our fighters, certainly not without putting Da Silva on his guard. He is counting on them being in position ready to take on the army."

"Is there any help we can give?"

"I'm taking the scrambler with me. I'll call you later."

Tigger said on an impulse: "Ganesh... count me in on this if I can do anything. Laxman did for Charlie, but I still reckon I owe him."

ooo

The village looked little different from the last time Ganesh had seen it some months before when he arrived with Dougal at much the same vantage point on the rim of a gully that ran along the edge of the village. It was a little after dawn, and the sun had risen just high enough to peep over the edge of the valley and light up the square in front of him.

Ranged along the gully were scores of fighters who had spent all night creeping carefully into position. More had taken positions on the high ground overlooking the village. Fighters who had been in the valley for months knew where guards were posted and had managed to truss and gag any who might cause trouble. But there were a lot of Da Silva loyalists left. They formed an armed cordon around centre of the square where Da Silva, standing in the same jeep that Ganesh had used to carry off the princess, was haranguing a crowd of some 200 worried-looking PA soldiers. A man squatted behind him, his fingers on the trigger of the machine gun mounted on the back of the jeep; in front of him, in an area clear of fighters, was an iron post. Clearly, he was to be the executioner. There was no sign of Laxman.

Snatches of Da Silva's speech drifted over to the unseen watchers: treason... betraying the revolution... murder of comrades... making deals with the enemies of the people. At one point he seemed to be accusing Laxman of fixing the previous day's dogfight and trying to save Ganesh's life. Finally, ominously, he began talking about a revolutionary court, and death. Some of the crowd looked around uneasily as they heard the sound of heavy artillery fire, almost drowning out the insistent hum of an engine.

But Da Silva seemed visibly to relax, presumably reassured that Laxman's men would be too tied up fighting off the assault to help the prince. He barked an order and Laxman was frogmarched onto the square, his hands bound behind his back; behind him, also under guard, were his commanders – evidently forced to witness what would happen to them if they did not toe the line. As they got close to the iron post, Ganesh picked up his scrambler radio and said: "Now!"

Tigger's Spitfire shot into the valley spitting gunfire and screaming so low over the square that it seemed he would knock people's heads off. Everyone on the square threw themselves to the ground to escape the onslaught but it took them some seconds to realise that the bullets flying around them were not coming from the Spitfire, which had fired harmlessly into the hills. It was coming from the ground around the square. The man at the machine gun was dead and his weapon was smashed; Da Silva was crouching behind the bullet-proof door of his vehicle, and anyone who raised their head risked having it shot off. Anyone, that is, except Laxman and his two commanders who were sprinting head down across the square towards the gully, their hands still tied behind their backs.

As the three escapees were helped into the gully by their rescuers, Da Silva's men began to rally, crawling to cover in the houses and firing blindly at their attackers. Da Silva managed to start his jeep without showing his head then drove furiously out of the square, calling on his men to make a fighting withdrawal up the valley. But his attackers did not want a fight; as far as most of them were concerned, Da Silva's men could go off and claim their amnesty or take their chances with the army. Apart from the shooting the would-be executioner at the machine gun, they had not been aiming to kill. After some shouted negotiations the besieged men were allowed to walk unmolested out of the village in the direction taken by their leader.

But Ganesh had not finished. He raced down to the airstrip, where Tigger had just sent the signal that would tell the army commander he could stop firing blank shells. "Can you lend me your Spit, Tigger? That bastard who killed my dad has taken off up the valley in his car. I'd like one more shot at him before he does any more harm."

"It's your country. It's your air force. It's your aircraft. My job is done," Tigger said.

8   Epilogue

The armour on Da Silva's jeep proved not to be impervious to cannon fire and the vehicle exploded with such force that Ganesh felt sure its owner must have helped himself to some of his precious arms cache after leaving the village There were those who claimed that Da Silva did not die, that he had somehow leaped clear when the Spitfire attacked. Ganesh did not believe it, knowing that such stories often emerge about notorious deaths. But as Henry said, all the best Biggles stories ended with a hint that the villain would survive to plague the world again.

Laxman's men accepted the amnesty, as did the bulk of the People's Army, encouraged by the fact that its political wing, the RMP, accepted two places on a committee deciding a program for reform – the party's first step towards embracing conventional politics. A core of hard-line killers descended into banditry. It was never absolutely clear whether, left to himself, Laxman would have accepted his sister's final peace offer. Da Silva had not given him a chance to state his views, submitting him instead to a farcical self-styled revolutionary court. Tigger stuck to his view that having attracted such a large and enthusiastic following after stumbling into revolutionary politics, Laxman did not know how to back out. In the event, his own men took the decision for him.

Laxman had been deeply affected by the battle. He told Tigger: "Those pilots in my flight that got killed... their politics were crazy, they were wild, they made me feel uncomfortable, but we had lived and trained together for months and we were comrades. I hated to see them die like that."

And he was sure he had not shot Charlie down. "I fired

318

but I didn't hit him. He pulled round so tightly that I thought he might get a shot at me but he seemed to spin round and fall out of the sky. Then I spotted a Spitfire chasing one of my men and I went after it, not knowing it was Ganesh. I dived and got a quick burst, and he turned in on me like Charlie did and I caught sight of his face – and the ME going for his tail. I shouted a warning. It just came out. I couldn't stop myself. I felt physically sick when his aircraft was hit and felt like giving up. But we had a set plan that if we got split up we would rally above your airfield to take another shot at you when you returned to base. The other ME headed there and I couldn't let him go there alone. You know the rest."

It turned out that Laxman was right: he had not killed Charlie, which meant that he was technically not guilty of murder, and so could go free under the amnesty. Naturally this conclusion was widely dismissed as a whitewash to save the prince even a nominal jail sentence, but it was backed by independent experts. Dougal's last dogfight had caused a sensation in Britain, where formal inquests were held into the deaths of the two veteran airmen; as a result what was left of their aircraft and their bodies was subjected to detailed forensic analysis, which showed that as far as could be ascertained Charlie's aircraft had received not a single hit. Doctors concluded that he had a heart attack under the combined stress of the g-force and battle. The coroner recorded a verdict of death by natural causes but one newspaper columnist was less charitable, suggesting that Dougal had effectively killed his friend by exploiting his loyalty to draw him into a fight for which he was manifestly unfit. This was denied by Charlie's wife, nobly if less than persuasively. She said Charlie died at his friend's side, as he would have wished, and that with Dougal facing an unequal battle he would never have forgiven himself if he had not gone to help.

The coroner recorded an open verdict on Dougal's death, declaring that it was not possible to know whether he committed suicide. That was fair enough, but Tigger was sure that Dougal had killed himself, tipped over the edge by Charlie's death. It was tempting to think that the root cause lay in that long-ago train crash that killed his brother, and that he had finally succeeded in his attempt at suicide by combat. But if he'd been driven solely by a death wish he would have died long ago. Experts testified that he was probably suffering from what doctors treating Vietnam War veterans were beginning to call Post-Traumatic Stress Disorder – long-delayed combat stress, compounded in Dougal's case by the buried trauma of his brother's death. But PTSD victims were typically terrified of battle; Dougal appeared almost to have an appetite for it. Perhaps the answer lay in something Charlie said: "Some men will always run towards the sound of gunfire. Some out of duty, some because they like a fight, some because they want to die, and some because it's the only way they can face down their fears."

Dougal's reticence about the involvement of the British intelligence service gave another clue to his state of mind. An official, talking privately after the inquest, confirmed that Dougal had provided air cover for Solung at the request of the British government. He agreed that Dougal should have told Tigger, being as his life was on the line. It was strange behaviour for a man who normally took a pride in keeping no secrets from his comrades. Tigger concluded that Dougal no longer had the psychological resources to deal with the consequences of leading men into combat. He could face the prospect of his own death, even welcome it, but he avoided any talk that would confront him with the possibility that a friend might die. It was the poor judgement of a damaged man who in retrospect seemed to have been cracking up even before they arrived in Solung.

Laxman had demonstrated that he was a better leader than politician and he seemed to accept the fact, leaving the negotiations over reform to others. This also meant that he was not tarnished by the inevitable letdown when it was realised that reform would be a long process that could not possibly satisfy everyone, and he remained a hero to the poorer sections of society. But it was Ganesh who emerged from the saga with his reputation most enhanced; he was depicted as a low-born man turned national saviour, a symbol of a nation reborn, and his story was taught in schools.

Tigger too found himself in the embarrassing position of being idolised in a country where celebrity could reach the point of apotheosis. His joust with Laxman had been simplified into a myth of how he had held his fire to secure peace. Tigger was more inclined to think that he had simply balked at firing on a friend. But the fact was that he did not have a conscious motive: like Laxman when he shouted a warning to Ganesh, he had acted without thought.

The princess, in a long phone call to Tigger after the battle, observed only half jokingly that this must have been the first battle in history in which the opposing sides tried not to kill each other – and that perhaps they had all been affected by the dream of the ridiculous man. Tigger would have none of it. "That sort of thing only happens in story books," he said. "We were lucky, that was all. We were lucky Ganesh was there to sort things out."

Henry had become a familiar face on TV news channels and was already getting offers of work. He planned to stay in Solung for the royal wedding and coronation, dealing with the media, and promised to be on call for similar work in future. But his main plan, as he put it, was to plug back into London and see what happened.

Tigger couldn't wait to get home. He saw the princess only once before he left, when he went to the palace to receive a second medal. The meeting was easier than he had feared. She was no longer the woman, or rather the girl, he had known. She was mistress of a court, and the formality that surrounded her made it easier for him to distance himself. Raju shook him firmly by the hand, their eyes met, and an uncomfortable moment had passed.

She said: "You know we can't thank you enough for everything you did, Tigger."

He said: "It was nothing like as difficult as the job ahead of you."

"Have you any idea what you are going to do?"

"See what the world has got to offer a redundant warrior."

"I'm sure it has a lot to offer you. I do hope we meet again."

And that was it.

ooo

Except, of course, that Henry had the last word. Two years later he and Tigger were back in Solung to celebrate the birth of a son to the king and queen. Tigger, hand in hand with a young woman, was in love again. "Look at us," he said. "The world turned upside down two years ago and here we are again still standing as if nothing has changed."

"Some things never change," Henry said. "As it happens, I wrote a song about it." He picked up his guitar and sang:

Don't you ever get to dreaming
of those golden days of yore,
when the stars were heaven's windows
and your sweetheart lived next door,
when a girl was spice and honey
with puppy-dog tails foresworn
until the springtime reached the meadow
and the blue boy blew his horn.

Cos it's the same old love,
it's the same old game,
the more it changes
the more it stays the same.
It does.

There are times it gets confusing,
there are times it leaves you cold,
there are times it makes you happy,

there are times it tears your soul.
You can read your fortune smiling
or you can let it get your down,
but you know it makes no difference
cos the world keeps spinning round.

And it's the same old love,
it's the same old game,
the more it changes.
the more it stays the same.
It does.

There are things your gran could tell you
about the pain of days gone by
and that love was never easy
and that love will never die
though the ways of old are changing
it's the joy that has to be
it's what holds the world together
it's how one and one make three

So don't you ever get to pining
for those days of long before
when the moon was made of blue cheese
and the soldiers sang to war
Cos the bee still finds the flower
and the seed finds ground to grow
and the spring still warms the meadow
and the bud finds room to show

And it's the same old love,
it's the same old game,
the more it changes
the more it stays the same.
It does.

Appendix 1

Conflicts in Vietnam and Northern Ireland dominated headlines in 1972, the year in which this book is set. In Northern Ireland, militants on both sides of a sectarian divide had over the previous three years transformed a righteous and unlosable civil-rights campaign into an unwinnable (by anyone) quasi civil war that lasted three decades. British soldiers, originally sent in to protect civilians, became entangled in the madness. In January 1972 a unit fired on a protest march, killing 14 innocent people, an event remembered as Bloody Sunday. Peace in the region remains fragile.

Britain stayed out of Vietnam but US involvement escalated from 1961 when President Kennedy sent in large numbers of GIs to counter communist troops fighting to take over the country. In March 1968, seven years before the end of the war, GIs ran amok in the village of My Lai, killing more than 500 women, children and old men. Here is Henry's song about it, *Ballad of a soldier*:

Well Johnny was a soldier boy
who went to fight for his country
He took his gun
and a photo of his mum
when he sailed across the sea
I want to stay alive said he
I will no martyr be
But I don't see why
you should mourn if I die
if it helps the world to stay free

The enemy stood protected in a wood
At the top of a deadly hill
And if anyone dare
Show his head in the air
His foe was no slow to kill
But Johnny said "it's only once I'll be dead
Just give me some covering fire
If you stay here
I can take them from the rear
Where the cover goes up higher."

His first grenade sent three to their grave
And his next three killed twenty five

The enemy corpses
filled the bloody copse
but there were nineteen left alive
And all but one Johnny slew with his gun
before they had time to fly
And with a bayonet cut
he skewed the last in the gut
Poor man took twenty minutes to die

Oh my boy my Johnny boy
I would not know your face
Where is that boy I knew
so kind and full of grace?

On Johnny's chest they pinned a bravery crest
and then sent him back to the war
And the more he fought
the more Johnny thought
things were so simple as they'd seemed before
Until in the end
he couldn't comprehend
foreign enemy or foreign friend
The more he said that we can count as dead
the fewer we'll have to defend

Well children cried as mothers died
with their babies in their arms
But they looked in vain
for the soldier's pain
cos these gunmen
had no qualms
If guilt should die with innocence
who cared whose blood would spill?
But murder was too mad a word
So they called it overkill.

Oh my boy my Johnny boy
I would not know your mind
Where is that boy I knew
so loving and so kind?

Oh mother dear I'm dying out here
with your tears so far away
You can tell the town

I didn't let them down
cos I'm bound for a hero's grave
My end began
when I asked a man
where I could find the enemy
He turned around, threw his body to the ground
And then fired his gun at me.

They taught you to die for your country
with words like love, honour, obey
They gave you your life and your reason
gave it to throw it away

They taught you to take your direction
from good men who knew what was right
who taught you that killing was sinful
then told you to go out and fight

Appendix 2

"... like the kids dying in Vietnam right now. The wars never stopped. They fragmented into smaller wars." (page 238) Naturally Henry wrote a song about it, *The Twentieth Bloody Century*:

It was World War One we were called to the gun
with the summer blooming high in the meadow.
And time after time we went down the line
as the blossom surely goes where the wind blows.
Oh the bells that were rung
and the songs that were sung
as we marched to the drumbeat of duty!
And oh how they cried
as their darling ones died
in the twentieth bloody plentieth bloody century!

No never again then came the refrain
with the grieving still too raw for
forgiving.
For the blood that was spilt a new world must be built
we must fight for a land fit to live in.
Oh the fine words they'd lend
any means to their end
as they danced to the music of glory!

And oh how they cried
as their darling ones died
in the twentieth bloody plentieth bloody century!

When World War Two screamed its
infernal machines
gave the killing a terrible level.
There was no side could claim so
exclusive an aim
as to separate goodness from evil.
No woman nor child
could be spared from the wild
fire of bomb, bullet, atom and factory.
And oh how they cried
as their darling ones died
in the twentieth bloody plentieth bloody century.

Then they fought for the rich and they fought for the poor
and they fought for muddy tyranny and freedom
And they fought for their need
and they fought for their greed
and gave guns to their brutalised children.
They fought 'cos they ought
and they fought 'cos they fought
and they bullied the meek and hungry.
No strength left for tears
for the dying of their dears
in the twentieth bloody plentieth bloody century.

Oh when promise when you may call us again
when a war may seem the least of two evils,
when the foe's at the gate
or the beast stalks the streets
then poor Johnnie must go for a soldier.
But beware of the yen
for excitement in men
and wild youth seeking causes to die for.
Mind those young men who will
on a mission to kill
become so many slaughtered to sigh for.

And so on to the 21st century. See my song *The Poisoner*,
available on major streaming sites.

Printed in Great Britain
by Amazon